"Dear God,

"My country and the British developed it," Nathan Stand told the sea captain. "That thing can wipe out a whole city."

Garrison pulled a 9mm Luger from his pocket. "Out of my way," he grumbled. "This is my business now." Stepping from the bridge, he called to the men clustered on the deck. Hesitantly, Nathan Stand backed toward the rail.

Falstaff's face stiffened in annoyance. He moved into the open. The pistol in his hand coughed three times. All three bullets thudded into Garrison's chest.

Stand threw himself over the rail. The sea closed over his head. Bullets ripped into the water around him. The current caught him and he was upon the rocks. Like a pinball, he bounced from one boulder to another, fighting landward, the white, frothy surf closing over his head again and again. Finally, he caught hold of a pinnacle of stone and dragged himself onto the shore.

A rubber raft pulled away from the trawler, moving fast under the power of an outboard motor. O'Conner was in the bow with a rifle in his hands.

Stand scrambled up the slope. The land swept away from the sea in smooth, gentle hills. He cursed vehemently. There was no cover, not even a tree in at least half a mile. He had to face them here.

THE
FALSTAFF
CROSS

JOHN KERN

LYNX BOOKS
New York

THE FALSTAFF CROSS

ISBN: 1-55802-083-7

First Printing/July 1988

This book is published by Lynx Books, a division of
Lynx Communications, Inc., 41 Madison Avenue, New York,
New York, 10010. The name ''Lynx'' together with the
logotype consisting of a stylized head of a lynx is a
trademark of Lynx Communications, Inc.

Printed in the United States of America

0 9 8 7 6 5 4 3 2 1

For Susan, who is everything

MKNAOMI: The acronym of a covert CIA program. For twenty years, the CIA secretly developed and stockpiled vast quantities of chemical and biological warfare weapons. These included shellfish toxin, cobra venom, the germs to cause anthrax, tuberculosis, encephalitis, among others. Allegedly, the collected amounts of shellfish toxin and cobra poison alone were sufficient to kill tens of thousands of people.

In 1970 all such chemical and biological weapons were destroyed by order of President Nixon.

In 1975 CIA Director William Colby revealed before the Select Senate Committee that the CIA had disobeyed the presidential directive, and had secretly kept its stockpile of certain poisons. He said that what the CIA kept had amounted to "only a couple of teaspoons."

Plausible denial: The practice of withholding complete information from the President and/or other high officials, thus ensuring that they may honestly plead ignorance of any actions that are later proven to be illegal, or otherwise embarrassing.

THE
FALSTAFF
CROSS

CHAPTER 1

BEN MINGLETON straightened at the wheel, sensing a change in the sea. The swells were quickening and he heard a bass rumble add counterpoint to the beat of the *Keegan*'s diesels. It was the thunder of surf on distant rocks. Peering through fog, he saw the immense shadow of a looming cliff. The stone rose like a black wall marking the end of the world. A chilling vision, especially on such a dead man's night, with the cold gray mist swirling like tormented ghosts.

Mingleton shivered at the thought and superstitiously crossed his chest. He knew many fine men had died on those rocks, finding the place to be truly their world's end.

The chill passed quickly though. There was too much to feel good about. It had been a perfect crossing, rain squalls and fog all the way—weather to warm the heart of any smuggler. The pressure was dropping, promising a blow, but Mingleton was sure he'd have time to escape the coming gale. Besides, the dirty weather guaranteed that he had the sea to himself. Only madmen ventured out on such nights. Or a sane man with the best of reasons. Mingleton had fifty thousand good reasons—in pounds sterling. And now that money was nearly his. All that remained of the night's work was to meet Sim Richards's tug, transfer a few crates from the *Keegan*'s hold, and be off. Back to Wick before dawn and no one the wiser.

Mingleton smiled to himself. Ah, what a lovely business.

Where else could a man earn fifty thousand quid for so little effort? He thought bitterly of his father, a fisherman who had fought the sea every day aboard this same bucket, and whose only reward had been an early death from sheer exhaustion. In his last days Mingleton's father had hands so gnarled and broken, he couldn't hold a copper coin, even if he'd had one.

Not for his son, Ben, no way. *What do you think of the lad now, Da? Fifty thousand quid. You never saw that much in your whole life, did you?*

Still a few minutes to go. Throttling down the engine, Mingleton sat back and lit a cigarette, trying hard not to stare at the clock. It was a losing battle. His nerves were jumpy, and it nagged him that he couldn't put a finger on the reason. It wasn't just the money, though for sure he was excited about that. No, it had to be something else.

Maybe it was the cargo. It shouldn't have bothered him, though—he'd hauled weapons before, though seldom. Whisky and cigarettes were his usual trade. Gun runners were a different crowd. Too many foreigners for one thing, he reasoned, and not a one of 'em could be trusted for a straight deal, even when a bloke could get past their strange chatter and suspicious ways.

Like the bugger he'd taken the crates from tonight. The mousy little kraut had talked a bloody blue streak, grunting and waving his soft little hands, going on and on, barely taking a breath. About the guns, mostly. He told Mingleton the entire history of the guns he was smuggling. Like he thought the Scot would care. Mingleton didn't think it mattered more than a fart in a windstorm, but he listened. The man was paying good money, so he listened.

Originally, so the kraut had said, the machine pistols had been stolen from the private stores of an oil-rich king in the Jebel Shammar. "So you see, we take from the rich," he grunted. "Like your Robbing Hood, yes? No harm, the Arabs have enough guns to kill each other a hundred times over. These will not be missed."

Mingleton had bit his lip, and kept himself from pointing out Robin Hood had been a bloody Englishman. At least, in their disdain toward Arabs, he and the kraut were on common ground.

The guns had been smuggled from the Mideast packed inside wooden crates. Well-placed bribes added grease to the rails and guaranteed that no customs official experienced a sudden curiosity.

From there, so the story went, the guns were carted through Turkey and Yugoslavia, to wind up finally in Switzerland. They sat cooling until the proper time to appear on the auction block. Men with soft voices and smudged passports came together in Zurich. The high bidder was an agent of the Erin Dawn, one of the newer splinter groups to emerge from the Irish Provisionals in the terrorist breeding ground of Belfast. Their buyer was a laughable fraud in a black wig and fire-red eyebrows. He sputtered German in a brogue so thick even the dour Swiss were hard pressed not to grin. The man's money was genuine, though, and he bid nearly twice that of his nearest competitor.

The next step was getting the weapons to Belfast. The Swiss merchants delivered them as far as Denmark, but they balked at directing them farther. They demanded an intermediary so if anything happened, the guns could not be traced back to Zurich. They had judged the amateur buyer and decided the possibility of something happening was not unlikely.

The Erin Dawn approached Ben Mingleton for the job. He was nearly perfect for their needs, a small-time smuggler with no police record and only a few previous connections with the arms trade. His services could be had for a relatively small sum. More important, with his Scots-bred dislike for the English, he had no qualms about providing the Belfast rebels with the means to continue their bloody struggle.

Mingleton stabbed out his cigarette and frowned, recognizing the source of his uneasiness. It all rang false now that he mulled it over. It was downright queer how much he'd learned in those few minutes in a Danish fishing village. The kraut had lied, that much was certain. All that history, nothing but a story. Of course it was no surprise to be lied to, but it was odd how intent the kraut had been about it. As if by telling him so much—too much, really—he had hoped to dispel Mingleton's natural curiosity, to make certain he wouldn't question the contents of those few wooden crates.

Yes, that made sense. Suddenly, Mingleton was sure of it; whatever lay in the *Keegan*'s hold wasn't contraband weapons. But what, then? What could be so important that they would worry so much about his nosing around? The idea raised the hairs on the back of his neck and a chill raced down his spine. He wanted to climb down to the hold and see for himself. But now the clock was against him. It was almost time for Richards to appear.

To hell with it, he decided. Whatever it was, it would be off his hands soon. Best to keep a blind eye and just get it done.

Mingleton slipped outside. The cold stung his face as he scrambled over the deck, setting drag anchors and tossing over a string of old car tires to act as a buffer when the two boats were tied off. After a brief, final check, he hurried back to the wheelhouse to get warm.

He took his place at the wheel, waiting anxiously for the final minutes to pass. His heartbeat blotted out the ticking of the clock. At last, as the moment neared, he grabbed binoculars and focused on a point near the base of the cliff.

The signal appeared exactly on time. A powerful lamp stabbed through the swirling darkness, switched off, then on again. After a ten-second pause, the series repeated. Mingleton let out his breath. All clear. With his own lamp, he flashed a return sign.

"Come on, Sim," he whispered. "No messin' about. Let's get this bloody business over and done with."

Moments later, a shadowy form poked through the fog. Mingleton felt his gloom lift at the sight of the tugboat. The *Maureen* came on, plowing through the swells like the tireless old workhorse she was, plodding but steady. Mingleton caught a glimpse of himself in the dark glass. His reflection was grinning.

With sudden energy, he threw open the wheelhouse door, then paused in the opening. He turned back, reached under the panel, and found the gun secured there by heavy metal clips. He hefted the pistol, a slim Browning automatic, then stuck it in his trousers and pulled his anorak down to cover it. Feeling truly ready then, he rushed out on deck.

Mingleton leaned into the wind, oblivious to the cold now as he watched the tug swing into her approach. Bringing two boats together on rolling seas was always dicey, but Richards came in without hesitation, feathering his engine against the changing currents, displaying a rare touch that somehow made it all look easy.

In just a few minutes, the boats were side by side. Mingleton tossed a line across, then jumped over himself. He timed his leap carefully so that the bobbing deck rose to meet him. It would be a bad night to break a leg through simple carelessness.

Mingleton tied off the stern. Richards was still in the wheelhouse. As he went past, Mingleton waved at the shadowy figure, then rushed forward to secure the bow. As he bent down and wrapped the stout rope around a cleat, he heard the wheelhouse door creak open behind him.

"Shag your old bones, Sim!" Mingleton shouted as he tightened the hitches. "Let's move along smartlike, eh. This is a big night for us, mate. The start of a whole new . . ."

Mingleton's voice trailed off as he caught the scent of tobacco, sharp and sweet on the damp air. And that was wrong, wrong as could be. Sim Richards never smoked.

Mingleton brushed his hands on his pants, comforted by the touch of the hidden pistol. Slowly, he straightened up and spun around. A man stood on the deck above, leaning on the rail. With a casual air, the stranger touched a match to his pipe. The flame's glow flickered across a wide, strong face, half shrouded by a heavy black beard. His hair was the same shade but for a long streak of silver above one eye. He was a rugged, imposing figure with eyes like smoked glass, cool and impenetrable.

"Who the hell are you? Where's Sim?"

The man puffed calmly on his pipe before answering. "You won't be seeing him for a while."

"And what's that s'posed to mean?"

"Your friend will be busy for a few days. With the police. They have a long list of questions to ask him. Such as what a retired tug skipper needs with a boathouse filled with arms and explosives. All stolen, as it turns out. You wouldn't know anything about that, would you, Mingleton?"

"What is this? Who are you?" the smuggler demanded again.

"My name is Nathan Stand. I won't be hurt if you haven't heard of me." He scowled as he watched Mingleton's hand creep toward the Browning. "Don't try it, Mingleton. Keep your hands in the clear and we'll get along fine."

"A friggin' cop, that's what ye are!"

"Let's skip the name-calling. That'll get us nowhere."

"A *Yank* cop! I can hear it in your voice. What does a Yank want with me?"

Stand shook his head, as if disappointed. "Let's not play games. We both know what's happening here. You're finished, Mingleton. This is the end of the killing for you."

"Get off. I never killed no one in me whole life."

"I had a feeling you'd say something like that. No, maybe you don't pull triggers, but you put guns in the hands of those who do. To me it's all one and the same."

"You're no judge, no jury, neither. Bugger you and what you think."

Stand went on in a soft flat tone. "You know, there was an incident just last month—that's what it's called in such places as 'Derry, an incident. A bomb exploded inside a chemist's shop. It killed three people. A woman and her twin daughters. Six years old, those girls were, Mingleton. Think of that. Six years old. When the firemen were through picking up, they had pieces of each child, but no way to tell what belonged to which."

"It's a rough old world, right enough," Mingleton said hoarsely. "But that has nothing to do with me."

Stand tapped his pipe on the rail, scattering ashes in the wind. "No? The Yard has a forensic lab in Cardiff. They have a fragment of that bomb there. It has your thumbprint on it, Mingleton. Clean and clear as you please." Stand blew once through his pipe, then put it away in a pocket. His eyes clouded with an undisguised loathing. "They found that fragment in what was left of the mother's skull."

"Lies! You can't stick that on me."

"Save your breath for the trial."

"Screw that. Nobody takes me to jail."

"That's your decision."

Mingleton stared at him for a long moment, then nodded thoughtfully. "So that's the way of it, eh?"

Stand nodded. "That's how it is."

"Not leavin' me much choice, are you?"

Mingleton made his move before Stand could reply. Springing from coiled legs, the smuggler feigned movement toward the rail, as if to dive into the sea. With a sharp turn, he darted back and launched himself headlong across the deck behind the cover of the boom winch. He rolled smoothly to land on his shoulders, and came up on one knee. The Browning magically appeared in his right hand.

Stand sighed, a weary sound of great sadness. His own gun was outside his coat, tucked in his left armpit, held there between elbow and rib. It took only a fraction of a second for him to grab the Colt and swing it to bear. He squeezed the trigger with a slow, steady pressure.

The sharp crack of the .38 splintered the stillness. Mingleton staggered back, a small neat hole opening in his chest. In the span of two heartbeats his anorak changed color.

The smuggler stared at the spreading stain as if mystified by its appearance. With a howl of rage, he raised his pistol, his hand shaking wildly.

Stand watched calmly, not moving. The bullet buried itself in the woodwork two yards to his right.

Mingleton cursed and spat blood. He glared at Stand with contempt, the expression petrified on his face forever. His legs went soft and he sagged to the deck, folding like a lowered sail.

Stand walked slowly down to the lower deck. He tossed the Browning over the side, then stood for a moment over the lifeless body. "You dumb bastard. What was the point of that?" He turned away, shaking his head in disgust.

Stand leaped across the short gap to the *Keegan*'s deck. He tugged open the hatch and dropped into the hold. The crates were there. They looked drab and ordinary for something that had already cost one man's life.

He gave them a second glance, puzzled. The boxes didn't look big enough to hold many weapons; the shipment couldn't be as large as they had suspected. He considered breaking one open to inspect the contents, but quickly discarded the idea. A few guns or a lot, what mattered was that these guns were going nowhere.

That thought twirled in his mind, nagging him. Could he really be so sure of that? The next logical step was to turn the guns over to the Company. But what would happen to them after that?

It all seemed clear to him. There was only one way to make certain these guns caused no harm. He would have to see to it himself.

Sliding into the space between the crates and the hull, he groped about and located the sea cocks. He opened the valves. Dark water streamed into the hold, ran across the planks to gather in the corners, and raced back upon itself, swiftly rising.

Stand hurried back to the tugboat, dragged Mingleton's body to the side, and dumped it onto the *Keegan*. The fishing boat ground against the tug's hull as it took on water. He wasted no time in cutting free the lines and steering the *Maureen* to a safe distance.

Stand left the pilothouse long enough to fetch a bottle of Black Label he'd discovered earlier in a galley cupboard. He returned with the whisky and set it down close to hand. Glumly he watched, and waited.

The *Keegan* was going fast. Already it was listing, bowing to the swells like a cowering servant. Stand took the bottle and walked out on deck. The pipe in his teeth was cold, but he didn't seem to notice. He waited quietly, his manner solemn and respectful.

The boat was slipping away. Waves slopped over the tilting deck. One of them carried off Mingleton's body like so much loose trash. Then, with a groan and the hiss of escaping air, the *Keegan* rolled and slid beneath the sea.

The bottle held only a few ounces of whisky. Stand gulped it all in one long swallow. For a time he watched the white bubbles breaking to the surface. Then his eyes were drawn to a small speck of color bobbing in the distance. Air had gotten trapped in Mingleton's anorak, it seemed, making it into a makeshift life jacket. The floating body was riding the tide, swept toward the jagged rocks at the base of the cliff.

Stand watched the lonely figure race landward until Mingleton's body disappeared. He threw the bottle into the sea and went below to search for another.

The long driveway was illuminated by electric lamps concealed in the branches of flanking trees. The thin, bare limbs of the cherry trees shivered in the breeze, but the maples were ablaze with autumn color. Their leaves, kindled with shades of red and gold, seemed especially bright against the dark backdrop of the night sky.

The cabdriver let out a low whistle as they passed rows of parked limousines. He pulled up next to a gleaming black Rolls, then spun around and inspected Stand with a puzzled gaze.

"Don't say it," Stand muttered. "Yes, this is the right place." He handed over a twenty and climbed out before the driver could gripe about his tip. The battered cab chugged away, the driver waving a fond good-bye with one finger. Stand shrugged and walked up to the house.

The man who opened the door was gray and slump-shouldered, with a face that suggested a daily regimen of chewing lemons. Stand's smile faded.

"Who're you?"

"I am Edwards, sir. The butler."

"You mean the *new* butler. Where's Charles?"

"I believe he's in Bermuda, sir. Is that whom you wished to see?"

Stand shook his head. "Mr. McWilliam."

The butler looked over Stand's jacket and faded sweater with open disapproval. "I'm afraid that's not possible," he said. "Mr. McWilliam is very busy at the moment hosting a dinner party. As you can see. Perhaps you could return some other time." He paused, then, with a starched smile, added, "If you would care to call for an appointment."

Stand took a step forward, his shoulders filling the doorway. He spoke slowly and gently, as if to a difficult child. "I mean to see him now, tonight. The old man may be having a party, but you and I both know he's presiding over the fun from his upstairs office. You can either announce me now, or watch me go up those stairs to find him on my own."

"Your name, sir?"

"Nathan Stand."

Edwards repeated the name silently, chewing it over with obvious distaste. He turned and walked stiffly to the hall telephone. Stand let himself in while the butler made angry jabs at the phone dial. The sounds of music and buzzing voices lured Stand a little farther down the hall. He edged up to the door of the ballroom and peered inside.

It was definitely one of the important Capitol Hill parties for which the McWilliam mansion was famous. The guest list could have been lifted directly from *Who's Who in Washington*. At a glance, Stand recognized two senators, a Pentagon general, and the secretary of state. A slack-jowled official from the Soviet embassy was sharing a plate of appetizers with a man Stand knew to be from the CIA. The two were chatting amiably, clearly with some pleasure. Both their faces were taut with the bland smiles of cuckolds.

A pointed cough drew Stand away. He turned from the party and let Edwards steer him back down the hall. There was a new deference in the butler's eyes and manner. "Mr. McWilliam will see you in a few minutes, sir. He says you should feel free to join the party while you wait."

"Nice of him," Stand said. "But no. I'll find something to drink and wait out on the terrace."

"Very good, sir. I'll call for you there when he's ready to receive you."

As quietly as he could, Stand slipped through the crush of black-tie socialites and headed straight for the bar. The bartender glanced at him with a bored expression, did a double take. His eyebrows lifted in suspicion. "You sure you're at the right party?"

"If you have malt whisky, then I'm close enough."

The French doors were open to the terrace, but the seasonal cold snap had led most of the crowd to gravitate toward the fireplace. Stand made it outside with only a few sharp looks at his scruffy appearance. He felt more at ease the moment he stepped into the cool night air. There were no floodlights on this side of the house and the sky was clear, stars bright on a field of black velvet. Dry leaves tumbled in the wind, their muttering a delicate undertone to the music that filtered through the open doors.

He sipped his drink and wandered out farther to inspect the grounds. A landscaper had altered the contour of the lawn since his last visit. Stand wondered who had ordered the change—he doubted the old man cared, except maybe for the small patch visible from the window in his office.

Stand assumed he had the night to himself, and didn't notice the woman until he nearly stumbled over her. She was sitting on a balustrade at the far end of the terrace, and her elegantly simple white gown glowed faintly in the moonlight. He edged away so as not to disturb her, but she got up and angled over to cut him off.

"Aren't you going to say hello?" she demanded.

"Well . . . hello."

"Nice start. Now say something else." Humor gleamed in her eyes as she watched him struggle for a reply.

Stand pointed to her shoulders, which the low-cut gown left appealingly bare. "You could freeze to death out here in that dress."

"That's true. You know, a true gentleman would offer me his coat."

"Really?" Stand said. "How interesting."

She waited an extra beat, then mugged a lost-child look of disappointment that broke his resistance. He took off his heavy tweed jacket and slipped it over her shoulders.

"Thank you, that's much nicer. It is cold out here; I'm glad you didn't take long to find me."

"What? I don't understand."

"C'mon. It's not that tough, is it?"

"You were waiting for me? I still don't understand. But I'm flattered."

"You must be easy to flatter," she said.

"Who isn't?"

"Good point." And then she smiled.

Stand suddenly realized she was one of the most beautiful women he'd ever seen. It was a result of that smile. On her face the expression was an occurrence of magic. Her features lacked the symmetry of perfect beauty. Her mouth was too wide and full-lipped, the nose a fraction strong. But when she smiled all the pieces fit. Her eyes grew to match the proportions of that generous mouth, and no man who gazed into their cool blue depths would notice the size or shape of her nose, anyway.

"You have me at a disadvantage," he said. "I mean, we haven't met before, have we?"

"No, but don't blame me. I've wanted to meet you for some time, Mr. Stand."

"How do you know my name?"

Her eyes held a brassy glint of mischief. "The mystery gets deeper and deeper, doesn't it? You do like women of mystery, don't you?"

"Not really. No."

"Spoilsport. All right, I'll try it again." She held out her hand. "Nice to meet you at last, Mr. Stand. I'm Jean Frost. There, you know my name and we're even."

"Hardly. I still have no idea what you're up to."

"I just want to talk. Is that so bad? Two strangers meeting, getting to know each other. Who knows? Maybe becoming friends . . ."

"You're still teasing," Stand grumbled.

Jean Frost laughed and raised one hand in semblance of a solemn oath. "No, that's really all I want. No ulterior motives, I promise."

"Then tell me how you know who I am."

"Oh, I know much more than that about you. In fact, almost everything."

"You couldn't."

"Is that a challenge? Let's see . . . full name: Nathan Duncan Stand. You were born in nineteen forty-nine, Drake's Bay, Maine. Your mother was American, your father Scots. You have a Ph.D. in literature. You served six years in the army, most of that time with the Rangers. Two tours in 'Nam. After the war you came back to Maine and taught lit at a small upstate university. You married Leah Morrison, an Irish citizen, and had a daughter, Melissa—"

"I think that's about enough," Stand said.

"How'd I do?"

"You got all that from the files, didn't you? You've seen my sheet."

"All of it," she said. "Your two-zero-one, POA, PRQ— both halves, I might add. The complete history of Nathan Stand."

He stared at her, beginning to comprehend. "You work for the old man?"

"Not exactly." She grinned, as if something about the question amused her. "You're close, though. Same game, different team."

"Langley?"

She nodded. "You're surprised. Why?"

"Forgive me. You just don't seem their type."

Jean gave him a flicker of that magic smile. "Thank you— I think. Actually, you're right—they never would have recruited me on their own. I slipped in through the back door, sort of. Through connections. I have great connections."

"You do, huh?"

"Uh-huh. the old man—as you put it—you see, he's my father."

Stand was taken aback. He sipped his drink and frowned

at her, not certain what to say. He had worked for McWilliam several years and could not recall the old man ever mentioning a daughter.

Jean laughed, enjoying his confusion. "You don't believe me, do you?"

"It seems odd I've never heard of you before tonight."

"Then you don't know Father very well. It's so much like him, never mixing business and family, everything in its own neat little compartment. If you want the whole sordid truth, I'm adopted. I was eight when they took me in. I'm sure it was Mother's idea. He and I have had a rough time ever since she died."

Stand nodded. He had fond memories of McWilliam's wife, a robust and unflaggingly cheerful woman whose untimely death had been a blow to all who knew her.

Jean continued. "I don't think he knew what to do with me once we were left alone. He's not a man who gets along well with kids, I suppose because there's very little child left in him. He never had much time for me, only business, always business. It was hard for him, I think, having me around. I reminded him too much of the time when Mother was still alive . . . and of the natural child they never had. I used to think he hated me for that, for not being more a part of her."

Stand shook his head. "You must know that wasn't true."

Jean smiled faintly and motioned toward his drink. "Would you mind if I had some of that?"

He handed her the glass and watched her sip the neat whisky. Wearing his coat, sharing his drink—these seemed disturbingly intimate gestures for two people who had just met. But then, he found her a disturbing woman in all sorts of ways.

She gave back the glass and glided to her place at the balustrade again, but didn't sit. For a long moment, she stared across the grounds, into the darkness, as if intently studying something far away. Then, as quickly as it appeared, the mood left her. She spun back to Stand and laughed self-consciously. "I'm sorry. Where were we?"

"You were telling me what you think of him—your father."

She sat down then, and drew Stand's coat more closely. "Well, of course I understand him better now. I know how hard it was for him. That he hurt as much as I did. He wasn't really avoiding me. He was avoiding pain."

Stand said softly, "Grief is a difficult thing. People find different ways to deal with it. Sometimes they get confused."

She looked up at him. "Yes, you'd know about that, wouldn't you? Grief is something you must know a great deal about."

Stand nodded. His voice rumbled in his chest. "Yes, I do. All too much."

Jean gave her head a coltish toss, flipping back her hair. "Well, what did I know about it back then? As a child, all I could see was that he kept me away. Always on the move, one boarding school after another, summer camps, educational tours, swimming in the Caribbean, skiing in the Alps. . . . It was like a rather frantic fantasy, every opportunity a girl could dream of, all the finest places. Everywhere but home."

She paused to take a deep breath. She stared past Stand, her eyes following a single maple leaf as it dropped from the tree and floated slowly down before being caught by the wind and abruptly swept away.

"I was a great disappointment to him," she said quietly. "I surrendered too easily."

"I'm sure you both did the best you could," Stand offered.

She nodded and looked about to say something more, but then her attention shifted from him. Stand followed her gaze and saw the butler coming their way.

"What is it, Edwards?" Jean asked.

"Sorry to interrupt, ma'am. Your father is ready to see Mr. Stand now."

"So soon?"

Her disappointment sounded sincere. Stand was pleased to hear it in her voice, and was surprised at how much it echoed his own feelings. He shrugged and smiled at her. "I'm sorry, but you understand . . . back to work."

"All alike, aren't you?" she said, but smiled back. "Don't worry, I do understand. I hope we'll have a chance to talk again sometime."

"I'd like that, too."

Jean handed back his jacket. She gave him a last fleeting smile, then turned and strode across the terrace, vanishing through the ballroom doors.

The butler coughed. "Sir, Mr. McWilliam is waiting."

"Do you know that woman, Edwards?"

"Of course, sir. Mr. McWilliam's daughter is a frequent guest here."

"A guest?"

"Yes, sir." The butler sounded puzzled.

Stand finished his drink and gave Edwards the empty glass. "All right, let's go."

"This way, sir. It will be quicker if we slip around the back."

Stand knew Edwards didn't want to take him back through the party, but he simply nodded. He followed the man around the corner of the house and through a grove of tall maples. In the moonlight the trees' colors were muted, plain. The wind was stripping the limbs, and leaves cascaded around them in an angry swarm. Already the ground was nearly covered. Their shoes crunched on the fallen bodies, reducing them to fine powder.

CHAPTER 2

DANIEL MCWILLIAM was a small, dapper man of fifty-odd years who looked as though he belonged in the display window of a funeral parlor. Stand was appalled to see how much the old man had deteriorated in the past months. His face seemed to have collapsed in on itself, retreating behind accordion folds of slackened flesh. His clothes probably hung better in the closet. Bruiselike blemishes darkened the backs of his hands, and he subconsciously hid them whenever possible. Apart from these few points of color, his skin was the pallor of week-old snow. Only his eyes remained undimmed, hard points of crystal buried in sockets that were sunken and masked in shadow.

He was dying. His cancer was so widespread that the doctors couldn't say where it had originated. They told him to check into a hospital and prepare for the end. McWilliam growled at the idea and said he would die later when he had more time. He went home, refusing to see a doctor again. He had already lived three months past their most optimistic predictions.

"People have been calling me *the old man* since I was thirty-three," he'd once said. "I'll be damned if I'm going to die before I can *earn* the title."

The old man was used to getting his way. He felt betrayed by his body and hated it for its fragility. He was not accustomed to failure. Nearly his entire life was a story of success.

McWilliam had been born into great wealth. His father had been an investment banker for twenty years before deciding he could play the market as well for his own benefit as for others'. He amassed a large fortune, then literally worried himself to death trying to keep it. Gambling with his own money, he discovered, was neither as easy nor pleasurable as playing with the funds of anonymous stockholders.

At the age of eighteen, McWilliam inherited twelve million dollars. What he did not inherit was his father's sense of frugal caution. Of itself, money held little interest for the young Daniel. By the time he was twenty-five, he was bankrupt. Undaunted, he started from scratch, using every hard lesson he had learned. In eight years he had amassed an even greater fortune, and was well on his way to becoming one of the wealthiest and most influential men in Washington.

But making money held little interest for him. He cared only for what it could do, how it could be used to make a difference. Politics was his true love, especially the forging of foreign policy. McWilliam had served in the O.S.S. during World War II, and the excitement of those years, a fascination with clandestine activities, never left him. The cold war suddenly made intelligence a vital concern, and the fledgling CIA found in Daniel McWilliam a willing and knowledgeable supporter. In time, he became more personally involved, serving three administrations as a secret advisor to the director of Operations.

The expansion of terrorism posed a new threat and set of pressures on the intelligence community. A new strategy was needed, instant response and total secrecy. The unwieldy bureaucracy of the CIA was ill-equipped to handle these needs. The director of Central Intelligence had a solution. He proposed the formation of a secret organization, one totally autonomous and devoted solely to counter-terrorism. The DCI knew full well the creation of a "secret police" such as he envisioned would be illegal. The potential for abuse was daunting, for a truly secret inner circle would be responsible to no one. But he weighed the hazards of such potential dangers against the present, very real dangers of terrorism, and made his decision.

The DCI reasoned there was a way such an organization could be made arguably legal: It would be privately funded. But by whom? What person in his right mind would donate untold millions of dollars with no prospect of financial reward, or even the solace of public recognition? The DCI had only one candidate. Daniel McWilliam accepted without a moment's hesitation. And the Office, a secret task force devoted to opposing the threat of terrorism, was born. From the moment of its inception, McWilliam lived for nothing else.

And now he was dying. It seemed that he was going away before the work had even begun. It felt like failure.

McWilliam rose and shuffled around the desk to offer his hand to Stand. The simple exertion cost him considerable effort. "Nathan, good to see you," he said, in a dry, wheezy voice. "Come in, pull up that chair. Did you just get back? You look all done in."

"I am tired. Sorry to bother you at this hour. I wouldn't have come tonight if I knew you were having a party."

McWilliam frowned. "Oh, that. Damned nuisance, parties, but they're important, you know. Get more accomplished in one night than in half the legislative session. Amazing how much easier these people are to deal with once you get a little booze in them."

"I met someone there, an interesting woman."

"Did you, now?"

"Her name is Jean Frost. She claims to be your daughter."

McWilliam smiled. "So you finally met Jean. What did you think of her?"

"I think you're a very lucky man."

"Yes. Thank you, Nathan. Now, then, tell me about your assignment. This was a tough one, wasn't it? You've been away a long time."

"Three months," Stand said.

McWilliam made a soft clucking noise as he made his way back to the desk and dropped gratefully into his chair. "That's a long time to watch over your shoulder. No wonder you look worn out.''

"You look well, though.''

McWilliam snorted. "Bullshit! I look like death on a hot plate and you damned well know it. Don't coddle me, Nathan. You've always told me what you thought, straight out. I like that. I get all the crap I can bear from those bureaucrats on the other side of the Hill. Don't you turn on me.''

"You're in a good mood tonight.'' Stand grinned.

The old man pretended not to hear. He shoved some papers aside, pushed up his horn-rimmed spectacles, and settled back with a heavy sigh. "All right,'' he said. "Let's hear your story. What happened over there? I've been getting the strangest signals from the Glasgow station. This Ops officer there, what's his name?''

"Brandon—Scott Brandon.''

"Oh, you have heard of him.''

"Of course,'' Stand said.

"I was just checking. You were supposed to coordinate the operation through him, weren't you?''

Stand nodded.

"Then can you explain to me why Brandon thinks you fell off the face of the earth? He issued a priority cable requesting a full scramble search for you. I have it right here. Listen to it. 'The contractor repeatedly failed to meet appointed contacts. All inquiries as to his location are negative. Elimination or capture by hostile forces must be considered probable. Recommend the contractor be classified as *missing and presumed dead*!' Now, what do you say to that?''

Stand shrugged. "I feel fine.''

McWilliam scowled and dumped the cable into the shredder next to his desk. He leaned forward, resting his elbows on the desktop, and glared over the tops of his glasses. "I see nothing funny about this. The DDO has been on my back about you every day for the last three weeks. He sees the reports, too, you know.'' The old man grabbed a stack of papers and waved them in Stand's face. "Look at this! All memos pertaining to your little adventure. Operations, Intelligence, Analysis, the NSC . . . I've got something from everyone but the head of the goddamned Department of Sanitation. All demanding the same thing—what's going on in Scotland, and when am I going to do something about it?''

"But you didn't," Stand said quietly. "Why not?"

"Because I know you. That's why not." McWilliam's face was red, and he needed a deep breath before he was calm enough to continue. "All right, Nathan. Let's have it. There must have been some reason for your behavior, good or bad. So what did you think you were doing?"

"It was a difficult job that required complete cover. I went underground because it was the only way."

"You couldn't break away once in a while to pick up a phone?"

"Brandon is an idiot," Stand said.

The old man sighed. "I presume you mean he's not a field man. Look, I know how you feel about desk men serving as principals. Let's not get into that again. Nathan, get this through your head—you are a contractor, and you will perform *as specified*. You cannot change the terms of your assignments to suit yourself. The stink you raised this time jeopardized the entire task force. The NSC was demanding to know where this contractor came from. If they had been able to trace you back to me . . . well, it's unthinkable. It would mean the end of everything we've worked for."

"I can appreciate that, sir."

"You'd better. I will not have this organization compromised because of one man's foolishness. I've had to warn you about this sort of thing before. Either you will do things our way, or not at all. Is that clear?"

Stand raised his head and spoke slowly, fighting to keep his temper in check. "I had been in Glasgow three days when I was approached on the street by a young woman. I was waiting for a cab and she just walked up to me and asked how the operation was going, if we had identified any of the smugglers yet, and when we were planning to bust them."

"And who was this young woman?"

Stand made a sour face. "The roommate of Brandon's girl

friend,'' he said. ''That ass was telling them both everything, feeding them the details of the operation like it was a bedtime story. Trying to give them a thrill, impress them with what a big man he was.''

''That's a very serious charge, Nathan. Are you sure he revealed real details? Maybe he invented his pillow talk from whole cloth.''

''Brandon doesn't have the brains to make anything up. No, I'm sure he told them the truth. The roommate knew enough about me to pick me out of a crowd when she just happened by.''

''Weren't these women vetted?''

Stand shrugged. ''How would I know? Probably they were when Brandon first started dating the one, but that was nearly two years ago. Besides, what's the difference? They don't sign secrecy acts. I'm not saying they would sell us out—it's what they could have spilled by accident that had me worried. Hell, Brandon's lover is a receptionist at a radio station. What would have happened if she'd opened her mouth near a reporter?''

McWilliam made a face at that, but withheld comment. He laced his fingers together and rocked slowly in his chair, frowning in concentration. ''Very well, Nathan,'' he said finally. ''I understand your feelings better now. Still, it's clear that you overreacted. You should have notified us of your problems with the assigned controller. We would have found someone more suitable.''

''There wasn't time. It would have taken too long to get a new man in place. They could have shipped those guns anytime during the interim. I cut Brandon loose because it was the only way. The penetration was tricky enough as it was. If the SAS hadn't done such a fine job of paving the way for me, it never would have come together as well as it did.''

McWilliam said, ''I gather, then, that the operation was a success?''

Stand looked at him, thinking it must be a joke. The old man, though, didn't seem amused. ''You don't know the results?'' Stand asked. ''I thought it had to have reached you by now.''

''Since my agents do not bother to inform their principals, the principals have nothing to report back to me.'' McWilliam shook his head and added, with pointed sarcasm, ''I did read in the *newspapers* that the British intercepted two freighters bound for Northern Ireland with cargoes of stolen arms and explosives. I assume—assume, mind you—that is the successful conclusion you've alluded to.''

Stand nodded, then lowered his eyes. ''There was a third shipment, a much smaller one. I handled it personally.''

''And how did you persuade the Brits to let you do that?''

''I didn't tell them about it.''

McWilliam fell back in his chair, seized by a sudden fit of wheezing. Dull popping noises rumbled in his chest, as if there was a hard little pinball crashing about inside his body, steadily racking up points. It was a full minute before the coughing subsided and he was able to catch his breath.

''Are you all right, sir? Can I get you anything?''

''You've done enough,'' McWilliam said weakly. ''No, on second thought, bring me a brandy. You know where it is.''

Stand got to his feet hesitantly. ''I thought the doctors warned you off alcohol.''

''Just bring it!'' the old man snapped.

Stand slid open a panel in the bookcase on the far wall. There were glasses and an assortment of crystal decanters inside. The brandy fumes made his throat tighten in thirst, but he fought down his own longing and filled only one glass. It didn't seem McWilliam was going to offer him any. He took the glass over and slipped it into the old man's dry, cold hand.

McWilliam tried to sneak a white pill into his mouth, but Stand saw it anyway. He didn't say anything. The old man slurped at the brandy as if it were scalding coffee. McWilliam seemed embarrassed by his own sputtering, and he put the glass down quickly. Gripping the desk, he straightened into an exaggeratedly erect pose. ''Thank you, Nathan,'' he said softly. "Let's continue. The truth now: What possessed you to pull a stunt like that?"

"It was only a minor shipment of automatic weapons. A few crates on a fishing boat, one smuggler, very small time. He had no previous record to speak of, but the Yard suspected him of working for the Provos before. He was thought to be involved in a bombing that killed a woman and her two young children."

"I see. And you took it personally."

"I did. You know how—"

McWilliam cut him off. "What I know," he said, "is that your reaction was reckless, unwarranted, and completely inexcusable. We are conducting an organized campaign against terrorism—we are not in the business of providing you with opportunities to indulge in a private vendetta."

"It was a simple job. I handled it."

"What if you failed? How many innocent people may have suffered because of your miscalculation? Your arrogance? Think about it. One mistake—there would have been nothing to prevent those guns from reaching their destination. By choosing to handle the job alone, you were gambling with the lives of others, and that is not what we're about, Nathan. I won't have it."

Stand's protests died in his throat. He nodded grudgingly. "You're right, sir. I didn't see it in those terms. I didn't think it through."

"A lot of good that does now," McWilliam grumbled. "What am I going to do with you, Nathan? I never know what to expect anymore. This sort of renegade action has happened all too often. You're becoming a genuine risk to this office—undisciplined, unpredictable. I can't tolerate much more. I won't have anyone in the field I can't trust. You understand me? *Anyone.*"

The two men fell silent for a long moment. Stand distractedly pulled out his pipe and filled the bowl with moist, black tobacco. He put the pipe between his teeth and was about to strike a match when he caught himself and looked at the old man. McWilliam motioned him on with a wave of the hand. "Go ahead. I'm not so far gone that it'll kill me to watch someone else smoke. At least one of us can still enjoy tobacco."

Stand touched the match to his pipe. Clouds of sweet blue smoke rose about his head. McWilliam sniffed, stared at his empty hands, then folded them together tightly. "All right," he said, "tell me what happened."

Stand spoke in a carefully measured tone, choosing his words at length. "I caught up with the guns off the Orkneys. I was aboard the tugboat that was supposed to load the weapons and carry them on the home stretch. The tug skipper was already in custody. We tumbled the police to him, or, actually, the SAS did. They found the boathouse where he was stockpiling contraband arms. That part went smoothly. He gave the police no trouble."

"Were these guns routed through the same middlemen as the two freighters?"

"No, these came through Denmark. It was thought to be a Swiss connection, but we'll probably never know for sure. The Company men messed up their chance to grab them when they were loading. That's why I decided to step in before they went any further. They were brought across by a Scots fisherman named Mingleton. He was the one sour note. I had to kill him."

"I see," McWilliam said simply.

"I gave him a chance to surrender, but he tried a stupid Hollywood stunt and pulled a gun."

"As an expert on stupid stunts, you probably had no trouble knowing one when you saw it." McWilliam smiled thinly.

"It was a waste, a needless waste."

McWilliam nodded, waited to see if there was more. After a moment, he took another slurp of brandy, then looked thoughtfully at Stand. "Well, all in all, I guess it could have been much worse. You did manage to smash the Provos' supply lines. The Brits came out of it with a success they can splash across the papers to show they're not backing down on the Ireland problem. The PM owes us one now, and she doesn't take her debts lightly. Not a bad result, I suppose.''

"Thank you, sir. About the rest of it . . . I'm sorry. For what's it worth to you. I suppose not much.''

"I know you're tired," McWilliam said. "I won't keep you much longer. But I want to tie up the other details. You don't trust Brandon—that explains why you didn't turn the guns over to him. So who did you leave them with?''

"Sir?''

"The guns, Nathan. The shipment you confiscated. What did you do with them?''

"They're gone.''

"What does that mean—*gone*?''

Stand said, "I disposed of them.''

McWilliam's eyes narrowed until they almost disappeared. "Are you serious? You took automatic weapons worth several thousand dollars and merely destroyed them?''

"I was supposed to prevent the guns from reaching the Provos. I accomplished that.''

"By destroying property that by rights belongs to the United States government!''

"The Office is hardly the government. Only a handful of men in the government even know this task force exists.''

"That's splitting hairs, and you know it. Incredible. You've outdone yourself, Nathan. Destroying those guns was a criminal act.'' McWilliam stared at him and shook his head. "Incredible.''

Stand's eyes grew cold. "I contracted to keep those guns from the hands of terrorists, not to steal them so our people could turn them back on the black market for their own profits.''

McWilliam stiffened. His voice was barely more than a whisper. "Where did you get such an idea?''

"From experience. Prove me wrong. I'd love to be wrong in this case. Do you know—definitely know—what would have happened to those guns once I turned them over to the Company?''

''You know I don't. Not exactly. The Company doesn't keep me apprised of *all* its plans.''

''You can guess, though. A fast paper shuffle and those guns would have been right back on the auction block. Same guns, same interested buyers . . . only this time *we're* the sellers. And that's supposed to make it all right. To their eyes it probably makes sense, simply good business. More funds to spread around quietly on the actions they don't want to appear in the accounting books. But I can't see it their way. What would have been the point of it all?''

McWilliam let out his breath in a long sigh. He settled deeper in his chair and slid his fingers under his glasses to massage the sinus points at the top of his nose.

''Maybe there is a particle of truth in your suspicions,'' he wheezed. ''I don't know. Neither do you, for that matter. The point is, whatever you may think, suspect, or imagine is unimportant. There's one thing you simply haven't gotten in your head. You do not determine policy. Your feelings about anything are immaterial. I like a streak of independence in a contractor; in fact, it's almost essential. But this time, Nathan, you went too far. I can't dismiss these actions as merely misguided. They were unforgivable. I won't permit this sort of thing to continue.''

''I understand, sir.''

McWilliam's head came up. ''Do you? I truly hope so. Because you brought it on yourself. You leave me no choice, Nathan. I'm taking you out of circulation.''

Stand grinned. ''As in missing and presumed dead?''

''Dammit! Do you see me laughing here? Aren't you listening? Don't think I enjoy this. I've protected you as long as I can. It's over, Nathan. From this point on, you are relieved from duty. I'm sorry, it's the way it has to be.''

Stand blinked as if something had fallen in his eye. ''You're serious about this?''

''I respect you, Nathan; I don't want to lose you completely. If you want, I'll try to find you a job with the support staff. A desk job, that's the best I can do, I'm afraid.''

"There must be something. Some other way."

"This is where it ends. I'll have to pull some strings to get you on with the support staff. Anyone else I would terminate here and now. If the DCI catches wind of this, he'll want both of our heads.''

"You might as well cut me loose now," Stand said. "I'll never make it as a desk man."

"That's what you think now," McWilliam said gently. "Give it some time, you'll see things differently. It may actually be a good experience for you to work with Langley. You might learn not to criticize them so freely. Their game is a lot more complex than the one you and I play.''

Stand shook his head. "I just don't like the way they do business. I don't like choosing my actions according to the political winds of the season, and I don't like bowing to the director as if every word from his lips is gospel.''

"Then you'll just have to learn to live with what you don't like. Face it, Nathan, they're the only game in town.''

"I'll think about it."

"Do that," McWilliam said. "Take your time, get some rest, think things through. Come see me when you've made a decision. I hope you'll give it a try.''

Stand go to his feet. Slowly, as if in a daze, he walked to the desk and offered the old man his hand. "I don't know what to say. I guess this is good-bye.''

McWilliam's cold fingers gripped Stand's hand with a strength that surprised him. "Take care of yourself, Nathan.''

Stand turned away quickly. McWilliam looked down and pulled his shirt cuff over the dark blotch on the back of his left hand. When he looked up again, Stand was gone. The door swung shut behind him with a solid thud.

McWilliam pulled a page from a file and peered down at it, but his eyes were blank, unfocused. For a long time he sat there, motionless, barely breathing. His head bowed lower, lower, and then the spasm struck. He coughed and clutched his chest as the pain shot through his lungs, each breath like a mouthful of broken glass.

Nathan had called him a lucky man. Well, lucky men died too. If anything, they just had more to lose when the end did come.

CHAPTER 3

TRAFFIC FLOWED smoothly along the broad avenues, but the bundled pedestrians clung together in tight packs, storming the sidewalks in broken-field runs, their heads bowed to the rain, cursing and stomping through the puddles as if hoping for something more substantial to kick. Jean Frost ducked into a coffeeshop and took a table at the back. She smoked a Winston and warmed her hands around an espresso while she waited. The place was doing a brisk business that morning as red-faced men and women ran in to swap grim predictions for the coming winter, roughly interchangeable tales of flooded basements, soaked auto distributors, and apartments without heat. Jean listened to the drone without paying any real attention. She picked out a second cigarette, hesitated, and stuck it back in the pack. She sipped her coffee and watched the door, waiting.

Jean was used to waiting for what she wanted. Nothing of real importance in her life had ever come easily. She permitted herself to savor and enjoy only those things that she had won through her own efforts.

She had shunned the Ivy League schools of her parents' choosing, and earned a law degree from a small midwestern college, where she could afford the tuition by working full-time as a courier for a private law firm. She determinedly refused to spend a penny of the substantial trust fund the McWilliams had set aside for her education. That money was spent *after* graduation, on travel, on a year of touring Europe while she considered what career and new challenges she would next pursue.

Fate made that decision for her, for it was on that vacation that she had met Gunter Holbein, a powerful Swiss industrialist. They fell in love and, after a whirlwind romance of four months, were married. It was the most impetuous act of Jean's life, and for three years she had no doubt it was the best decision she had ever made.

But gradually the romance waned. Jean was bored playing the role of a businessman's wife. She longed to start a career of her own, but her staunchly old-world husband wouldn't hear of it. They quarreled often, and Holbein spent less and less time with his young wife, claiming problems at work and a dozen other excuses that Jean didn't care to question too closely.

Then Holbein became gravely ill from congenital heart disease. Jean tried to lure her husband away from his work and rekindle the passion of their early years together. He seemed uninterested, and slowly they grew apart. Jean learned of her husband's death on the phone. He had died of a massive stroke, in the arms of his mistress.

Jean Frost-Holbein was again simply Jean Frost. She inherited a considerable fortune, but the money did nothing to soothe her pain. She returned to Washington and spent months without setting foot outside her father's house. McWilliam assumed his daughter was working through her grief. He could not know that she struggled to cope not with death, but betrayal. Jean never told him the truth of her sudden loss.

Finally, simply to fill her time, Jean began helping her father, serving as secretary and general assistant. She gradually came to see the appeal of her father's work, and for the first time she understood his single-minded devotion. For his part, McWilliam was pleased to find his daughter displaying a sharp mind and willing attention to the endless details of their secret work, so many of which could never be committed to paper.

As her father's health declined, Jean assumed greater responsibilities. Eventually McWilliam pulled strings to have her enlisted in the CIA, appointed as liaison between the Office and Langley. Jean thrived in her new role and the new attention from her father. In their shared devotion to the work at hand, they formed a bond that made Jean feel she might someday truly earn the love her father was so emotionally unprepared to display.

During these heady, hectic years, there had been no time for romance. Jean was consumed by her job and seldom sought companionship, or returned the attentions of the many men who admired her beauty. She doubted she would ever again trust a man in that way, giving fully of her body and love.

But eventually, like so much else, that, too, had changed.

The door of the coffeeshop opened and James Gregory burst inside, as always making his appearance an act of high drama. Jean imagined a fanfare of trumpets whenever she saw him. He paused inside the door and brushed the dampness from his overcoat, muttering an obscenity about the weather. The people near him laughed. He started toward Jean, weaving between tables. Jean stared down at her hands, blushing. Her heart pounded as if it would burst.

It amazed her, the power of his spell. She felt the same excitement at seeing him now as on their first night together. They had been lovers for nearly two years, but the thrill of infatuation and romance had never dimmed.

Gregory swept down upon her and sat. For a moment he simply stared into her eyes. She had the uneasy sensation he was examining her, peering into every secret corner of her mind.

"I thought we decided to be discreet."

"Relax, Jean. Nobody in this café is watching. They don't care about us. They're only concerned with their own boring boxed-in lives."

Jean glanced around. He was right. No one was paying them special attention. She had only imagined it. It was a disquieting revelation, how much this man's presence could distort her judgment.

He took her hand. "I missed you so much, Jean. It seems like we've been apart forever."

"It was only a couple of weeks," she said, hiding her pleasure at hearing him express her own feelings. She stared at his face, studying it with undisguised fascination. He had started to grow a moustache. It gave him a vaguely sinister air, the swaggering virility of a Latin film star. She reached out and teased the dark bristly stubble with a fingertip. "How did this happen?"

"You don't like it?" He stroked the whiskers fondly. "In a few weeks it'll fill out. Then you'll like it."

"I'm not sure I'll know you," Jean said, with a small laugh. "It makes you look very different."

"Good. It'll be exciting for you, like making love to a stranger."

Jean looked into his eyes. "I only make love to you. And it's always exciting."

"C'mon," Gregory said quietly. "Let's get out of here. I want to make love to you now."

Jean put a hand on his arm, stopping him when he started to rise. "James, please. We need to talk. So much has happened and I've been worried. . . . It's all turned sour, and when I didn't hear from you—"

"All the more reason to be alone. I've missed you so much, Jean. Come we'll have time to talk. After."

"James, please . . ." she muttered. It didn't come out the way she intended.

Gregory smiled and helped her to her feet.

James Gregory was living proof that in America, every man had the opportunity to rise as far as his will and determination could take him. He had enjoyed a dozen opportunities and wasted them all.

Approached by a CIA recruiter during his final year at Notre Dame, he had found the idea laughable. His future was already determined—had been since the moment of birth. He was to study law at the University of Florida, then enter his father's prestigious Washington firm. Gregory & Dawsone was a national institution, power brokers who hammered out contracts for some of the world's wealthiest corporations. Gregory's future was assured—fast living, easy rewards, and privilege. The idea of becoming an underpaid civil servant in some dreary embassy was no more than a bad joke.

One semester at Florida was enough to give him second thoughts. Gregory discovered that law required a dedication he wasn't prepared to give. It appeared to him as nothing but word pushing. He had no enthusiasm for it. He gazed at legal texts and saw nothing but dry, dusty sentences, meaningless strings of semantics. What he needed was excitement.

On a whim, he contacted the CIA recruiter and enrolled in the Junior Officer Trainee program. The work was demanding and, in its own way, every bit as dull as his legal studies. But this time Gregory stuck with it. It was six years before he received an overseas assignment in secret operations, but the prospect propelled him through the grueling years of training.

Intrigue, shadowy meetings in dark alleys, backstage schemes to alter the balance of world power—the lurid world of espionage appealed to him and his sense of drama. Gregory had always known he was a man destined for greatness. And here he discovered the perfect business for a man of his unique gifts. There was no telling how far he would go.

He went about eight miles. To the CIA headquarters in Langley, Virginia. Gregory was posted to a desk in Operations, the subdivision of Logistics and Support. He became a "plumber," a support officer for a string of second-field contracts—agents spying inside NATO nations.

And there his career foundered. Gregory came to realize that the day-to-day business of spying was as mundane and dreary as any other. He wasn't a spy, he was a shipping clerk, shuffling men and equipment from one place to another, processing requests, and dealing with an endless backlog of paper work. He toiled for ten years without distinguishing himself in any way.

While Gregory was no more than mediocre in his assigned

duties, he did become an accomplished master in another realm almost as important—in-house politics. Early on, Gregory learned that his only real asset was his attractiveness. His looks and easy charm made him a romantic figure to every woman in the vast Langley complex. Knowing this, he involved himself in affairs with secretaries, typists, personal aides, the women close to the men in power. What he learned from his stable of lovers—what they unwittingly revealed—gave him an overview of the Company that few could match. He knew almost everything about everyone else's business.

Stringing these women along, keeping them happy and unaware of one another, was not an easy task. It required a delicate touch, careful plotting, intrigue, and deception. It was almost like being a spy. In fact, he was a spy, he decided. A mole burrowed deep within the system, daily trading and acquiring secrets. This self-image pleased him.

For years he muddled along, pacified by the excitement of his carnal intrigues and the sense of power from his voluminous insider's knowledge. But gradually, Gregory began to find less and less pleasure in his secret passion. No spy had ever labored more successfully, learned more. But what use was this storehouse of knowledge? Where had it gotten him? The Company did not recognize his abilities, it had cast him aside, wasting his talents and his life. He deserved more.

Gregory began to wonder how he might better use his special skills for personal gain. The Company had had its chance. There were others who would not be so blind to his importance.

Jean clamped her legs around his hips and they rocked, harder, faster, until they were almost lurching from the bed. At a silent signal, Gregory rolled onto his back. He lay still, barely breathing. She straddled him, accepting his full length. He held out his arms, but she shook her head. Poised on her knees, she arched her back and rode him with short frantic thrusts. He moved with her, rising to meet her bucking hips.

They threw themselves at each other in a brutal frenzy, roused beyond thought by growing urgency.

He reached up and roughly squeezed her breasts, rolling the marble-hard nipples between his fingers. Jean hissed and tossed her head back. The air seemed to catch in her throat and her whole body began to shudder. She braced her hands on his chest and pounded with abandon, crying out as her body jerked in rippling convulsions. In the same instant, he felt his own tension crest. He closed his eyes, groaning as the spasms drained him. Jean moaned softly and collapsed atop him. Gregory idly traced the long hollow of her spine, stroking gently. Her body was hot and damp, as if a fire burned below the silken cover of her skin. He tenderly kissed the top of her head, then lay back with a sigh of weariness.

Jean's eyes fluttered open, wide with concern, as if she had heard something disturbing in the sound. "What is it? Did I do something wrong?"

"I was just thinking. A sorrow that we can't feel this way every moment of our lives."

Jean rolled onto her side and nestled her head in the crook of his shoulder. "Why not?" she murmured. "I do. Whenever I think of you my whole life seems perfect. Sometimes it seems so much like a dream it almost scares me. You know, as if it's too good to be real."

"It's not perfect. How can it be, when we're apart so much? I want it to be different, Jean. I want us to be together for real and always, the way we should be. The way we deserve."

She hugged him tightly. "I know. The last time at the house, I wanted to tell Daddy about you so badly. I thought he could arrange something for us, get you reassigned so we could work together more closely."

He stiffened, gripping her so hard that she winced in pain. "You didn't tell me you had spoken to anyone about us," he snapped.

"I didn't say anything. I just wanted to, that's all." She stared at him in confusion. "I won't mention it to him if the idea bothers you so much."

"Our feelings are our secret, Jean. Our business, alone."

"I thought you wanted the whole world to know about us," she said.

"I do, but the timing has to be right. I don't want anyone to get the wrong idea. Trust me, Jean, there are people who would twist it around, make it seem ugly, sordid, use our love against us."

"What people, James?"

"You know how this business is. These people know how to use secrets to put their thumbs on everyone and they don't like anything they can't control. They'll use anything to get whatever they want. We have to be careful, that's all."

Jean sighed. "For how long?"

He gently guided her head back to his shoulder. "I know it's not easy this way. I don't like it any more than you. But things may change very soon."

"I still don't see what would be the harm in your asking for a reassignment."

"It wouldn't work out," he said gruffly.

"But we would be together. That's what we want."

Gregory shook his head. "I couldn't work under your father. That's no way for us to start a life together, with me having to answer to him for everything I do. The Office is too small an organization for a man like me. There's no room to grow, no opportunities."

"I never knew you felt that way."

"I've told you before I wouldn't be comfortable there. You didn't listen, because you wanted me with you so much."

Jean nodded silently, accepting the rebuke because she knew it was true. Gregory had always been reluctant to join her in the Office. But she had always hoped he would see there was no other way. Their work was such a large part of their lives and made such demands of their time and energy. It seemed to her that the only way they could truly be together was to share those duties.

Gregory went on. "And there is another consideration. . . . Forgive me, darling, but your father may not live much longer. When he dies, you will be his successor. I love you, but I don't know how I would react to taking orders from you."

"It could work, James. We'd be a team. I know it might not be easy for you at first, but we would learn how to handle it. You always complain how you're wasted in your current post. Well, in the Office you would know you were doing something important, making a real difference in the world."

Gregory laughed bitterly. "I don't care about the world. I want to make a difference for me. My life is nearly half over, Jean, and what do I have to show for it? I want the rewards, the respect that's due me. Until I have it, I won't be deserving of you."

"What do you mean?" Jean said. "You don't have to be someone different for me to love you. I love you as you are."

"Let's drop it," Gregory said. "I don't want to talk about it right now, okay? Let's just enjoy being with each other while we can."

Jean started to protest, but he leaned over and silenced her with a kiss. At first she resisted, her lips stubbornly wooden. But he persisted and her resolve weakened, her lips softening, clinging hungrily to his. At the end, she pulled away from him with a sigh of sadness.

"What's wrong, Jean?" Gregory asked. "There's something troubling you, I can tell. Is there something you haven't told me?"

"Yes, James. We have to talk now. Seriously."

He sat up, resting his back against the headboard. "All right, I'm listening."

Jean pulled the sheet up and cuddled to him, as if seeking his warmth. She began hesitantly, avoiding his eyes. "I almost don't know how to start. We could be in a lot of trouble. James, what have you heard from Switzerland about that shipment I asked you to arrange? Do you know what's happened to it?"

He frowned. "Not much. I don't think it's arrived yet."

"I have reason to believe it was intercepted," she said. "I think it was confiscated in the midst of a major smuggling bust by the SAS and a contractor from Daddy's Office."

"You're the Company/Office liaison. Why didn't you know about that?"

"I didn't know you were going to route the shipment through a smuggler with ties to the Provos. That was a major mistake, James. You shouldn't have chosen Ireland for a way station. It could have been routed to America directly from Denmark. There was no reason to have it change hands in a nation where they're so concerned about smuggling."

"I didn't have a network I could trust in Denmark," Gregory protested. "Besides, the Danes are much too scrupulous in their customs checks. Once the shipment reached my people in Ireland, sneaking it into the States would have been a breeze. Getting something out of Ireland is no problem, as long as you're not trying to move it into Ulster."

"The scheme was much too cute."

He bristled. "You mean it's my fault."

Jean sat up, retreating from the sting of his voice. "I didn't say that. I just wish you had talked it over with me before you charted the shipment that way. We could have thought of something that wasn't so involved, that didn't rely on professional smugglers."

Gregory rolled his eyes. "Look, Jean. You want to sneak something halfway around the world, you don't call Federal Express. You have to deal with smugglers, and yes, they're crooks and untrustworthy, but what other choice do you have? This wasn't a simple transport problem you handed me. There were layers and layers of deception involved, mostly to fool the smugglers themselves. You give me something to move—you won't even tell me what it is—but you say it's imperative that no one, even our own people, be aware of the transaction. Did you think a job like that was going to be easy?"

"Calm down, darling," Jean said. "I'm not criticizing you. I'm merely trying to understand where it went wrong. It's important that we both be clear about this in case . . . well, there's no telling what might happen."

Gregory stared at her. "You're worried about an investigation, aren't you? Goddammit! I can't believe you screwed me over like this!"

"James, please—"

"This whole thing was your idea."

"I know. I'm sorry. I never should have gotten you involved."

"Involved in what? You trust me to do your dirty work, but not to know what it's all about. God, Jean, you're just like all the rest of them." Gregory rolled away from her, sat on the edge of the bed, and held his head in his hands. Jean reached out to him, but he pushed her hand away. "Leave me alone. Haven't you done enough?"

Jean blinked, fighting back tears. "James, give me a chance. We're in this together, you know."

"Great. That makes it a real loving experience, doesn't it?"

"I said I'm sorry. You don't have to bite my head off."

Gregory spun around, glared at her. "What have you gotten me into? You owe me an explanation, Jean. When is this thing going to blow up in my face?"

"I don't know," she muttered. "There's still a chance it may all blow over."

"What blow over? For chrissakes, Jean, talk to me. What was in those crates?"

"If you'll be quiet for a minute and give me a chance, I'll explain it," she said.

Gregory nodded grudgingly.

Jean told him how Stand had caught the smuggler, taken the shipment, then, on his own initiative, disposed of it. Gregory's mood brightened as the story unfolded, and when she finished, he smiled as though greatly pleased.

"So what's the problem?" he asked. "Darling Daddy has fixed everything for us."

"It's not that simple."

"Why not? We lost the shipment—that's regrettable, of course, but under the circumstances, it's better than turning up in a Company investigation. And Nathan Stand, the contractor who caused all this trouble, is gone, too, out to pasture where he can't stir up any more hassles. All the ends are neatly tied off. It's beautiful, really. I don't see where you could ask for a better result, everything considered.''

Gregory walked slowly around the bed, stealing a proud glance in the mirror at his lithe, muscled body. He stood over Jean until she looked up. Then he leaned down to kiss her.

Jean pushed him away. She stared at the floor, then got up and pulled on her clothes. Gregory stretched out on the bed, watching her dress, his expression sullen and withdrawn. She came back, started to sit on the edge of the mattress, but changed her mind and dropped into a chair across the room.

"What is it now?" Gregory hissed, his tone weary and exasperated. "Jean, it's nothing to worry about. You lost the shipment, but otherwise we slipped out of this still smelling sweet."

She looked up at him and shook her head. "It's not over. We can't let this thing rest until we know what Stand did with the shipment."

"You said he destroyed it."

"I'm convinced he didn't. For one thing, the shipment is not so easy to dispose of. That's the reason I was moving it in the first place, sending it to a place where the disposal could be handled under scientifically controlled conditions."

"What the hell is it?"

Jean sighed. "And second, if he had tried, we would know about it. This thing is dangerous, James. There would have been a disaster if it had not been disposed of properly. We have to find out where it is."

"So make Stand tell you," Gregory said simply.

"If only it were that easy." Jean smiled wanly. "Daddy fired him over this incident. If I start to ask what he did to the shipment, he'll become suspicious."

Gregory stomped over and stood in front of her, forcing her to look up at him. "I think it's time you told me what was in that shipment. I agreed not to ask questions when you first approached me. We're in this together, so I have a right to know. I'm not sticking my neck out any further until I do."

She nodded. "You're right. I didn't want to tell you before, only because it was better that way, safer for both of us."

"Tell me now," he said.

Jean looked away, found her purse on the floor, and pulled a pack of cigarettes from it. She lit one and drew in the smoke hungrily.

"I thought you were going to give those up."

"I know, I know. I can't be a saint right now, James. This isn't easy for me either, you know."

Diplomatically, he backed away, giving her time to form her thoughts. "Whenever you're ready, darling," he said gently. "Just tell it to me in your own way."

Jean told him. Gregory listened in silence, fighting hard to conceal his growing excitement.

CHAPTER 4

THE FOG slithered in like a snake, coiling around every pebble and crag on the shoreline. Silently, it crept up the rock toward the lone figure on the edge of the cliff. Nathan Stand's gaze was distant. He stared out to sea. Nothing showed on his face, no hint of what he saw. In one hand he held a bottle, but he made no move to drink. He didn't move at all, even as the fog approached, whispering up his legs and swirling around him.

The mist swallowed everything in its path. It settled over the island, the land vanishing as if it had never existed. There was only the fog, blank, the color of stone or of silt at the bottom of an ancient sea. Dead. Empty.

Finally he stirred, shaking himself as if awakening from a dream. Hesitantly, he raised the bottle and drank. Then he took one step forward and let it drop from his fingers.

He moved off when he heard the splash. Even in the blinding fog, Stand walked quickly, confidently, knowing each step, every stone, by heart. He found the stairs leading to the sea and started down. The steps were slick with beaded moisture. Twice he slipped, skinning his shins and sliding several feet before he caught himself. But he persisted, groping and feeling his way. And when the planks of the pier thudded under his boots, he was almost running.

* * *

Stand took the *Walter Scott* north to clear the island, then swung her bow toward the distant coast of Maine. The swells were gentle, the wind at the stern just a whisper. He thought he might outrun the fog, but it was everywhere, dark and impenetrable. He couldn't see more than five meters in any direction. Beyond that, the world dropped off to nothing.

He sat back and took his hands from the wheel. The boat went on, unguided, closing on the shore. After a brief moment of hesitation, he reached out and shuttled back the engine, then cut it off.

The stillness was sudden, total. There was only the steady beat of his heart, and the pulse of the sea, strong, constant, relentless. It was so quiet he could hear the rasp of his own breathing. With sudden hunger, he lit his pipe and inhaled deeply. The narcotic sweetness raced through his veins.

He was as drunk as he'd ever been. His body glowed, every nerve humming with electricity, and he'd never felt so alive. It was an ironic thought, and he laughed aloud.

He brought out a tamper and pressed down the charred tobacco in the bowl of his pipe. Normally this motion was automatic, but this time his fingers fumbled badly, and hot ash spilled out over his lap. He cursed and brushed himself off, then repeated the procedure slowly, with exaggerated caution.

He struck a match and got his pipe going again. Before the flame died, he touched it to a candle. The wick flared into life, the glow spilling across a nearby object. A photograph in a gold-edged frame sat above the instrument panel.

In the picture a woman and child had their heads together as if sharing a secret. Their eyes shone as they looked at the man behind the camera and laughed. The girl was a scaled-down copy of her mother. Their smiles expressed the same surprise at being caught in a moment of silliness.

Stand sat, entranced. The flickering candle was reflected in the exact center of his dark eyes. He couldn't look away from the picture. He knew it better than he knew himself, but he stared at it in wonder, as if it were new and unexpected. Minutes passed. Then the picture misted over and the spell was broken. He blinked but couldn't clear the moisture from his eyes. He was surprised he could still cry. He thought he had no tears left.

Must be the booze, he decided. The alcohol was working its magic. As he sat there, he felt a strange heaviness pressing down on him. He could barely move. But everything else did. The cabin walls began to spin.

Stand reached to slide the picture closer, but the thing wouldn't hold still. He tried to grab it and almost fell from his chair. It took effort to sit straight again. His body felt like stone. Everything was blurry, as if the fog had penetrated the wheelhouse. The walls spun faster and he felt himself sinking, falling into a whirling vortex where time and reality faded. He closed his eyes, welcoming it.

The sound cut through the haze that clouded his mind. He listened and heard it again. A low somber knell. The warning buoy. His heart quickened. The sound was very near.

The clang of the buoy was joined by a deep grumble and loud sporadic cracks like cannon fire. The noise grew stronger. He felt the air shudder from the force of it.

He felt the boat heeling, caught in the current, dragged helplessly landward. There were only seconds left.

The Serpents, the local seamen had named this place, one of the most rugged landfalls on the Atlantic seaboard. It was a spiked bed of growlers, submerged stones that could tear a steel hull like cheesecloth. The channel between the rocks was a winding nightmare, so narrow in places that the clearance for a boat like the *Walter Scott* was measured in inches. The Serpents' name came from the distinctive hiss of a bore hole in the great rock at the head of the maze. And for the certain swift death that sound promised.

Stand heard it now. He trembled and cursed himself for his fear, but his voice was lost in the violent din of the breakers. The cabin tilted around him. A screech sounded below as the hull scraped off the first hidden growler. Stand was thrown roughly to one side. The boat skinned by, then righted itself in a stomach-turning lurch. The candle fell from the table and sputtered out.

Sprawled on the floor, Stand looked up and saw the picture of Leah and Melissa rock on its frame, then topple over. He stared at it. All at once, his mind was clear. He knew what he had come to discover.

With sudden determination, Stand threw himself back behind the wheel and pressed the ignition. The diesels fired into life. He threw open the throttle and spun the wheel hard over.

The boat responded sluggishly, coming around in a grim fight against the current. The hiss of The Serpents was deafening, but Stand ignored it, his face set in concentration. He counted the seconds, listening to the beat of the pounding surf. The timbre of the sea suddenly deepened. In that instant, he spun the wheel back to starboard and held on.

There was one bad moment when the boat took a hard glancing blow. The impact echoed with a clappered ring of heavy metal. Stand knew he'd struck the wreckage of the *Tamara*, a sunken freighter. The *Walter Scott* was thrown to one side, listing so hard that the sea stormed over the deck, dragging her down. With heart-stopping slowness the boat righted itself, shrugging off the fatal burden.

Then suddenly he was through. The violence faded behind him and the boat skimmed through calm, deep water.

He pointed her to the east and set the diesels at a slow, steady pace. The danger was past. He felt no elation, only a numbness of crushing exhaustion. He looked for the fallen picture of his family, located it on the floor in the back of the cabin.

He dropped to his knees and touched it tenderly. The glass front had shattered, obscuring the faces with a webwork of jagged lines. In a rage, Stand tore at the glass with his bare fingers. Blood from his cuts dripped on the picture, blotting out Melissa's smile. He froze, gazing at the image in horror.

The picture slipped from his trembling hands. He kicked it across the cabin, then scrambled, crawling, to the opposite wall. He backed into the shadows, struck by the knowledge of his brush with death. He was not ready to die. That was all he had come to find out.

Time passed, as relentless as the sea, and the currents of both swept him farther away. Stand huddled in the corner gazing at nothing, his eyes blank. He knew there was only one path back to life left open to him. But for the moment, he was content to drift, waiting for the end of the long black night.

On Innesmore the weather was always changing. It was one of the things Stand liked most about the island. Innesmore was a spit of rock barely a mile and three-quarters round, situated near the mouth of the Bay of Fundy. On a clear day he could see the silhouette of Nova Scotia to the northeast. A similar line rimming the seas to the west was the coast of northern Maine. In the mornings he sat at the table, drank his coffee, and watched through the tall bay windows the fishing boats laboring out to sea. He knew each one by sight, and sometimes climbed into the lighthouse to follow a favorite by means of the telescope mounted there.

The lighthouse was perched atop a cliff on the island's north shore, surrounded by a ring of stunted pines. They were all that grew on the bare slopes, where the winter wind cut like a scythe. There were squirrels and snowshoe hares in the forest beyond the house—how they came to the island, no one knew—but apart from their company, he was alone.

Stand had first come to the island eight years before, the year that Leah and Melissa died. It was a time he barely remembered, a black void of continual drunkenness. The real keeper of the lighthouse was an old family friend. When he retired that year, he had asked Stand to take his place. Stand had no occupation then. He had left the college to spend the year in a drunken haze, trying to deaden his grief by not remembering at all.

"You've drawn a rough lot," Karl Penny had said. "But you gotta beat it out, lad. A man has to be tougher than his fate. Get outta this town, it's no place for the likes of you. Too many folks here with a stake in you losing. You'll never get past all that hate inside you long as you're around so many easy targets."

Stand had avoided the old man's eyes. "I don't know, Penny. I don't know if I can make it alone."

"Ha! You been alone, lad, since the day you was born. Time you got used to it. There's nothin' in this world a man can't face up to, once he's learned to live with hisself."

Stand promised to think about it. Instead, that night he did exactly what he had been doing for most of that long black year. He went out and got drunk, then picked a fight with the biggest opponent he could find.

A solid year of steady drinking and few meals had left Stand a skeleton at that time, barely strong enough to raise his fists. He was a poor match for even the lowliest opponent, but almost every night he picked a fight with someone. The rough fishermen had come, in their own way, to understand how he was using them to punish himself, and they learned to ignore his challenges. Beating him down had gotten boring.

That night Stand chose to heckle a group of lumbermen from the far northern range; tall, burly men hardened like steel. Stand singled out the largest of the bunch and started provoking him with insults, pestering him like a buzzing gnat.

To his credit, the logger tried to put him off. He bought Stand a drink, asking him to take it away somewhere and leave him alone. Stand accepted it, then splashed it across the man's face. The lumberman knocked Stand halfway down the room with a single swipe of his arm. Stand picked himself up and roared back into the fray.

That pattern repeated itself for nearly ten minutes. Not to miss the fun, the logger's friends soon joined in, taking turns at pounding out the troublesome drunk, who kept coming back for more.

The big logger was a more gentle man than his appearance suggested. He pleaded with Stand in a whisper, "Stay down, damn you. Give it up, man. We don't want to kill you."

By this time, Stand had suffered multiple rib fractures and his face looked like raw meat. But he bared his teeth in a grim smile and staggered back into their midst, still swinging.

The logger saw there was no other way. He ended it with a boot to the face that rolled Stand's eyes into his skull. He crumpled and sagged to the floor. This time he did not get up.

It was the best thing that happened to him. Karl Penny visited Stand in the hospital. He urged Stand to accept the lighthouse post. Stand, numbed by Percodan but otherwise sober for the first time in weeks, had sense enough to accept. He expected no miracles, but knew he had to try something to break the downhill skid. At least on the lonely island, he might survive long enough to find his way back to life. The island became his prison. He sentenced himself to solitude there, in the full knowledge that he might never escape.

Eight years ago. He had lived there ever since. Even after Daniel McWilliam had found him and put him to work. It could never be a home, but it was all he had. On those lonely windswept shores, Stand was safe from others, safe from the harm of his own drunkenness. Safe from everything but the past.

The skies had carried through on their threat. The soft morning rain had become a full-blown gale. The fishing boats had run back to the harbors, tied off, and were riding it out. The wind moaned through the pines, whipping them back and forth, their thin needles shaking free and taking flight like a cloud of locusts.

Stand was still in his place by the windows when the radio set in the main room crackled and came to life. "Farragon to St. John. Changing course to lay over at Yarmouth till 0600 tomorrow. Please advise home office."

The St. John radioman replied in a terse, bored voice. Stand didn't bother to listen. He monitored the ships' radio traffic more out of habit than interest. His father had owned a marine salvage operation, one of the riskiest ways in the world to scratch out a living. Besides the hazards of sea and weather, there were cutthroat competitors with whom to deal. Ships in trouble usually accepted the aid of the first salvage man to reach them, so a distress signal was the starting gun for a grim race.

In Stand's childhood home, the radio was never off. Even as a young boy, he was expected to monitor the signal traffic for the first hint of trouble at sea. It became a lifelong habit. To him, the chatter of seagoing radiomen was as pleasantly nostalgic as a favorite old song.

He would have liked to go out for a walk around the island, but the storm made the prospect unlikely. So he stayed at the table throughout the day, watching the sea through the windows, and drinking often enough to keep a pleasant buzz. The lighthouse was nicely laid out with modern furnishings, but Stand spent almost all his time by the windows, where he had a sense of space and light. He couldn't bear to be in a room without windows. Elevators made him sweat. Claustrophobia was a minor discomfort that he had dealt with all his life. It wasn't so much a physical aversion to close spaces as a silly but still troublesome notion that he might never escape.

When he was a boy, Stand had avidly pored through accounts of refugees who had escaped the Nazis by spending years in attics, cellars, or caves. The idea of those dark cramped spaces left an impression on Stand that he couldn't forget. He was never able to enter a room without sizing it up, wondering what it would be like if he had to remain there the rest of his life. No room was ever big enough.

He had a book spread open on the table, but didn't try to read. He merely sat and gazed at the sea and the black clouds. A sheet of rain moved across the horizon, blurring the line between sea and sky so that they merged into one.

His eyes were blank, far away. He had an old fruit jar for a glass. He opened the bottle and topped off the jar without paying attention, familiar motions requiring no thought.

Somewhere beyond the storm, the sun pivoted and began its slippery fall toward dusk. The gale continued, unabated. The wind shrieked like the drawn-out cry of a man falling toward a bottomless unknown. Stand's head drooped toward his chest and he tumbled over the edge of consciousness into sleep.

The memories were there. They came, unbidden, in a familiar dream. . . .

It was a fairy-tale land, green and lush, with skies the blue of tropic seas. There were flowers everywhere, the blossoms so bright and lovely that his eyes ached to take them in. The hills were like ocean waves, flowing smoothly into the distance. It was quiet, still as the hush before dawn, the wildflowers swayed in a breeze that had no voice.

Stand looked around, bewildered. It all seemed familiar yet strange, like a friend one had not seen in many years.

He wandered through the high meadows, his body feeling light and airy, almost as though he were floating. He didn't question the odd sensation. Somehow it seemed natural and right. He came upon a tree, an old broken elm growing alone in the middle of a field. It cast a thin gray shadow, as if it were of too little substance to stand against the light. His eyes widened in alarm. He knew this tree and it didn't belong here.

Then he saw the train. At first he thought it must have driven into view, but then realized it had been there all along. He must have missed it, for the train was dead on the tracks. It looked as if it hadn't moved in some time. Hesitantly he drifted toward it. The train lured him closer, compelling him in a way he could not identify.

Suddenly the sky went dark. The storm came from nowhere, and the hills grew pale in a flash of lightning. A crash of thunder stopped his heart. But the thunder didn't fade, it continued to crackle, growing louder, the sound sending a shiver down his spine. All at once he knew why. It wasn't thunder at all. It was gunfire.

Stand tasted the sour bile of fear. Warily, he continued toward the train. His limbs felt heavier, his steps labored and clumsy. He couldn't take his eyes from the train. The din of gunfire grew louder. Without thinking about it, he suddenly knew from where it was coming.

Then he heard the screams. It was as if the sky had opened up and rained elemental terror. The sound was everywhere at once; an ugly wailing, harsh, raw, rising whole octaves above the normal range of human voices.

Stand was running. He heard footsteps in the grass behind him, but he didn't turn to see who was there. He had a strange chilling sense that he wasn't being followed but pursued. It didn't matter. He knew only one thing mattered. He had to reach the train.

The screams were deafening. More voices joined in, raucous and painfully shrill. Stand kept on, struggling as his legs grew even heavier. He felt an odd resistance, as if the earth had grown soft and clutched at him. He tried to run, but his legs wouldn't move. The air itself pushed him away. It got harder the closer he got to the train. It took all his strength to cover the last few yards.

At last he stumbled up and seized the handle to the door of the car. The screaming inside mounted to an unbearable howl. Wretched terrified voices, screeching in jangling glissandos to a treble pitch of madness. And the cough of gunfire was cold, mirthless laughter.

Stand flung open the door.

The voices broke, shattered by an abrupt silence. Stand gasped. Inside, there was only darkness. Nothing.

He staggered back a step, shocked and disbelieving. He looked again and saw something that froze the blood in his veins.

It was moving.

The darkness oozed through the open door and spilled upon the ground. He gagged. The stench assaulted his nostrils, a choking miasma of ancient decay. The muck flowed toward him. Everything it touched vanished. He tried to run, but his legs wouldn't respond. The darkness was upon him already, a black wave rising to bury him alive. His mouth opened in a scream, but there was no sound. Nothing at all.

Stand awoke with a start. He groaned and heard the sound oddly muffled. It was then that he realized he was slumped over with his face plastered against the tabletop. He sat up stiffly and massaged the tingling numbness in his cheek. One hazard of being a drunk.

Still shaken by the dream, he stared out the windows and saw it was growing dark. He got up quickly and turned on the houselights. The big lamp in the lighthouse tower had already switched on, automatically triggered by an electronic sensor. He watched the broad beam sweep across the sky and shine on the glowering clouds. Like a photographer's flash, the light caught them for an instant, froze them in sharp relief, then moved on.

Stand moved toward the kitchen. He had taken only two steps when he froze, halted by a startling sound.

Daddy.

Stand spun around sharply. "Melissa?"

The answering silence was deep, unbroken. Slowly he came to his senses.

It happened so often that Stand wondered if there wasn't more to it than imagination. It always occurred in unguarded moments when his mind was drifting between conscious thoughts—suddenly he would hear a voice call his name. It was never more than that, single word, but it would ring so clearly, the voice so instantly, utterly recognizable, that it seemed too real to ignore. Maybe it was just an aberration of the mind, a neural echo from sometime long ago. He didn't want to know. It was his daughter's voice, and wherever it came from, he felt some comfort at the sound of it.

Stand was so affected by the experience that when he heard his name called again, it took a moment for him to realize the voice was real. He walked to the radio set and fine-tuned the frequency. The speaker buzzed with Karl Penny's nasal voice.

"Karl Penny to Nathan Stand. Come in, Innesmore station."

Stand threw the switch to transmit. "Right, Penny. Innesmore here. Go ahead."

"Took you long enough. What's going on? Got your nose in the bottle again, lad?"

Stand sighed. "What do you want, Penny?"

"It's not me what wants anything. That McWilliam fella called for you again. He said to get yourself to Washington, quicklike."

"You're sure about that, Penny?

" 'Course I'm sure. I'm old, but I'm not stupid. Mentioned something about a second chance. That mean anything to you?'

"Almost everything, Penny," Stand said.

CHAPTER 5

STAND GOT out of the cab and walked up the long drive. There were only two cars parked outside the mansion this time, a gray Porsche and a long black hearse. Stand paused a second, staring at the limousine, his mouth dry. Then he went up to the house and knocked on the door. It opened swiftly, as if someone had been standing on the other side. That someone smiled, rather magically.

"I see we both got our wish," Jean Frost said.

"I'm sorry. What?"

"You're staring, Mr. Stand. Did I startle you?"

"I expected to see Edwards . . . you don't look like Edwards."

She laughed. "Well, thank you for that. I gave him the day off. Edwards is reliable and efficient, but he's not especially pleasant to have around. Come in, Mr. Stand. What can I do for you?"

"Your father asked to see me. This is a nice bonus, meeting you again."

"Thank you," she said. "Daddy's resting at the moment, but I'm sure he'll be glad to see you as soon as he wakes up. Would you mind waiting?"

"If it's no trouble."

"Of course not. I was hoping we'd get to talk again. Let's go into the library. I just have to finish one small matter and then we can be alone."

She led him down the hallway and turned into a large sunny room with bay windows and a glass door leading to a patio. Books were stacked along every wall, the shelves stuffed from floor to ceiling. There was a fire going in a stone hearth, and four overstuffed chairs were grouped around the warm glow. A man peered around the back of one of the chairs, and got to his feet as they entered. He was a slim hawk-faced man, with gray brooding features and a mournful expression.

Jean grinned as the two men sized each other up. "Let me introduce you," she said. "This is Mr. Straker, of Straker and Sons Mortuaries. Mr. Straker, Nathan Stand."

Straker offered his hand in a solemn manner. "Stand, is it? Are you a relative or a friend of the deceased . . . that is, of the family?"

Stand's alarm showed. Jean whispered in his ear. "Don't worry. Daddy's fine. We just have to think ahead."

Stand nodded and turned back to Straker. "Actually, I'm a business associate. But I like to think I'm a friend as well. I'm sorry if I've interrupted your business."

"Not at all. Mrs. Frost and I were nearly finished, anyway. Just a few more selections to make."

"Really, Mr. Straker," Jean said. "I think I'd like a little more time to consider the choices you've given me."

He nodded sympathetically. "Very commendable. But remember, if you decide to select either the Perma-view or Cryogenic options, we shall need at least two weeks' notice."

Jean managed a rather grim smile. "I'll do my best to make a timely decision. Mr. Straker. Now, let me see you to the door. Make yourself comfortable, Mr. Stand. Have a drink if you like. We'll just be a minute."

Straker offered her an arm. Jean took it and they walked out slowly, as if to a measured cadence. She glanced back at Stand, grinning and trying not to laugh.

Stand shuddered and went immediately to the liquor cabinet. There was an opened bottle of brandy already out. His hand moved toward it. Then he caught himself and backed away. He stood there, licking dry lips, until he heard Jean return.

"Oh, God, am I glad that's over." She sighed, then stopped when she saw him poised over the cabinet. "Are you sure you wouldn't like a drink?"

"A single drink might not do it," he said. "Forgive me again for interrupting your business with . . . whatever that was."

"Well, at least we can make ourselves comfortable," she said. She pointed to the chairs. Once they were seated, Jean opened a cedar box and pulled out a cigarette. Seeing this, Stand started to fill his pipe. Jean watched him and smiled. "Daddy used to smoke a pipe when I was a little girl. I always loved the smell. But then, he smoked almost anything—pipes, cigars, cigarettes. He loved tobacco. I imagine that's how his cancer started."

Stand paused and looked at her. "Then why do you smoke?"

"I'm a hopeless addict, too. It's one of the few things we have in common. I know I should quit—his condition certainly gives me a good reason—but didn't someone once say a good reason is the worst reason to do anything?"

"I don't know," Stand said. "I suppose someone or other has said something like that . . . but what reason did he have for saying it?"

Jean laughed. "You're right. Why do we do the crazy things we do? I'm a strong believer in destiny, that our lives are ordered and predetermined. It's not a particularly comforting thing to believe in, but it does give me someone else to blame."

"And what does your destiny hold for you?"

"The same end for all of us," Jean said, then shook her head and made a face. "Forgive me, I'm being maudlin. This business with Straker upsets me more than I like to admit." She smiled and threw her cigarette into the fireplace.

"Do you have any idea why he wants to see me?" Stand asked.

"I do, yes. But I think I should leave that for him. Tell

me, have you had any second thoughts about your last assignment?''

"What do you know about that?"

"Nearly everything, really. It's part of my job to know all of our operatives' activities.''

"I had no idea I was being watched so diligently.''

"I'm sorry about what happened,'' she said. "About your disagreement with Father. Do you intend to tell him what you did with the stockpile?''

"I don't know that I would have called it a stockpile.''

"You know I meant the guns.''

Stand frowned. "You ask a lot of questions. I don't see why that should concern you.''

A telephone on a nearby table buzzed softly. Jean went over and picked it up, talked briefly, then hung up and motioned to Stand. "Well, you'll have your chance now. He's awake and ready to see you. Come on, I'll walk you up.''

Stand got to his feet. "That's all right. I know the way.''

"No, I insist.'' She took his arm and steered him to the door. "I wouldn't want to miss this.''

"What do you mean by that?'' he asked.

She just smiled and gave no answer.

Stand followed her into the warm, paneled office. The old man didn't rise to welcome him, but his smile seemed genuine. He pointed to a chair, and Stand sat down. Jean took the chair next to him. The old man nodded to her without a word.

"So, Nathan, I see you got my message.''

"That's why I'm here. Though I still don't believe it.''

"What's that?'' McWilliam asked.

"I've never known you to back down on a decision before, sir. I thought my termination was final.''

"And well it would be,'' McWilliam said gruffly, "if I had my way about it.''

Stand shook his head, confused. He raised his pipe to his lips, but then noticed the new addition to the office furnishings, a wheeled cart with a tank of oxygen. He quietly put the pipe away in his pocket.

"But you do have something for me?" Stand asked. "Your message said something about a second chance."

"That's so. I just wanted it clear to you that I make this offer against my better judgment."

Stand looked at Jean. She had a wry smile on her lips.

"All right, Nathan," the old man said. "Let me spell it out for you. Something has come up, a rather urgent situation with one of the Company's double agents in East Germany. He has to be pulled out and Jean has persuaded me that you are the best man for the job."

Stand glanced at Jean again, but her face gave away nothing. He turned his attention back to the old man. "Why me? This doesn't sound much like an Office worry. The Company has plenty of people who can handle that job. Why don't they take care of it?"

"The DDO is not convinced the cauterization is necessary. Let me tell you the situation. This agent is a rather low-level provider, a major in the East Berlin section of the KGB Office of Financing. He's a cautious type, afraid to steal very much, and he doesn't have access to much that usually interest us. But his field reports are sometimes useful in confirming other information, so the Company has continued to string him along."

"That's changed somewhat in recent months," Jean said.

McWilliam looked at her and nodded wearily. "Yes, why don't you take it from there?" he said. It was clear that even the effort of talking was hard on him. He was breathing heavily, each exhalation emitting a faint whistle.

Jean turned in her chair to face Stand more directly. "A few months ago, this agent was transferred to a branch of KGB Special Actions. He started to come across financial records of past KGB covert activities, including some signs that they sponsored the bombing of the Dutch embassy in nineteen-eighty-three, the Swissair hijacking in eighty-five, and the murder of Adolph Kleist, the president of Deutschland International Investment Federation. These were all believed to be independent terrorist actions, so the possibility of a Soviet tie-in got us pretty excited.''

"Us, meaning the Company?" Stand asked.

Jean nodded. "At first Division Seven was in an uproar. It seemed too good to be true. Suddenly, a low-level unpromising contact starts providing top-grade material, really impressive stuff. Of course the agent knew what he was on to and he started making bigger demands for larger payments. And Seven played along with him.''

"Where does the Office come into it?" Stand asked.

"I'm coming to that. Of course, I kept Daddy informed of that situation all along, because this information tied in directly to the Office efforts against terrorism. Anyway, Seven began to get suspicious of this windfall. Things started to go sour in the German section. Agents were tumbled, our surveillance teams watching Soviet operatives were being eluded by their targets with alarming frequency, and the Soviet signals traffic was suddenly altered, suggesting that they were definitely up to something.''

Stand nodded thoughtfully. "So the conclusion was that this agent was responsible?"

"That seemed a likely explanation," Jean said. She glanced at her father as he let out a soft moan.

McWilliam shifted his weight in his chair, a pained expression on his face. He finally managed to make himself more comfortable, and waved at them self-consciously. "Sorry. Please continue, Jean.''

"Nathan and I could conduct the briefing somewhere else if you'd like to rest," she said, looking concerned.

"I just had a rest," McWilliam snapped. "Get on with it.''

"All right," Jean said softly. "As I was saying, Seven concluded that the KGB had tumbled to this agent and were feeding him the information.''

"Turned him?" Stand asked. "Or just using him?"

"Definitely using him. Seven was sure they were running a litmus test, feeding the information just to see if we would react, but letting him think all along that he was stealing it without their knowledge. In the process, they managed to expose a lot of our German station's network. So the DDO decided to cut him loose. It was obvious the man's usefulness had ended.''

"Sounds like a wise decision." Stand frowned. "But I still don't see where we come into this. Why don't they just pull him out and end it all?"

"There's a catch," Jean said. "Ops is certain the KGB is waiting for them to do exactly that, baiting a trap to snare any part of our network that tries to go after him. The Berlin desk is dead set against making a move, and the DDO concurs. They won't risk any more damage to the German network. Simply put, the agent is on his own."

"A fine way to reward a man for years of risking his life on our behalf," Stand grumbled.

"He knew what he was getting into when he started. If he didn't then, he does now. And he's scared."

"Sounds like he's got a damned good reason to be," Stand said. He saw Jean smile faintly at that, but he ignored her and turned to the old man. "This stinks. How does the Company expect to stay in business if they don't hold up their end of the bargain?"

McWilliam met his eyes evenly. "Put bluntly, this man is not worth the risk. I believe the DDO is entirely justified in his decision to cut him loose. It's unfortunate, but sometimes hard decisions must be made."

Stand looked back and forth between the two, turning the thoughts over carefully in his mind. When he spoke, his voice was bitter. "I presume," he said, "that all this is leading up to you sending me after him. You said I was the perfect man for this job—what did you mean? That the perfect man to send after someone you've already given up on is a man you also consider a loss? Is that it? Send Stand, because it won't matter much if we lose him."

The old man said softly, "There is an element of that in the decision, of course."

"Thanks a lot."

"We're in a tough business, Nathan. We must talk frankly.

The truth, however unpleasant, must be faced. And you are always free to refuse.''

Jean broke in quickly. ''In any event, there are better reasons for choosing you.''

Stand glared at her. ''That's right. He said you were the one behind this. How kind of you to think of me.''

''As I was saying,'' she said softly, refusing to react to his sarcasm, ''there are other reasons for selecting you. First, you know this agent, Mr. Stand.''

''Who is he?''

''Hans Reiger, code name Castle.''

Stand nodded. ''I know him. Our association was brief, and it suited me that way. Not much spine, or brains either, for that matter. He's the kind of man the KGB could easily turn. I don't have any trouble believing he's the one to blow the German station.''

''Yes, we knew you had run into him before. More important, he knows you. He'll trust you. And that's helpful because at this point he's so frightened and paranoid that it would be impossible for a stranger to gain his confidence.''

''All right, I'll accept that. What's the other reason?''

''It's possible that not all the information he has stolen is fabricated. And any true intelligence concerning Soviet ties to terrorism would be extremely valuable to the Office. Reiger's last communication indicated that he had stumbled onto something very important. We must go after him, even if it turns out to be nothing.''

Stand snorted. ''Reiger probably made it up just to raise the stakes to make you think he's worth pulling out.''

McWilliam nodded. ''We have, of course, considered that possibility. Nevertheless, I believe it's worth a try. Even if the worst should happen and Reiger takes a fall, it'll have been worth the effort.''

''That's your idea of the worst case?'' Stand said dryly. ''I think the worst would be if they kill *me*.''

Jean smiled and touched Stand's arm. ''Don't worry. After all, I'll be there to protect you.''

Stand stared at her. ''What?''

"I said—"

"No way. Think again."

"What's the matter?" McWilliam asked.

"I don't need anyone to watch my back." Stand's eyes were dark and cold. "I'll fetch Reiger for you. But my way. And that means I go alone."

"Absolutely not," Jean said. "It's out of the question."

"We're talking about pulling an agent out of East Berlin. An agent the KGB may well be using to bait a trap. That's not a job for amateurs."

"We are all professionals here," Jean said coolly.

"You're not going across the Wall to deliver a memo or negotiate a budget increase. You order things done and you make big decisions, so you think you know what this business is about. You don't—not that end of it."

"I'm well aware of your feelings about staffers and field agents, Mr. Stand. Despite what you think, I have been in this business a considerable time, and I do know something of the risks involved. I do not demand them lightly of others, and I haven't made this decision lightly either."

"Why you?" Stand asked.

"Because this operation is my initiative. I'm responsible."

Stand shook his head in disgust. "No. That's my flat answer. I won't risk being killed because of an amateur's mistakes. You don't know what you're demanding. An operation in East Berlin is like treading through a minefield on snowshoes—one wrong step is all it takes."

McWilliam coughed loudly to get Stand's attention. "That is enough, Nathan." His sunken eyes were blazing. "You forget, you are not in a position to make demands. Jean feels it is important for her to accompany you on this assignment and I concur. Those are the terms and they are not negotiable. You can accept or you can return to that grim island and the empty pit of alcohol and despair that is your life. There the matter ends. Yes or no?"

A vein throbbed visibly at Stand's temple. He stared at the old man and said softly, "You're not pulling any punches this time, are you?"

"Like the DDO, I am prepared to cut my losses as necessary. This is the last time, Nathan. I will not come to you after this. There is only one second chance."

"You'll need me again," Stand said.

McWilliam nodded gravely. "Undoubtedly. We will need you again, but we will live without you."

Stand got to his feet. He nodded and said quietly, "Then here is where it ends."

He turned away and walked slowly to the door. Jean and her father exchanged a look. Then the old man cleared his throat. "It's a shame, Nathan," he said. "I didn't tell you what information Reiger has stumbled upon."

Stand paused in the doorway and glanced back. "Forget it, I'm not interested."

"Really? I thought you would be. He's gotten a lead on Falstaff."

The door slapped Stand on the back as he spun around. "You're serious?"

Jean nodded. "That's right."

Stand let out a slow breath. He eased the door shut and quietly returned to his chair. He leaned forward intently, a dark light burning in his eyes.

"Tell me," he said.

"The purpose of terrorism is to terrorize." They were the words of a man named Vladimir Ilyich Lenin. A simple phrase, often repeated.

Falstaff had taught the world what it meant.

Stand knew all about him—at least, what little there was to know.

Falstaff was a bomber, the most indiscriminate of assassins. His victims were faceless innocents, ordinary people with the bad luck to be in the wrong place at a horrible time. An airport, a restaurant, a factory—there was no pattern to his choice of targets. They were nearly always public places, filled with people going quietly about their business. Then, with one tick of a clock, their quiet lives were shattered.

His talents were much in demand. In a period of four years, Falstaff had worked for the Irish Provisionals, the Turkish People's Liberation Army, the Basque ETA, and on several occasions for the PFLP—Popular Front for the Liberation of Palestine. His ties to these revolutionary groups were, as best anyone could judge, purely mercenary. Political causes did not interest him. He was simply a craftsman.

The stories about him were many, the facts few. His background was charted only by rumor and supposition. Some experts believed he'd been trained in Camp Matanzas, the Cuban terrorist school on the outskirts of Havana. Others suggested the Patrice Lumumba Friendship University in Moscow, a KGB-conducted school that recruited youth from the Third World. Many of them arrived expecting to be trained as doctors. Instead, they were trained in the arts of terror.

Falstaff was a complete mystery. No one could even say what he looked like. The few men who had ever seen him were either dead or too frightened to come forward. Only one man had ever tried to turn witness against him. The Turkish police found the informer on a lonely hill overlooking the Black Sea. He was naked, bound with a strip of tape across his mouth, and his hands and feet were secured to a tree by spikes. The man was delirious, half dead from sun and exhaustion. His eyes were wild and he struggled, as if frightened of his rescuers.

Until they pulled off the gag. Molded to the underside of the tape was a small charge of plastic explosives. Three policemen were severely wounded. Of the informer, there was barely enough to bury.

Falstaff never needed to repeat the warning. He was free to wander the globe, moving from one site of unrest to another, as silent and deadly as a virus.

These things, Stand knew—as did most of the world. The mysterious assassin was a celebrity. Newspapers ran stories about him monthly, French and British television had produced documentaries that aired to large audiences, and in

America three major film companies released movies loosely based on the bomber. The public shuddered with a perverse delight and clamored for more, but there was precious little to offer them. All that was truly known about Falstaff's legend were the names of the victims he had slaughtered in a bloody trail across half the world.

Stand chewed his cold pipe, waiting. The old man had guessed right—he was definitely interested. Stand had strong feelings about Falstaff. He wanted to see him dead.

At a cue from her father, Jean began. "We shouldn't get our hopes up too much, but there has been a development that seems very promising. The Company has gotten it hands on a man named Sergei Yanov, who claims to have assisted Falstaff in a recent bombing. He won't reveal details yet, but says he has seen Falstaff personally and can provide us with a physical description."

"And the Company thinks he's telling the truth? How do they know he's not just another crackpot?"

"Until a few days ago, Yanov was a Soviet operative. He was submerged amidst the Russian emigré community in Italy. Last week he walked into our embassy in Rome with enough stolen KGB paper work to make our analysts believe he is who he says he is. Some of the documents were very sensitive. None of it concerned Falstaff, but it was still top-grade stuff."

"Unless the Soviets gave it to him as play material," Stand said. "A small sacrifice to help him buy into our good graces. Why should he suddenly decide, out of the goodness of his heart, to give us this? It smells like provocation."

McWilliam broke in. "This Yanov had a good reason for going private at this time. He didn't just wake up and decide he'd like to visit Disneyland."

"What reason?" Stand asked.

"He's scared. As Jean told you, this man has had personal contact with Falstaff. The thing is, that wasn't supposed to happen. Falstaff realized Yanov had seen him, and he tried to silence Yanov permanently."

"So that's why he defected? To win our protection?"

The old man nodded. "Yanov has been living in fear, waiting for Falstaff to come back and make a better job of it. He refuses to talk until he's brought to the States and given total protection. The Rome station has been sitting on him while the documents he brought were confirmed. Apparently, they checked out, because now they're preparing to bring him over."

Stand sat quietly for a moment, letting it all sink in. Then he looked at Jean and asked, "How does this all tie in to Reiger? What does he have to do with Falstaff?"

Since Stand so vehemently rejected her participation in the operation, Jean had become distant and guarded. All signs of her warm smile had vanished. She replied now in a tightly controlled voice.

"Reiger told us his information linked Falstaff to an incident in Düsseldorf a few weeks ago. That happens to corroborate what little Yanov has told us. It's not much, but it seems unlikely to be a coincidence. It justifies going after him."

"What incident in Düsseldorf?" Stand asked. "I don't remember a bombing there recently."

"That information is classified. You'll be fully briefed if you accept the assignment."

McWilliam leaned forward, his elbows resting heavily on the desk. "There you have it, Nathan. What is your answer?"

"On your terms?"

"That is the only way."

Stand gazed down at the floor. Jean's chair creaked as she sat back, turning away with a small sigh of restrained anger. A silence lingered, broken only by the faint whistle of the old man's labored wheezing.

Finally, he looked up at McWilliam and gave a reluctant nod. "All right, your way. Anything for a shot at Falstaff. I want him."

"So do we all, Nathan," the old man said softly. "I'm glad you'll be able to assist us toward that end." He coughed, clutching at his chest. He took a small white pill from a plastic container, this time making no effort to hide it.

Jean stood and motioned to Stand. "Then it's settled. I'll take Stand to Langley. I'll complete his briefing there and pull together the necessary background materials. No reason to waste any time. We'll start immediately."

McWilliam nodded weakly. "Good luck to you both."

Jean walked to the door and frowned when she saw Stand hadn't moved. "Come on, Mr. Stand. We're done here. Let's allow Father to get some . . . to go back to work."

"You go ahead," Stand said. "I'll be down in a minute."

Jean hesitated, her face dark with anger. Then she threw open the door and vanished outside. Her heels clicked sharply on the hardwood floors. The door swung shut, muffling the sound.

McWilliam moaned softly and gazed at Stand. "That was not wise, Nathan. Jean is a formidable woman. You would do well not to antagonize her."

"What's really going on here?" Stand demanded. "Why did you go along with this crazy idea of her accompanying me? It's insane to jeopardize a delicate operation with an unqualified amateur."

"I see no reason to explain my decisions to you, Nathan. The matter is settled."

"You know damned well the risks multiply with more people involved. It doesn't make any sense. This is your own daughter. Why are you so anxious to put her in a dangerous situation where she doesn't belong?"

"I said the matter is closed." McWilliam sighed. "You know the conditions. If you don't choose to abide by them, you can save us a lot of grief and back out now."

Stand shook his head. "I want Falstaff. If this is what it takes, I'll find a way to cope. I want that bastard's head."

McWilliam stared at him, his expression troubled. "Revenge, Nathan? Is that really all it means to you?"

"It's enough. It doesn't bring my family back, but it does give me a reason to live on without them. Without that, I have nothing."

"Your passion has always amazed me," the old man said. "You're too smart a man to live by such a narrow-sighted code. Hate is no reason to live, Nathan. It's a destroyer of life. This hatred in you is an ugly thing; it festers and consumes you like a cancer."

Stand's eyes narrowed as he climbed to his feet. "I'll take your word for that," he said. "You're the expert on cancer. But you're wrong. We're both dying in our own ways. Don't confuse yours with mine."

McWilliam gazed back impassively. "I suppose we both have our own unpleasant truths to deal with. If I was wrong, forgive me."

Stand frowned, puzzled by McWilliam's uncharacteristic moodiness. The old man met his eyes.

"You'd better go now, Nathan. I don't think she's in a mood to wait around for you."

Stand hesitated a moment longer, then quietly let himself out.

Jean was waiting by the front door. As Stand approached, she took his overcoat from the hall tree and tossed it at him. "About time," she snapped. "What were you doing, trying one last time to convince him I'm incompetent?"

"I never said that."

"No? Then who was that arrogant, proselytizing bastard shooting his mouth off up there for the last twenty minutes?"

Stand shrugged. "Is this a trick question?"

"Don't play cute with me. I want to know where the hell you get off. What was the idea of telling him I'm an unqualified amateur?"

"I get the feeling you're angry about something. 'Course, I could be mistaken."

"Fuck you."

"Nope," Stand said thoughtfully. "Definitely not mistaken."

Jean's face glowed scarlet. She waved a fist under his nose, and then, with a growl, she spun away. She yanked open the door. It crashed against the inside wall. She stormed out, slamming her hand on the hood of the Porsche as she went around to the driver's side.

Stand closed the door quietly, then called to her. ''I admit it, I was worried about working together. But I think we're getting off to a nice start, don't you?''

CHAPTER 6

THE DRIVE seemed one of the longest of Stand's life, which was odd considering the speed at which Jean drove. She ignored him. Staring straight ahead, she swerved from lane to lane, passing other cars as if they were standing still.

"Shouldn't we get clearance from the tower before trying to take off?" Stand asked, but the joke fell flat. Jean didn't speak to him the whole way.

They roared up a parkway with an impressive view of the Potomac. The few weeks of prime autumn color were past, and the trees along the river were brown and bare. The traffic ahead slowed and Jean pulled off on an exit marked "Bureau of Public Roads." They entered the one-hundred-forty-five-acre tract that was the home of the CIA. Stand caught glimpses of a surrounding fence, twelve feet high and topped with barbed wire. Along most of the perimeter, the fence was hidden by clumps of forest.

Soon, the headquarters loomed in their view. It was seven stories high with winged additions forming a loosely shaped "H." The building was huge but of no particular architectural distinction. It made Stand think of an enormous college dormitory. He mentioned this to Jean, and she told him that was the effect the designers had hoped to achieve. She looked at him in mild surprise. "Is this really the first time you've been here?"

"Yes, that's right." He had had a more sarcastic reply in

mind, but she was finally speaking to him, and he didn't want to get her angry again. "You've worked here for a long time, then, I take it?"

"It seems that way sometimes, but it's only been five years."

"What did you do before then?" he asked.

"We already more or less covered my background, didn't we?"

"Some of it."

"Enough of it," she said.

"Does your husband work here, too?" he asked, knowing that such intelligence-community marriages were not uncommon.

She frowned at him. "I'm a widow, Mr. Stand. I thought you knew that."

They drove through a long parking lot and found a space about a quarter-mile from the building. Stand got out and stretched gratefully. The sports car was not designed for a man of his size. They strolled toward the building. Jean seemed more comfortable now that she was in her own territory, but Stand still kept a cautious distance.

They entered the wide main lobby. It was an impressive open foyer with a high ceiling and wide marble columns. Just inside the door was a security desk manned by three uniformed guards and flanked by rows of television monitors. One of the guards sauntered over as they stepped up. "Hello, Mrs. Frost. What can I do for you today?"

" 'Morning, Harry. This is Nathan Stand. He'll need a visitor's pass. You should have the clearance papers."

"Stand, huh?" the guard mumbled, sorting through a pile of manila folders. He held up a file triumphantly. "Looks all right. Papers check out. We'll just have to get him a badge."

Stand gave the guard the pass he'd been issued at the perimeter gate. The guard had him take a chair in front of a red curtain. Stand was barely seated when a light flashed in his face. The guard took out the film and slid it into the slot of a processing machine. "Okay, that wasn't so bad, was it?"

Stand blinked, his vision still spotty from retinal afterimages. "I hope you got my good side," he said.

"I'm not a miracle worker."

"How long, Harry?" Jean asked.

" 'Bout five minutes or so. Walk around some if you like. Just don't let him wander off until he gets the badge."

Jean and Stand paced around the lobby like people waiting for a bus. She halfheartedly pointed out a few of the sights. On the north wall of the lobby was a somber memorial of engraved stars, honoring CIA employees who had died in the service of their country. Farther along was a bas relief of Director Allen Dulles. He was seen in profile, with his head surrounded by a large circle. There was something vaguely familiar about the image.

"He looks like he's posing to be stamped on a coin," Stand said.

Jean nodded. "That's an old joke around here. This is called the 'plug-nickel portrait.' "

They drifted aimlessly, killing time. The lobby echoed with footsteps as men and women of all descriptions tromped through. The cavernous halls swallowed the murmur of their conversations. No one spoke to Jean or Stand. Few even glanced in their direction.

They wandered across to the other side. A verse from the Bible on the south wall was etched: " 'And ye shall know the truth and the truth shall make you free.' John 8:32".

"Nice," Stand said. "Where do they keep the bowling trophies?"

Jean sighed. "C'mon, I think it's been long enough."

They walked back to the security desk. The guard handed Stand a newly developed identity badge. Stand scowled at the photograph. The long dark beard was familiar, but the face above it was haggard, drawn, a much older man than he remembered seeing in the mirror.

"Not bad, huh?" the guard said. "I think you look almost lifelike."

Jean grabbed the badge and clipped it to the breast pocket

of Stand's jacket. She took his arm and dragged him away. "Come on," she pleaded. "I have a meeting in a few minutes with the Finance department, and if I'm late, Bill Sidlowe will use it as an excuse to turn down my requisitions."

"I thought your father bankrolled the Office expenses."

"Officially, yes. But the Company does pick up the tab for some things, like payoffs to foreign nationals, purchase of special equipment, some travel costs, incidentals, anything that can't be directly traced. The arrangement suits both parties—it saves Daddy money and it gives the Company a way to watchdog our operations."

She hustled him down a long hallway. They turned a corner and there was another corridor, just as endless. Jean glanced at her watch and stepped up the pace.

"I thought the Office is supposed to be total secret," Stand said. "How secret can it be when expenses show up on an accounting ledger?"

"Our costs are a drop in a very large bucket. And believe me, if you knew how convoluted the payment system is, you'd never worry about it."

"But it still means the Office is funded by tax dollars."

"Not at all," Jean said. "All our money is skimmed from the legitimate profits of proprietaries. You'd be amazed how many of the front companies have become genuinely lucrative. We do especially well in the Third World."

They went around yet another corner. Jean showed no sign of slowing down. "Are you sure we're not going around in circles?" Stand said. "This building can't go on forever."

"Almost there," Jean replied. "We're a little out of the way."

"Any more out of the way, we'd have to bring passports."

She stopped and opened an unmarked door. It opened onto another hallway, but this one was dimly lit, the overhead lights widely spaced. Thin red panels on the walls glowed faintly as they passed.

"Heat sensors," Jean said, anticipating his question. "This is a top-security area. We already passed through a metal detector and there are low level X-ray stations at various points. Nothing comes through here, in or out, that they're not aware of.''

Halfway down the hall was a glass booth. A security guard inside came to his feet as they approached. Jean stopped outside the booth, unclipped her badge, and pressed it to the glass. She motioned to Stand. "You, too. We can't go anywhere until we're cleared.''

Stand held up his badge as instructed. The guard picked up a photoelectronic gun, the kind clerks used in department stores to read computerized price codes. He ran the muzzle across the two cards, and a light on the counter glowed green. He waved them on.

Stand smiled at the guard. "Thanks, nice talking to you.''

Jean pulled him away. "Don't bother. He can't hear you. That place is totally sealed off.''

Stand looked back, feeling a shudder of claustrophobia. "It's like a damned fish tank.''

"Believe it or not,'' Jean said, "that's one of the toughest jobs to get. That guard is one of an elite few. It takes almost six months to run the background check. His whole family has to be cleared, even relatives he's never met. They run spot checks on all his acquaintances periodically and he's fluttered probably twice a month.''

"Polygraph tests?''

"All Company employees face the polygraph at least once a year. It's no big deal, really.''

The corridor jogged right and they came to an elevator. A guard stood by the door, armed with both a handgun and a small-caliber rifle. His face looked as if it would break if he ever smiled. He punched numbers on a key pad and the door slid open.

Stand followed Jean inside. There were no buttons to push and no floor indicators to be seen. The elevator moved so smoothly and quietly that the motion was almost imperceptible. The door whispered open and Jean rushed out. She went down the hall and opened the third door on the right.

After traveling all that way, the place was something of a letdown. It could have been the headquarters of any modern insurance agency. The floor was covered with a thin brown carpet that muffled their footsteps. Inlaid fluorescent lights blazed from a low acoustical-tile ceiling. File cabinets were jammed against every wall, and in the odd spaces between were teletypes, clacking away quietly inside Plexiglas cages. There was a plain metal desk at each end of the room, and in the center were two cubicles with computers and printers.

Stand looked around uneasily. No windows. The room was cramped and colorless. He couldn't imagine spending eight hours a day there. It was like the inside of a discarded refrigerator.

"This is it," Jean said. She checked her watch and made a face. "I've really got to run. You should be all right on your own for a while. Just make yourself comfortable."

Stand nodded mutely, his throat dry. He glanced across the room as a young man appeared in the door to an outer office. He sported large aviator-style glasses, and wore jeans and a loud striped shirt with no tie. His lanky blond hair fell to his shoulders and was hooked behind his ears to keep it out of his face. He looked all of seventeen years old.

"There you are," the youth said to Jean. "I wondered if you were going to make it in today. Did you forget your budget meeting?"

"I'm on my way now," she said. "This is Nathan Stand. He's going to help us bring out Reiger. I need to brief him on what we know about the Düsseldorf incident. Watch over him, will you? I've got to grab the requisition specs and run to Finance."

"On my desk. I already pulled them for you."

Jean smiled warmly. "Jerk, you're a lifesaver." She plucked a stack of folders from the near desk, then raced back to the door. "Wish me luck."

"With Sidlowe," the youth said, "a gun would be more appropriate."

Jean looked thoughtful for a moment, then shook her head. "No, too tempting." She opened the door and vanished down the hallway.

"Does she run around that way all the time?" Stand sighed.

"Hey, man, you just saw the whole franchise. That lady works harder than anyone, and she does things right. She's special. You work with her awhile, you'll feel the same. I'd do anything for Jean. I mean that, and I'm usually a real asshole when it comes to getting along with other people. Ask anyone."

Stand laughed and shook hands with the grinning youth. When he pulled his hand back, he found the palm blackened.

"Sorry 'bout that. The ink smears on the printouts."

Frowning, Stand took a sheet of typing paper off the near desk and cleaned the ink from his hand. The youth watched him with an amused expression. "So you're gonna pull out Reiger, huh?" he said. "She say your name's Stand?"

"That's right. I didn't catch your name."

"Alexander Jerkanlostoklovitch."

"What?"

"Just call me Jerk. Everyone does."

"How'd you ever get a security clearance with a name like a Russian fan dancer?"

Jerk shrugged. "They want experts on Russian linguistics, they have to search deeper than the Smiths and the Joneses. Anyway, the Jerkanlostoklovitch family is American to the bone. My great-great and not-so-great grandparents left Russia in the eighteen-fifties and carried the proud family name to the land of the brave and the free."

"Carried it with both hands, I'd imagine."

"And banjos on their knees, you got it." Jerk grinned again. The expression was never off his face for long. "But, hey. Enough about me. What say I show you around the place."

"Okay."

Jerk turned and waved one arm in a broad sweeping gesture. "There. What do you think of it?"

"Isn't there a window anywhere?" Stand asked.

"Sure. Three flights up, second room on the left. If you

stand on the back of the toilet, you can almost see the sky. Any other questions?''

Stand looked around, feeling uneasy. ''I'm glad I won't have to be here long,'' he said. ''What do you know about Reiger and some incident in Düsseldorf? Somehow, it's all supposed to connect to Falstaff.''

''I could tell you a few things,'' Jerk said. ''But I don't know how much Jean wants you to know. Guess I better leave that to her. How 'bout we have a cup of coffee? You could handle that, couldn't you?''

Jerk pulled out the top drawer of the nearest file cabinet. Inside was a ten-cup Mr. Coffee and a pile of plastic mugs from various fast-food restaurants and covenience stores. He topped off a yellow mug with the logo ''Donut Beat All'' and passed it to Stand.

''Sorry there's no cream or sugar. I'm not supposed to have the coffeemaker either, but the commissary is way at the other end of the building and security gives you a hard time when you go back and forth all day.''

Stand took the coffee gratefully. He had made a breakfast of two neat Scotches, and the liquor had soured his stomach, leaving him drowsy.

''Why don't we take a load off?'' Jerk said. He pointed to the chair behind the far desk. ''Make yourself to home.'' He took his own chair from behind the other desk and wheeled it across the room. Then he plopped down and kicked back, resting his sneakers on the edge of the desk.

The swivel chair was small and groaned under Stand's weight. He settled in gently, like a man getting on an amusement park ride.

''Comfy?'' Jerk asked.

Stand grumbled. ''Very funny.''

The young man took a candy bar from his shirt pocket, unwrapped it, then waved it at Stand. ''Like half of a Snickers?''

''No, thanks.''

''Suite yourself.'' Jerk bit off a large chunk of the warm chocolate and worried it between his teeth like a dog with a chew toy. He gave a small shudder of pleasure and smiled with brown, goo-smeared teeth. "You sure you don't want some?"

"I don't think so," Stand said. "I'd hate to get hooked. Before you know it, you're into the hard stuff."

Jerk nodded thoughtfully, as if it had been a serious statement. "You noticed that, huh? You think candy's addictive? I wonder sometimes. I can't drink coffee anymore without one of these things."

Stand started packing his pipe. Jerk watched him for a minute, then licked his fingers clean and sat back with his hands folded behind his head. "I used to smoke," he said, his expression wistful. "I used to go through a couple packs a day. That was before I came here. I liked cigarettes, you know. People say they're nasty, dirty-smelling things, but I liked 'em. Thought I couldn't live without 'em. Then one day, Sheila—that was the girl I was living with then—she says to me: 'Jerk, I don't want to marry you because your breath stinks, and I don't want to be the wife of a walking trash fire.' "

"And that convinced you you should quit?"

"Nah. It scared me, though. I mean, I never even thought about marrying her. I don't know where she got that idea."

Stand waited for him to continue, but Jerk merely sipped coffee and played with his candy wrapper, rolling it into a tight ball.

"Well?" Stand asked finally.

"Huh?"

"Is that it? Was that the end?"

Jerk shrugged. "Sure. Sheila left me a little while after that. I just stopped smoking by myself once she was gone."

"That's a wonderful story, Jerk. Very moving."

Jerk swung his arm in a perfect hook shot, tossing the rolled-up candy wrapper into a wastebasket clear across the room. He grinned. "Two!"

Stand smiled. "You seemed to have had lots of practice at that."

"Office champion, two years running."

They were both caught off guard when the door swung open. Jerk's feet thumped to the floor. "Jean! I mean . . . hi, Jean. I didn't expect you back so soon."

She frowned. "So I see." She walked over and dropped the requisition folders into his lap. "You can refile those . . . when you manage to find a spare moment."

"Sure thing," Jerk said. "Uh . . . how'd you wind up the meeting so quick?"

Her breath hissed out slowly between clenched teeth. "It doesn't take long to say no. And they've had lots of practice." She sniffed at the hanging blue clouds of Stand's pipe smoke, then turned and scowled at him. "You seem to have made yourself right at home."

"No problems so far, thank you."

"I'll get the paper work, and then we can start your briefing—that is, if you and Jerk are through with your little coffee klatch."

Jerk stepped up beside her. "We were just getting to know each other a little better."

She fixed him with a look that wilted the grin on his face. "You," she said softly, "I'll deal with later. Stand's presence here was not an invitation to take the day off. I expect to see some work from you. And I do mean now, if it's not asking too much." She turned sharply and marched into the outer office, slamming the door with a crash.

Stand shook his head. "That woman is harder on doors than anyone I've ever known."

"Yeah. Musta been some bad meeting," Jerk said.

"Or maybe it's just because she doesn't like me."

"Yeah, could be that, too."

"Thanks, Jerk," Stand said. "Thanks a lot."

Jean came back in with a small stack of papers. She wheeled out a chair and sat down across from Stand. "Here's the Suspected Activists file from the day of the incident," she said. "You might as well start there. You only need concern yourself with the parts circled."

Stand took the SA file and started to read. This was a daily compilation of reports relating to the whereabouts and activities of persons around the world suspected of terrorist involvement. Since the Office's sole function was counter-terrorism, the Company shared this report with them on a daily basis, though with a certain begrudging reluctance.

Despite Jean's orders, Stand skimmed through several other pages before focusing on the circled portions. It was a disheartening exercise. The lengthy report made him realize what little impact they had made, how terrorism was still growing at an alarming rate. In Japan the Rengo Sekigun was stirring. In Central America more Cuban-trained activists appeared every day. Turkey was under siege, torn by riots and street violence orchestrated by anarchist underground groups, over thirty in number, which threatened to cripple that impoverished nation permanently.

The file on the many splintered factions breeding hate and death in Northern Ireland would take almost an hour to sort through. The material on Palestinians would take even longer. The situation among Islamic fundamentalist factions was a hopeless muddle of divided allegiances, petty rivalries, and murderous in-fighting. Stand felt sickened by it all.

Finally, he concentrated on the reports from West Germany. Apparently, there had been a bomb scare in Düsseldorf, but the event had attracted little attention. A bomb had been planted in a train station, but the bomber had made an anonymous call to the police, tipping them off in plenty of time for them to clear the area and locate the device.

This apparent act of contrition was interesting enough, but what was particularly curious was that German demolition experts had determined the bomb would never have gone off. It was not a dummy, in the usual sense. it contained a genuine charge of Composition C-4, a gray puttylike plastic explosive made primarily of RDX, the major component of conventional military bombs and artillery shells. The bomb was also rigged properly to its timing device. At first glance, it appeared expertly constructed and entirely lethal. But on closer inspection, it was discovered that the pentaerythritol tetranitrate in the blasting cap appeared to be contaminated and rendered inactive. This was odd, for the blasting cap showed no external signs of wear. In any event, PETN was impervious to moisture. After lengthy analysis, they decided that it was not contaminated, but *replaced*. The bomb had deliberately been designed to be inoperable.

It was a bewildering amount of effort for someone to go to merely for a hoax. No one took credit for the bomb scare, and the event barely made a ripple in public notice. So what had been the purpose of it all?

When Stand finished with the report, Jean motioned the young man to join them. "Go ahead, Jerk," she said. "Tell him what you came up with."

Jerk nodded eagerly. "Well, the thing I noticed is how this bomb still managed to screw things up, even though it never went off. It made me wonder if maybe that was the whole purpose of it in the first place."

"Screwed up what?" Stand asked.

"A Company operation. The German station had a big meet planned that day with a potential defector. It wasn't scheduled to go down in the train station itself, but they were routing the guy to the meeting by train. When the police cleared the station, the Russkie got nervous and ran back across the Wall."

"So you think the bomb was planted there to kill the defector?"

"No, I think it was just meant to scare him off. And it worked. It sent him running back home, where the East Germans can either arrest him or prepare to follow him the next time he's approached. A fishing trip to see how many of *our* people they can net. It's more subtle than killing him, and that's why it's hard to prove. I can't get anyone but Jean to really listen to me."

Stand frowned, tugging on his beard as he thought. "If that was the bomber's real aim, then it means he had to know in advance that the Company was going to transport the defector by train."

"That's right," Jerk said softly. "It means they have someone on the inside."

"It could have been just an unfortunate coincidence."

Jerk's eyes were large and round behind his heavy glasses. "Yeah, that's possible. But what if it wasn't?"

Jean had passed along Jerk's suspicions, but they had received no response. The Intelligence department staff was sitting on his report, she explained. They questioned the value of an appraisal by a lowly Russian linguist. In effect, they shuffled his report aside, claiming flatly that they had their own people to make such evaluations, and didn't need anyone's help, thank you. In true bureaucratic fashion, his initiative was met with a cold eye of suspicion.

"I still don't see the connection to Falstaff," Stand said. "Are you saying that he was the one who planted this dud in the train station?"

"You got it. I'm dead sure of it."

"It doesn't sound like Falstaff's style," Stand protested. "He doesn't fool around with this sort of game. He kills."

Jerk shook his head. "Maybe he never has before, but he did this time. Look at the forensics report on the bomb—it had his handiwork written all over it."

Stand pulled the report from the file and glanced over it. "What is this about sand?" he asked.

"That's what convinced me," Jerk said. "Something about it rang a bell. I did some checking through the computer and found I was right—in every single bombing attributed to Falstaff, some traces of sand have been discovered."

"But what does it mean?"

"It's how he creates the cross."

"You lost me again," Stand said. "What cross?"

"Yeah, that's right, I guess you couldn't know about that. You see, Falstaff always signs his work. He places sand in the bomb housing in the form of a cross. When the bomb goes off, the sand flies out in this particular pattern, and *voilà!*—You have a giant bas relief cross imprinted by the force of the bomb blast. Some artists in the southwest United States have made a name for themselves doing this same sort of thing, using explosives to create sand-blasted metal sculptures. You can make the designs very intricate."

"I never heard of this before. You say Falstaff always leaves this cross shape in his bombings?"

"Always," Jerk said. "The guy must have a real ego problem—he wants us to know when a bombing is his work. We've managed to keep it quiet to prevent copycat bombers from muddling things up."

"Then there's no doubt when a bombing is definitely Falstaff's."

"Absolutely none. We know every job he's pulled, but it hasn't helped us find him. It just tells us who to blame after the killing's over."

Stand nodded a grim acknowledgment, then glanced at Jean. "But you think we can get to him through Reiger?"

"Don't you see it?" Jean asked. "Falstaff pulled this job on behalf of the Soviets. So Reiger's claim that Falstaff had figured in some reports he was able to steal might well be truthful. And if the Soviets were able to hire Falstaff, they must have known how to contact him."

"So you think there's some truth to the rumor that he's been Soviet-sponsored all along?"

"There could well be. In any event, this would bring us closer than we've ever been before. If there's even the smallest chance of learning something about Falstaff, we have to follow up."

"I'm sold," Stand said. "When do we leave?"

"Tomorrow morning," Jean said. "The longer we wait, the more frightened Reiger will become. We have to move quickly, before he does something foolish."

Jerk looked up. "We? Does that mean you're going, too, Jean?"

"That's right," she said.

"But why? You're gonna leave me here all alone?"

"She thinks I need a nursemaid," Stand said gruffly.

Jean smiled thinly. "That's not quite true. But yes, I will be accompanying Mr. Stand on this assignment, so I'm counting on you to hold the place together while I'm gone. You should have plenty to keep you occupied. You'll hardly miss me."

"Yeah, sure," Jerk mumbled.

Jean glanced at her watch. "Well, I'm going to finish up here and go home to pack and get as much rest as possible. I think you should try to do the same, Mr. Stand. Jerk, since you'll be putting in some long hours in my absence, why don't you wrap it up now and go home early? Are there any last-minute problems you need me to clear up?"

Jerk chewed on a fingernail as he thought. "Well, yeah, I think you oughta look at the situation with the penetration of the new Rumanian network."

"Why? What's going on there?"

Jerk straightened and brushed his hands on his shirt. It left a faint indigo trail across the brightly striped fabric. He didn't seem the notice. "I did what work I could on that, but I didn't think you'd want me to spend too much time on it until we were sure what our involvement would be. I've learned that our man is going to be used purely as a shill. Ops is setting up the penetration their own way and giving me the runaround. I'm dead sure they only asked for a contractor so they could have someone to burn as a diversion."

Jean said softly, "Stepping out of your place again, Jerk? It's not your job to make assessments of Operations procedures."

"This is not a wild-haired guess, Jean. The Division Seven desk as much as told me straight out what they're planning. The cocky bastard didn't think it would matter. They always get what they want anyway."

"Damn!" Jean hissed. "I've told Ops again and again I won't tolerate having our people used that way. I have to have a long and very heated talk with the DDO about this. I won't put up with it."

"Try to have that talk soon," Jerk said.

"Our contractor's been there only a few days. You think he may be in trouble this quickly? Should we cauterize him?"

Jerk nodded. "Get him out now—if it's not too late already."

Jean smiled dimly and put a hand on Jerk's shoulder. "All right. I'll have Daddy take it up with the DDO while I'm gone. He should be able to make him see our side of it. Thanks for telling me, Jerk. God, it steams me when they try to pull this sort of thing. I sometimes wonder who our real enemies are.''

Jerk's pale face reddened from her attention. "You go on, Jean," he said. "Don't worry 'bout a thing. I'll take good care of the place while you're away."

She smiled and glanced at her watch again. "Yes, I better get moving. Lock up everything, won't you?"

She rushed into her office and reappeared shortly with her purse and a coat over one arm. "Oh, Jerk, Mr. Stand's motel is on your way home. Would you mind dropping him off?"

"No problem, sure."

"Okay. Good luck." She looked at Stand. "And I'll see you in the morning. I'll come by for you around nine, all right?"

Stand nodded.

Jean waved and turned to leave. Just as she started to spin, James Gregory appeared in the doorway. She brushed into him, and he caught her around the waist to save himself from being run over.

"Oh, James, I'm sorry."

"Don't be," he said, flashing white teeth. "We should meet this way more often." He seemed content to leave his hands on her hips, but Jean pulled back, blushing and seeming abnormally flustered.

"Did you need something?" she asked.

"I wanted to talk with you over a few matters of mutual concern. Do you have a minute?"

Jean toyed with her hair, brushing a few loose strands back into place. "Actually, I don't. I'm sorry, James. I was just leaving."

"Then I'll see you to your car," he said smoothly. He held the door for her, pretending to ignore the gaze of the other two men. Jean walked out and he followed her.

"James Gregory," Stand said. "What's he doing here?"

"You know him?"

"I dealt with him a few times in the past. His incompetence almost got me killed."

"Yeah," Jerk said. "I don't like him much either." He opened the file cabinet and turned off the coffeemaker. "Well, I guess that's a wrap for today. Are you ready to go?"

Stand got to his feet. "You won't have to ask that again."

Stand walked beside Jerk as they trekked through the long parking lot. He sighed and gulped in the cool air, relieved to be outside and away from that cramped closed-in office. He didn't pay any attention to Jerk's chatter until suddenly he stopped beside a wheeled junkyard in the vague shape of a car.

"What do you think, isn't she a beauty?" Jerk said, running his hand affectionately over a gleaming chrome bumper. The bumper was the only thing on the car that did gleam and it was held in place by strips of wire. The body was a metallurgist's nightmare, a conglomeration of steel, lead, tin, and something that looked suspiciously like aluminum foil. The dents and dings and blemishes were held together solely by rust.

Stand took a deep breath. "Nice car, Jerk. Did you build it yourself?"

"Get real. This baby's a classic. I bought it from a stock-car racer in Georgia."

Stand peered closer. Large white numbers were in fact still faintly visible beneath layers of peeling paint. "Are you sure it will get us home?"

"You kidding? She once finished twelfth at the Firecracker Three Hundred. Climb in and hold on."

The top was either down or missing. Stand thought it was probably a convertible, but knew that might be wishful thinking. The appearance of a stock-car racer was maintained by a heavy roll bar. Even the roll bar was dented. That didn't make him feel any better.

He got in hesitantly. The interior was stripped to the bone, two bucket seats, steering wheel, tachometer, and a gearshift with a knob shaped like a upthrust fist. There was a radar

detector mounted where the dash should be, and Jerk flipped
it on as they rolled out of the parking lot. The shocks bot-
tomed out with a spine-wrenching clank when they crawled
over the first speed bump.

Then they were on the highway and still crawling. Jerk
hunched over the wheel, his face grim with concentration,
but they never nudged over the speed of a wind-up toy. Stand
laughed and settled back in his seat, relaxing. Jerk drove like
a ninety-year-old grandmother on Quāāludes.

"What's so funny?" Jerk asked, glaring at him suspiciously.

"Nothing. I was just enjoying myself. Nice day for a ride."

Jerk grinned happily. "Yeah, me, too. I get such a kick
out of this, the roar of the engine, the wind in my hair—God,
I love driving. Hold on to your hat now. I'm gonna crank this
baby up."

There were twelve cars stacked behind them at the first
exit.

Stand insisted Jerk drop him off outside the entrance to the
motel. He climbed out stiffly and waved good-bye. The car
crept back onto the highway, backfired in a belching farewell,
and slowly rattled into the sunset.

Stand trudged wearily through the complex until he reached
the last building at the very rear. He let himself in and
stretched out on the bed, staring blankly at a spot on the
ceiling. It was always like this before an assignment, a feeling of overwhelming fatigue, a crushing numbness. It was
his way of preparing himself mentally, clearing his mind,
making it a blank before the time came when he would have
to concentrate, totally aware and alert every waking moment.

The sun was setting in one corner of the window, a faint
red glow bleeding color from the cedars on the distant hill-
tops. The twilight was pale and without warmth. With a
groan, Stand got to his feet and picked up a small paper sack
on the dresser. There was an ice machine at the end of the
building, but he didn't feel like bothering with the trip. He
twisted the seal off the bottle and went back to the bed.

An hour passed and darkness crept up the window, then slipped inside. Stand watched it slither into the corners. He shivered and took a drink. It was the last night of drinking. Tomorrow he would stop and he would not drink again until the assignment was completed.

The darkness crawled to the bed and touched him where he lay. He looked into its face, knowing what he would find, knowing it had come for him. He drank a toast of greeting.

CHAPTER 7

THE TOURISTS fell silent as they entered the columned hall. They peered up at the statue with expressions that were childlike in their open wonder. The marble figure of Lincoln cast a powerful spell, suggesting strength even in repose. It was barely twilight, but the day was dark and gloomy.

Gregory joined the tourists, pretending to admire the memorial. His hands were jammed in the pockets of his overcoat, his shoulders hunched as if he were feeling a deep chill. Despite his pretensions, he looked very much like a man who wanted to be somewhere else.

Martin Ronn stepped around a column and moved up behind Gregory without a word. Gregory jumped.

"What's the idea, sneaking around like that?"

"You seem nervous tonight, my friend. Is there something troubling you?"

"You know damned well there is. Why did you have to pick such a public place for the meeting?"

Ronn smiled and tilted his head back, studying the statue's bearded countenance. "I find it a most admirable site," he said. "In my country, Lincoln is respected as the most visionary of your Presidents."

"That's just wonderful. Now what about the money?"

"You will have your money, my friend, when you have given me something to earn it. Your reports lately have been of little use to us, James. You cannot expect full payment for trifles and simple gossip. You must bring me more.''

''What about the information I gave you in the last drop? About the shipment they tried to smuggle out of hiding? That should be worth a lot. It's the most fantastic thing I ever brought to you.''

Ronn nodded grudgingly. ''It is certainly an incredible story, if true.''

''I tell you it is true!'' Gregory blurted. ''I know it is. I handled the transportation arrangements myself.''

''That may be so, but you have given me only an extraordinary allegation. There is nothing concrete for me to make use of. Your contract agent made rather a mess of things. If you could deliver this stockpile to my hands, then that would be most rewarding. For that, I would be very generous indeed.''

''But I told you, the contractor destroyed the stuff.''

Ronn's voice was flat and unemotional. He continued to stare at the memorial, avoiding Gregory's eyes with a show of disdain. ''I think not,'' he said. ''I am of the same mind as your woman friend. If this substance is what she claims it to be, then it is not so easily destroyed. You must try harder to learn precisely what this man did with the stockpile and its exact location. I want that substance, James. The acquisition of the stockpile would please my superiors very much.''

''What could you do with a thing like that?''

''There are many possibilities. An accident might be arranged in the Third World, perhaps, or in one of the Central American nations where your leaders have chosen to interfere in the natural rise of socialism. Yes, an embarrasing accident that would reveal to the world the ruthless extremes your nation will use to attain your goals.''

''I think I get the idea,'' Gregory said softly.

Ronn shrugged. ''It is but one possibility. In any event, the decision as to its use would be left to others. You don't really care what we do with it, do you, James? You are not experiencing—what do you call it?—a crisis of conscience?''

Gregory looked away quickly. "I don't give a damn what you do to them?"

Ronn reached inside his coat and brought out a small flat package of old-fashioned Russian cigarettes, brown cardboard tubes filled with fine-cut tobacco. He pinched one tube carefully, then lit it with a gold Dunhill lighter. Gray acrid smoke curled up around his face.

The tourists left and a group of young schoolchildren was ushered in under the watchful eyes of a hurried teacher. Ronn smoked and watched the children, his normally stonelike face softening.

"I have two children of my own," he said. "Did you know that, James? They are both nearly grown, and I have not seen them in over five years."

"What? I wasn't listening." Gregory was watching the schoolteacher's rather prominent bust line as she bent over to scold a child quietly for bickering with a playmate.

Ronn frowned and dropped his cigarette, ground it out beneath his heel. "Nothing, it was not important. What progress have you made on the other matter I spoke to you about?"

"About the Office? No, nothing yet."

"You must try harder, James. You are in a unique position to bring us proof to expose the treachery of this secret wet squad."

"It's counter-terrorist," Gregory protested. "It's not the same as one of your assassination teams."

"Semantics. It is an inner circle operating without the knowledge of your own leaders. To expose this to the world would be an unparalleled success for me. I mean to have that success, James. You must bring me the evidence I need."

"I told you, it's tough. The place is guarded tighter than a bank, and they take special precautions with their paper work. There's no way I can get my hands on anything without it leading directly back to me."

"You are resourceful. I know you will find a way." Ronn's voice was soft, but there was an edge to it that made Gregory shiver.

The teacher was herding her students back outside, and Ronn turned to fall in behind them. "Come," he said. "We have been standing around here too long. Walk with me."

The wind snapped at them the moment they left the shelter of the building. Gregory clutched at his coat, pulling the collar up around his ears. Ronn looked about somberly, his gaze distant and wistful.

"Your autumns are pale and dreary compared to those we have in Russia. I think I miss the Russian fall more than anything but my family."

"You can have it," Gregory muttered unhappily. He glared at the gray scudding clouds. "I hate this. It's only November and it feels like it's going to snow."

Ronn studied the sky, his expression thoughtful. "No, I think not," he said sadly.

They walked for a ways until they were out of earshot from the students. Ronn paused and glanced around casually. It was the deeply ingrained habit of an experienced operative. As he seemed to admire the Washington cityscape, he scanned for signs of unwanted followers. He shrugged and moved off again after only a few seconds.

"I want to know more about this contractor," Ronn said, "the man who disrupted the transfer of the stockpile. You say that his superiors have punished him for his actions in this incident?"

"Yeah, they did, but he's back now. Jean talked her father into giving him another chance. She arranged it so she and the contractor could work together. They're on their way now to West Germany."

"What do they hope to accomplish there?"

"I don't know, exactly. She didn't say. I don't think the mission is really anything important, just something Jean trumped up for an excuse to get the contractor alone."

"I see. So your woman friend hopes to use this opportunity to win his confidence and learn the location of the stockpile."

Gregory nodded, the movement almost imperceptible with his chin buried inside his coat collar. "Yeah. That's what she's got in mind. She'll probably pull it off, too. Jean's smart. She knows how to get what she wants.''

"I hope so," Ronn said. "Your friend may prove to be a most valuable ally. I want to be kept fully apprised of the progress she makes. Notify me the moment you learn anything new.''

"Sure. It may be a week or two, but we'll turn up something. Things are going about as well as we could hope for. All we gotta do is give Jean a little time to work on him.''

Ronn smiled and patted Gregory on the shoulder. "Very good, James. You have taken steps on your own initiative to uncover the facts I must have. I am pleased with you. I will wait to see what this woman can learn from the contractor. But if you have uncovered nothing within a few weeks, then I shall have to take steps of my own. I mean to have that substance, James, even if it requires more direct action.''

"What would you do?" Gregory asked.

"You need not concern yourself with that now. I hope that the woman will learn what we need to know through more subtle means. The irony of her laboring on our behalf amuses me. You surprise me, James, with your efforts.''

Gregory moaned miserably as the wind whipped around them. There was a slight tremor in his voice, though he tried to sound tough and determined. "Then it ought to be worth something," he said. "If you're so pleased, show your gratitude.''

"Certainly, James." Ronn did not bother to disguise the loathing in his voice. "You have earned your reward, my friend.''

Gregory looked at him, a gleam of excitement in his eyes. "Where will you leave it?''

"A drop will not be necessary," Ronn said. He pulled a white envelope from his coat and slipped it to him. "You see, I was prepared. I knew you would not fail me.''

Gregory didn't hide the envelope, but hefted it in his hand, frowned, and started to tear it open.

"Put it away, you fool! Not here.''

"It doesn't feel like much," Gregory whined, but he tucked it away in a pocket as ordered.

"There will be more, much more, when you give me the information I have requested. I know you will work hard to please me, James. You will work hard and you will be rewarded with a great deal of money. And that is all you really care about, isn't it, James? The money?"

"Yeah, sure," Gregory said. He seemed genuinely puzzled by the question.

Jean leaned out and glanced down the aisle again. At last, she saw Stand appear in the hatchway. She waved. He came down and dropped into the seat beside her.

"Where were you?" she asked. "I thought you were going to miss the plane."

"I wanted something to read," Stand said, and held up three paperback books.

"Do you think you're going to read all those on this one flight?"

"I wanted to make sure I got at least one good one."

"I figured we would use the time to talk things through. We need to discuss the operation, make some plans."

Stand shook his head. "Not right now."

"You mean you intend to ignore me?"

"I don't feel like talking. Okay?"

"All right, you don't have to snap at me," Jean said. Gently, she settled her hand on his arm. "Look, I know you resent having me around on this job. But we're going to be together for a long time, so we might as well try to get along."

"We'll get along later," he said, turning away as if the matter was settled.

A shudder passed through the hull as the plane began to move along the tarmac. Stand edged closer, staring past her to gaze out the window. Jean squeezed his arm to get his attention, but he continued to stare outside as if oblivious to her presence.

"What are you looking at?" she asked.

"Nothing." Stand began chewing on the stem of his pipe. A small white muscle twitched on the side of his face.

"You're not going to be like this the whole time, are you? What's with you?"

Stand didn't seem to hear her. The plane hesitated at the end of the runway, the engine roar mounting. Stand's breath whistled faintly through his empty pipe.

A flight attendant strode down the aisle and paused beside him. She leaned down and tapped him on the shoulder. "I'm sorry, sir. No smoking. You'll have to put that away."

Stand scowled. "I'm not smoking. There's nothing in it. Can't you see that?" His voice was so harsh that Jean cringed in embarrassment.

The young woman, though, seemed unaffected. "Yes, sir. Still, it would be much safer if you would put it away until after takeoff."

"Safer for who? I'm not bothering anybody. Why don't you go give someone a pillow or something?"

The attendant smiled easily, unperturbed. "All right, sir." She gave up and hurried off to her duties.

"What was that about?" Jean demanded in an angry whisper.

Stand ignored her, staring blankly out the window as the plane shot down the runway.

Only then did she notice how his hand was shaking, clutching the paperbacks and twisting them out of shape.

The plane lifted smoothly from the ground and angled steeply into the sky. Stand's breath escaped in a long sibilant hiss.

Jean patted his arm gently. "I'm sorry," she said. "I didn't realize."

"Don't make a big thing out of it, okay?"

"Have you always been afraid of flying?"

"I'm not afraid of flying," he said. "I'm afraid of pilots. I don't like being out of control, stuck back here with the baggage where I can't see what's going on."

Jean laughed. "Well, maybe next time you can ask them to let you sit in the cockpit."

"No good. I've tried that before."

She shook her head, trying to contain another laugh. "You're really something, you know that?"

He smiled thinly and put the misshapen paperbacks in the magazine flap of the seat in front. "I'm okay now. It only bothers me on takeoffs and landings."

"So are you ready to discuss the assignment?"

"If you like," he said, sounding reluctant.

Jean glanced around, then put her elbow on the armrest and leaned close to him, speaking in a whisper. "Did you think it over last night? I suppose you have some definite ideas on how it should be done."

He nodded. "I did, and I do."

"Well, how do we get him out?"

"*We* don't," Stand said.

Jean bristled. "Wait a minute. Don't start that again. Whether you like it or not, I'm a part of this operation, and I'll be right there with you every step of the way. You're not going to push me aside, so just get that idea out of your head."

"If you'll give me a chance," Stand said, "I'll explain. I meant *we* as in you and me—I'm not going in after him, either."

"I don't understand."

"Look, we know the KGB is probably using Reiger to lure us into a trap. We all agreed that's likely. I don't intend to walk into a trap. The only way to get Reiger out safely is to have someone else do it for us."

Jean frowned. "Who do you have in mind?"

"I know members of the German underworld. They cross the Wall every day, smuggling goods in and out of East Berlin without a second thought. They're prepared to handle a job like this in a way we could never hope to do."

"I don't like the idea of dealing with criminals."

"Nobody likes dealing with criminals," Stand said. "But everyone does. Often, it's simply the best choice—in this case, it's the *only* choice."

Jean shook her head and laughed, but it was a bitter sound, without mirth.

"What's the matter?" Stand asked.

"Nothing. I was just remembering when someone else told me much the same thing. I told him then it was wrong to deal with criminals, but he said it was the only way. And it ended up badly."

"There are always risks," Stand said, "some acceptable, some not. To walk into a KGB trap when we already know they're waiting for us would be simply stupid. I don't intend to spend the rest of my life in the Lubianka."

"But it'll never work. Reiger won't trust strangers. He'll never go with them."

"It won't matter whether he trusts them or not," Stand said. "They won't ask him to go for the ride. They'll snatch him."

"You're talking about kidnapping."

"I'm talking about getting him out safely, with our own hides intact. These people do this sort of thing all the time; there's a large and profitable trade in smuggling people across the Wall—anyone who can pay their price."

"There's a catch," Jean said. "We don't have that kind of money."

"We will soon. I decided on this course of action last night. I talked to your father and he approved. He agreed to forward the money. It'll be waiting for us in a drop site on the way to Lübeck."

Jean frowned. "So we're going to Lübeck, are we? Nice of the two of you to let me in on your plans."

"I'm telling you now."

"I don't know. I still don't like it."

Stand grated his teeth around the pipe stem, then turned to look her full in the eyes. "It's this way or nothing. I'm not going to cross the Wall. Not this time."

"With an amateur in tow? That's what you mean, isn't it?"

"That's part of it, yes."

"You really hate me, don't you, Mr. Stand?"

He shook his head slowly. "I don't hate you. I'm afraid of you."

Jean made a face. "Me? What's to be afraid of?"

"It's because you don't know the answer to that question," Stand said, "that I am afraid." He turned away, opened one of the paperbacks, and began to read.

Jean fumed in silence, pretending to stare out the window. But she watched him from the corner of her eye. It was a very long time before he turned the first page.

CHAPTER 8

THEY LANDED in Frankfurt and rented a car under the name of one of the four passports Stand carried. The passport was a real one, for complete passports were too difficult to forge, and nearly always detectable. The more successful technique was to alter genuine ones so that the description, photograph, and visa stamps appeared to match the new owner. Stand used the alias of Thomas Drake, an English professor of German literature. When asked why he was visiting Frankfurt, he said that he was there to study the home of Germany's greatest writer, Johann Wolfgang von Goethe. The inquisitive clerk seemed delighted at this, and gave Stand long-winded instructions on how to locate the Goethehaus, where the poet had lived much of his life.

They checked into a hotel in the south part of the city and paid for a week, giving special instructions that they were not to be disturbed while the professor was working. They knew no one would find it odd that the bed in the room of the professor's lovely young assistant would not appear slept in after the first night.

They slipped out early the next morning and headed north through an angry storm. Cold rain slapped at the car like pellets, splattering the windshield in drenching waves. They drove at a crawl through traffic-clogged streets, Stand cursing and swiping the fogged windshield with his hand. The heater put out more noise than heat, and it was not until they had left the city behind them and were racing along the autobahn that it finally cleared the misty patterns of their breath from the glass.

An hour into the country the rain slackened. Their eyes were drawn to the east, where a seam opened in the clouds and a sliver of golden light broke through. The clouds fell away like torn cloth, splitting to reveal the sun. In an instant the gloom was burned away, withering at the touch of a brilliant fire.

They were so taken with the sudden spectacle that Stand slowed the car for a better look. "Incredible," he said. "That sort of thing makes me wish I was a poet."

"Why didn't I bring a camera?" Jean said. "I never have it when I need it."

Stand shook his head. "A picture would never do it justice."

"But you think poetry would? Words could never capture a moment like that."

"I'll bet you don't read much poetry, do you?"

"Never," Jean said.

"Why not?"

Jean shrugged. "I just never cared for it much, I guess. I mean, it's always so solemn or downright sad. What's the point of all the melancholy?"

"Good poetry is about seeing everything with a sharpened eye, not just sadness."

She stared at him with a curious gaze. "A poem for all occasions. You really were a lit professor once, weren't you?"

"Is that so surprising?"

She nodded. "I never really thought of you that way. It doesn't seem to fit you, the man you are now, the things you do . . . I mean, professors are supposed to be doddering old fuddies, with bad clothes, dumpy wives, and cynical attitudes."

Stand made a face. "Are they? College must have been a wonderful experience for you."

She leaned back and curled her legs up beneath her, yoga-

fashion, and studied him with a penetrating, absorbed look.
He flinched when he caught her at it.

"I wish you wouldn't do that," Stand mumbled.

"Do what?"

"Look at me like that. It makes me feel you're seeing
something I'm not aware of."

"What's so bad about that? Maybe you're too guarded,
maybe you should let me see more of the man inside."

"It makes me fell odd . . . exposed, sort of."

She grinned. "Maybe that's what I'm doing—undressing
you with my eyes."

Stand frowned. "You say the damnedest things sometimes."

As a joke, her comment was something of a clunker, but
it somehow eased the tension between them. Like the breaking of the storm, they felt a gloom suddenly lifted. Jean continued to stare at him, her expression intent and thoughtful.
Then, finally, she shook her head.

"No, I just can't see it," she said.

"See what?" He feigned alarm. "How undressed I am?"

"No, not that." She laughed. "I was still trying to picture
you as a teacher. I can't imagine you in a classroom, droning
on about Beowulf and Lady Chatterbury while the kids stare
out the windows and nod off."

"Lady Chatterbury?"

"The Bath lady. You know who I mean."

Stand groaned. "I'll bet your lit professors ran for cover
when they saw you coming."

"You're not far wrong," Jean said. "Let's just say literature was never my strong suit. I never could see the point of
it. What good is it, really? I mean, it seems so dry and unimportant, especially these days. There's so much to learn
about what's happening in the world right now, day-to-day
changes in science, politics, technology. Things you really
need to know. Stories are kind of fun, and a good way to kill
time when you're all alone, but that's about all I see in them.
Who cares what cadence Shakespeare used in his sonnets,
what pretty words he strung together to impress a lady friend?

What relevance does that have to our world? No, thanks, I prefer facts—hard, cold facts."

Stand was quiet for a minute. He steered the car into the other lane and passed a slow-moving truck. They went around a gentle curve and the view of the sun breaking through the clouds slid off behind them, out of sight and now forgotten.

"What good are those facts of yours," he asked finally, "unless you know how to interpret them in proper context? That's something literature—or any real art—accomplishes. It expands your outlook, makes you witness and experience things you might never know in your own narrow world. So then you can approach those precious facts from different angles, ones you might never otherwise have considered, or even been aware of."

Jean sighed. "Okay, I'm convinced—that you were a professor, I mean. You have the rhetoric down. Still, you're just talking about a way of thinking. The way I see it, thinking about something is different from doing it. Academics strike me as people who are content to sit and let things happen around them. I'm not made that way—I have to go, to act, to make things happen."

Stand felt a genuine annoyance. "It's not like that at all," he said. "Reading is not a passive activity. I will never understand that attitude. The very act forces you to think, to weigh matters, consider your own opinions—to learn. How can you consider thinking and learning a trivial activity?"

"Yes, I see your point," she said. "But I believe you learn most by doing, by acting. Give me a man of action any day."

Stand clicked the stem of his pipe against his teeth. "Action matters, of course. The impact we have on others is measured through our actions. But the most important act is choosing *what* we do and will not do."

Jean shook her head. "I don't understand that. Is that an excuse to rationalize doing nothing? You don't buy that, Nathan. I know you don't—you couldn't, because you're not content to sit by and let the world go to hell. You fight back. Everything you've done, your entire career, shows that you believe in taking action, in trying to make a difference."

"There's probably a simple explanation," he said.

"And what's that?"

"I'm shallow."

She frowned and stared at him, a shadow of annoyance darkening her eyes. "I'm serious," she said. "When you destroyed that shipment of guns, that was an act of defiance, of intolerance for a situation you hated."

"Was it?"

"Are you saying it was just the snap decision of a shallow mind?"

"Maybe it was," Stand said. "What difference does it make now?"

"Why are you so defensive? Why won't you talk about it? I just want to understand you. What harm could it cause to tell me about it now?"

"I don't want to talk about it. For better or worse, the thing is done, over with. Just drop it."

"You must have a reason for being so secretive. Is it that you're afraid you'll give something away? Is that it, Nathan, is there something you don't want the rest of us to know?"

He grumbled. "Why won't you leave it alone?"

She gasped and snapped her fingers as if the thought had just occurred to her. "I know what it is . . . you didn't really destroy those guns, did you? That's what you're afraid you might give away—the fact that they still exist."

He scowled. "Where did you get that idea?"

"I'm right, I know I'm right. I can see it in your face. Now, how could you have . . . I got it. The guns were on a boat, so the easiest way to get rid of them was to sink them. You sent them to the bottom of the sea. That's it, isn't it?"

"What's with you and those guns?" Stand growled.

"Stop being so stubborn. You said yourself it can't make any difference now."

Stand shook his head firmly. "To no one else. But it would to me. Give it up, Jean. I'm not going to tell you anything."

"You're just like him, you know it. Both of you so damned bullheaded."

"Your father?"

"Yes. You're both so stubborn, the only way to change your mind would be with a brain transplant. Oh, in so many ways you're total opposites, but it's like you have the same center, a similar core. The same toughness . . . you're a killer, too, aren't you, Nathan?''

"What do you mean by that?''

"I meant the question literally—you have killed people, haven't you?''

He frowned and nodded stiffly. "You know I have.''

"That's it, then,'' she said. "That's how you two are the same. Oh, he's never killed anyone—not personally, I mean. He never pulls a trigger. He leaves that to people like you. But at the bottom of it all, he's still responsible, isn't he?''

"What are you getting at?''

Jean uncurled her legs and drew her knees up to her chest. She rested her chin on her knees and gazed off distantly. "I just wonder at the unfairness of it. He gives orders, makes people do things like that, but he never has to dirty his own hands, doesn't have to feel involved.''

"You're dead wrong,'' Stand said. "Your father doesn't take his responsibilities lightly. He's only in the business because he cares. He cares a lot. At times, I think he cares too much.''

Jean stared out the window on her side. She raised one hand and pressed it to the glass as if to confirm its strength, substance. The droplets of rain that still clung to the outside were animated by the passing air, running in long shuddering trails, colliding, coming back together, constantly changing form.

"I suppose you're right,'' she said at last. I suppose it isn't easy on him. He tries not to show it, but his illness worsens and he . . .'' Her voice trailed off as she took a deep breath.

Jean was staring at the water-beaded glass. Her breath formed small clouds of moisture on the inside. "The cancer is eating away at him, almost literally. It's amazing, sometimes you can actually see a difference one day to the next. He's withered, dried up. Like his insides are slowly disappearing.'' She tugged at her collar, as if a cold hand had just touched her neck.

"It's a tough way to die. I feel for him."

Jean shivered. "It's eerie, you know. This sounds terrible, but I'm glad to be away for a while, to escape having to watch that. It scares me. God knows how he must feel. He refuses to talk about it, never lets on. But he must be scared, don't you think?''

"I don't know. Probably."

She turned to him as if in sudden anger. "Then why won't he let anyone help him?" she snapped. "Why does he push as all away? Keep working, keep pretending. Is the damned job so much more important than us, than what's happening to him?''

"How do you expect to help him?" Stand asked. "He's dying. That's something everyone has to do for himself. Work is simply his way."

"But it's always been like that—the job first, and everything else second. He never had time for anything or anyone else.''

"Including you?" Stand asked softly. "That's what you mean.''

"I love him. He means more to me than anything else in the world. But he keeps his feelings tied up inside. I never know what he thinks. I would do anything if I could just be sure he feels that strongly about me.''

"Have you ever told him that?"

Jean turned away quickly. "Let's just drop it."

"Whatever you want."

They drove on in silence, the hushed pause of sudden tension. Both looked to the other for the simple sounds that would break it. But neither spoke. They sat stiffly, avoiding each other like a long-quarreling couple whom words had failed, and silence was all they had left to share. The stillness draped around them like folds of heavy cloth, smothering them under its weight.

* * *

They entered Lübeck through the Holstentor, a fortified gateway with twin towers that looked straight out of a tale of armored knights and fair maidens. After checking into a hotel they strolled around, taking in the sights. Everywhere there were somber buildings of dark, glazed brick that had stood for centuries against the fury of wind and weather on the edge of the cold Baltic Sea. The Gothic buildings were staid in comparison to the ornate designs found elsewhere in Germany, but their brooding appearance was an accurate reflection of the people who had built them: stolid, serious, and sturdy.

Stand and Jean walked quietly, talking seldom. By unspoken agreement, their dispute of the day before was forgotten, but they still had little to say. Finally, tiring of playing tourist, they left the city for a quiet walk on the beaches.

The horizon was a blur, and the dark sea fading into a blank grayness at the edge of sight. Its vastness was imponderable, as endless as the sky. The sea was angry. It slapped at the pale sandy shore with a mounting ferocity. The wind, too, was bitter, roaring at them in deep-throated gusts that became shrill as it swept inland.

They walked with their heads bowed, but otherwise ignoring the gathering storm. Stand moved away from Jean and sat down on a large slaggy stone. He pulled out his pipe and blew through it once, then held it in his lap as if forgotten. His hand trembled from something other than the cold.

"What is it?" Jean asked. "Is there something wrong?"

He seemed not to hear. His eyes were slowly scanning the breadth of the sea, as if he was watching, waiting for something to appear.

Jean sat down beside him. He looked up as if startled. "What?"

"Tell me, Nathan," Jean said softly.

"I came here once before," he said. "With Leah. It was our first year together, before Melissa was born."

"To this very spot?"

He nodded and let out his breath slowly.

"That must have been a long time ago."

"Yes," Stand said. His voice was dull, lifeless.

"What was she like, your wife? Tell me about her. You never talk about your family."

"No." Stand turned and motioned with his head. "Why don't you go back to the hotel? I'd like to be alone for a while."

"So you can sit here and feel sorry for yourself? You've done that long enough, Nathan. What good does it do?"

"Please leave me alone. What I feel is none of your business."

"Don't do this, Nathan. We were starting to get along like two normal people. Then you crawl into this cold shell and spoil everything. Don't treat me like this, not now. We need to know we can trust each other."

"Will you please go away?"

"I'm not moving," Jean said. "I want to know what's going on with you."

"Why? What difference does it make?"

Jean stared out across the black water, as if hoping to find whatever it was he expected to see. Then she spoke again, her voice soft, almost a whisper. "I know the memories hurt," she said. "I know how much you must have loved her. But I'm counting on you, Nathan. You're not going to break down and start drinking again. You've got to promise me that."

"Actually, that sounds like a damned good idea."

"No, Nathan," Jean said sharply. "Why do you torture yourself this way? Do you think it'll change anything? It won't. She's dead, Nathan. Both of them are dead. Nothing can bring them back to you because they're gone. And killing yourself little by little won't bring you any closer to them."

"What do you know about it?" Stand grumbled.

"I know. A lot more than you think. You're not the only person in the world to lose someone you loved."

He frowned at her. "It's not the same. You got over it."

"And you can't? Is that what you're going to say? That's garbage—you just don't want to get over it. You'd rather have an excuse to drink, to pity yourself. You want the truth, Nathan, I think you're glad they're gone. What excuse would you use if they were still alive? Tell me that.''

''Are you through?'' Stand growled. ''Go on, get out of here.''

''Or you'll what?'' Jean shot back. ''People have been too easy on you, Nathan. It's about time someone told you the truth. They're gone—you lost them and they're gone. Your obsessive mourning isn't romantic and noble—it's just stupid—it's a betrayal of everything they ever meant, of the love they once had for you.''

The hard briar pipe snapped in his hand. He angrily tossed the two pieces into the sea. ''Dammit! Will you shut up and leave me alone!''

She sat still, flinching at the lash of his voice, but not retreating. ''No,'' she said gently. ''Nathan, I do understand. I know exactly what you're feeling. I've been there. You feel guilty for continuing to live without them when you thought you never could. Well, you can . . . you have to. It's the only choice you have.''

His voice was sharp, raw, dredged up from some open sore deep inside him. ''You think you know it all. You know nothing. What would you have me do? Pretend that they never lived? Go on as if nothing had happened? I can't do that—I won't forget them. If I hold on to them, their memories, so tight . . . then in some way, they're still with me. I won't let go, not for you, not for anybody.''

''The bottle is the only thing you won't let go of. Where does it stop, Nathan? How long do you think you can live in the past? How long can you hide?''

''That's all I'm going to take from you,'' Stand snapped, jumping to his feet. ''Who gave you the right to judge me? It's my life, dammit! Mine.'' He peered down at her, his eyes as dark and ominous as the gathering storm. ''Stay the hell out of it.''

Stand turned his back to her and stomped through the sand to the water's edge.

Jean sighed and called softly after him. ''Nathan, I'm sorry. I was wrong. You're not killing yourself. You don't have the guts. If you really want to die, then get it done. Otherwise, get on with the living, the hurting, just like the rest of us.''

He ignored her, gazing out over the sea and the black, threatening skies.

After a minute, Jean got up and walked away.

Every hour Jean checked his hotel room, but he was never there. She sat up, trying to read one of Stand's paperbacks, but the words kept blurring and running together. Finally, she set the book down and drifted to sleep in the chair.

The sound seemed to reach her from somewhere far away. She got up, blinking, and went to the door. Stand came inside, glanced around at the darkness, and quickly flipped on the light. Jean winced and rubbed her bleary eyes. ''What time is it?'' she muttered.

''Midnight.''

''Where have you been all this time?''

''That doesn't matter. Go sit down, I'm sorry I woke you.''

''No, that's all right,'' Jean said. Her eyes cleared and she studied him with concern. ''Are you okay?''

''I'm sober, if that's what you mean,'' Stand said gruffly. He moved to the window and drew the curtains, then sat down in the chair where she'd been sleeping. Jean watched him warily, then settled on the edge of the bed.

''Do you have a cigarette?'' Stand asked.

''Is that what you came here for? What about your pipe?''

''I broke my pipe,'' he reminded her. ''Give me a cigarette.''

''Don't have any,'' she mumbled. ''All gone.''

He cursed and stared at the brimming ashtray as if considering one of the half-smoked butts, then made a face and pushed the tray aside.

''What do you want, Nathan?''

''I'm going now. I'm going to make the deal with Pharaoh.''

''So late?''

''This is just about the time he starts stirring. I did some checking around. I'm pretty sure I know where to find him.''

Jean stood up. "All right, let me get my coat."

Stand shook his head. "That's not a good idea."

"Nathan, don't start—"

"Please listen to me," he said. "I'm not trying to cut you out. I intended all along to meet him by myself. I figured to sneak out and take care of it before you knew what I was doing."

"So what are you doing here?"

"I decided to be up-front with you. It didn't seem right to go behind your back."

"Well, that's a switch. What brought about this change of heart?"

Stand sighed and held up his hands. "Please just hear me out."

"Save your breath," Jean said. "The plans we make with this criminal concern us both, so I intend to be there. No arguments. Is that clear enough?"

"I know we're in this together, but this end of it is mine." He silenced her objection with a quick motion. "No, let me explain. It's not because of anything I think or feel. The man we're going to deal with, Pharaoh, he's a strange character—a dangerous one. And something you need to know is that he hates women, especially strong independent women like you. Not a mild dislike, a crazed irrational revulsion of all females."

Jean's face was a rigid mask. "You didn't bother to mention that anytime we discussed the plans, did you?"

"I thought I could talk you out of going."

"Well, you were wrong. Forget it, Nathan. We'll just have to deal with someone else."

"There is no one else. Pharaoh is the king of smugglers in this region. Nothing moves in or out of East Berlin without his knowledge. If we try to deal with an underling, he'll think we're cutting him out and we'll have an underworld war on our hands besides the rest of our worries."

Jean got up and paced around as she thought. "How sweet of you to share this with me at the last minute," she said.

"You knew how tough it would be for me to drop the whole thing after we've come so far."

He nodded. "I admit it, that's exactly what I thought."

She stopped at the far end of the room and her mouth twisted into a sour grin. "Well, you were right. We can't drop it, not now. But I'm not staying behind."

"Jean, it doesn't make sense to jeopardize our chances by confronting him with the thing he hates most in the world—namely, someone like you."

"He's a grown man, he can learn to live with it. Our money will help soothe his discomfort."

"It's a mistake," Stand said. "It'll only complicate things. You don't know how difficult Pharaoh can be."

Jean looked at herself in the mirror and pushed her already short hair back behind her ears. Then she turned and looked pointedly at Stand. "I understand difficult men," she said. "I've had a lot of practice lately."

CHAPTER 9

JEAN STAYED close to Stand and didn't say a word. She wore a heavy fisherman's sweater and a Timberline parka, with a wool watch cap over her hair. She had carefully scrubbed away any trace of makeup. As a disguise, it was a complete failure. Stand swore and told her to stay behind him and out of sight as much as possible.

They walked into a run-down section of the waterfront a short distance from the docks where tall, heavy cranes worked through the night. The noise was deafening, with the grinding of heavy machinery and the cries of the loaders as boom arms swung crates into the holds of long cargo ships.

Their footsteps echoed with a dull clatter on the cobbled walkway, separated from the water by a low stone seawall. The district was a marked contrast to the rest of the city; it was a scene of complete devastation. The buildings were leveled to rubble, hollow shells burned out and flattened beyond repair. The darkness was nearly complete, broken only when an occasional slash of light from the docks spilled out among the abandoned ruins.

Despite herself, Jean shuddered, all her senses revolting. It was a filthy place, with garbage piled around the buildings, even more bobbing in the surf below the sea wall. Rats scurried about freely; some of them, large as kittens, raised their heads and glared defiantly, their yellow eyes steady and unblinking.

She sensed the same look in the faces of the men they passed. Small groups in ragged clothes, sitting atop the seawall or huddled in the alleys, shared a bottle and smoked sour-smelling hand-rolled cigarettes. Their eyes were bitter with an unsensing animal hatred, an instinctive wary distrust of all that moved through the dark haunting underworld.

Stand paused by the door of an ancient two-story stone warehouse. The windows were boarded over, the walls chipped and crumbling. He inspected Jean briefly and tugged the cap down to her eyebrows. "This is it," he said. "Still glad you came?"

"This is no time to be smug," she muttered.

"Stay close to me, keep your head down, and whatever you do, don't talk to anyone."

She nodded, swallowing hard. "I don't think I'll be tempted to mingle."

Stand opened the door, then pushed Jean back as she started to enter ahead of him. "I think Emily Post will forgive me this once," he said.

Inside, they stopped to let their eyes adjust. There was just enough light to enhance the gloom without really pushing it away. The interior of the two-story building was hollowed out to form a single cavernous room. The few overhead lamps hung from a bare framework of iron girders twenty feet from the floor. Cobwebs hung thick as theater curtains. It was a nightclub, but with no more atmosphere and allure than a coal mine.

There was a crudely fashioned bar running the full length of the far wall. It was there most of the men were clustered; rough, burly men in faded clothes, with unshaven faces. They hunched over their drinks like figures in a still life, barely moving, seldom talking. All they had to say to one another had been said before, many times.

A few men sat at the tables grouped around a low stage in the corner. Stand motioned to Jean and started toward them.

The smoke and stench of sweat and urine had Jean's eyes watering. She blinked and squinted to make out the figures at the table Stand was headed for. One man appeared young and slender, the other so fat his bulk spilled out over both sides of the straight wooden chair.

"Which is he?" she asked. "The big one?"

"Hard to miss, isn't he?"

A lank-haired woman moved away from the bar and veered between the tables to intercept them. She stooped like a hunchback and dragged herself along, leaning heavily on the tabletops. She wiped her hands on the tail of her faded wool shirt, then stepped in front of him and straightened with apparent difficulty. Her nose had been broken several times and would never be straight again, but the pale skin of her face was still youthful, unlined.

"*Guten Abend,*" Stand said.

The woman glanced at him, then swept her gaze over Jean. A glimmer of hostility sparked in her dull eyes, and she curled her lips in a sneer. "Take your lady to do her slumming somewhere else," she said to Stand. "This is not a place for tourists. We are not here for your amusement."

Stand spoke sharply in the harsh guttural German of a Berliner. "French brandy. A new bottle, unopened. You understand?"

The woman pinched her nose and sniffed loudly. "*Ja?* And maybe some caviar for the princess?"

Stand pointed a finger at the fat man. "Over there. For Pharaoh."

The woman's eyes fluttered wide. "*Verstehen,*" she muttered, and moved off with sudden energy.

"You do have a way with women, don't you?" Jean said.

"Hush," Stand snapped. "Let's get this over with before that witch tells the whole grimy lot about you."

As they wove their way to the table, Jean studied the man called Pharaoh. At least she *thought* it was a man—what he resembled most was a walking pile of laundry. Pharaoh wore at least six shirts of all descriptions: denim, flannel, two wool Pendeltons, and one that might have been silk. Nearly all were unbuttoned and hung over his round body in twisted folds, bunched and incredibly wrinkled, as if they'd been washed and then put on before they were dry. As she drew closer, Jean amended that thought—they looked too filthy to have *ever* been washed.

As Stand neared the table, the fat man glanced up. His eyes grew round and he spoke softly with a rumbling foghorn voice, "By God, I knew I smelled an Amerikaner somewhere in the city. Pharaoh's nose is never wrong about the scent of money. It attracts me like a cloud of delicate perfume." He laughed and clapped Stand on the shoulder. "Sit, my sweet-smelling Amerikaner, sit down."

The fat man waved a hand at his friend. The young man scowled insolently and moved aside, making room. He was a thin, wiry man with the glazed eyes of a junkie. A knife scar trailed down one cheek, gleaming palely against his ruddy pockmarked skin. He had the look of a thug, wearing hostility like a badge of honor. He nursed a drink and masked his resentment by pretending to ignore Stand, as if he had sized him up and judged him unworthy of attention.

Stand pulled over a chair and sat next to Pharaoh. Jean took a place behind Stand, shielding herself from the fat man's view. Pharaoh chuckled and punched Stand again playfully. Stand smiled thinly. "You seem cheerful tonight," he said. "Especially for a dead man."

"Who said that Pharaoh was dead?" the fat man growled.

"I did. In a report to the Company."

"You said this to the CI and A?"

Stand nodded. "The last administration decided to clean house and rid the Company of all involvement with known criminals. They ordered field agents to turn in reports on any criminal associates, so the information could be handed to the police in the respective countries to aid in prosecution. It was their way of weeding out undesirables."

"They called Pharaoh an undesirable? Who is responsible for this insult?"

"The German *polizei*. There was a select group of troublemakers that they wanted very badly. Your name was high on the list."

"Yes? What number?"

"If I remember correctly, it was three or four."

Pharaoh's face fell in disappointment. He patted his enormous belly. "I am embarrassed they took Pharaoh so lightly. But after all, I have not been well. My stomach troubles. I suppose three or four is not so bad for a sick man."

"Your stomach would have troubled you more on prison food if I had told them the truth."

Pharaoh bowed his head gloomily. "So you lied to them for me. For Pharaoh, you took the risk. You reported that I was dead . . . and they believed you?"

"I doubt it," Stand said. He smiled. "I told them you were buried in a small churchyard in Zwicau, and they could check it out if they liked, but that it would take a crane to lift you from the grave. I guess they figured it wasn't worth the bother."

Pharaoh rocked with laughter, then abruptly grew silent, staring over Stand's shoulder. The waitress was approaching. She froze a few feet away as his eyes swept over her with withering contempt. "What is it?" Pharaoh barked. "I didn't summon you, woman."

She darted forward, dropped a bottle of brandy on the table, then hastily stepped back. "Your friend ordered me to bring this, *mein herr*. I hope I have done right." She scurried away, glancing off tables in her haste.

The fat man snorted, then looked at the bottle and let out his breath in a loud sigh. "Nathan, my friend, you remember everything. It is too generous, this gift. You humble Pharaoh. And when I have nothing to offer you in return."

"We'll get around to what you can do for me," Stand said.

"Of course." Pharaoh chuckled. He broke the seal on the bottle, raised it under his nose, and sniffed with a grand show of pleasure. "As you say, we will get around to the purpose of your visit. But first we will share this delightful gift. Have a drink, Nathan, and also for this shy one who stays so close to your back. Come, we will all drink to the memory of Pharaoh, who died so young and in the full bloom of his manhood."

The fat man shook with laughter and rocked back on his chair. He stole a glance quickly past Stand. Suddenly, his hand snaked out, seized Jean's chair, and dragged her into the open. His eyes grew cold. "Nathan, what treachery is this?"

Stand sighed. "Meet Jean Frost."

Pharaoh glared at her, his face twisted in revulsion. He shuddered and spun angrily on Stand. "What do you mean by this? Why have you brought this creature here?"

The young thug had been drinking quietly, bored and distracted. Now he sat up, staring at Jean with sudden interest.

Pharaoh slapped the table in front of the young man, so that he started and looked up resentfully. "What are you doing?" Pharaoh hissed. "Take your eyes off the little bitch. I will not have you sully yourself with the likes of that."

Jean glared at the fat man and leaned forward intently. Without looking, Stand reached back and patted her insistently on the knee. Grudgingly, she eased back, shielding herself behind Stand.

"What is she doing here?" Pharaoh demanded again.

"She is my associate," Stand said quietly. "And my friend."

"Your whore, you mean."

The young man shifted his chair, moving out of Pharaoh's reach to a place where he could see Jean clearly. His head swayed drunkenly on his shoulders and his lips parted in a wide leer. Jean's stomach tightened. The thug's eyes were jaded and cruel, cold as a reptile's.

"How much did she cost you? She is very pretty."

"Get away from her!" Pharaoh raged. "Do you forget what I have told you? Keep your hands off her."

"Stop it, both of you!"

The men were shocked into stunned silence as Jean came to life, snarling and shaking a fist. "That is enough!" she cried. "I won't take more of this from any of you. I will not be shoved aside and stared at and talked about like I'm not here. Do you understand that?"

Pharaoh hissed and looked at Stand. "Nathan, I will not have your whore speak to me in this manner."

"I will speak to you any damned way I please," Jean said.

"I don't know what you have against women, Pharaoh, and I don't care. Your arrogance makes me laugh. You may be king in this place, but look around you. This place is a sewer. What floats to the top here is not cream."

The fat man sucked in a breath and sat very still. Beads of sweat had formed on his brow. His eyes did not waver from Jean's face, even though he spoke to Stand. "Nathan, this foulmouthed creature has gone too far. No woman may speak to me thus. She continues to live only because of my friendship to you. But I suggest you take your whore away from here, and quickly, I should think."

The drunken young man leaned over and tugged a lock of Jean's hair from under her cap. He toyed with it, holding it up to the light. "Forget him," he said in a throaty whisper. "I like to hear you speak. Your voice is a lovely sound. Come away from this place with me and I will make your lovely voice say things you never dreamed of. I will show you things, and you will scream for me to do them again and again. Yes, you will love these things and you will beg me to do them to you."

He reached out again to stroke her hair. Coolly, Jean grabbed his little finger and bent it back toward his wrist. With a cry of pain, the thug snatched his hand away.

"Touch me again," Jean said, "and I'll take that finger and cram it down your throat."

Pharaoh's arm lashed out and knocked back the thug as he reared up from his chair. "Get away, Horst! I told you, I will not have you touching the filthy little beast."

The youth scowled and cowered under the fat man's rage. He drew back, simpering and sucking on his injured finger.

Pharaoh took the bottle of brandy and pushed it across the table to Stand. "I have shown enough tolerance for one night. Your whore's behavior offends me, Nathan. Take your gift and leave me. I'm sorry, but we can no longer be friends."

"Then I am sorry, too," Stand said. "I had hoped to do business with you, business that you would find very simple and profitable."

Pharaoh waved dismissively. "I told you our friendship is ended."

"Do you take money only from friends? I need your help, Pharaoh, and you know from the past that my money is always very good." He paused, smiling. "Actually, the money is Jean's. Maybe taking it from her would help ease your discomfort."

Pharaoh stared at him, then chuckled softly. "Maybe this is so. But Pharaoh's price is more expensive to people who are not his friends."

Stand nodded. "Of course."

"All right, Nathan. I will listen to you. Tell me what this business is you need of me. And I will tell you how much it will cost."

Stand pointed to the young man. "What's your friend's name?"

"He is Horst."

"Tell Horst to go powder his nose."

Pharaoh turned to the young man and said quietly, "Leave us, Horst. Go tell that shrew woman to begin cooking my evening meal."

Horst climbed unsteadily to his feet and glared at Stand and Jean in turn. One finger absently traced the ridge of his long scar. Then he turned and stumbled across the room to join the crowd at the bar.

Pharaoh turned to Stand. "Now you will do me the same courtesy and tell your woman to leave."

Stand shook his head. "She stays with me."

"I think my price will be very high," Pharaoh said, scowling in displeasure.

"I'd have been surprised if it wasn't," Stand said. He poured a large measure of brandy into a glass and slid it over to the fat man.

Pharaoh belted it down like bitter medicine. He pushed the empty glass aside, then produced a silver snuffbox from the pocket of his outermost shirt. He poured a mound of brown powder onto the back of his hand, raised it to his nose, and inhaled quickly. He pinched his nostrils together and sniffed even louder, then sighed and sat back with his hands folded across his belly.

"I grow weary, Nathan," Pharaoh said. "Tell me what it is you want from me."

"There is a man in East Berlin. We want him brought out, delivered here to Lübeck. It's important that he leave quickly."

Pharaoh dabbed at the traces of snuff still clinging to the underside of his nose. "I assume that your friend in the East would prefer not to announce his departure to the border guards?"

"My friend," Stand said, "does not know that he will be leaving. I would like it to come as a surprise."

"I see. Who is this man? Where will I find him?"

"His name is Hans Reiger. He is a major in the KGB Office of Finance." Stand handed over a photograph taken from Reiger's 201 file.

"You resort to stealing a worker of the opposition?" Pharaoh asked. "I do not remember you doing such a thing before. This man must be very important."

"He's one of ours, Pharaoh. He's in trouble and we want to get him out. The Soviets may be waiting for someone to come for him, so it will have to be done quickly, and without attracting attention. Once he learns where he's going, he won't be much trouble for you. It must be done soon; I would like it to happen within the next two days."

The fat man shrugged. "This is but a trifling matter. I have men who go across every day as you go to your jobs in America. You disappoint me. It is nothing."

"How much will nothing cost us?"

"Twenty thousand dollars, Amerikaner."

Stand shook his head. "Too much."

Pharaoh spread his hands and smiled sadly. "You may cross over and deal with this man yourself anytime you wish. There are buses if you do not wish to drive yourself, with guides who will show you all the beautiful sights. All for a pittance. I hope you will find the visit an enjoyable one."

Pharaoh poured himself another drink and gulped it down as quickly as the first.

"Five thousand," Stand said. "That's fair; the going rate is three."

"There are unusual expenses in this case," Pharaoh argued. "There are the fees of the men who will transport your friend, sedative drugs to keep him quiet, several vehicles, bribes for the border guards—these things take time, and you have left me none. It is too much. For this price you would leave poor Pharaoh grasping at pennies."

"Seven thousand five hundred. But that is the top price. No more."

Pharaoh studied Stand's face and sighed resignedly. "You take all the pleasure out of haggling," he complained.

"I refuse to haggle."

"That is what I mean."

The waitress who had served them appeared on the small stage, accompanied by a small dark woman with a violet birthmark on her face. The two women stared across the heads of the audience and began to peel off their clothes.

Pharaoh scraped his chair around, turning his back to the stage. "You are a hard man, Nathan," he grumbled. "All right, seven thousand five hundred. But I will take the money in advance."

Jean nodded and dug a hand into her coat pocket. Stand saw her and warned her off with a sharp look. Pharaoh watched the exchange and smiled to himself.

"You can pick up the money at our hotel tomorrow," Stand said to Pharaoh. "Half then, the second half when Reiger is delivered to us."

The fat man mugged a sad face. "This distrust grieves me, Nathan. When has Pharaoh ever cheated you before?"

"I've never given you the chance," Stand said.

The two performers had finished removing their clothes. The dark woman had prominent stretch marks on her belly. She turned to the waitress and slithered her hands over her body. The two women embraced and began to dance slowly with each other, kissing with wet, open mouths while their hands stroked and fondled pale flesh. Occasionally, the dark women would stop and spank her partner hard, leaving a bright red welt. Stand saw Horst move to a table closer to the stage, staring up with glassy eyes.

Pharaoh watched the young man for a moment, then twisted his thin lips in a grimace. Abruptly, he pushed away from the table and climbed to his feet. He swayed as if his legs could not support his enormous weight. "We have a deal, Nathan," he said. "I will deliver this Reiger to you by noon the day following tomorrow. A man named Stadl will contact you. You will give him the money, and he will tell you where to pick up your friend."

Stand nodded, his face dark, troubled. The fat man turned and waddled off. His hips undulated jellylike as he moved, bumping into the tables and chairs, knocking them askew.

Jean let out her breath as if she had been holding it the whole time. "What are you waiting for? Let's get out of here."

Stand placed a restraining hand on her shoulder. "Hold on. Something's wrong here."

"Everything's wrong here. That's why I want to get out."

Stand looked around anxiously. The young man named Horst had disappeared. "You don't understand. Pharaoh just went to a lot of trouble to do something he seldom ever does."

"What's that?"

"Move," Stand said. "He normally stays in one place all night."

"I don't blame him," Jean said. "Did you see the way he walks?"

"Leaving so early is out of character. He holds court in this place like a king on a throne. Everyone doing business with Pharaoh comes to him. It's a point of pride. So why did he hurry off this time?"

"I suppose it was my charm and endearing social grace," Jean said.

"I don't like it. He's up to something." He stared at her

and frowned. "You brought the money with you, didn't you? What the hell did you do that for?"

"I thought we were going to pay someone to nab Reiger for us. I didn't know kidnappers worked on credit. You never told me to leave it behind."

"He knows you have it," Stand said grimly. "I saw his eyes light up when you went for your pocket. I don't like it; I have a rotten feeling in my gut."

"Can't we worry about this just as well back in the hotel?" Jean asked. She stared up at the two women on the stage and shuddered. "You really know how to show a girl a good time, Nathan. But if it's all the same to you, I'd just as soon call it a night."

Stand glanced around once more, then nodded tightly. "Let's go. But keep your eyes open and stay close."

Once outside, Jean gratefully gulped in the sea air. Even stinking of garbage and engine oil, it was a relief after the stench in the warehouse.

"Watch your step," Stand said. "The fog's getting heavy."

They trudged cautiously through the darkness, covering about a block. They were only a short way from the lighted docks when Stand suddenly halted in his tracks.

"What is it?" Jean hissed.

"The rats," he said. "I don't hear them anymore."

"I hear something."

Footsteps ticked on the cobblestone walkway. Three shadowy figures stepped into their path. One figure angled toward Jean. A shiny stiletto glinted in his hand. Jean looked up to see a familiar leering smile.

Horst cackled. "Hello again, pretty woman."

"I think I just figured out what Pharaoh was up to," Stand said quietly.

"I'm so happy for you," Jean said.

Stand moved slowly to one side, edging away from her. The two strangers moved with him. Horst stayed with Jean, waving his knife in her face, forcing her to retreat toward the alley.

The two men separated, preparing to jump Stand from both

sides. One was bare-handed, the other brandished a length of chain, casually swinging it by his hip. Stand had no doubt which one he would deal with first. There was no room for mistakes. One slip and they would finish him.

The men closed in patiently, certain of their advantage. The man to Stand's side flicked his chain like a whip, grinning as it cut through the air with an evil whistle.

Stand let them drive him back until he felt the seawall against his legs. This was the moment they would come, he knew. Like rats, they would swarm in once their victim was cornered.

In that instant, they heard a short scream as Jean cried out. The two brutes grinned at each other. While they were distracted, Stand scrambled onto the seawall and balanced himself as he took off along its top. It brought him close to the bare-handed man. He grunted in surprise and dove at Stand's legs.

The man stretched out along the top of the wall as he caught Stand's boot, pulling him up short. Stand had expected this and caught his balance easily.

The man cried out with glee as he tried to twist Stand's ankle. Stand countered by simply sitting down, hard, as if he were closing an overstuffed suitcase. He let his full weight drop on the man's head and shoulders. The man's face smashed into the stone wall with a thunk like a bursting melon. The fingers on Stand's ankle grew slack.

Stand rolled off the limp body and caught himself on hands and knees. He had lost sight of the second attacker, but now heard the whistle of the chain close behind him. He threw himself down just in time, the chain passing so close he felt the breath of it ruffling his hair. Chips of stone flaked off the wall in a shower of blue sparks.

Stand rolled away quickly, scrambling to regain his footing. He could hear Jean and Horst scuffling in the alley. He chanced a look in their direction, but could see nothing through the fog.

With a wild roar, the man came after Stand, swinging the steel chain in a wide deadly arc. Stand lurched back, barely evading a blow that would have staved in half his ribs. The end link still nicked him.

The man grew bolder. He lunged at Stand again, swinging the chain and laughing with crazed delight. Stand ducked under the flickering steel, then threw himself to one side as the man followed with a backhand swipe to cut the legs from under him.

Stand fell back, dodging and feinting, but again the rough links cut him, wrapping partway around his thigh. He staggered as if struck by a hammer, his leg momentarily numbed, and it was all he could to keep his footing. A quick strike would finish him, but the blow did not come.

To Stand's surprise, the brute hesitated. Smugly assured, he took a moment to rest. His chest was heaving from the effort of swinging the heavy chain, and he doubled over, resting his hands on his knees while he caught a breath. He smiled arrogantly at Stand, feeling no rush to press the battle when the outcome seemed so apparent.

In that moment, Stand sensed his opponent's weakness. Instinctively, he understood that a man was drawn to the weapon he himself feared most.

Stand watched the man straighten and take a final deep breath. He grinned and swung the chain in small circles, like a ball player on his way to the plate. He seemed to enjoy the anticipation of the final blow. Without hurry, he stepped toward Stand, taking the chain back in a long steady backswing.

Stand's heart was pounding, but he forced himself not to retreat. Not until the last second, when the man bounded in, cocking his arm the last few inches, did he move. And then he lunged, not away from the stinging chain, but toward it.

It was as Stand suspected. The man's eyes widened in disbelief, and for a fatal second he hesitated. Instead of completing his swing, he drew the chain back, protecting it from Stand's grasping fingers. In doing so, he left the rest of his body open and vulnerable.

Pulling out of his feint, Stand drove his knee into the exposed solar plexus. With a whoosh of sour breath, the man doubled over. Stand followed with an open palm strike to the side of the head. The man crumpled, smacking the ground full length, his face resting on Stand's foot. Stand shook him off angrily. The man made no sound.

Without a second look, he spun away, rushing toward the alley where Jean still struggled. The sound of a scream pointed the way through the fog.

Jean retreated slowly into the darkness of the alley. Horst followed, lazily swinging the knife. Jean screamed again, not out of fear, but because she sensed Horst liked it. He was like a cat toying with a mouse, wanting to prolong the fun. The more frightened Jean appeared to be, the longer he was willing to play. She hated seeing the leering grin on his face broaden, but it was not hard to force herself to play along. The sound came easily to her lips.

"I am glad you haven't lost your voice," Horst cackled. "I have been looking forward to hearing it." He pressed forward, waving the knife. Jean retreated. "Don't run away, pretty woman. You will thank me when we are together. It will be an experience you will never forget."

Jean backed away, one hand groping behind her as she stumbled against the piled garbage. Her eyes never left the swinging knife.

Horst leered and stuck one hand into his trousers, fondling his genitals. "You will like me very much," he hissed. "I have so much to offer a woman like you."

Jean sneered. "Play with them while you can," she said. "Touch me, you'll have to keep them in a box."

Horst's grin faded. Suddenly, he leaped at her, the knife slashing at her face. Jean threw herself back, colliding with a metal trash can heaped with stinking waste. She and the can both toppled over. Jean cursed as the garbage poured over her.

Horst towered above her, laughing. "Perhaps Pharaoh was right," he said. "He says women have such a nasty odor. You smell like a pile of dung, my pretty little woman." He reached down to snag a handful of hair, but Jean slapped his hand away.

"Keep your filthy hands off me!"

Horst drew in a breath as if stung. His lips curled back over his teeth, and he raised the knife high.

In desperation, Jean grabbed the lid of the garbage can and raised it just in time to deflect the plunging blade. Horst grunted and stabbed at her again. Jean used the can lid like a shield, again avoiding the jabbing point.

With a crazy laugh, Horst danced on his toes, lunging at her again and again, stabbing without real force, almost playfully. He assumed an exaggerated swordsman's pose, with his free hand curled by his ear. Lunge and thrust, cut, parry, and feint. He skipped around her, enjoying the game, laughing insanely at each hollow thunk as Jean countered with her shield.

Jean regained her footing, and the next time Horst stabbed at her she parried, then changed her grip on the metal lid and slammed it into his grinning mouth.

Horst staggered back, surprised and bloodied. He daintily dabbed a finger at a split lip. The wildness in his eyes grew cold and hard. He spit blood onto the cobblestones and raised the knife in a more serious underhanded grip.

Jean dug into her coat and pulled out a large stack of money and tossed it on the ground at his feet. "There, that's all of it. Take it."

"I will," Horst said softly. "And then I will take you." He bent down to pick up the bound bills.

Jean took two quick strides and lifted her foot in a drop kick aimed at his crotch. Horst swung his arm across, knocking her aside. Jean lurched off balance, tumbling to the ground. Horst picked up the money and waved it in her face, grinning with delight. "And now, it is your turn, my pretty."

"Horst."

Horst swung around quickly when the soft voice called his name from the entrance of the alley. He glared when Stand stepped out of the fog. "You."

Stand watched the grinning man drop into his knife fighter's crouch. Slowly, pointedly, Stand pulled the drawstring of his parka hood out one side so that about three feet of it hung down. He took an end in each hand. "Come on, Horst," he said gently. "I'm ready for you. Show me what a big man you are."

Horst lunged at him, bringing the knife up from the ground in a slashing arc at Stand's chest. Stand stepped aside, letting the blade pass by. Then, as Horst's momentum carried him close, Stand moved in and slipped the string around his neck, spinning to pull it tight. Horst gagged as Stand threw him over a shoulder like a sack of potatoes, then left him dangling from the string around his throat.

Seeing her chance to help, Jean moved in again. She repeated the drop kick, this time burying her toe in his crotch. Horst let out a scream so high and shrill it was almost beyond hearing.

Stand let go of the string and Horst fell to his hands and knees. He clutched at himself, panting breathlessly, his face white.

"You did that pretty well," Stand said.

"Thank you."

Horst fumbled for something hidden in his coat. Stand kicked him in the face. The German's eyes rolled back in his head, and he rolled over and lay still.

Stand picked up the fallen money and handed it to her. "Anything else you need?"

Jean nodded and took his arm, trembling as the shock started to sink in. "Yes. Take me out of here."

Pharaoh's man came to them early on the second day. He was a tall, formidable-looking man, older than Horst, and much more down to business. "Pharaoh is very displeased with you," he said. "You have caused him much worry and loss of respect."

"What about Reiger?" Stand asked.

Stadl nodded. "We have brought the man, as you wished. Pharaoh is a man of his word. The contract has been completed."

They followed Stadl down to the beach. There was a van parked amid the dunes. A man sat on the sand a few yards away, smoking a cigarette and cradling a submachine gun in his lap. He got up and pointed the gun in a very businesslike manner.

"Open the van," Stadl ordered.

The guard threw open the rear door, and a man who had been leaning against it toppled out. It was a middle-aged man, with thinning hair and half-frame bifocals still perched on the end of his nose. There was also a four-inch slit under his chin where his throat had been cut.

"This is the man you asked for?" Stadl asked.

Stand nodded. "That's Reiger."

"The money, please."

"Just a minute," Jean said. "You expect us to pay for a dead man?"

"Pharaoh has kept his word. The man Reiger was brought to you."

Jean bristled. "What kind of a trick do you—"

She was silenced by the sound of the man drawing the bolt on his submachine gun. Stand looked at the armed man, at Stadl, then sighed and nodded to Jean. "I guess next time we'll have to be more specific about our demands. Give them the money."

"Nathan, do you really—"

The man raised his weapon. Stand said softly, "We're really not in a position to argue."

Stadl smiled. "Very wise, Mr. Stand. As you say, we could easily kill you first and then take it."

Jean hesitantly held out the wrapped bills. Stand took them from her and pushed them into Stadl's hand. "Take a message to Pharaoh for me," he said.

"As you wish."

"Tell him that if he ever tries to cross me this way again, I will come back with a very dull knife and make a woman out of him with a few well-placed cuts."

Stadl's face grew pale. "I cannot tell Pharaoh this."

"No, I don't suppose you can," Stand said sympathetically. "Did you bring a shovel?"

"Yes. We provide a complete service," Stadl replied. He pulled a shovel from the back of the van and gave it to Stand. "It has been a profitable morning. I hope we shall do business again. *Auf wiedersehen.*"

Stand just smiled. Stadl and the other man got into the van and drove away. Stand watched them until they were out of sight. Then he took off his coat and started rolling up his sleeves.

"Is that all you're going to do?" Jean asked.

"Did you have something else in mind?"

"That man just stole seventy-five hundred dollars and killed one of our agents, and all you're going to do is dig a hole?"

"Yes," Stand said. "Glad we got that straight. What would you have me do? Run after Stadl and get myself shot?"

"No," she said hesitantly.

"Go back looking for Pharaoh and get myself shot—plus have various portions of my rather personal anatomy mutilated by Horst and his little pocket cheese-slicer?"

"No."

"Place an emergency call to the President and ask to have the marines raid Lübeck?"

"No."

Stand sighed. "Well, then, Jean, just what would you have me do?"

"Shut up and give me the shovel."

CHAPTER 10

THEY PARKED on a country road far out in the Virginia hills. The lights of the Washington skyline glowed dimly on the horizon, washing out the edge of the sky, but over their heads the night was endless. The stars shimmered like sputtering candles, small brittle fires, fragile and yet eternal. The wind swept through the trees in a mournful voice, whispering a sad promise of winter.

They held each other tightly and kissed. Jean laid her head back with a sigh as Gregory's lips moved to the gentle slope of her neck. Her skin tingled under his warm breath. Then his hands were searching, stroking, slipping inside her blouse. He let out a cry of pain and pulled away.

Jean laughed, the mood broken. "What happened?"

He cursed and rubbed his thigh. "Your car bit me."

"Porsches aren't made for love, I guess." She tenderly massaged the place on his leg that had gotten pinched between the bucket seats. "Poor darling. Let's just sit back and enjoy the night together."

Gregory grumbled, "I guess we'll have to."

"Don't be a grump. This is fun. I haven't done this since I was a teen-ager. It's so lovely out here, just the two of us, the night, and the stars. I feel like we're the only two people in the world. It's so quiet and peaceful."

"It wouldn't be if I had room to get hold of you."

Jean laughed. "Yes, it's exactly like when I went parking

as a teen-ager. The boys seemed to have six hands and they were all hormones. God, that seems a long time ago.'' She turned and looked at him with a thoughtful smile. ''I bet you took lots of girls out parking, didn't you?''

''I seem to remember doing this a few times,'' Gregory admitted.

''A six-pack of beer or a bottle of sweet wine and we felt so wicked. I always think of sin as having that same gagging sweetness. You remember the taste of that stuff for the rest of your life. What a time that was. The simplest moments were overwhelming. Life had sharp edges everywhere and we thought we were experiencing sensations no one had ever known before.''

He slipped an arm around her shoulders and pulled her close. ''You're in a strange mood tonight.''

She looked away and her voice was soft, barely more than a whisper. ''I'm just thinking, looking back and wondering if it all should have been different. If I did the right things, if I could have gone some other way.''

''What would you have changed?''

''I'm thirty-one, James. Oh, don't look at me like that—I know it's not so old, but for a woman it's a point when she has to ask hard questions. Biologically, I don't have that many years left. Sometime, not so long from now, I'll discover the chance is gone forever.''

''Are you saying you want to have a child?''

''I don't know. That's the terrible thing, I just don't know. I used to be so certain I would. When I was growing up, I knew that was all I would ever need or want. A man who loved me and a child of my own, one person in the world I could truly belong to—me to her, and her to me.''

''Her?''

She smiled. ''Or him. I'd love a little boy all the same. But little boys grow up to be men, and I've seen too much of what men become.''

''You're just saying these things because you've had a rough week.''

''That's putting it mildly.'' Jean sighed. ''I felt so damned helpless, you know. Here we spent all that time and effort, all that money—and then they murdered that poor little man for no reason at all but to get back at us. It made me think about how fragile life really is, how it can end so suddenly, so easily. I guess that's why I'm in a funny mood tonight."

"That's all right, darling. Tell me all about it. Tell me everything."

"No," Jean said. "I don't want to do that. You have enough worries of your own without having to listen to mine."

"But I like that you share them with me," Gregory said. "That sharing's what love is all about. Everything that troubles you concerns me as well."

Jean sat up, giving her head a toss. "No, they're my problems. I'll have to learn to deal with them myself."

For a minute they sat, staring out across the dark hills, listening to the night. An owl cried somewhere in the forest as it pounced on some small furry prey. They heard a brief commotion, a thrashing and crackling of twigs, then only silence. Gregory turned to face her, his expression grim.

"What about the problem we really do share? Did you manage to learn anything more from Stand?"

Jean shook her head. "He didn't tell me a thing. He's very guarded. It wouldn't be wise to press him too hard. I couldn't bring the subject up very often or he would have gotten suspicious. Anyway, we were pretty busy."

"Yeah, so I gathered," Gregory said. "Well, it didn't work; we'll just have to try something else. There must be something you could do to make him open up to you."

Jean laughed bitterly. "What do you want me to do—sleep with him?"

"Of course not. Not you, darling. I was wondering, though, if he would be susceptible to the attention of another woman, someone we introduced him to."

"I don't think so, James. It would take a hell of a woman to make him forget his dead wife. She's been gone for years now, and I'll bet he's never even looked at another woman in all that time. No, I just don't think it would work."

Gregory shrugged. "Well, whatever you say. It was just an idea. We have to come up with something. You tell me what would work."

"I don't know," Jean said. "Look, it's been some time now and no one has learned of the stockpile yet. I'm tempted to let it lie and forget the whole thing."

"You're the one who told me we can't do that. The stockpile is too deadly, the potential for disaster is enormous, and I don't mean merely a political embarrassment. You know what could happen, Jean. Think of the thousands, maybe millions, of innocent people this thing could harm. Could you live with yourself if that happened?"

She lowered her eyes. "You know I couldn't."

"All right, then. It was our blundering that created this mess. We're responsible. One way or another, we have to be the ones to clean it up. We'll never be able to rest until it's done. That's how I feel, and I'm sure in your heart you feel the same."

"You're right, James," she said softly. "I'm ashamed of myself. You look right at the truth, and don't turn away even when it's unpleasant. What would I ever do without you in my life?"

Gregory kissed her slowly and gently. He held her chin and peered into her eyes. "Don't worry, darling. You'll never have to know. I'm here, and I'll always be here for you."

"Oh, I'm so sorry, James. I didn't mean to sound like a crybaby."

"Then you'll continue to work on him?" he asked.

She nodded. "I'll think of some way to make him talk."

"Is your father getting suspicious about your sudden interest in Stand?"

"I don't know. I've had a funny feeling about Father for a few weeks now. It was odd how easily he let me talk him into giving Stand a second chance, and he didn't bat an eye when I demanded to accompany Stand on the assignment. Daddy never changes his mind so readily. It was almost as though he was expecting it, as though he knew there was something more important at stake."

"You think he knows about the stockpile?" Gregory asked.

"It's possible, I guess. He's up to something, but I can't figure out what. He's been acting strangely around me lately, asking a lot of questions. Suddenly, he's taken a real interest in my personal life. He even asked me about you."

"He knows about us?"

"Apparently so." Jean frowned. "He picked a damned awkward time to become the concerned parent."

Gregory groaned. "Don't you see? He knows. He's snooping around, gathering evidence against us. The whole thing is going to blow up in our faces."

"No, I don't think so. He may have learned we moved the stockpile, but he has undoubtedly figured out why. And he won't say anything about it to anyone—he can't, not even to me. It would all be for nothing if he reveals knowledge of our action. He knows that better than anyone. He'll keep whatever he knows to himself, you can count on that."

"Good." Gregory stretched and yawned loudly. "It's been a pleasant evening, darling, but I'm tired and I know you are, too, after your trip. Are you ready to go now?"

She took a last glimpse at the view, hiding a frown of disappointment. She grabbed the key and started the car. "How about my place? Can you stay over?"

"Not tonight, my love. I'm going out of town tomorrow. I have to catch an early plane."

"You didn't tell me that. Since when do you work over the weekend?" She stole a glance at him from the corner of her eye. "I mean, it is because of work, isn't it?"

Gregory chuckled. "You sound jealous, darling. What did you think, that I was going to fly across the country to meet another woman? Relax. I've told you there is no one in my life but you."

Jean drove down the dark country road, gravel spitting up from the tires. A cloud of dust rolled up behind them, blotting out where they had been. "I'm sorry," she said. "It's hard for me not to be jealous sometimes. I know how other women look at you, how much they would like to be where I am now. But I do trust you, James. I hope you know that."

"I do, Jean. I love you, and I want nothing more than to be worthy of you."

Jean drove slowly, wanting to prolong the time they had together. Gregory watched her and smiled to himself, pleased with the night's work.

The next morning Gregory drove to the airport. He checked his bag, had his ticket stamped, and chatted with a pretty attendant while he waited to board the plane. Finally, the ten-forty-seven to Denver was called. He took his seat and waited ten minutes, then went into the restroom. When he came out, a tall man with dark hair was in his seat. Gregory went by him without saying a word, and quietly left the plane.

He found the car exactly where Ronn had said it would be. The keys were under the bumper, held by a magnetic clip. He drove out of the airport, bypassed Washington, got on 270 and headed north through Maryland. Following Ronn's instructions, he left the highway twice and proceeded by rural roads. Once he drove through a small town, turning down several side streets, then pulling into a driveway and doubling back. No one was following him.

He got back on the highway and drove for another half hour, pulling off on a country road near the Pennsylvania border. He continued along the graveled back roads until he came to a crossing. Off the road, by a fence post, was a dented and apparently discarded Coke can. Gregory picked it up and shook out two coins, a penny and a nickel. He took the penny and replaced the nickel, then put the can back where he had found it. He drove on to the site the signal had indicated.

He parked the car just inside a long winding dirt driveway that snaked through trees to a distant farmhouse. By the base of the mailbox was another dented Coke can. Gregory put his penny into the can, then walked up the drive for a quarter-mile and slipped into the trees. He waded through the brush and came to a pond. He sat down on a rock and took out some doughnuts he'd bought at a 7-Eleven along the way, and prepared to wait.

A half hour later, he heard Ronn approaching, rattling the coins inside the soda can to announce himself. The Russian dropped down beside him, his face flushed and breathing heavily. He immediately lit one of his smelly cigarettes, then finally looked at Gregory. "Good day, my friend. I see you found the instructions clear enough."

"Why all the bullshit?" Gregory asked. "Nobody knows about us. I didn't have to waste the whole weekend just to meet with you."

Ronn frowned. "We have been practicing this trade for many years. It seems elaborate, but that is its function. You must not deviate from the instructions at any cost, James. I hope that is understood."

"Yeah, all right. As long as you pay me, I guess you can call the tune."

Ronn smoked for a while in silence. He tapped the ashes from his cigarette onto the ground, then kicked dirt over them with a heel. "Fine, James," he said. "Now, tell me what news you have to report."

"I found out what they were up to in Germany. Jean's people have been trying to track down the person who planted a bomb in the Düsseldorf train station a few weeks ago. One of the Office clerks got a crazy idea that it was placed there to disrupt a meeting between the Company and an East German defector."

"An inspired guess."

Gregory stared at him in astonishment. "You know something about that?"

"I am aware of the person he seeks, and the role he played in that incident. I will tell you no more than that. It need not concern you."

Gregory cursed under his breath. "I can't believe it. That little twerp is really on to something. I thought he was just trying to win brownie points with Jean."

"Brownie points? I do not know this expression."

"Please her, win her favor. You know, do something more than expected of him."

"Ah, yes, I see. So how did this lead your woman friend to West Germany? What did they accomplish there?"

"Not much," Gregory said. "It all turned sour for them. They tried to sneak out a double agent from the KGB Finance Office, but the German gangsters they hired got mad and slit his throat. They got the agent, but he wasn't much good to them dead."

"A Finance officer," Ronn said. "You're certain of that? What did they hope to learn from him?"

"He was gonna lead them to the man who planted that bomb, but, like I said, they never got to ask him, so it was all for nothing."

Ronn smiled. "What about the contractor? Did your woman friend get him to reveal the location of the stock-pile?"

"Nope, that was a bust, too," Gregory said. He told Ronn about Stand's continued reluctance to discuss the stockpile, and how Jean had failed to learn anything new. And he told him that the costly failure of their mission, resulting in the death of an agent, meant Stand was back in retirement, this time for good."

"How is this man acting now?" Ronn asked. "Does he appear unhappy and bitter over the loss of his career?"

"He's been drinking pretty hard ever since he got back. Jean told me that much. I guess he's been staying over in Washington a few days, hoping to talk McWilliam out of canning him. So far, McWilliam won't see him—he's really angry about the way they botched the assignment. I think we can safely assume Stand is out of the game for good."

"I think I will arrange for someone to meet this man," Ronn said.

"You gonna try to turn him? Forget it."

"Why do you say this?"

"Because he's a stubborn son-of-a-bitch, that's why. He'll just laugh at you."

"No matter," Ronn said. He tapped out the rest of the ash from his cigarette, then put the burned-out cylinder into his pocket. "I shall decide if the approach is warranted."

"I still don't think it's a very good idea."

"Your objection is noted," Ronn said sharply.

Gregory scowled and brushed some powdered sugar off his coat. The doughnuts had left him thirsty and he was tired of sitting out in the wind.

"Let's get this over with," he said, handing Ronn a small canister of film. The prints would show the paper work for the Rumanian operation, and details of a planned shipment of arms to Nicaragua. Gregory was a willing informer but a timid thief, and that was all he had been able to steal in recent weeks.

"Thank you, James," Ronn said, with exaggerated politeness. "Is there anything else you have to tell me?"

"Just one thing. I don't know whether it means much or not, but I got the idea from the way they're acting that it might be important. The Company has gotten hold of a new defector, someone who went private a few weeks ago. Came to us of his own volition, in Italy, I think. They're preparing to slip him into the country soon, making accommodations for a long debriefing."

"And what is so exciting about this particular *seksot*?" Ronn asked, using the Russian word for an informer. He sighed disinterestedly, and pulled out another cigarette.

"I don't know, really. They're being very tight-lipped about the matter. I just thought it was kinda funny because he's supposed to be a Russian operative, but they keep referring to him as the Italian."

Ronn looked up, the smoke catching in his throat. "Sergei Yanov? Is that the name?"

"Yeah, I think so. That sounds right. Yeah, I'm pretty sure that's him. Who is he, anyway? What's so important about the guy?"

"He is a pig, a traitor who sells himself and his comrades to save his own worthless skin." Ronn smiled to himself at the irony of saying these things to his informant. "So, the Italian has reappeared. He has eluded us these many weeks, but at least he emerges from his hole."

"I was right, huh? This is important?"

"Yes, James. You have pleased me very much. Tell me, where do they plan to interrogate the Italian?"

"One of the grinders in the Washington area. I don't know which one."

"That is not very helpful. Your people have many safe houses in the immediate region. We cannot hope to watch them all."

"I think it's in Virginia. I heard someone mention it was near the Farm."

Ronn nodded. "Well, that is something. When will the traitor arrive?"

"Soon, probably in the next few weeks, that's all I know."

"That is not good enough. I must have specifics—time and place, and method of transport. You must give this matter your special attention, James. I want to know everything, and quickly, before they move him."

"I don't know," Gregory said hesitantly. "You already have me doing too much. And this kind of thing is risky. I can't get that information through my usual channels, and I don't like sticking my neck out any further than it is already."

Ronn stepped close to Gregory. He slipped an arm around his shoulders in a friendly way, then suddenly his hand closed around Gregory's throat.

"You will do as I demand," he said. "I will tolerate no more of our petty excuses. You belong to me, James. Do not forget that, my friend." His fingers clamped around Gregory's neck, squeezing like a vise. The American squirmed, his eyes watering in pain, but Ronn held him easily.

"All right, stop it! I'll get it, you know I'll get it."

Ronn smiled coldly and released him. "Yes, James. I know you will. I never doubted it."

"You'll get what you want," Gregory said, still breathing hard. "Just lay off the rough stuff. You don't need to do that."

"I am sorry, James. It was necessary to impress upon you the importance of this matter. You are correct, though—this is a dangerous task, so I think you will deserve an especially large payment. Keep that in mind.''

''Yeah, sure.'' Gregory brushed off his trousers and looked around anxiously. ''That's all I had to tell you. I'm sick of sitting around out here in the boonies. Can I go now?''

''In a moment,'' Ronn said. He buried the ash of his second cigarette, then put the smoke-charred tube in his pocket. He looked up and spoke in a slow, thoughtful tone. ''I have something of my own to tell you. I have been recalled to Moscow. I shall be leaving soon, and someone else will become your controller.''

''Why are they sending you home?''

''I do not know. The decision was just announced, and no explanation was offered. It is not my place to question the orders of my superiors.''

''Who will take your place? Someone from the embassy?''

''It is possible,'' Ronn said. ''I don't know, because matters are somewhat confused right now. When your President recently expelled a number of our diplomats, our operations were thrown into a state of chaos from which they have not yet fully recovered. Your controller may be one of the embassy residents, I cannot say.''

''When will I meet this new person?''

''These matters have not yet been arranged.'' Ronn sighed wearily. ''You will be informed when it becomes necessary. In the meantime, you must concern yourself only with the duties I have given you. This is very important, James. You must not fail me.''

Gregory smiled crookedly. ''Want to make a big splash before you leave, huh?''

Ronn's face was a hard mask. ''That is all. You may go now. Your money is hidden on the alternate site. You can pick it up tomorrow, as arranged.''

''Okay, sure,'' Gregory mumbled. He stood there a moment, looking as if he wanted to say something more. Instead, he shrugged and moved off slowly through the brush.

Ronn stayed behind. He smoked and gazed through the

woods with a melancholy air. The sun touched the tops of the trees and he watched the shadows lengthen. The wind had died, and the water of the pond was smooth and still. He tossed a pebble and watched the ripples fan out, but quickly the water glazed over again, as if the disturbance had never happened.

CHAPTER 11

MARTIN RONN dropped into a chair by the windows and watched the haze of twilight settle over the Washington skyline. The weekend was over. The travel and constant alertness had left him weary, but his mind would not let him rest. So much to do, so many problems yet unsolved, and now his time here was growing short.

It was his favorite hour, when dusk softened the edges of the city and gradually it became a panorama of lights: the streetlights, the glow at the windows of suburban homes, the passing car lights, and the steady crisp colors of neon. So much light. The Americans turned back the darkness with an energy that stunned him.

It was amazing how active these people were at night. In Moscow it was different. Of course, people went out for concerts, plays, movies—how his people loved their cinema— but there was less of this frantic running about. The night was usually an occasion for friends and talk. People tended to gather in one place and remain until the talk and vodka were drained. The Americans were always moving. Even at night they were seldom still, rushing here and there as if motion itself was their main passion. Ronn wondered sometimes why they had homes at all.

Yet he had to admit, it was this same quality—this vitality—that he found most admirable in the Americans. As a nation they were headstrong, arrogant, and of course ideologically confused. But as a people, they were energetic, adventurous, and honest in a naïve fashion that both amused and disturbed him.

No other people could match their spirit, their eagerness to tackle a problem, simplemindedly refusing to admit there was anything they could not solve. The Americans symbolized his nation as a bear, and Ronn had to agree there was some truth to this likeness of a lumbering giant. But if that was so, then he likened America to a wolf, cunning and hungry, constantly on the prowl.

Even a wolf must be respected. Ronn had been in Washington for five years, and despite himself, he had come to love the city. He loved the broad tree-lined avenues that reminded him of Leningrad, the staggering system of paved roads on which any citizen could travel, the supermarkets with a wealth and variety of foods such as he had never known existed.

There was also much about America that he detested—crime, unemployment, drugs. And most of all, the political apathy of its citizens, an ideological chauvinism that made them ignorant, even incurious, about the rest of the world. The average American knew little more about Ronn's nation than about the surface of the moon. In a country where so much information was available and uncensored, they cared more about television stars and rock musicians than about the people who shared with them the major responsibility for the world's destiny.

Still, despite these misgivings, Ronn was saddened by his reassignment. He was going home, back to Moscow. It would be good to see his family, but he would miss this strange land and all its perplexing contradictions. Most of all—though he was not proud to admit it—he would miss the excitement, the challenge of his life as a spy. The professional issues troubled him most. He had spent years building a network that was unrivaled. But now, through what appeared a completely arbitrary decision, it was all to end.

Ronn lit a cigarette and stared out at the brooding twilight. He faced a disturbing dilemma. The network would have to be handed over. He did not matter as much as the legacy he would leave to his successor. The work must continue. But whom could he trust with the product of his labors? The situation at the embassy—as he'd told Gregory—was chaotic. There was no one there he felt to be worthy. Who, then?

The more Ronn considered the problem, the more frustrated he became. There seemed no answer. But he would have to select someone, and soon. If he didn't, Moscow would choose for him, and that was unthinkable. They would give his network to someone like Rysorkov, a young fool on the embassy staff of residents who could barely put on his shoes in the morning without consulting Moscow first. Yes, that would be Moscow's choice. They would prefer someone without the streak of independence Ronn had displayed, a puppet they could easily control. And it would be a disaster.

Ronn's thoughts were also disturbed by a more immediate problem. The Americans were close to discovering his part in the gambit at Düsseldorf. Ronn had been loath to help the East Germans, but the request had come from Shaelinsky, the director of the Spetsburo, the bureau of special tasks that answered only to the Central Committee. To refuse such a *papakha*—a "big hat"—was tantamount to suicide.

"You must understand the nature of our position," General Shaelinsky had said. "We cannot risk using one of our own experts to place this bomb. Our negotiations with the West are in a delicate stage just now. If the West Germans trace the bombing back to us, it would make a shambles of our efforts. The secretary is adamant that this shall be avoided at all costs."

"I see, Comrade General. What is it you wish from me?"

"I am told you are in contact with the man called Falstaff. He could handle a job of this sort quite easily. You must dispatch him to Germany at the appointed time and carry out the sanction as I've described to you. Make certain he comprehends that the bomb is not to be detonated. This is imperative, Vdovushkin. The bomb is to be a threat only; under no circumstances do we want an incident that will embarrass us."

"I will speak to him as you wish," Ronn had said. "But please understand, Comrade General, I do not control Falstaff; he goes where he pleases and undertakes only the assignments that he wishes to."

The general had snorted. "Offer him whatever he wants. You have the complete backing of the Central Committee. Whatever he demands will be made available to you."

"It's not that simple, sir. I doubt there is really any price that would tempt him if he did not care for the assignment."

"Nonsense. No more backtalk, Vdovushkin. You have your orders. See that they are carried out."

"Yes, Comrade General." Ronn had given up. There was no way to explain a man like Falstaff to Shaelinsky. It was like trying to make a sleepy overfed zoo animal understand the mind of a jungle cat.

But to Ronn's surprise and considerable relief, Falstaff was taken with the idea. "It is an interesting task," he said. "To leave a bomb that is not meant to explode, but which must appear that it shall. It will take someone of my skills to make such a thing convincing. You were right to come to me with this challenge. Yes, I think it could prove amusing."

Ronn had been appalled. He could not fathom how anyone, even a madman, could think of such actions as amusing. But then, Falstaff's mind had always been beyond his comprehension. It was only an accident of fate that had brought them together a long time before.

Falstaff was an anarchist. He had no politics, no ties to Russia, or to any country. He cared for nothing but the pursuit of his own legend. He had performed his deadly services for Ronn before, but only when an assignment appealed to him because of a unique challenge, or an opportunity to create a spectacle of killing that would attract the world's attention.

Ronn knew him from a time and place that were so different, it barely seemed real to him anymore, the Patrice Lumumba University. Ronn had been an instructor in that notorious school and he was one of the first to recognize the talents of a student recruited from the Basque separatists. His name was Antonio Auramuño, and he quickly distinguished himself, showing a particular skill in the crafting of homemade bombs.

One day, disaster struck. Auramuño was learning to increase the effectiveness of simple TNT by carefully directing the force of the blast when a defective detonator went off prematurely. The explosives had been contained inside an electric circuit box—the lesson being concerned with how to paralyze the power source of a targeted building or factory— and it was only the metal shell of the box that saved his life.

The door was blown into his face. Like a knife, it flayed the skin to reveal a gruesome mask of blood and bone. Some instinct had made him raise his hands at the critical moment, and they, too, were laid bare. The concussion knocked him flat on his back, and he stared up with eyes that were white and terrified. He was somehow still conscious. That had horrified Ronn, for he could see the fear in the young man's eyes, the knowledge that in a single moment everything had changed, nothing could ever be the same for him.

Ronn had held him, spoke tenderly the first words that came to mind. He said that the boy would live, that to survive tragedy was the sign of a special destiny, that somehow he would be better for having come so close to the face of death. Ronn knew his words were false, that the youth could see through him, and he hated himself for it.

That was the last Ronn saw of Auramuño. They carted him off to the hospital and he never returned to the school. It was rumored that he had died in surgery, but no one could say that was true. Ronn didn't have the heart to make a more official inquiry. He knew what he would find—no one had ever survived such a blast. If the boy, through some miracle, still lived, he would be hopelessly crippled, a wasted shell of what he once had been.

Years later, when Ronn had been posted to the embassy in Paris, he was approached on the street by someone he thought to be a stranger. It was Auramuño, his face completely altered by plastic surgery. He was so unlike the student Ronn remembered that at first he believed it was some sort of cruel joke.

"So you doubt me?" the stranger had asked with a laugh. "Well, perhaps you are right to do so. Auramuño is dead. He ceased to exist on the day he lost his face. That man is gone forever."

"Who are you, then, and what do you want with me?"

"I want to help you."

"Why?"

"Because, Professor, it is because of you that I came to understand the great significance of my second life. You showed me the way to the truth. It was you who made me what I have become."

"And what is that?" Ronn had asked. "What have you become?"

"As Christ arose after crucifixion, I was reborn in the wake of an explosion. Created in death, and that is my calling, my fate. Before I am done, all the world will know my message, and they will tremble. My new name, the name of the man who was born on that fatal day, is Falstaff."

Ronn had felt a chill settle in his spine. The shadowy figure called Falstaff was already known to the world. Now he was certain this poor creature was mad.

"So you still do not believe me, Professor?" Falstaff asked. "You try to hide your doubts, but nothing escapes me. No matter. You will come to know the truth. Watch the events that will unfold tomorrow and you will see how well I learned my lessons."

The next day, as the Russian ambassador was riding to the embassy, a bomb exploded inside his limousine. The bomb was so skillfully directed that the ambassador was torn apart while the driver, just a few feet away, escaped with only scratches. The heavy limousine, armored against gunfire and bombs from the outside, had swelled up like a balloon, but did not rupture. It was a masterful demonstration of a tightly controlled blast pattern. A group of Ukrainian nationalists claimed credit for the kill, but Ronn learned from the French demolition experts that the bombing bore the distinctive stamp of Falstaff.

They explained how it was possible to use explosives to

create a particular design. Sand was spread atop the bomb in the desired form or within the bomb housing. The force of the explosion literally sandblasted an impression of that shape onto any surface it contacted but did not destroy. The police confided a fact that had been concealed from the public, that Falstaff always used this method to leave a distinctive mark, a signature in the form of a cross. That symbol was clearly impressed on the roof of the limousine in the ambassador's blood. Ronn shuddered as he recalled the stranger's crazed talk of being reborn in the way of Christ. Christ, who died on a cross.

That evening, when Ronn finally made his way home, the stranger was waiting for him outside his apartment. "You believe me now," he said. "I see it in your face."

It was true. Now Ronn looked closer and he could see something familiar in those pale eyes. He could even see faint traces of scars left by the surgery that had resculpted his face. He believed, and he was afraid.

"Well, Professor, were you impressed with your student's work today?"

"You killed a good man," Ronn said. "He was a friend, and a loyal worker for the cause of socialism. Is this how you would repay Mother Russia?"

"I owe no allegiance to Russia. I have no masters. Politics bores me. I kill because it is what I was born to do. It is my destiny."

"The police know that Tardokiroff's death was your handiwork. It is not safe for you here."

Falstaff laughed. "So they know. I am surprised they caught on so quickly, but that is good. I wish for my work to be recognized."

"Your use of this signature is foolish. It will lead them to you eventually."

"I have nothing to fear. They will never find me." With that, Falstaff held up his hands. "Look, Professor. These hands that were all but destroyed. Look closely. What do you see?"

Ronn frowned, bewildered. He saw nothing unusual. There

were faint ridges where skin had been grafted to replace dam-aged flesh, but otherwise the hands appeared quite ordinary. Here and there, a few small hairs grew in odd places like the tips of his fingers, but surely that was not . . .

Then he saw it. Ronn seized Falstaff's hands and brought them closer. He looked up in astonishment. "Your palms are smooth, you have no lifelines."

Falstaff nodded, smiling. "And no fingerprints. All that belonged to the man you knew before was burned away in the heat of that explosion."

"Like your face."

"Just as my face was changed. Even you did not know me when I first approached you. I am a totally new man, with no past. The man Auramuño is dead. The records in your own country say so. It was how they chose to cover the em-barrassment of my accident. A dead man will never be sus-pected. I am not of this world. Falstaff is untraceable."

"Then why have you revealed yourself to me?"

"I wish to make an arrangement with you. We may be very useful to each other, Professor."

Ronn disputed that point angrily. "I steal secrets. I am not involved in killing."

"The skill in these hands is too valuable to ignore. You will find occasions to use my services. I guarantee it."

And Falstaff was right. Over the years, Ronn had reluc-tantly called upon him. It became known to a small circle of his superiors that he had ties to the bomber, and they had no compunction about using him. For his part, Falstaff nearly always accepted the jobs, enjoying the opportunity to preen for his former teacher. It didn't matter to him where he struck or whom he killed—it was all the same. Each strike added to his legend, spread chaos and fear, and that was all he cared about.

Ronn sat in his apartment and smoked one cigarette after another without tasting them. The room had grown dark but he didn't mind. He felt comfortable in darkness. He had spent much of his life there. Falstaff was becoming a problem.

Ronn knew he would have to tell him that they would never meet again. But beyond that was a greater worry—the business with the Italian.

Ronn had used Falstaff for the Düsseldorf deception against his wishes, and now his reluctance was proving to be justified. The Americans were getting close to the truth because of some minor detail they had noticed in that episode. They could not put the facts together in a way that would lead them to Falstaff, but that would soon change, once they began talking to the Italian. Sergei Yanov. How Ronn had come to hate that name.

Yanov had defected to Italy in the summer of 1981. His defection raised a minor stir in the press that year, for he was a colorful character who affected the pose of a dandy, and loved to praise his new homeland. He was a darling of the media, featured in magazines and on television, and was often asked to serve as a representative for the growing ranks of Russian emigrés in Rome and Milan. For a time it seemed he was everywhere. Then, in the way of celebrity, he gradually faded from public view and was more or less forgotten.

The KGB had raised a great fuss at the time over Yanov's defection, then backed off, seemingly content to cut their losses. The truth was they had nothing to fear from the Italian. He was a full colonel of the KGB. In secret Moscow files Sergei Yanov's record was stamped with a one-word summary: *NASHI*—meaning "ours."

The Italian still served his Kremlin masters. His defection was part of a carefully planned long-term penetration. As a trusted member of the emigré community, he was often enlisted to aid new dissidents to leave Russia illegally. He would inform the KGB of these potential defectors, and they would quietly disappear before their hopes could be realized. No one suspected Yanov's treachery—there were many ways such schemes could fail, and no one could doubt the sincerity of his disappointment when one of his charges was captured.

Besides serving as a double agent, Yanov occasionally performed as a cut-out or a support man, passing messages, procuring materials, and assisting Soviet operatives in the field. It was in this role that he was enlisted to help in the deception bombing by Falstaff.

Yanov's task was simple. He merely had to deliver a car to an appointed place along the Konigsallee, the major boulevard in the heart of Düsseldorf. The car's trunk was filled with materials for the bomb Falstaff would personally construct. It was a routine dead drop, but Yanov was not content to follow the accepted procedure. He decided to hang around and see for himself that the exchange went smoothly, a nearly fatal mistake.

It was a warm day and the Ko, as it was popularily known, was crowded with people out to enjoy the sun, leaving the office district on one side of the waterway to stroll by the elegant shops and cafés on the other. Yanov mingled with the crowd, then took up a point across the boulevard where he could watch the car to see who came for it. He waited, growing bored, but then at last he saw a tall man with a pale face move toward the vehicle. Curious, Yanov drifted closer.

The man inserted a key and opened the door. Then suddenly he froze, his gaze locking on Yanov across the square. Yanov had never seen this man before, but he realized the agent had recognized *him*. The stranger glared at him with a rage that Yanov would never forget.

The agent ducked into the car. Before Yanov knew what was happening, the car lurched into motion, tires squealing, and raced directly at him. Yanov stood paralyzed by disbelief. Each second seemed to pass in slow motion, every sensation forever sealed in his memory. The hum of the crowd was pierced by the roar of the car's engine as the man rammed it into a higher gear. It bore down on him, and he could clearly see the man's face behind the wheel, his eyes steady and cold. A woman screamed, and then Yanov was thrown off his feet, saved at the last moment by an alert bystander. The car screeched past, missing him by inches, and then was gone.

Yanov returned to Italy, badly shaken. He could not understand why the agent had been so intent upon killing him.

But he remembered those cold pale eyes, and he felt certain the man would try again. With that threat looming over him, he began discreet inquiries. He learned that the controller on the operation was Victor Vdovushkin, a KGB operative who also went by the name of Martin Ronn. The information was only a rumor, but it was enough for Yanov. That same day he cleared out all his records and walked into the American embassy.

For years, Yanov had heard rumors that Vdovushkin was controlling the terrorist bomber known as Falstaff. A sick feeling of dread in the pit of his stomach made Yanov certain that the stories were true, and that the man in Düsseldorf had been Falstaff himself. It made sense. He understood now why the man had tried to kill him. No one had ever seen the terrorist's face and lived. And now Yanov had seen him. So he ran. This time his defection was genuine.

Ronn thought over all these facts again, everything that had been troubling him since the traitorous Italian had vanished. Now it appeared the Americans had him, and soon they would begin an extensive interrogation that would give them, among other things, their first physical description of Falstaff. The terrorist was insane with anger over Yanov's betrayal. He had been pressuring Ronn for weeks to help him locate and kill the Italian, but they had never been able to find him. Now, finally, he had resurfaced. Killing him would not prove easy. The Americans would protect him as if he were the President himself. It was an incredible piece of luck that Gregory had discovered that the Italian was in American custody.

Ronn groaned and stretched out wearily, closing his eyes. Gregory. There was still the question of what to do about him. So much to do and so little time. Gregory, Falstaff, the Italian—all such pressing problems that he could not concentrate on one while the others were yet unsolved. They tumbled about in his mind, kept getting tangled, intertwined.

His eyes shot open. It was so simple. The three problems were connected. Falstaff was threatened by the American secret Office and by the Italian—Gregory was Ronn's link to both of these elements. And someone had to be chosen to take over running Gregory. The answer was obvious. Falstaff would become Gregory's controller.

Ronn smiled. There was a certain elegance to the simplicity, the directness, of the scheme. The more he thought about it, the more it appealed to him. Falstaff would protest at first. He wouldn't care for the bother of running an agent. But Gregory was Falstaff's only hope of finding the Italian and silencing him forever. He could not ignore a chance like that. Once the Italian business was settled, Falstaff could do whatever he chose to with Gregory, cast him loose or continue to use him to stay one step ahead of the American counterterrorist efforts. Gregory would never know he was reporting directly to a terrorist.

Yes, that was it, Ronn decided. He would leave the rest of his network to be handled by Moscow. Only Gregory, his most sensitive source, would become Falstaff's concern. There was another element to the plan that pleased Ronn greatly. It effectively removed the danger of compromise for the Soviets. Even if the worst happened and Gregory were uncovered as a traitor, he would have no visible ties to Soviet operations. The Americans could never publicly admit one of their own was serving terrorists. If it ever came out, Russia would appear an innocent bystander. It would be an embarrassing scandal for the Americans, a disastrous setback for their intelligence community.

Ronn poured himself a glass of vodka in a spirit of celebration. It was the perfect solution. Persuading Falstaff might be difficult, but he had no doubt he would succeed. Falstaff would see the beauty in a scheme that involved such intricate layers of deceit. Gregory, in betraying his country, would be himself betrayed, an unwitting pawn in a game of cross and double cross.

Ronn smiled. Double cross. Yes, Falstaff would like that.

Stand took a beer and found a table near the back. It was still early in the evening and not yet crowded. Danker's was a downtown bar and grill on Washington's E Street, near the national theater. Because of location and its congenial atmosphere, it was favored by many workers from the Justice Department, the IRS, the FBI, and the Secret Service. On any given night a large proportion of the drinkers were lawyers, judges, and customs agents, enjoying the relaxed setting and a chance to swap professional gossip.

Stand felt at home among these men and women in their uniform gray suits. Their hair was all neatly clipped, their shoes smartly polished, and their eyes looked as if they had been awake for days, which in many cases was probably true. Their faces were haggard, but their voices were clear and rang with passion, intense people discussing issues about which they cared. They assumed the pose of serious drinkers, with elbows firmly braced on the tables, and the bar hummed with the trill of their easy laughter. The worst cutups were often the judges—a reaction to the pressure of maintaining a stiff, dignified facade all day.

Stand smoked his pipe and drank the beer slowly, determined to stay sober until his business there was concluded. He had just finished the mug and signaled for another when he saw her come through the door. Jean Frost looked crisp and serious in her own gray suit, and her face had the same weary expression. She wove her way toward him, pausing to wave at friends and chat briefly with a few others.

She stopped at the bar and got a drink, then made her way toward him. As she came over, Stand got to his feet and pulled out a chair for her. Jean smiled and lifted her eyebrows in surprise.

"Why thank you, Nathan. That's a courtesy I'd almost forgotten." She stared at him, then laughed. "Sit down, you're making me nervous. Makes me wonder what you want from me."

He smiled back. "No ulterior motives, I promise."

"Well, that would make you the only person I've run into lately who didn't want a piece of my hide. What a day." She took a sip of her whisky and let out a long sigh. "You don't know how much I needed that. Or maybe you do. What do I know?"

"It's all right, Jean. We both know I'm a drunk. You don't have to mince around it."

"No, I didn't mean that at all," she said. "I just meant that you know what I'm talking about, you know how crazy a day at the Office can be."

"Not at the moment."

She looked up quickly. "I'm sorry. I seem to be saying all the wrong things."

"Never mind," he said gently. "Tell me about it. What are the latest events at Mother K?"

Jean shook her head. "That's one expression I never use to describe Langley. It sounds too warm and homey for a place where I spend all my time getting knifed in the back."

"That bad? You look like you'll pull through okay."

"Thanks, but I wasn't so sure for a while. You remember Jerk's suspicions about the Rumanian operation? He was right about all of it. Ops was using our contractor just to have someone to burn to distract attention from their own penetration. I spent the afternoon screaming my head off at the DDO . . . for all the good it did."

"No use, huh?"

Jean sighed. "It was like beating my head on a brick wall. I thought I could count on Daddy to support me, but he sat back and didn't help at all. I know he's as angry about the situation as I am, but he made me argue the case alone."

"Your father may not be around to support you much longer," Stand said softly.

"I know. Maybe that's what he had in mind, letting me learn to fight my own battles. Who knows what he was up to? But it was just so damned frustrating. 'Little lady, who are you to tell me how to run my operations?' That's what that pompous windbag said to me! Can you believe it? 'Little lady'!"

"I guess he didn't know who he was up against."

Jean frowned. "Now I *know* you want something—that's the second nice thing you've said to me. All right, Nathan, what is it?"

A waitress brought Stand's second beer. He took a drink

quickly, then sighed and sat back. "That shouldn't be so hard to figure out—I want to see your father."

"Uh-huh, I thought so," Jean said. She looked past him, watching a group of noisy FBI agents at the bar. "I don't know if I can help you with that. You know how he is once he's made up his mind."

"If he would just listen to me for a few minutes, I know I could make him give me another chance."

"He says you had your second chance. And blew it." Jean looked down at her hands on the tabletop. "I'm so sorry about that, Nathan. It was my fault, what happened to Reiger. You never would have had that trouble with Pharaoh if I hadn't forced you to take me along."

"No, the fault was mine," Stand said. "I knew what would happen, but I didn't do what I felt was right. It was my indecision that made it all go wrong."

Jean looked up at him. "I read your report," she said softly. "You didn't mention the way I fouled up by showing them the money. Why did you do that?"

He shrugged. "It didn't seem important."

"Not important? They tried to kill both of us because of the money. That's how the whole thing went sour, but you just skipped over it."

Stand gulped down the last swallow of beer. He had forgotten his resolve and downed the second one very quickly. He toyed with the mug, hefting it and sliding it around the table, fighting the impulse to order another. "The little details don't matter," he said finally. "What's important is that I was supposed to be in control of the situation. I wasn't—I let it go bad and a man died because of me."

"Because of *us*," Jean corrected him. She reached out and touched his hand, making him look up at her. "I appreciate you trying to protect me. But it isn't fair for you to take the blame. And I told Father that. I told him what really happened, all of it."

"And what did he say?"

Jean hesitated. "Pretty much what you did—that you knew better and messed up. He was really shook by the idea of me in Pharaoh's den of thieves. It scared him, I think. That's probably why he came down so hard on you. I'm sorry, I guess my participation made things worse for you in a lot of ways."

Stand nodded thoughtfully and refilled his pipe. He was struggling with himself to keep from ordering another drink. Jean sipped her whisky and borrowed Stand's matches to light a cigarette. She glanced around the barroom in a distracted manner, then suddenly perked up when James Gregory appeared at the entrance. She raised a hand to wave at him.

"Look, there's James. Let's have him join us."

"Let's not," Stand said.

Jean caught herself and dropped her hand before Gregory saw her. She watched him saunter over to the bar. Then she turned and frowned at Stand. "You don't like him, do you?"

"No, I don't."

"Why not?"

Stand sighed. "What difference does it make?"

"He's really very nice, once you get to know him."

"Yes, I hear you know him pretty well."

Jean raised her head proudly. "I love him. I love him very much."

Stand took back his matches. He held them over his pipe to improve the draft and get it going again. Then he tossed them down with a weary gesture. "Then I'm happy for you. It takes all types. If you two get along, well, fine. My opinion shouldn't matter."

"No, I guess it doesn't," Jean said, but she smiled, to make sure he didn't take offense. A gleam appeared in her eyes as she watched Gregory across the room. He was drinking at the bar, bantering with a couple of customs agents. He didn't seem to have noticed her yet. Jean watched him eagerly, but he was engaged with his friends and didn't look her way.

Neither Jean nor Stand took any notice when a slender, hawk-faced man entered the barroom and took a table by himself. It was Martin Ronn.

Jean finished her drink and glanced impatiently at Stand,

drumming her fingers on the table. It was obvious she wanted to conclude their business so she could join Gregory. "Well, Nathan," she said, "was there anything else? What exactly did you want from me?"

"Just what I said, to ask you to talk to your father. Persuade him to see me, give me a chance to explain myself."

"I really don't know what good it would do."

"What if I promise to tell him where to find those guns from the Belfast shipment?"

Jean stiffened. She stared at him, Gregory momentarily forgotten. "Are you sure you want to do that? I thought you were dead set against giving that away to anyone."

"Would it help? Do you think he'd go for it?"

"I don't know," Jean said hesitantly. "Those guns are a thing of the past, pretty well forgotten by now. I doubt he cares much about them anymore."

Stand frowned. "Everyone seemed very curious about them a few weeks ago. Especially you."

Jean coughed over a mouthful of smoke and stabbed out her cigarette. She met his eyes and nodded grudgingly. "It just seemed such a waste for you to sacrifice a career over them. But that's all over with. It would probably only stir up more trouble to dredge up that issue again."

"Mention it to him," Stand said. "I'm desperate. I need my job back. It's all I have. I still feel strongly that those guns are better off undisturbed, but if he wants them bad enough to hear me out, then I'll do it. I'll turn them over, but only to him, no one else."

"Okay, Nathan. If that's how you feel. But I don't know if I want to approach him about it right at this time. He's very busy, you know. He already has too many worries."

"That's all right. I'm going to be gone for a few days myself. I need some time to think things over, make up my mind about this. Just give him the offer. I'll contact you when I get back."

Across the room Gregory moved away from the bar and paused for an instant near Ronn's table. He tipped his head in Stand's direction. Ronn nodded. Gregory kept going, heading for the door.

Jean glanced up anxiously when she saw him leave, but she stayed a moment longer. "Where are you going, Nathan? In case I need to contact you."

"A long way. To see someone from a saner time."

"To Ireland? Your family?"

He smiled faintly. "You think you're pretty smart, don't you?" He saw Jean staring at the door where Gregory had vanished and waved a hand at her dismissively. "Go on. You might still catch him."

Jean got up. "Thank you, Nathan," she said. "I'll do what you ask. I promise." Jean grabbed up her cigarettes, stuffed them in her purse, and moved off hurriedly.

Ronn watched her disappear through the door. Then he got up and casually made his way out. He walked about half a block until he spotted Gregory and Jean. They held each other, talking in low voices, then kissed and climbed into their separate cars.

"See you in a few minutes," Jean said. Then her Porsche roared off down the street. Gregory's car pulled out and followed. Ronn smiled to himself and went in search of a cab.

Ronn stood in the shadows outside Gregory's apartment until he saw the headlights sweep across the garage door. He waited to see that Gregory was alone, then stepped onto the porch. Gregory walked up, whistling to himself. His tune ended on a sour note when he saw Ronn. "What are you doing here?"

"Inside," Ronn said curtly. "We need to talk."

"I don't like you coming to my place. What if somebody sees you here? It's the middle of the night, for cripe's sake."

Ronn said nothing, and Gregory saw he would not be dissuaded. "All right, get in quick," he said, and opened the door.

Ronn walked inside and flipped on the light, then dropped into a chair. He had his hands in his pockets and seemed content to leave his coat on. Gregory walked over slowly and sat on the couch, unnerved by Ronn's silence. "All right, what the hell's going on?" he asked. "You told me we were never to meet in the open like this."

"I will ask the questions," Ronn said sharply. "Events have accelerated, and I deemed it worth the risk for us to meet this way one time only. Now, you saw the woman, did you not? What did you learn from her?"

Gregory frowned and slumped down in the couch, throwing his feet up on the coffee table. "She's worried about Stand," he said. "He's thinking about telling McWilliam the location of the stockpile."

"Yes? And why has he experienced this change of heart?"

"He wants his job back, and hopes that will persuade McWilliam to take him on again."

"I see. And the woman—what does she intend to do about this?"

Gregory shrugged. "I don't know. I mean, she doesn't know. There's nothing she can do except maybe kill him, but then nobody would know where the stuff is. So we're caught in a hard place."

"When does he intend to see his superior?"

"Not for a while. Stand told Jean he's going to leave for a few days, go somewhere to make up his mind if he really wants to go through with it."

"And you know where this place is he intends to go?"

"Jean's pretty sure he's going to Ireland," Gregory said. "To a little town called Clarerea. Stand's wife was from there."

Ronn nodded. "Good. That will do nicely."

"For what?"

"That is something you need not know, James. But it is time that I took more direct action against the troublesome Mr. Stand. He has been in our way quite long enough."

CHAPTER 12

THE AIR was damp and close, sour from the muck that spewed from the factory smokestacks that surrounded the village. Dim streetlights cast a jaundiced glow to the pools of water dribbling between the cobblestones. Nightfall brought a deepening chill that chased the locals to their pubs, and the streets were silent but for the droning mutter of the rain.

Stand paused on the footbridge and opened a bottle of Jameson. The liquor burned at the back of his throat and he grimaced, then replaced the lid carefully and put the bottle in a pocket of his coat.

His steps quickened. On the other side of the bridge was the park. The park—that was what they called it here, though Stand felt it hardly deserved the title. In truth, the cemetery was little more than a vacant lot, a tiny patch of grass and a few stunted trees. Row housing loomed high on both sides, casting shadows in which little grew.

The rusty gate squealed in protest to his touch. He moved into the lot, staggering drunkenly, picking his way as if looking for a soft place to fall. It was tough going at any rate, especially in darkness. The grass was overgrown and choked with fallen tree limbs, a tangle that snarled his legs so that he nearly stumbled with each step.

Leah had loved that spot. When she was a child, she had played there nearly every day. It was the only place in the village that was green and full of life, a small bit of nature amid the gloomy soot-darkened buildings. It would have saddened her to know how the villagers had let it go untended. Still, he had respected her wishes. It was better than the proper site on the northern edge of town, right outside the wire fence of a factory.

In the center of the lot was a lonesome elm, ancient and withered, sagging like an old woman under its own weight. He went to his knees at the base of the trunk and dug his fingers into the mound of leaves gathered there. The pile of mulch clung together stubbornly, but he fought it with a fierce determination. His breath rasped. He worked faster, almost desperately, his fingers scratching and clawing at the mire.

At last he touched stone. Carefully now, he cleared the last of the sticky mess, brushed away the dirt until the smooth face of a marble block was clean. Bending lower, he traced one finger along the engraved words that he knew so well: Leah Norah Morrison Stand—Melissa Rae Stand.

Suddenly he smashed his fist against the stone. His knuckles came away skinned and bleeding, but he raised his fist and slammed it down again. Then again, over and over in a maddened frenzy, as if trying to drive the stone deeper into the earth. A soft cry broke from his lips, but he kept pounding, time after time, and stopped only when he dropped from exhaustion.

Tears blurring his eyes, Stand sprawled over the ground, his face touching the cold stone. He passed out.

He awoke with a sudden start. He sensed rather than saw movement in the darkness. Reacting instinctively, he threw himself to one side. Something whistled past his ear.

The attacker grunted as his leather sap glanced off the marble tombstone. Stand lashed out blindly at the sound. His hand struck something solid, a thigh or hip, and he knew it had done little damage.

The man came at him again. This time Stand's eyes had cleared. He saw the heavy bag of metal shot swinging at his face. He ducked under it, twisting clear, grabbed the man's wrist, and pulled back with all his weight.

The attacker cried out, yanked from his feet into an awkward somersault. He struck hard on his back, flopping and trying to break free, but Stand held him in an iron grip. He gave the arm a vicious twist and was rewarded with a shrill scream. He felt the wrist in his hand become dead weight as the attacker's arm separated at the shoulder.

Even as he writhed in pain, the attacker continued to fight. His free hand moved toward his waist, clutching at a holstered revolver.

Stand saw the gun and reacted. There was no time for halfway measures. Coiling his leg, he drove his foot at the man's face, concentrating all his weight and strength. His boot hammered the man's jaw, snapping his head back, and his neck broke with a sound like a dry twig. The man crumpled, his head drooping loosely like that of a poorly stuffed doll.

Stand sat up, shaking his head. He sighed wearily and dragged himself to his feet.

The bullet screamed past his face. Chips of bark exploded from the tree behind him.

He went down again, fast, just as a second shot spit dirt in the place he'd been standing. He pressed his face to the grass and crawled to the dead man, groped, and found the gun still in the dead man's hand. He tore the Webley revolver from slack fingers. Feeling better with the gun, he cautiously raised his head and peered around.

Nothing moved on the dark streets. Stand watched and waited, his heart pounding in his chest. His pulse raced each time a leaf was rustled by the wind. He lay completely still, feeling tension settle over his muscles like a cold, sodden blanket. It was a battle of nerves now. One of them would break soon.

Stand heard a sudden flurry of footsteps fading. The sniper was fleeing.

Stand jumped up just in time to glimpse a shadow detach itself from the darkness and sprint through a pool of murky light on the far side of the street. He took quick aim and snapped off a shot at the retreating figure.

It was a hasty shot, wide and harmless. He knew the moment he squeezed it off that he had missed, so the muffled cry startled him. He was even more surprised to see the fleeing sniper tumble and sprawl across the cobblestones.

It didn't seem right. He was sure the shot had missed. He bolted for the street, crashing through the tangle of grass and debris, but the sniper was up again, moving before he reached the fence. Stand was barely in time to see his assailant reach the far side of the footbridge and disappear, limping noticeably. It would be useless to pursue him. Worse, it would be dangerous. There were too many places in those tight streets and alleys where a man could hide or turn to stage an ambush.

Wearily, Stand dropped the gun to his side. He turned back to search the dead man's pockets for a clue to his identity, but lights were snapping on in houses up and down the street, and a police siren howled in the distance. He didn't need to listen to know which way it was headed.

Stand jammed his hands in his coat pockets. He went only a few steps when he yanked out one hand and swore bitterly. A fine cut on his finger dripped blood. The bottle in his pocket had smashed into jagged slivers, and his coat and trousers were soaked with whisky.

He spun around angrily and glared at the homes on the street, all of them with their lights burning brightly. No one had yet ventured outside.

Stand shook a fist in the air. "Come out, you spineless cowards!" he screamed. "Come out! Or will you forget this, too?"

With a contemptuous growl, he turned away, walked to the footbridge, and crossed over to the tangled maze of streets that led to the village. His footsteps made no sound, and in a few moments he vanished, melting into the shadows with the ease of a man all too familiar with darkness.

"I don't care what time it is," Stand barked. "People are shooting at me. He can damned well get out of bed. Get him."

The embassy staffer retreated from Stand's rage. "I called

him," he said in a trembling voice. "He'll be here, he told me he would."

Stand frowned and edged to the window, peering out at the quiet Dublin streets. Dawn edged over the rooftops and the sky had the pale cast of dried bone. He leaned his head against the sash and rubbed his burning eyes. Fatigue made him feel heavy and slow, his body aching as if he had been worked over with a hammer. It had been nearly six hours since the attack in Clarerea, and he had been on the move throughout the night to reach the Dublin station in the first hours of dawn.

He heard the door open and swung around. The man was heavyset, with gray stubble on his cheeks. His hair was still uncombed and his tie was thrown together as if done in the dark, with the ends widely uneven. He smiled tiredly at the staffer and motioned toward the door. "All right, Jimmy, thanks for calling me. I'll take it from here."

The staffer glanced briefly at Stand and muttered, "Good luck." Then he hurried out. The click of the lock was loud in the quiet room.

The man ran his fingers through his tousled hair, then shrugged off his raincoat and dumped it on a chair. He walked slowly toward Stand and offered a handshake. "I'm Carter, chief of station here. You're Stand, I take it."

"That's right." The man's handshake was firm and strong, pumping slowly, as if he were weighing Stand's response and judging him through his grip. "Sorry to get you out of bed so early," Stand added.

"Forget it. All a part of the job. Nothing bad ever happens in the daylight." Carter's eyes appraised Stand frankly with an open stare. "You could have knocked me over with a feather when Jimmy said a guy stormed in out of nowhere and claimed he was Nathan Stand."

"Why is that?"

Carter gave him a bland half smile. "It's not the first time I had your name on my mind," he said. "I was with the Ireland end of that smuggling detail you pulled off with the

SAS a month or so back. That was a nice piece of work. The reports said you had a lot to do with it.''

"The SAS did the real work," Stand said. "I just helped pull the pieces together.''

"Well, whatever. I saw some strange follow-up reports that said you had something to do with another thing that's been on my mind. Seems you stopped some guns headed for a group in Belfast that call themselves the Erin Dawn?''

"Yes, that's right," Stand said.

Carter scratched his head, his eyes narrowing under heavy lids. "Well, that's a funny thing, you know. Because I've been spending the time since then trying to catch a lead on those folks. Fact is, no one here has ever heard of them. I've browbeat every snitch and sniffed into every dark corner in Ulster, but I can't turn up a scent anywhere. It's like they showed up from no place and then disappeared after doing nothing.''

"I don't know what to tell you. That's what our informants said they called themselves. I stopped the guns and that's the last I had to do with it.''

"Seems funny, though, don't it?" Carter drawled.

"The shipment cost them top dollar. Maybe we broke their back financially.''

Carter smiled. "We can always hope, can't we? But now here you are, and it sounds like you got yourself some kinda trouble.''

"That's what I call it when people shoot at me," Stand said. "It was in Clarerea, up in the north, and I was—''

Carter held up one finger to silence him. "Let's take this into the briefing room," he said. "You know what they say, the walls have ears.''

Stand nodded. They walked into a small plain room where a long conference table took up most of the space. There were four framed pictures, one on each wall. One was a portrait of the President, another of the current DCI. The third was a photo of Chief of Station Carter at some sort of reception, posing with the two men from the other pictures grinning like old chums. The final picture, oddly, was a print reproduction of the Mona Lisa. Stand preferred this last picture—the smile seemed more genuine.

Carter motioned Stand to a chair. "I need some caffeine. What about you?" He filled two mugs with tea from a pot in the corner, dolloped cream in them, and brought them to the table. "Sorry I don't have coffee," he said. "I been on this station for twelve years. Guess I'm gettin' more Irish than I realize."

Stand drank the tea greedily. It was hot, and strong enough to wake the dead, which was close enough to how he felt. Carter slid two ashtrays across the table. He pulled a pack of Three Castles cigarettes from his coat and set them next to the tray. Then he folded his hands together and looked at Stand.

"Now, then, let's get on with it. It'll be a while before I get any field reports to check on your story. I didn't have a man in the area, but I sent someone up there soon as Jimmy called. We should hear something in an hour or so."

Stand nodded and pulled out his pipe. He frowned when he felt the lightness of the tobacco pouch. It was empty. "Could I steal one of those cigarettes?" he asked Carter.

"Sure, help yourself. So why don't you fill me in on your eventful night. Clarerea, huh? What were you doing in a pissant place like that to begin with?"

"It's a long story," Stand said. "My family is buried there. I went to visit the grave site."

"Oh. Sorry to hear that. Still, it seems sort of a funny thing to do, visiting graveyards in the middle of the night."

Stand frowned. "I was drunk, all right? Is that what you wanted to know?"

"I was wondering when I'd get an explanation for the delicate aroma of your hundred-proof after-shave. You reek of whisky, Stand. What'd you do, take a bath in the stuff?"

"I had a bottle in my pocket. It broke in the scuffle."

"Yeah, this scuffle—tell me about that."

"There's not much to tell," Stand said. "One man jumped me. When he started to pull a gun I had to kill him. Then a second one started shooting from across the street. He took a couple shots at me, than ran away.''

"You get a good look at this second person?'' Carter asked.

"No, he was too far away.''

Carter took out one of the cigarettes and held it over the ashtray. He carefully broke it in two and then started shredding the first half, letting the tobacco spill out.

Stand stared at him. "Trying to quit?'' he asked.

Carter nodded. "It's my wife's idea. She sent me to some clinic—they said to break them up like this whenever I want to smoke. It's supposed to help. It doesn't.''

"Save some for me, all right?''

"Sure,'' Carter said. He finished breaking up the cigarette, then brushed the crumbs off his fingers. He stared at his empty hands for a second, then folded them together again. "Did you see what direction the guy ran off?''

"No,'' Stand said. "Just away.''

"Okay, forget him for a minute. The other one, the guy who jumped you—what can you tell me about him?''

"Not much. It was dark and it all happened very fast.''

A phone on the table buzzed softly. Carter picked it up. "Excuse me a second.'' He spoke into the phone receiver. "Yeah, this is Carter. . . . No kidding! You got there quick. What'd you find? . . .'' He listened for a minute, then looked up at Stand, his eyes hard. "You sure about that? . . . What are the police doing on this thing? . . . Okay, do what you can to clean it up with them. Stay there as long as it takes. I want copies of everything they turn up, especially forensics. Stay on it, Joe. I'll keep after it from this end.''

Carter hung up the phone. Slowly, deliberately, he took out a cigarette and lit it, then inhaled deeply.

"What is it?'' Stand asked. "You learned something.''

Carter nodded tightly. "Yeah, you could say that. Everything looks pretty much like you said. They found the guy who jumped you. Joe says he's beat up something awful. Bruises on the leg and back. Arm clear out of the socket, and his neck snapped in two. Somebody did a number on him, all right.''

Stand frowned at Carter's tone of voice. The station chief's attitude had changed, and he seemed suddenly hostile. "What's the problem?" Stand asked. "What did he tell you?"

"I just want to understand all this," Carter said. "We got one dead man who looks like he's been through a meat grinder. Now here you are, and you don't have a scratch on you. How do you explain that, Stand?"

"I already told you what happened."

"Yeah? Well, you tell it to me again. You explain it to me real good."

"What is this?" Stand growled.

Carter drew in a lungful of smoke and exhaled it with a long sigh. "All right, Stand. You can play innocent if you want to, but the game is up."

"What the hell are you talking about?"

"We got a positive make on the guy you say attacked you," Carter said. "He is—or, rather, was—Shawn Kelso. Name mean anything to you?"

"No. Should it?"

"Kelso was a knuckle dragger for the Provos. A bad animal. His specialties were kneecapping and bone-breaking. They used him whenever they wanted to make an example of someone—you know, a little demonstration to keep the troops honest."

"I don't get it," Stand said. "Why would the Provos want to make an example of me?"

"An interesting question. Why don't you just come clean now and save us both a lot of trouble?"

Stand's face darkened and his hand clenched into a fist. His voice was soft and tightly controlled. "You'd better be damned sure of yourself before you start talking to me like that."

Carter smiled. "What happened, Stand? Did I touch a nerve?"

"What the hell are you getting at?"

Carter took a last puff on his cigarette, burning it down to the filter. He made a face and tossed the butt into the ashtray. "Let me lay out the facts the way I see them," he said. "A little scenario, just to see how it plays. Let's say some American agent—an Office contractor, for example—decides to cut himself into the action in Ireland. Who knows why he does that? Maybe he just wants more money, or maybe he's been a sympathizer for their cause all along. You have an Irish heritage, don't you, Stand?''

''Scots.''

Carter nodded thoughtfully. ''Well, pretty close. Anyway, let's suppose this man wants to work on behalf of the revolution. So he offers his services. Now, the Provos are a suspicious lot. They might just as well decide to shoot this gift horse in the mouth, so to speak. Our contractor needs something to offer them, earnest money of a sort, something valuable to prove to them that his heart's in the right place. So I ask you, Stand, what does he come up with?''

''This is your story,'' Stand grumbled. ''You tell me.''

''Guns,'' Carter said, smiling thinly. ''The perfect gift for revolutionaries who have everything. A nice fat shipment of Russian machine pistols, let's say.''

Stand shook his head. ''It won't wash, Carter. I was a big part in helping to smash their supply lines, remember?''

''Yes, there is that. But those shipments were ones the SAS had already tumbled to. There wouldn't be much our contractor could do to prevent that operation from going through. But there was another opportunity for him, a shipment of Russian machine pistols that he intercepts. And then the guns conveniently disappear.''

Stand said softly, ''Got it all figured out, don't you?''

''What happened, Stand?'' Carter hissed. ''Did you get cold feet at the last minute? Or did you suddenly turn greedy and demand more money? What did you do to make them turn on you?''

''Stuff yourself,'' Stand said. ''I told you what really happened. Or doesn't the truth have any place in this little scenario of ours?''

Carter glared at him. He flipped a switch on an intercom.

''Get Mason in here now.'' He sat back, folding his hands

behind his head. "Oh, yes, the truth. There maybe a few holes in my story here and there, but for the most part, it reads pretty well. Explains a lot, actually. Why some of the targeted groups in that crackdown escaped scot-free, why a dummy organization called the Erin Dawn appears overnight and vanishes just as quickly. Yes, I think it's a very interesting story, indeed. I can't wait till the folks in Langley get a chance to hear it."

The door banged open and a uniformed marine stepped inside, holding his rifle high.

Stand glared at Carter. "You're making a big mistake."

"I think the mistake was yours, Stand. You made it when you came in here with that cock-and-bull story, demanding protection from the people you double-crossed. You can remedy that mistake now by giving me the truth. Or you can wait till an interrogation team arrives to begin a formal investigation. Believe me, you'd make things easier on yourself if you played straight with me now."

Stand reached toward Carter's cigarettes, then paused and looked up questioningly. Carter nodded. "Go ahead," the station chief said. "Make yourself to home. 'Cause one way or another, Stand, you're gonna be with us for a long time."

Stand lit a cigarette, then tapped the lighter on the table in a nervous rhythm. As he did so, he spun the flame setting to high.

"What's the matter, Stand? Getting fidgety?"

Stand smiled. "I'm always squirmy around incompetents. Afraid it might be contagious."

Carter snatched his lighter back angrily and motioned to the guard. "Take him away. Get him out of my sight."

The guard stepped up and prodded Stand in the back. "C'mon, you heard the man. Move it or lose it."

Carter stuck a cigarette in his mouth and mumbled around it. "Good-bye, Mr. Stand. I'll see you again soon when the question-and-answer boys arrive." He flicked the lighter. Flame shot up in his face, nearly a foot high. Carter shrieked and dropped the lighter in alarm. The guard laughed.

Stand flung himself back into the guard, driving an elbow into his stomach. The man slammed into the wall and doubled over. Stand brought his hand down on the exposed neck and the marine sagged to the floor, out cold.

Carter gasped and jumped to his feet, just as Stand tore the rifle from the marine's hand. He swung it around in one smooth motion, smashing the butt into Carter's face. The station chief fell back in his chair, then toppled over like a felled tree. The chair smacked onto its back with Carter's feet dangling in the air, the cigarette still clinging to his lip.

Stand tossed the rifle onto the table, then headed for the door. He hesitated, then went back and gently pried the burning cigarette from Carter's mouth. Stand tapped it out in the ashtray and shook his head at the unconscious station chief. Quietly he let himself out and locked the door behind him.

Jean rolled over and groped sleepily for the telephone. She raised the receiver and croaked something sounding almost human. A familiar dry cough on the other end startled her into alertness.

"Jean, wake up. This is important. I want you clear-headed."

Jean rubbed her eyes and squinted at the clock on the night table. Five-forty-five A.M. She moaned softly and sat up straight. "All right, I'm with you. What's up?"

McWilliam's wheezy voice crackled through the phone. "Stand has gotten himself into big trouble. The DCI has declared him a renegade and ordered a full intensive search. They've got Justice preparing a warrant as we speak. The stations are being notified to consider him armed and dangerous."

Jean ran her fingers through her hair, pushing it back tightly. All traces of sleepiness had vanished. "What did he do?" she asked breathlessly.

McWilliam told her of the Dublin station chief's suspicions.

Jean whistled softly. "He's really gotten himself in deep

this time, hasn't he? You don't really believe Stand was working for the Provos, do you?''

"Absolutely not," McWilliam snorted. "The idea's preposterous. There's something going on, Jean. I've had a bad feeling in my gut for weeks. I don't know what it is, but I think Stand may be involved in something much bigger and more complex than we suspect.''

"What do you want from me?" Jean asked.

"Find him. You worked with him, spent more time with him than anyone else recently. If anyone has a line on what's going on in his head, it must be you. Find him, talk to him, bring him back quietly, Jean. Promise him my own personal protection. I have safe houses even the Director of Operations doesn't know about. I'll keep him out of harm's way until we can figure out what the hell is going on.''

"All right," Jean said. "I'll do what I can. But I can't guarantee he'll listen to me even if I do manage to find him.''

"Listen carefully," the old man said. "I hate to say this, but it is entirely possible that Stand really has cracked up. He is a very dangerous man. If his grasp of reality has slipped, he could make a great deal of trouble for all of us. Jean, I am giving you full contract autonomy. If you find any reason to suspect that Stand represents a danger to the Office or to our nation's interests, you are to act with any means necessary. *Any* means.''

"I understand," Jean said softly.

There was a moment of silence. Then McWilliam's voice was gentle, unlike any tone she had heard him use before. "I'm sorry to ask this, Jean. I really wish it didn't have to be you. For God's sake, be careful. Stand has a way of finding trouble, and when you catch up to him, you may wind up in something very messy. Please watch out for yourself.''

Jean laughed uneasily. "Don't worry, Daddy. I'm a big girl. I know how to take care of myself.''

"I know you do. But please, be especially careful this time. I don't know how I would live with myself if any harm came to you. You're very important to me, Jean. I'm proud

. . . I mean, I think you should know—I've always been very proud of you.''

Jean held out the phone receiver and stared at it in a daze. She shook her head and blinked, as if she were looking at something she couldn't quite bring into focus.

For the first time, she started to feel scared.

CHAPTER 13

GREGORY STOOD up when he heard movement in the brush. Ronn made his way slowly up the wooded hillside, limping and favoring one leg. "What happened to you?" Gregory asked. Ronn sat down on a rock looking flushed and weary.

"I stumbled and turned my ankle. It is nothing."

Gregory smiled down at the Russian. "You're getting old and soft, Martin."

"Thank you, James. I am glad I came all this way to hear you say that." He winced and gently altered the position of his foot. "But maybe it is so." He sighed.

Gregory jammed his hands in his pockets and stomped his feet, looking around the wooded scene with distaste. "Why couldn't we meet somewhere warm?"

"It was especially vital to meet somewhere private this time. This is what you may call an auspicious occasion."

"What do you mean?" Gregory asked.

Ronn just stared past Gregory, his gaze fixed on something behind him. Gregory turned and saw a man step into the clearing. He was tall and slender, with very pale skin and eyes that seemed bleached of any real color. It was Falstaff.

"Hey! What's going on?" Gregory asked.

"This is the last time you and I shall meet," Ronn said. "I wish you to meet your new controller."

Falstaff walked over slowly to join them. Gregory stuck

out a hand in greeting, but Falstaff ignored him. "What's the matter?" Gregory grunted. "You too good to shake hands with me? It wouldn't kill you to at least act friendly."

Falstaff stepped directly in front of the American, stood face-to-face with him, only inches separating them. "Understand this clearly, James Gregory," he said. "We are not friends. You betray all those who call you friend. I have no need of friends, especially such a traitorous one as you. You disgust me."

"Yeah? Well, I'm not feeling too crazy about you either," Gregory shot back.

Ronn pushed the two men apart. "Enough. It does not matter what you think of each other. The two of you serve a common goal."

Gregory scowled and shook his head. "No way. I won't work with this clown. Find someone else."

Ronn turned angrily on him. "You do not give orders. You will do as I command."

"Forget it. If you're clearing out, then all bets are off. This is where I call it quits."

"You cannot quit, James. The choice is not yours to make."

"Oh, no?" Gregory hissed. "Just watch me." He turned to storm away.

Ronn called after him in a soft voice. "You will not fare well in prison, James. A pretty-faced man such as you will find life in your federal institutions most unpleasant."

Gregory stopped and looked back over his shoulder. "What are you talking about?"

"That is how your country punishes traitors," Ronn said. "I believe incarceration for life is the usual sentence."

"You can't threaten me. You try anything against me, I'll turn you in, go to the Company with the whole story."

"And you believe they will forgive you for conspiring with the enemy?"

"I'll tell them I was stringing you along," Gregory said. "That I fed you phony and worthless material just long enough to gather evidence against you. It would work, too.

You would be the one facing jail time. They'd come down hard on a foreign spy.''

Ronn laughed. "James, you understand so little of this game. You truly think they would forgive you for all of the information you have stolen in the past years?''

"They'd never know I took it.''

"But of course they would," Ronn said. "They would know everything, because I would tell them.''

Gregory's face fell. "You wouldn't do that. You're tough, you'd never give in to them.''

"Don't be foolish. I would tell them whatever they wanted to know. There is no reason to resist. My part would be complete. They cannot change what has already been done. They would interrogate me for several months—a year, perhaps—and then I would be traded for one of your people in custody in my country. I would go home, exactly as I am about to do now, only a bit later. It would be inconvenient, but bearable. For me. For you, I'm afraid it would be a somewhat different story.''

Gregory paled. "But that's not fair. You're the spy. I just did whatever you told me to do.''

"Spies are accepted as a necessary evil. Traitors are never forgiven. Wake up, James. It is how the game is played.''

"It's not fair," Gregory mumbled again, visibly shaken.

"Fairness has nothing to do with it." Ronn said. "Enough of this foolishness. Now you understand the position you are in. I will be gone, but your work will continue. This man will be your controller, and you will do as he says because now you know the consequences of failure.''

Falstaff stepped up, forcing Gregory to look at him. "Let us not speak of failure," he said. "You will not fail me, James. You will not even think of such things.''

Gregory sighed. "Do you have a name? What do I call you?''

Falstaff smiled coldly. "You may call me Nazareth. A fitting name for a new beginning.''

"Whatever," Gregory mumbled. He looked back and forth at the two men, then shivered and hunched his shoulders inside his coat. "Can we hurry this along? I'm freezing to death out here."

"Certainly," Ronn said. "To business. What do you have to report?"

"Stand has gotten himself a lot of attention all of a sudden. He killed a man in Ireland someplace. I don't know all of the details."

"Forget that," Ronn said. "I know of the incident. Tell me of the reaction. What has happened since it occurred?"

"Stand's on the run," Gregory said. "The entire Company is out to get him. They found out the guy he killed was a Provo heavy and they decided Stand had been dealing with them. They tried to lock him up for questioning, but he broke away and is on the loose now."

"Your people had him in custody, but they let him escape?"

"That's right. He took out two men and strolled out of the embassy like it was nothing. There's no telling where he is now."

"Your people are such bunglers," Falstaff chortled. "It amazes me sometimes that your nation still exists at all."

"Tell me about it," Gregory muttered.

Ronn spoke to Falstaff. "This contractor has been a considerable thorn in my side. He complicates matters at every turn. You must find him, for he alone knows the location of the stockpile."

"Jean has been assigned to locate him," Gregory said. "I've arranged time off and I'm going with her."

"And I, as well," Falstaff said. "I will follow you, and you will keep me aware of your progress. This is most important, James. The contractor must be found and made to reveal the secret of the stockpile. I have plans for this substance and I mean to have it."

"What are you going to do with it?" Gregory asked warily.

"You will be told when the time comes."

Ronn broke in when he saw Gregory bristling at Falstaff's tight-lipped response. "You have done well, James. It is good that you arranged to take part in the search for the contractor, very good. I am pleased that you showed such initiative. Anything else?''

Gregory lowered his eyes. ''I think they've already brought over the Italian. I tried to find out when he was being moved, but the security was too tight.''

''Forget the Italian,'' Falstaff said. ''He is nothing.''

Ronn stared at the terrorist in astonishment. ''Why do you say this?''

Falstaff waved his hand in a gesture of disinterest. ''Yanov is a mere nuisance. He cannot harm me. And he will be disposed of once the stockpile becomes mine. Everything depends upon that—it is the key to everything.'' He turned to Gregory. ''How does your search begin?''

''We fly to Dublin tomorrow.''

Falstaff nodded. ''That is good. Wherever the search leads you, I shall follow. When you and the woman have located the contractor, I will be there to take over. That is all. You may go now.'

Gregory scowled and looked at Ronn as if for confirmation. The Russian nodded. ''Good-bye, James,'' he said quietly.

''I won't see you again?''

''No. I return home soon. To Moscow and my family. It will seem a quiet life after all I have known. But perhaps I am ready for it.''

Gregory shook Ronn's hand. ''Good luck to you.''

''And to you, James.''

Falstaff frowned at the display of sentiment. He motioned abruptly to Gregory. ''Go now. We will leave after you.''

Gregory glared at him, then turned and stomped off as if only too happy to comply. The terrorist watched him until he was out of sight, then glanced at Ronn. ''You have softened, Professor. I think you treat the American too kindly. He will perform better under a firm hand.''

''You will find it is better sometimes to stroke a dog than to kick it. The lowest cur will turn on its master when it has been cuffed and beaten too long.''

"Yes, you have changed," Falstaff said, staring thoughtfully at Ronn. "I think your leaders were wise to recall you."

Ronn grimaced and climbed to his feet. "Perhaps. I shall miss the excitement and the power of secrets, it's true, but I have no heart anymore for manipulating other men. It requires an arrogance and certainty of purpose that I no longer possess. I know the Americans too well to hate them."

They trudged down the hillside, Falstaff slowing his steps to keep pace with Ronn, who still favored his injured ankle.

"I hope you will be content in your new life," Falstaff told him.

Ronn nodded. "I suppose that is exactly what it will be— a completely new life. I hope I am ready for it." He climbed in the car and drove away, slowly traveling the winding road down the hill.

Falstaff watched the car with an absorbed expression. He reached inside his coat for a small radio transmitter. He raised the aerial and flipped a switch. A small red light began flashing.

"Good-bye, Professor." He pressed the button.

The air was split with a resounding roar and the car on the road below erupted in a ball of fire. It veered wildly and crashed through the guardrail, tumbling end over end as it glanced off the slope in a long skittering slide. It came to rest at the bottom of the cliff. A second explosion sounded. Flaming debris flew out in all directions.

Falstaff shuddered with an almost sexual pleasure as he imagined the release of Ronn's soul to the netherworld. "Yes, Professor," he whispered. "You will be happy, I think. I feel it."

The terrorist drove down the hill and stopped the car at the place where Ronn had gone over the cliff. He got out and made his way to the bottom of the canyon. Ronn's body lay in a bed of tall weeds, where it had been thrown from the car. It was badly charred, with tattered scraps of clothing smoldering and spitting sparks into the grass.

Falstaff smiled. He poked at the body with his toe, straightening the way it lay, then pushed the legs together.

Carefully, he arranged the arms until they were each pointing straight out from the sides.

"This time, Professor, you shall be my sign."

He left the burning body lying with arms outspread, in the form of a cross. He climbed up the slope to his car and drove slowly away. Heavy black smoke billowed up behind him, blotting out the sun.

The morning showers had stopped and clouds scattered like beggars chasing a gold coin. The sun burst through the autumn gloom. London looked unprepared. Like much of Europe, the city wore its age with a self-conscious dignity that was better suited for gray somber days. The people on the streets looked up with expressions that were vaguely distrustful, not prepared to revel in the warmth, but steeling themselves for when it would suddenly end.

Stand walked aimlessly, content to drift with the crowds. Straying down Carnaby Street, he merged with the shoppers and tourists who packed the popular and pricey mecca of fashion. Teen-aged girls bounced from shop to shop, sharing conspiratorial whispers and laughing with abandon. Their energy radiated in a cloud around them, as did the scents of their oversweet, generously applied, perfumes.

He wandered through Soho, moving quickly past the famous Palace Theatre in Cambridge Circus, then along to Gerrard, where he paused outside the house once occupied by the poet Dryden. North along Shaftesbury to Dean Street, he found the house where Karl Marx had lived during his years in England. The house had been refashioned into a restaurant.

Stand thought he was simply roving without direction, but then he found himself on the southeast corner of Soho Square. He stopped dead in his tracks. Across from him was the House of Saint Barnabas. Suddenly he knew he hadn't been roaming at all. He had subconsciously followed the same route he and Leah had taken, the one time they had come to England as tourists.

Stand felt an ache so sharp that he nearly doubled over

from agony. The memory of Leah was strong in this place. He could almost see her as she had been that day, laboring over a sketch pad, drawing the house.

"How real would I be to you," she had said, "if someday I was gone? Would you remember?"

"Where are you planning to go, Leah?"

"I don't know. I'm just in one of my silly black Irish moods. Feeling mortal and sad because it all goes so quickly. You would forget me, Nathan. It's all right, I know you would, but I forgive you."

He knew she was wrong, but he never told her that.

A long black cab glided to the curb in front of Stand. He looked up sadly, and the memory slipped away. He glared at the driver for tearing him from the past.

"Sorry, mate," the cabbie said. "Thought it looked like you wanted a ride."

I do," Stand blurted. "I shouldn't have come here." He climbed into the backseat and sat rigidly, his eyes still locked on the grand old house.

The driver peered over his shoulder. "Goin' to keep me in suspense, are you?"

"Oh, sorry." Stand pulled a copy of the London *Times* from his coat pocket. It was folded to the Classifieds. He read off the address from an ad about a room to let.

The driver frowned. "Bloody big spender, aren't you? You could walk there faster than it takes to turn a cab 'round."

"Then drive around awhile. Anywhere. An hour or so. I don't care."

"You mean that?" The cabbie was suddenly all smiles.

"Get going."

They drove off. Stand didn't look back, though it took all his willpower not to.

The cabbie dropped him at the address on Greek Street. He accepted his fare and tip with a brief uneasy smile. Stand had refused to talk while they had driven in aimless circles. The moody silence had unnerved the driver. Despite the large fare, he delivered Stand before the promised hour was up and sped off quickly.

The house was an old two-story brownstone with weathered wood trim in vaguely Victorian lines. It was bordered by an Indian restaurant on one side, a pub on the other. Stand gazed longingly at the pub. The heady aroma of stout ale was heavy in the air. He licked dry lips, hurried up to the house, and rang the bell.

The door opened instantly and a little girl of about seven or eight smiled at him. She wore a school blazer and pleated skirt, and her long brown hair was soft and straight. She toyed with a strand of it as she studied him with a disturbingly frank curiosity.

"Hello," Stand said. "I'm here to see your mother—"

"My mum is taking a bath," the girl said with grave seriousness. "You are supposed to come in and sit down and be comfortable. You can have a drink if you want. She says to tell you she'll be right down."

Stand smiled awkwardly. "Hold on. I'm not sure you—"

The child brushed past him onto the stoop. "I'm sorry, but I have to go. I mustn't be late. There's going to be a fight."

"A fight? Where?" Stand tried not to laugh. The child had the serious, intent manner of a small undertaker.

"Uh-huh," she said. "Jason Evers is going to have his teeth knocked out."

"How do you know that?"

"Jason Evers called me an Anglo-Saxon Amazon this morning, and I'm going to hit him. I don't think he should get away with calling people names, do you?"

"Do you hit everyone who calls you a name?" Stand asked.

"Yes, I do."

"Even when you don't know what the name means?"

The girl had bounced down to the sidewalk. Now she paused and looked back at him. "It does mean something bad, doesn't it?"

"Not really," Stand said.

She looked disappointed. "I guess you think I shouldn't hit him, then, should I?"

Stand shook his head. "Probably not."

She brooded over that for a moment, then shrugged. "Oh, not to worry. It probably is best this way. He is the teacher's son, you know."

Stand nodded with great seriousness. "You've made a wise decision, I think."

"Thank you." She gave him one of those openhearted smiles that only a child seemed capable of doing. "You seem like a nice sort, Mr. Bickley. You see that my mum has a smashing time tonight, won't you?"

"What?" But she was gone before Stand could gather his wits. He watched her bound along the sidewalk and disappear around the corner at the end of the block. His heart ached with a familiar pain. Melissa would have been only a few years older than this child.

He took one step inside and called out, but no one responded. The mother must still be in the bath. Stand decided to follow the child's orders and let himself in.

It was a fairly typical British home: small rooms with too much furniture. The chairs were old and needed recovering, and the dining table had one short leg, which was propped up by a stack of books. There were books everywhere, in fact: stacked on shelves along the walls, piled on the coffee table, more atop the television, all neatly arranged. The furniture was dusted and shining, as if recently polished. It was a home that showed much care, neat and tidy without being fussed over.

Stand sat down in the living room and idly picked up a book left open on the coffee table. It was a British edition of a Russian emigré novel. Stand glanced at a few pages, then began to read with interest when he was interrupted by a scuffling noise in the hallway. He got to his feet as a woman entered the room, wearing a terry-cloth robe and vigorously rubbing a towel through her hair. She was a small, compact woman with a trim figure and attractive features. She avoided looking at him and quickly moved into the dining room.

"I'm terribly sorry about the delay, Jeff," came her voice from the other room. "I know I shouldn't have taken the time for a bath, but Mrs. Staffield had the heat on in the office all afternoon and I nearly smothered. Now you're on the jump to leave, and I'm still a mess."

"Don't rush on my account," Stand called.

A face peered timidly around the doorjamb. She glanced at Stand, then hurriedly yanked the towel off her head. "Who the devil are you? How did you get in here?"

Stand shuffled his feet, but stayed in place, wary of alarming her. "I'm sorry if I startled you," he said. "I called, but I guess you didn't hear me. Your daughter told me to come in and wait."

"Lynnie told . . . Where is that child?"

"She went to settle a score with someone who had called her a name."

The woman groaned and slumped back against the doorframe. "Oh, that's all I need now. She was supposed to wait for me. By now it's probably too late."

Stand smiled. "Don't worry. She decided to let Jason Evers keep his teeth."

"She did?"

"We talked it over. I think I made her realize that hitting him wouldn't exactly be right, or in her own best interest."

"You did that?" She sighed, and some of the tension left her face. "It would seem that I'm in your debt."

"It was no problem," Stand said. "You have a charming daughter, Mrs. . . . ." He recalled the name in the newspaper ad. "Mrs. Foster, is it?"

"Yes, Meghan Foster." The woman came tentatively closer and sat on the arm of a chair across from him. "You still haven't explained who you are and what you're doing in my home."

"I suppose I have two missions here," Stand said hesitantly. "First, I'd like to inquire about the room you have to let."

She smiled with relief. "Oh, I see. That's different, isn't it? And what's your second mission?"

"I'm supposed to see that you have a smashing time to-night."

"You're what?" The wariness was back in her eyes.

"That was a joke," Stand said quickly. "Your daughter again. She told me to see that you have a nice time this evening. I believe she had me confused with someone else—a man named Bickley?"

She put it together and smiled with resignation. "That child. She'd run my entire life if I let her. What am I to do with her?"

The question was left hanging when they heard a pounding at the front door. Meghan Foster jumped up, panic in her eyes. "Oh, that will be Jeff. And now I'm even more late." She ran toward the stairs, calling back to him, "Be a dear and show him in, would you, Mr.—"

"Stand."

"I'm sorry to ask you. But please. He'll be furious with me. Please tell him I'll be right down."

Stand had no chance to protest. Like her daughter, Meghan Foster moved quickly when she had something to do and there was no stopping her. The pounding at the door grew louder and more impatient. Stand sighed, went to the front door, and threw it open.

The man on the stoop was a middle aged, balding, and definitely surprised to find Stand frowning back at him. "Who are you?" he demanded, making it sound more like a complaint than a question.

"You must be Jeff," Stand said. "Come in and make yourself comfortable. You can have a drink if you like. Mrs. Foster promises she won't be a moment."

With a rumble of displeasure, Bickley marched past Stand and into the living room with the air of a conquering general surveying territory claimed in battle. He started to sit, thought better of it, and darted about the room like a ferret, assuming one self-conscious pose after another. He examined the titles of the books, the hanging pictures, even inspected one table lamp. He picked up a toy of Lynnie's and studied it with the gravity of an expert appraising a rare vase. He jumped when he accidently flipped the switch and it came to life in his hands.

Stand said gently, "Why don't you relax? I'm sure she's nearly ready."

"Nearly?" Bickley pulled out a pocket watch on a long gold chain. "Look at the time, sir. What's she doing with herself?"

"She's getting dressed."

"Whatever was she doing undressed?" He studied Stand suspiciously. "And how do you come to know of this undressing business, you . . . whoever-you-are?"

Stand dropped into a chair, weary of making a pretense of politeness. He didn't care for Bickley and his suspicious questions. "If you must know, she has been taking a bath. And I've been waiting to see her about a room she has to let. I hope to become her boarder. Is there anything else you would like to know?"

Bickley glared at Stand, his mouth forming around some unspoken words. Then he clamped his mouth shut and looked aside. Meghan Foster appeared at the doorway. She was still in her robe, but had discarded the towel. Her hair was damp and hung in short tangles.

"Here I am, Jeff," she said, a little too brightly. "Sorry to keep you waiting. You've met Mr. Flann, have you?"

"Stand. Nathan Stand."

"I'm sorry. I'm afraid I didn't hear you well before. I was preoccupied."

"Don't worry, I understand."

Bickley rattled his watch chain like a maraca. As soon as he was certain he had their attention, he donned an aggrieved expression. "Good Lord, Meghan. It's nearly half past, and you look as if you were dragged from a sinking ship. We'll never make it to the Danforth in time. I have to go back to the office sometime tonight, you know. It's only for you that I tried to squeeze in the dinner."

"Why don't you do that?" Meghan Foster said gently. "Go back to the office, I mean. I still have business to discuss with Mr. Stand. I don't want to keep you if you have work to finish. I appreciate the offer, but couldn't we make it another night?''

"But I made reservations.''

"I'm sorry, Jeff. It's just not a good night. Please try to understand.''

Bickley glanced pointedly at Stand, then spoke to her in an injured tone. "I understand perfectly well. Much better than you think. Good night, Meghan. Don't bother to see me out.''

He turned and stomped away, his heels clicking on the hardwood floors. Neither Meghan nor Stand moved until they heard the slam of the front door. Then they glanced at each other uncertainly. Meghan let out a long sigh. "That was bloody awkward.''

"I'm sorry if I caused any trouble," Stand said.

She dropped into a chair, as if exhausted. Her hand waved feebly in the air. "No, please. I'm the one who should apologize. You must think I'm a terrible person.''

"Why would I think that?''

"Because I just used you in quite a cold, calculating manner. And I don't even know you.''

Stand smiled. "You didn't really want to go out with that strutting pigeon, did you?''

"I didn't hide it very well, did I?" she said, laughing softly. "I tried all day to think of an excuse to break the date. I don't know why I ever accepted in the first place. He must have caught me in a weak moment.''

"Dinner at the Danforth is enough to tempt the strongest person," Stand offered.

She smiled faintly. "Yes, I'm sure it's everything they say it is. Wonderful food. And no doubt I would have gobbled everything in sight. Ignoring Jeff, only pretending to listen to him. A perfectly awful way to behave. So of course I would have come home burdened with guilt and indigestion to top it all off. Don't mistake me. Jeff is a kind man, and he was generous to ask me, but he's just so—''

"Dull?''

"Hopelessly so.'' Meghan laughed. "All he really wants

is a willing ear. He talks on and on about his former wife
and how horribly she treated him. His divorce was years ago,
and it's still the only subject he likes to talk about—other
than himself, of course.''

''So why do you see him?''

''I don't know, really. I haven't thought about it. I suppose
I feel sorry for him. He's such a sad little man, and his wife
did treat him quite badly.''

''But what do you get out of it?'' Stand asked.

She grinned. ''Besides indigestion, you mean? I suppose
very little. I don't know why I bother, except that he is always
pestering me for a date and after a while it just seems too
much trouble to refuse. He can be very intent. I do hope I
didn't upset him too much this evening.''

''I wouldn't worry about him,'' Stand said. ''He had the
injured look down pat. I'll bet he practices in the mirror.
Why not? It suits him. Some women respond to that. He
hooked you with his sadness and he'll hook others. If you
ask me, he likes playing the victim.''

Meghan shook her head. ''My, you size up people very
quickly, don't you, Mr. Stand? I must be out of my mind,
discussing my private relationships with you, and here we've
barely just met.''

Stand smiled. ''I don't mind.''

Meghan didn't seem amused. She stood up and tied her
robe together more firmly. ''Nevertheless, I believe this conversation has reached an end. Would you care to see the room
now? It's just up the stairs.''

She led him upstairs. There was a bathroom just off the
landing, the ''loo,'' as Meghan called it. To the right was
Meghan's room, and on the other side was Lynnie's. There
was a table in the hall with a vase containing fresh cut flowers
and above them hung a collection of framed watercolors, the
technique somewhat crude, but painted with boldness and
obvious emotion.

Stand caught her watching him and made a guess. ''Did
you do these?''

''When I have time,'' she said. ''I've done better since,

but haven't gotten around to framing them. There's never any time since Lynnie started to grow. I'll get back to painting someday."

"I hope so," he said. "You have talent. I like them."

She shrugged as if the matter was not important, but he could tell she was pleased. She steered him down the hall. "Your room—that is, if you take it—is at the end. It's not much, I'm afraid. It's rather small."

She opened the door and stepped aside, letting Stand enter. The room was like the rest of the house, slightly cramped but clean and comfortable. A four-poster bed took up most of the floor space. There was an electric heater built into the near wall. The other furnishings included a small chest, a nightstand, and a dresser pushed against the far wall near the window so a person could sit and gaze at the street.

The dresser was littered with five flat, open boxes. Stand glanced at them and saw that they all contained thick stacks of typewritten pages.

"Excuse me," Meghan said quickly. "I forgot I'd left those in here."

"These look like manuscripts," Stand said. "Do you write as well as paint?"

"No, these aren't mine. Well, they are mine to work with, but I didn't write them. I brought them home to proof. You see, I'm an assistant editor for Meese and Barker, the publishers. There's always so much to do, I bring work home a lot of the time. I like to go over them up here so I can hear Lynnie if she needs anything in the night."

Stand picked up one manuscript and leafed through it. He read a few paragraphs and frowned. "You have your work cut out for you on this one."

Meghan laughed gently. "That one doesn't belong with the others. It's not an M and B book, it's a novel that my husband wrote."

"Your husband is a writer?"

"My husband is dead, Mr. Stand. He left Lynnie and me about five years ago. Went out to buy cigarettes and never came back. Sometime after, I received word that he had died in an auto accident.''

"I'm sorry," Stand said.

"No, that's quite all right. I always knew something like that would happen. Just a matter of time. My husband was drunk and ran off the road. There was hardly a time when he wasn't drunk. I consider it a blessing that no one else was hurt in the crash.''

Stand set the papers back down. "Forgive me for criticizing his work. I was out of line.''

"Not at all. You're right about the book—it's dreadful. It would take more than my blue pencil to save it. Bill wanted so much to be a writer, but he never really enjoyed the writing itself. He would sit here for hours, often all day, most of the time staring out the window and imagining excuses for his lack of progress. And getting drunk, of course. He claimed he was writing the Great American Novel. As you can see, it's American, but far from great.''

"Your husband was from the States, then?"

Meghan nodded. "Like yourself. Oh, there's no mistaking the accent, I know it well. Bill was from Kansas. Have you ever been there, Mr. Stand?''

"A few times.''

"I always wondered what it's like there, what Bill was running so hard to get away from. He said he wanted enough distance between him and America to gain perspective. The truth is, he never looked at anything very hard but through the bottom of a bottle. You should know, Mr. Stand, if you're thinking of taking the room, there's no drinking here. I won't have alcohol in my home.''

"I'll take it," Stand said.

"Pardon?''

"The room. I'd like to stay here, if you'll have me.''

"Just like that?" Meghan asked. "But are you sure? We haven't even discussed a price yet.''

Stand shook his head. "Not necessary. You don't seem the type who would cheat me. I'll pay you whatever you think is fair.''

Meghan frowned and glanced behind her, as if half expecting someone to step in and take over for her. "I don't know, this is so sudden. I mean, I don't know anything about you yet, do I? How long would you be staying?"

"I'm not sure," he said. "A week or two. Let's say a month. I'm here to see about a business matter, and I'm not certain how long it will take."

"What sort of business is that, Mr. Stand?"

"Personal," he said. "Very personal."

CHAPTER 14

STAND HAD been resting for about an hour when he had a visitor. The knock on his door was loud and insistent. He had a suspicion about who had come calling. Lynnie Foster stormed in before he could reply.

"Mum says you're not Mr. Bickley," she said. She sounded like a judge passing a harsh sentence. "You spoiled everything. I was going to stay over with my friend Karen and watch the telly. But when Mum didn't go out, I had to come home."

Stand struggled to keep from smiling. "I'm sorry, Lynnie. I'll try not to let it happen again."

The child flopped down on the bed beside him. "That's all right," she said. "Are you going to stay with us for a long time?"

"A few weeks, maybe. Is that okay with you?"

"Are you an orphan? Don't you have a home of your own?"

"I have a nice home, Lynnie. But it's far away from here, in the United States."

The child's face lit up with excitement. "In Hawaii?"

"No, not in Hawaii," Stand said. "Where I live, it's cold and wet and foggy a lot of the time."

"Oh. That sounds like here." She bounced on the bed once, then leaped to her feet. "Well, I'm going to go eat now. Are you hungry, mister?"

"You know, Lynnie, if we're going to live in the same house together, we ought to be friends. Don't you think so? Why don't you call me Nathan?"

"Okay. Are you hungry, Nathan?"

"A little bit," he said.

She smiled and took his hand. "Good. Then you can come down and have shepherd's pie with us."

"I think we should ask your mother first, Lynnie."

"No, she sended me up here to ask you to eat with us. She told me to be real sneaky about it. Was I sneaky enough, Nathan?"

Stand laughed. "I never suspected a thing."

Meghan stood back to check that everything was in its place. A moment later, Lynnie dragged Stand into the room and directed him to the table. "Sit here, Nathan, next to me," the child ordered.

Meghan smiled at him. "I see you received the invitation, Mr. Stand."

"A very sneaky little girl told me there was shepherd's pie down here that could not be believed."

"It's hardly that good. But there is plenty, and you're welcome to share it."

Lynnie tugged at Stand's sleeve. "C'mon, Nathan. Sit down."

Meghan raised an eyebrow. "Nathan, is it?"

"Of course," Stand said, nudging the child with an elbow. "We're old friends now. Aren't we, Lynnie?"

The child nodded vigorously. She climbed up on her chair and hurriedly plopped heaping spoonfuls of meat and pastry onto Stand's plate. "Eat it all up, Nathan," she commanded. "Mum makes good pie." She chewed a large bit animatedly to show him how it was done.

"Calm down, luv," her mother scolded softly. "Give him a chance." She turned to Stand and smiled helplessly. "She's not used to having someone new around. I'm afraid you'll have to put your foot down, or she'll run you about like a perfect little dictator."

"I don't mind," Stand said. "I'd forgotten what it's like to be around children since . . . actually, I'm enjoying it."

The shepherd's pie was as good as promised. Stand hadn't realized he was hungry until he tasted it. He finished his plate in short time and, with Lynnie's beaming approval, helped himself to more.

They ate quietly for a few minutes. Meghan seemed nervous and only picked at her food. Finally, she pushed her plate away and looked up at him. "Do you come to London often, Mr. Stand?"

"About two or three times a year. It depends."

"On this same personal business of yours?"

He had wondered when she would get back to that. "No, not always," he said. "There are other commitments that bring me here sometimes. Related to my work."

"And what sort of work is that? I'm not sure you've explained that yet."

Stand said quietly, "I prefer not to talk about it—if you don't mind."

Meghan frowned. "Really? What sort of Yank doesn't like to talk about his work?" She tapped the table with a nervous gesture, jangling the silverware. Taking a deep breath, she stared at him until he met her gaze. "Forgive me, but I really must insist that you tell me. Understand my position. I won't have someone in my home who can't be honest with me. What am I to think? For all I know, you could be a criminal."

"I am not a crook," Stand said, in a very bad Nixon voice. He forced a dry laugh. "If you were an American, you'd think that was funny."

"I know quite well what you meant. It's not funny. Please answer me, Mr. Stand."

Her eyes were cool and unflinching. Even the child had caught on to the tension in the room. Lynnie stopped eating and watched them with wide eyes.

"Very well," Stand said. "My work, if you must know, is simple survival. Getting from one day to the next. That may not sound like much, but it's enough for me, at least for now.''

"I don't understand."

"I am retired, Mrs. Foster. I haven't worked for some time now. I hold a doctorate in American literature. Before this, I taught at the university level. But I have been forced to put that behind me."

Meghan brightened a little. "A professor? But that's grand. You seem awfully young to be retired, though. Are you saying that you got the sack?"

"No, not really," Stand said. "I was forced to retire because of a . . . a disability. A medical condition. That's what brings me to London occasionally. I receive treatments here—treatments which are not available in my own country."

"Heroin?" Meghan asked softly.

Stand shook his head. "No, Mrs. Foster. I am neither an addict nor a terminal patient. My condition is not so serious as that, though it is troubling. Please don't think that you and the child are at any risk. My trouble is definitely not contagious."

Lynnie had grown bored. Their voices had softened, the moment of tension past. She finished her meal and was squirming in her chair. "Can I be excused now?" she asked her mother. "It's time for my favorite show."

"All right, darling. Clear away your dishes, there's a good girl."

The child jumped up, grabbed her plate, and looked over at Stand. "Will you watch the telly with me, Nathan?"

"Maybe later," he said. "I think your mother and I still have a few things to discuss."

With signs of minor disappointment, she raced from the kitchen. Soon the noise of the television and Lynnie's laughter came drifting in from the living room.

Stand looked at Meghan. "Well?"

She fidgeted in her chair, a bit like her daughter had done. "You know what I want to ask," she said. "This disability of yours—what is it, exactly? Some kind of cancer? I mean, how are you affected?"

Stand shook his head. "That is what I meant when I said my business was personal. I don't want to be rude, but it's really none of your business. I don't see that the unpleasant, very personal malfunctions of my body need be your concern."

"It's not AIDS or anything like that?"

"My condition is a personal disability. It's not related to any disease. Simply put, certain parts of me do not work as they're supposed to."

"I see," Meghan said, blushing slightly. "Thank you for telling me. I'm sorry to bother you with so many questions. I will respect your need for privacy. It won't happen again."

Stand nodded gratefully. "You had to ask. I know that. It must be worrisome, having a stranger around your house."

"I am a little nervous. You're our first boarder, Mr. Stand, and I think it will take some getting used to."

With that, it seemed they had reached some sort of settlement. He helped her clear the table and offered to dry the dishes, but she told him they could wait until later. She brewed a pot of tea and they took it into the living room to watch television with Lynnie.

After a while, the child fell asleep on the floor. Meghan took her upstairs to bed. Stand picked up a book from the coffee table and noticed the Meese and Barker imprint. He read for a few minutes. Meghan returned and saw that he was reading.

They discussed literature for a very long time. He had not enjoyed an evening so much in years. The time passed without their notice, and before they knew it, it was almost midnight.

Meghan gathered the teacups and and got slowly to her feet. "I hate to break this up. But I'm going to nod off at work tomorrow, and Mr. Barker frowns on that sort of thing."

"My fault. I shouldn't have kept you so long."

"Don't be silly. I haven't enjoyed book talk so much in ages. We never seem to talk books with any pleasure at work and never at all when we're away from the office. Then we usually gossip about co-workers." She laughed. "As I suppose, Jeff will be spreading stories about me tomorrow."

"And now you'll go in looking sleepy and bleary-eyed. I suppose that won't help much."

She stopped, disturbed by the thought, but then merely shrugged. "Well, let them think what they want. They will, anyway."

Stand looked at her admiringly. "You know, you are a delightful woman, Mrs. Foster."

"Trying to win points with your new landlord, Mr. Stand?"

"If I do, so much the better. But honestly, I can't tell you how much I enjoyed your company."

A significant look passed between them. Then they both glanced away awkwardly. "I had better check in on Lynnie," Meghan said. "Good night, Mr. Stand."

"Your daughter calls me Nathan. I wish you would, too."

She smiled softly. "All right, Nathan. And you call me Meghan. But I warn you, don't ever call me Meg. I'll plant my foot in your backside. I can't abide how men always shorten women's names to make them cuter. My name is Meghan, and you're welcome to use it. Well, good night again."

"Good night . . . Mrs. Foster."

She laughed. "Coward."

She went up the stairs and he heard her footsteps overhead, then silence. He sat back down and picked up the book again, but his mind was racing and the words on the page were just a blur. He got up and walked to the window, parted the curtain, and stared out at the night. Fog had crept in. There was nothing to see. His thoughts were as blank as the darkness beyond.

For the first time in a long while, Stand slept through the sunrise. He woke to find he had the house to himself. A steaming bath almost lulled him back to sleep, but he fought the temptation and padded back to his chilly room, cursing the British aversion to central heating. Downstairs, he found

Meghan had left him a pot of tea in a knitted cozy, and a plate with two bran muffins. He ate his breakfast with a lazy, indulgent pleasure while reading the *Times*.

Stand's mind was clear, the result of several days without a drink, but his body felt heavy and weary with a deep lassitude. He was tempted to sit around all day and read, perhaps wander to the shops and buy some groceries to repay Meghan's kindness with a meal waiting for her when she came home from the office. He imagined her smile of surprise, a good meal, and then a pleasant evening playing games with Lynnie. After she went to bed, he and Meghan could talk and . . .

No. Stand caught himself. They were a charming family, but they weren't his. And he wasn't here to lose himself in the comforts of a warm home. There was work to be done.

Stand walked for several blocks, then stopped at a phone booth and dropped in a coin. He dialed a ten-digit number, a direct line into the offices of MI 6. He heard the click of a recorder in the background as a deep voice answered gruffly. "Sherman, here. What is it?"

Stand spoke slowly, trusting Sherman to recognize his voice. "Good day, sir. I was given your name by a mutual friend, and he told me that you might be interested in our company's new form of life insurance. It's an unusual policy that I think you might find rather intriguing."

"What's the idea of bothering me here?" Sherman barked. "You bloody salesmen are all alike. I've got a job to do here, mate. I don't have time for this nonsense."

For the moment, Stand thought his friend hadn't caught on. But then he was back, and Stand breathed a sigh of relief. "Who gave you this number?" Sherman demanded. "I know, it was James, wasn't it? I'm going to give him a piece of my mind when I see him. No, make that two pieces. I'll park him down and give him a bloody thrashing that he'll never forget."

"I'm sorry to have disturbed you, sir," Stand said. "Please

forgive me. But if you do ever wish to invest in life insurance, I hope you will call—''

The line went dead abruptly as Sherman slammed down the phone. Stand smiled. He glanced around to get his bearings, then took off in the direction of St. James's Park. It was still a long time until two o'clock, but he wanted to take a good look around before their meeting.

Stand stood in the bushes and watched a man wander up casually and take a seat on a park bench. He was in his late fifties, heavily built, and looked even rounder in his bulky wool overcoat. The collar was open enough to reveal a blue blazer over a starched white shirt with an Oxford tie. His hair was thin and unnaturally long, combed over a wide bald spot that showed pink scalp on the top of his head. He patted the hair in place self-consciously and watched a female jogger go past in a Goretex stretch suit that left nothing to the imagination. He watched her till her jiggling buttocks were out of sight, then took out a bag of nuts and munched them with a bored expression.

Stand left his place and wandered around in a wide circle, looking carefully for any signs of surveillance. Satisfied that they were not being watched, he hid in the brush behind the park bench. He saw Sherman take a handful of nuts and toss them on the ground. A small flock of pigeons landed near him and began pecking at the scattered nuts. Sherman glanced around furtively, then wound up and flung more nuts at the pigeons, throwing hard, as if trying to gun them down.

''Sodding birds.'' Sherman grunted. Then, in a soft voice, he said, ''You can come out, Nathan. I'm quite alone.''

Stand emerged from the brush and sat down on the other end of the park bench. He smiled but didn't look directly at the other man. He took the lid off a paper cup of tea and watched with amusement as Sherman continued to attack the pigeons.

''I think you stung one that time. You'd better keep an eye out overhead the rest of the day. He may try to get back at you.''

"The city belongs to the sodding pigeons," Sherman grumbled. "You should see what they do to my car. Stupid beasts. Tell me, Nathan, if you were a bird and could fly anywhere you pleased, would you live in this bloody place?"

"I appreciate you meeting me," Stand said. "I presume you've heard by now."

"The memo was on my desk yesterday. You've made a right mess of things this time, you know."

"How bad is it?"

"They're saying that you've flipped your bonnet, gone raving starkers. A lot of words like rogue and renegade are being bandied about. They describe you quite well, actually."

"And what do you think, Sherman?"

A rueful smile curled the Englishman's lips. "I've always known you were crazy. It just surprises me that it took so long for the others to see through your thin veneer of civility."

Stand sipped his tea and frowned. It was cold and bitter. "Seriously," he said. "Are they looking for me? Is there any chance they'll back off?"

Sherman chuckled. "They accused you of going over to the opposition. So what did you do? Talk to them like a reasonable human being? No, you beat up two of your own people, then ran off like a common thief. Not the sort of thing they're likely to forget or forgive. Bad form, Nathan."

"You don't believe what they're saying about me, do you, Sherman?"

He shook out the last two nuts, cocked his arm, then watched sadly as the pigeons flew off to a safe distance. He put the nuts in his mouth and crunched them, then licked salt from his lips.

"Sherman?" Stand prodded.

The Englishman sighed and brushed off his hands. "No, Nathan, I know better. I don't think you have enough brains to be greedy. You play these silly games because you really believe they make a difference. More's the pity."

"Thank you," Stand said. "Do you have any idea if they suspect I'm in England?"

"They found the boat you stole. The plane booking to Rome didn't fool anyone. Oh, I wouldn't use that passport again if I were you. And thank heaven I'm not. You're a very famous man at the moment, Nathan. You wouldn't believe the ruckus you've stirred up. The CIA is doing its invasion routine, marching about like storm troopers, stepping all over the toes of the lads at Five. There's always been bad blood there, but this is making it worse. Five resents the Yanks' attitude and are out to prove something by nabbing you first. It's like a bleedin' football match, and you're the ball."

Stand swore softly. "You're certain the Company believes I'm here? Are they concentrating on London?"

Sherman looked up at the gray sky and scowled. "They're not here for a holiday in the sun." He spied a flock of pigeons flying low overhead. He crumpled the sack into a tight ball and tossed it at them. "Bugger off, you filthy beasts."

"Sherman, I need your help."

"Don't say that, Nathan, please. I'm already in the muck up to my chin just for meeting you. It would be my pension if this was discovered. There's a villa waiting for me on a Mediterranean island, someplace warm where the sky is actually blue and the sun is strong enough to warm even these old bones of mine. It's all I've worked for, the only thing I have to believe in. There aren't many years left in me. I can't risk losing that. I won't, Nathan."

"Please, Sherman. You know I haven't gone crazy."

"You have if you think you can change my mind. Drop it, Nathan. You want my advice, clear out now. Go somewhere warm and put it all behind you. It may take awhile, but they'll forget you."

"But I won't," Stand said. "I won't forget and I won't run. If you can't help me, all right, I can do it myself. I have to. I'm being set up, Sherman. I don't know why, or who's behind it, but something is going on, and it has to be something big. It's for damned sure about something a lot more important than me."

Sherman bowed his head until his chin rested on his chest. He stayed like that for a full minute, saying nothing. A lone pigeon strayed up and pecked at the ground near his feet, within easy kicking distance, but he didn't move. At last he sighed and his head came up slowly. "All right," he said. "What do you want me to do?"

"Thank you," Stand said quietly. "You won't regret this, Sherman."

"I do already. I'll meet with you one more time. Those are the ground rules, Nathan. Whatever information you need me to dig up, I'll find it and bring it to you. We meet once more, but one time only. That's where it ends."

Stand nodded. "That's fair. You're a better friend than I deserve."

"That's true. Now, what's the job?"

"I need you to go to Switzerland," Stand said. "I want you to track down the source of some stolen weapons. They were smuggled into Belfast in October, delivered to a group called the Erin Dawn. I don't know much except that they originated in a clearinghouse in Zurich. Find that clearinghouse and everything you can about that shipment."

Sherman groaned. "Do you have any idea how many arms dealers there are in Zurich?"

"I know I'm asking a lot," Stand said. "But this is right up your alley. If anyone can find them, you can." He handed Sherman a slip of paper with nine numbers on it. "Here's the access code to an Office slush fund—there's nearly half a million dollars in it. That should buy you some immediate attention."

Sherman nodded and tucked the paper away in his coat. He said dryly, "I assume I'm not spending the money, just letting them know I have it."

"Right. The Erin Dawn threw a lot of money around loosely when they made the original purchase. I'm sure the responsible clearinghouse will be eager to do business again. Just make it known that you're in town, shopping for more of the same. They'll probably come to you."

"What's so special about these guns?" Sherman asked.

"I don't know. That's what I need you to find out." Stand paused thoughtfully. "Don't tell them it's guns you're after," he said. "Be vague. Say only that you're looking for more like the last shipment."

"You think it's something other than guns?"

"It has to be," Stand said. "I don't know what, but it has to be something else. That shipment has caused too much trouble. Everything has gone wrong since the moment I intercepted those guns. Somehow, there has to be a connection."

Sherman stared quizzically at him. "You intercepted these weapons? Don't you know what they were? Why all the trouble to find out about something you already have in custody?"

Stand sighed and tossed his paper teacup in a trash can. "It's a long story, Sherman. The guns are not accessible for inspection. It would be very difficult to get to them again. It might become necessary, but I'd rather not go near them unless that's the only choice. I won't consider that until I see what results you can come up with."

"I see. This sort of thing may take a few weeks, Nathan. Can you stay out of sight for that long?"

"I'm in a safe place. I'll lie low and stay quiet until I hear from you. You know how to contact me when you come up with something."

Sherman flicked a piece of lint off his overcoat and leaned back, staring up at the sky. He craned his head, scanning back and forth, as if searching for the sun somewhere behind the clouds.

"All right, I'll do this for you. Switzerland in November. It will probably be cold. I must be getting old, Nathan. These days I'm cold all the time. I never used to mind it, but now I can't get warm."

Stand looked down and said nothing, disturbed by his friend's moody tone of voice.

Sherman went on, speaking softly, as if to himself. "There was a time when I loved this sort of thing. When I was young this business was so exciting. Secrets—we loved having secrets, stealing secrets. It was thrilling, it made us all feel special, important. Now that feeling's gone. Too many secrets, so many that they don't mean anything anymore. Not yours or mine, or even the nation's. They're just commodities. That's a terrible feeling to lose, Nathan. There are some things a man shouldn't know about himself . . . one is how bloody little his secrets matter.''

"Sherman . . .''

The older man looked up and made a face. "I know, I know. I digress; another sign of age. Don't worry, I'll pull it off, Nathan. Still a few tricks left in the old boy . . . don't know how many, but a few.''

"I won't forget this,'' Stand said softly. "I knew you were the right man to trust, Sherman.''

The older man laughed bitterly. "Trust? I can't remember the last time I heard that word used. I hardly know what it means.''

A flock of pigeons flew by overhead, the sound of their beating wings like a soft footstep in the night. Sherman glanced up at them and twisted his face in a scowl.

"Look at those stupid animals,'' he muttered. "Up and down, over and back, round and round in circles. You know why I hate those soddin' birds so much, Nathan? Because they're so damned free. They can fly, just lift up and go anywhere they please. But they don't.'' He sighed and shook his head as if it were very heavy. "What a thing to waste, that sort of freedom.''

The two men looked up quietly. The white birds stood out starkly against the gray sky. They glided playfully, soaring higher, then dove back toward the earth.

CHAPTER 15

GREGORY WALKED out of Jean's flat and shivered in the thin cold light of dawn. Jean had left the hotel and rented the flat when the search for Stand dragged into weeks. Gregory stayed over most nights, though he had kept his own hotel room for appearance's sake. It was a pleasant place in a quiet neighborhood, but that presented a problem now, for Gregory was left without a car and there was little hope of finding a cab in this residential area.

He stood for a moment, his mind groggy with sleep, pondering the solution. Jean's car was parked outside the flat, but he knew if he borrowed it he would hear about it from her. The relations between them were strained enough already. Gregory was finding it more of a problem to keep Jean convinced of his affections. The fact that they were working together only seemed to compound the difficulties. She was obsessed with the job at hand, and Gregory was not impressing her with his contributions. More and more, she snapped at him or ignored him in a pointed way. She was having second thoughts about the man with whom she was in love.

But she still had no reservations about him in bed. Gregory smiled to himself at the thought. As their search bogged down in frustration, Jean clung to him at night, becoming a more desperate and demanding lover. In this, at least, he was still able to please her.

Gregory sighed and started down the sidewalk. There was

nothing to be done but to walk a few blocks to catch the subway. He turned the first corner when he was startled to see a cab coming his way. He waved excitedly and the long black car pulled over to the curb. He opened the back door and then froze. Inside was the man he knew as Nazareth.

"What are you doing here?" Gregory asked.

"I have not heard from you," Falstaff said. "Get in, James. I wish to hear a report."

Gregory frowned and climbed in beside him. Falstaff signaled the driver and the car pulled away slowly.

"Why have you not told me of your progress?" the terrorist demanded.

Gregory raised his eyebrows and tipped his head pointedly toward the cabbie.

"You may talk freely," Falstaff said. "The driver is a deaf mute. You see, I am a man who thinks of all precautions. Face me and he will not read your lips. Now answer me."

Gregory shrugged. "There's nothing new to report. We're still stalled. No one has seen or heard anything of him. I'm not sure I really believe he's in the city at all."

"Your personal beliefs are of no value to me. You will confine yourself to facts. The woman has sent an operative to Scotland, has she not? For what purpose?"

"How did you know that?"

Mockery gleamed in Falstaff's colorless eyes. "Do you think your people are the only ones with spies? I know everything, James. I watch you both, you and the woman. There is never a time I am not watching you."

Gregory's breath caught short. "You mean, like last night, you saw . . . with Jean? You bastard."

"Your romantic dalliances are of no concern to me. Tell me what the woman is doing. What is her interest in Scotland?"

"Jean sent someone to arrange security at the testing site where the stockpile originated. She's afraid Stand may figure out where his trouble started and stick his nose into the background of the Erin Dawn shipment."

"She has a high regard for the contractor Stand's resourcefulness,'' Falstaff said. ''I see no reason to justify this belief. The man has done nothing. He hides like a frightened animal gone to earth.''

Gregory shook his head. ''Stand won't be content to lie low for very long. It's not like him. He'll do something to stir things up, sooner or later. And when he does, we'll be ready.''

''I hope that for once you are correct, James. I have made plans for the stockpile, important plans, and I grow impatient. All is in readiness, but I can do nothing until your people locate him.''

''We're doing our best,'' Gregory said lamely. ''I promise you, it won't be long.''

Falstaff scowled and turned to stare out the window. He gazed moodily at the gray city awakening around them. ''I feel as trapped as Stand must,'' he said softly. ''I do not like staying in one place so long a time. It wears on me, the grinding monotony of this search. I cannot bear it much longer.''

''Yeah, I know,'' Gregory said. ''That's the only consolation—knowing that wherever he is, Stand has to be feeling the same. Trapped and lonely. It must be a miserable way to live.''

''Yes,'' Falstaff said. ''I suppose it must.''

Meghan sang softly to herself as she rinsed and dried the lunch dishes. She didn't know the words. It was one of the pop songs from the radio that she heard every day without really listening to it. It was actually sort of pleasant standing there, letting her hands labor over the dishes automatically, making happy noises while her mind wandered freely.

She did a double take, catching herself. What a funny thought—imagine *enjoying* doing the dishes. Something strange was going on with her, she thought, no doubt about it.

It was a Sunday afternoon, and this was usually the time she set aside to finish extra work so that she could begin the week at the office one step ahead. There was a lot of editing still to be done on a new manuscript, but try as she might, Meghan couldn't keep her mind on the task. She was enjoying the afternoon at home too much to want to slip into a world of fictional characters whose lives, problems, and happy moments were not hers.

The thought struck her with its simple clarity. She was happy. There wasn't any need to worry about work now. Right now she was home and content, and that was all that mattered.

She was still humming the tune when she finished the last plate and the door swung open. Lynnie bounded in, followed by Stand. Meghan smiled and turned, drying her hands on a cloth as her daughter ran over and hugged her around the waist. "Mum, I went jogging!" she said excitedly.

"You did?" Meghan said, and then saw that Lynnie was wearing a new gray track suit and clean white running shoes. "What's this?"

Stand stepped forward and laid a wrapped parcel on the counter. He was wearing a larger version of the same clothes, and had a wool watch cap over his hair. He grinned sheepishly. "We changed at the store and jogged back home. You can't walk when you wear running clothes, you know. It's an unwritten law."

Lynnie did a dizzying pirouette for her mother's inspection. "What do you think, Mum? Don't I look fast? We ran all the way back. Only walked once."

Meghan smiled uneasily. "You look wonderful, darling. But where did you get them?"

"I've been feeling the need for exercise," Stand said. "Been sitting around too much, getting lazy and slow. Lynnie helped me choose my outfit, and wouldn't you know it? They just happened to have the exact same thing in her size."

"I want to go show Karen," Lynnie said. "Can I, Mum?"

"Okay, honey," Meghan said reluctantly, biting her lip. She watched the child race through the door and across the alley to the neighboring flat. Turning from the window, she picked up the bound parcel, then glanced at Stand. "These are her other clothes?" she asked in a dull voice.

Stand nodded and sat at the small table where they ate their meals. He folded his hands together, listening to the silence and feeling her eyes upon him. He looked up and sighed.

"You're upset, aren't you? Did I step out of bounds by buying her the outfit?"

"She's delighted with it, that's obvious. But really, Nathan, I can't afford to give her everything she wants."

"It's a gift. I didn't mean for you to pay for it."

Meghan shook her head. "It's too much. I can't accept that from you. No, I'll write you a check. I insist."

He frowned. "Why? She was happy to get the clothes, and it made me happy to buy them for her. Why can't you let me do this for her?"

"It's too generous. You must see that."

"No," he said. "I don't. It's not a big thing. I can afford it. I'm not trying to spoil her. I won't do it again if it upsets you."

Meghan sat down beside him and absently rubbed a finger at a blemish on the tabletop. "But you do spoil her," she said. "Not usually like this, not by buying her things, but with your time and attention. You play with her and read to her and take her out for walks."

"I like being with her. She makes me happy and I like doing what I can to make her happy."

"She dotes on you so much that sometimes it makes me feel inadequate as a parent."

"That's silly. You do everything for her."

"I'm supposed to," Meghan said. "I'm her mother."

Stand touched her hand and looked into her eyes. "You've been both her mother and father for so long, maybe it's hard for you to give up any part of her."

"You're not her father, Nathan. You're just a man who happens to rent the upstairs room."

He stared at her for a moment, his eyes sad. "I had hoped I was becoming more than that."

"That's just the problem. You are. You're becoming so important to her. What's she going to do when you go away?"

"Maybe I won't have to," he said. "Not for a while yet."

"But you will. Someday you will leave us."

Stand's breath stalled. Reluctantly, he nodded.

"What will she think when suddenly you're gone?" Meghan asked. "Don't you see how much harder you're making it? What will she do then?"

"Remember," Stand said.

Meghan shook her head. "It's not enough, Nathan. You can't build a person up, love her, make her learn to love you, and then expect her to be content with a memory. It's must not enough."

"I know. But sometimes it has to be."

"Not for my daughter," Meghan said firmly. "I know you wouldn't do anything to hurt Lynnie, but it will hurt her, Nathan. You must see that."

He nodded slowly. "But what am I supposed to do? Stop loving her? I can't do that. Loving her is too easy, so natural. She's so much like—" He caught himself and lowered his eyes.

"Like what?"

"Nothing," he said. "Forget it."

Meghan stared at him and reached out to touch him, then stopped and wrung her hands together as if she didn't know what to do with them. She sat up straighter, almost visibly steeling herself. "Nathan, may I ask you a personal question?"

"Of course."

"Are you divorced? I mean, it seems clear that you were married before."

He looked up. "What makes you think that?"

"I'm not sure. It's just a sense I get. Partly, it's because you are so easy and natural with Lynnie—as if you've had children of your own. And because you settled into our home so comfortably. The way you help out with the little things, and always know what to say or do, as if you've been through all of it before. I'm sure you've been married, but you don't wear a ring and you never speak of a wife or family."

He let out a long breath. "I'm not divorced, Meghan. I'm a widower."

She asked gently, "And there was a child?"

Stand swallowed hard. He nodded, as if the motion itself caused him pain. "A daughter," he said. "Her name was Melissa. She was beautiful, just like her mother. She was a lot like Lynnie, about the same age when . . ." His voice trailed off, and he shook his head.

"How did they die, Nathan? An accident? Illness?"

"No," Stand said sharply.

"No, what?"

"No, I don't want to talk about it. That's all I want to say."

Meghan sat motionless. His voice stung, but she gazed back calmly at his burning eyes. "One more question, Nathan. I must know one thing."

"You've pried enough."

"One question. Am I right to trust you?"

That stopped him short. "You think—"

"I don't know what to think. Answer me."

Stand looked at her, and there was a pain in his eyes that was almost unbearable to witness. His voice was almost inaudible. "Meghan, I will never do anything to hurt you or Lynnie. You must believe that."

"I do. That's good enough for me. I do trust you, Nathan. It's not always easy, though. You have so many mysteries. You keep so much to yourself. I just needed to hear you say it, and to see in your eyes that you mean it."

She pushed back her chair and stood up. "I think I'll make some tea. Would you take some with me?" She lit the fire under the teapot, then looked back at him. "I am sorry, Nathan. About everything."

He nodded stiffly. "Yes, so am I."

They shared the tea and a few sponge cakes, talking seldom, and then only about trivial matters. They were edgy around each other, awkward and uncertain of what to say, so mostly they said nothing at all. After a while, Meghan put on her reading glasses and went to work on a manuscript she'd brought home from the office. Stand smoked his pipe and tried to read a book, staring at the same two pages until he couldn't take it anymore. He stood up and quietly slipped out of the room.

Meghan barely seemed to notice, and remained absorbed in her reading.

After Stand walked out, she pushed the manuscript away and dropped her glasses on the table. She wrapped her hands around her mug of tea and stared at the walls with a blank expression.

The silence followed him up the stairs and into his room.

The nightmare was familiar. He had lived through its variations a hundred times before, but its power over him was undiminished. It started as it nearly always did.

Daddy!

The shrill cry made Stand's heart race. He spun around, glancing about anxiously. Everything was black, a total cloaking darkness, as if he had been struck blind. He held out his hand, but couldn't see it. The air was clammy and close—it had a *feel* to it, a texture, pressing against his skin. Panic clamped his throat. It was like being submerged, drowning in a black, bottomless sea. There was nowhere to turn, no light to struggle toward, nothing but the relentless pressure of the enveloping darkness.

Daddy, where are you?

The voice was closer now, so close that it seemed to originate inside him, but he sensed that it came from somewhere else. Suddenly the hairs rose on his neck. A gust of wind blew across him with a foul odor that swelled his nostrils. Stand turned slowly, and she was there, a tiny pale figure barely more than three feet tall. Her eyes were open and alive.

Daddy!

A breathless moan broke through his clenched lips. "Melissa? It can't be. . . . Oh, dear God, it's you."

The child moved closer, drifting like a cloud, making no sound. Stand was paralyzed by the sight of her. Her face was the color of bone, sallow and bloodless. She was draped in a flowing white gown that hid her body, and which seemed

to glow with some eerie ethereal light of its own. She glided
silently closer, and his throat choked, as if he would never
breathe again. She couldn't be real, though he wanted so
much to believe that she was.

She stopped and looked up at him, close enough to touch.
He saw now that she was crying.

"Melissa, what is it? What's wrong?"

*Daddy, please make them stop. Don't let them hurt me
again. Make them go away. Daddy!*

"Who, darling? Who's hurting you? Where are they? Why
can't I see them?"

Her eyes were dull and dark. They looked straight through
him and beyond.

He ached to touch her. He wanted to reach out and pull
her into his arms, to hold her and never let go, but he couldn't
move. The foul odor was so strong he felt nauseated. He
heard a faint rumble like distant thunder, an odd rolling mutter, ominous in the otherwise total silence. The noise frightened him instinctively, for reasons he couldn't grasp. It grew
louder and he realized the sound was voices—mad, tortured
voices. The din became deafening, and it was everywhere,
echoing in his skull till he thought he would burst. He was
surrounded by voices, screams, shrieks, the piercing cackle
of insane laughter.

Stand fought to turn away, but he was trapped. There was
something holding his legs, clutching at him. He looked down
and realized it was the darkness itself. His spine turned to
ice. It moved.

It was like being buried alive by drifting sand. The pressure grew stronger around his legs. It swirled around his
calves, tugging as it crawled higher.

With horror he watched Melissa's legs disappear. She was
sliced in half, her torso suspended in space. Stand screamed,
adding his voice to the maddening howl.

The darkness rose to her neck. Melissa looked up at him
again, her eyes empty, the pupils bleached as white as her
skin. In a terrible flat voice, she repeated the words that
haunted his every moment.

Please make them stop killing me, Daddy. Daddy, why won't you come for me, Daddy?

Then the darkness closed in and she was gone.

Stand jerked awake, the scream in his throat like a half-swallowed razor. The darkness was still there, and there was a weight on his chest, pinning him down. In terror, he arched his back and lashed out blindly.

"Nathan, stop that! Calm down, it's over. I'm here now. Wake up. Everything's all right."

Slowly, his senses returned. Panting, he fell back, exhausted. The darkness had changed. He could see shapes, the outline of a woman looming over him.

"Leah?"

"No," she said gently. "It's Meghan Foster. Calm down, Nathan. It's over now. It was just a dream."

"The darkness . . . why is it so dark?"

"Easy, now, I'll take care of it." She reached across him and flipped on the lamp next to his bed. Light and color blurred his eyes. Then the room swam into focus, hard-edged and real. Meghan grinned down at him. "I never thought a big man like you would be afraid of the dark."

His eyes darted about, still fearful. "What's holding me down?"

She blushed. "I am." She was straddling his chest, her legs pinning his arms to his sides. With sudden embarrassment, she rolled off and straightened the robe over her nightgown. "I was afraid you'd hurt yourself," she said quickly. "The way you were struggling and thrashing about . . . I didn't know what else to do. You're not hurt, are you?"

Stand pulled his arms out from the blankets and waved them around, reveling in the freedom. There were clean red blemishes on his biceps, the imprints of Meghan's fingers where she had held him. He glanced at the marks and frowned ruefully. "You're a strong woman."

Meghan smiled. "Farm girl. Peasant stock, you know. A strong back and rocks for brains, my Da used to say. How are you feeling now?"

He sat up, shaking his head groggily. "Worn out. I'm sorry about this. Did I scare Lynnie with my carrying-on?"

"Don't worry about her. She's snoring like a sawmill. That child could sleep through an earthquake." Meghan pulled her robe together and sat down on the foot of the bed. She looked away hesitantly, then made up her mind.

"Your dream. It was about your daughter, wasn't it? You called her name over and over. It was awful; you sounded terrified."

"It keeps coming back. I've had it a million times, but it never gets easier."

"Nathan, you don't have to answer me if you don't want to, but I have to ask."

"What?" he asked warily.

She took a deep breath. "Your personal business, it's not a medical condition at all, is it? I've watched you for weeks. You seem healthy as a horse. It has more to do with this, doesn't it, with your dreams, the bad memories?"

He nodded grudgingly. "You're perceptive, as well as strong."

"You must have loved her very much."

His face was etched in lines of pain. He closed his eyes and breathed in and out slowly. "Yes, very much," he said. "Of course I did. She and Leah were everything to me, a whole world."

"Tell me about them. It might help, you know."

Stand laughed bitterly. "Talk and you shall be healed. Pop psychology, the great fad of the hopelessly bored. Nobody solves their problems these days, they exploit them for sympathy or attention. My id is bigger than yours. No, Meghan, the world has enough problems without having to listen to mine."

"I'm not the world, Nathan. And you're just avoiding the issue."

"That's what life is all about, pretending we don't know how it really ends."

"You fake," she said gently. "You're not really as cynical

as you try to sound. You're hurting, and you have a right to. The hurt was real, and you're scared. It's only natural.''

"And how do you come to these conclusions, Mrs. Freud?''

"I know what I see," she replied, ignoring his sarcasm. "And that is a man who loved his family so deeply that without them, he can't sleep nights. Or act in a civil manner when the talk gets personal. A man who tortures himself with a mistaken belief that he can keep them alive by never talking about them, never admitting that they're dead.''

Stand blinked. "You don't mince words, do you?''

"Not concerning things I care about. Or people.''

He frowned as if confused. "Why do you care about this? About me?''

She smiled shyly, her body stiff, unnaturally still, as if poised on the edge of some fearful chasm. Her voice was soft and low. "I'm a perceptive woman," she said, "but I don't understand everything, least of all my own feelings. But I know that I care for you, Nathan. And I don't like to watch you in pain.''

"I'm sorry I can't be different for you, Meghan. But I don't believe talking would change anything.''

She moved then, shrugging and looking away. It was as if some delicate support within her had shattered. Her whole body seemed to deflate, soften. "All right, Nathan," she said. "It's your pain, you don't have to share it. But don't talk to me of change. You're afraid of it, so much so that you can't even speak.''

"Talk isn't change. It wouldn't help.''

"Maybe not. But how far have you come through silence?" Meghan got slowly to her feet. "All right, I'll leave you alone. Are you ready to have the light off again?''

His hand brushed hers aside as it moved toward the lamp. "No, please.''

She nodded sympathetically. "I understand. We all have darkness in our lives, Nathan.''

He looked at her and took a deep breath. "Meghan, please don't go.''

He was trembling. She stood over him, gently touched his brow, brushed his hair where it spilled above his eyes. "It's all right," she said softly. "I can stay as long as you wish."

The words came out of him in a rush. "I'll try, Meghan. Really. I'll tell you what happened. You deserve that much."

"Not for me, Nathan. You don't have to. You don't have to tell me anything to make me stay."

"No, I want to. I want to try, if you're sure. : . . It's a long story."

"We have all night," she said.

The room was cold and she wore only a thin nightdress and robe. It seemed the most natural thing in the world when she pulled back the blankets and slipped in beside him. Stand sat up with his back against the headboard. Meghan lay next to him, her body a long line of heat all the way to his toes. It felt as innocent as two children snuggling together, seeking and offering warmth.

Stand closed his eyes and began to talk.

CHAPTER 16

HE SPOKE haltingly at first, dragging the words out one at a time. "It happened in Ireland," he began. In a little village called Clarerea. That was Leah's childhood home; her mother still lived there, in the same house where Leah grew up. They hadn't seen each other in years, the whole time we were married. We lived in America, you see. Leah always dreamed of going back to visit, even more so after Melissa was born. Leah's mother had never seen her grandchild.

"Then we learned that her mother's health was failing. We decided this was it, she had to go, whatever it took. Leah was so excited, even more than Melissa, I think. The two of them spent weeks packing and repacking, talking about what they would do and see, getting themselves so worked up they could hardly wait for the day to arrive."

"Didn't you go with them?" Meghan asked.

"No," Stand said. "I couldn't get away. It was the middle of the semester. We had hoped to go during summer break, but Leah's mother was so ill we couldn't wait. We were afraid she couldn't hang on long enough. As it turned out, Leah's mother lived three months longer than Leah did. And when she saw her granddaughter for the first time, Melissa was in a casket."

"Oh, dear God."

Stand frowned. "God had nothing to do with it. Or if He did, then He's a god of cruelty, and I have no use for Him."

"Nathan, you don't mean that."

"I don't know what I mean anymore," he said. "I had faith in something once—in the absolute rightness of the life we were building together. But that was stolen away."

Meghan touched him gently. "You'll find something else, Nathan. Someday. What happened when they went to Ireland? Was it the IRA? Something to do with the war in Ulster?"

Stand nodded and went on in a gravelly voice. "Clarerea is near Belfast." He focused on the memories and spoke more easily.

"Leah and Melissa took the train. I can just imagine how excited Melissa must have been. Her first train ride. And in a strange new country, her mother's homeland. Leah had a hundred sights to point out, memories to share with her. A grand adventure for them both."

Stand fell silent, hesitating. Meghan looked up and started to say something, but the look on his face made her keep still. After a few moments he started again, but it was in a different voice, a growl of bitter hatred.

"There were six of them," Stand said. "Young bullies. They called themselves Sons of a Free Tomorrow, or some such damned thing. They claimed they were acting on behalf of the revolution. It was a sham. They were nothing but thugs, greedy thieves looking to get rich quick.

"They stopped the train just outside the station at Clarerea. It was still out in the countryside, where there was no cover for anyone to approach without being seen. They herded thirty passengers into one car and held them as hostages. The brakeman was sent into the village with their demands. One million pounds was what they wanted, and a plane to fly them anywhere they chose. An hour later they sent an additional demand to free two Irish prisoners in British jails. It was an afterthought, a lame effort to make others believe they were revolutionaries, instead of the common criminals they were."

"I remember it from the news reports." Meghan shuddered. "Your wife and daughter were both taken as hostages?"

Stand nodded.

"And you were still halfway around the world. When did you find out what had happened?"

"I'm not sure I should tell you," Stand said. "You'll think I'm crazy. It was the strangest thing. I was in a class, leading a discussion of Hemingway. Suddenly, for no real reason, I had an awful, sickly feeling. I knew something terrible had happened. I ran straight out of the class. The students must have thought I'd gone out of my head. In a way, I guess I had.

"I started calling all the news services. Nobody knew anything. They thought I was a lunatic. Finally, I got a response from Reuters. The stringer was a little spooked by my call, I think. 'Good God, man!' he said to me. 'The story just broke a few minutes ago. How could you know?' "

"What did you tell him?" Meghan asked.

Stand shrugged. "What could I say? I couldn't give him an answer. I didn't even try. I hung up and drove straight to the airport. I caught the first plane out and was in Ireland before the hijackers killed their first hostage."

Meghan stared at him with an expression of horror. "You got there in time to *watch* it happen?"

He nodded tightly. "That's all I did, step aside and watch. That was my crime. I surrendered to those bastards long before anyone else did—by failing to take action."

"Stop it," Meghan said. "That's nonsense. What could you have done?"

"I could have saved them. I saw how it could be done."

"Nathan, you couldn't possibly—"

Stand shook his head. "There is a lot—so much—you don't know about me. Before becoming a teacher I was in the army. In the special forces—what in this country you call a commando. I was trained for such events as hostage situations. We saw tougher things in Vietnam. It's not an idle boast. I could have done something."

"That was not the war, Nathan, and Ireland is not Vietnam. These terrorist events are different. You may have been a capable soldier, but the police and the SAS deal with these things all the time. They had to be better prepared for the situation than you were.''

"Oh, they were there, all right," Stand said. "There was no shortage of people willing to take charge. The police stepped in and made sure I kept my distance. They were good at that part of it, keeping others away. But in dealing with the terrorists, they were useless. In way over their heads.''

Meghan frowned skeptically. "I can't believe it was left up to the local police. Didn't they call in specialists?''

"They called in their experts. So-called specialists. They were like termites. Everywhere you stepped there was a young officer with a public-school accent, a title as long as your arm, and a hundred reasons why he should be the one to take charge. Everyone wanted to prove something. They all saw the hijacking as the one big case that would shoot them up the promotion ladder.''

Meghan shivered and pulled the blankets higher. She could feel the tension in his body and the intensity of loathing in his voice.

Stand went on slowly. "They spent two days arguing among themselves. Two whole days. On each of those days, the hijackers killed a hostage. They shot them and threw the bodies out on the tracks so the press could take pictures. The first victim was an old man, the second a young woman. By that time the public was outraged. Even those ass-covering bureaucrats knew they had to do something.''

Meghan touched his arm gently. "You sound as though you hate them as much as the terrorists.''

"I have enough hate to go around.''

"But they were trying to help.''

"They were amateurs.''

"And you weren't?'' Meghan asked lightly. When Stand didn't answer, she looked into his eyes. What she saw there made her tremble.

Stand continued. "I know how it appeared to them. To the police I was some bothersome crazy American. I couldn't even explain how I came to be there. How could I tell them that I'd flown halfway around the world because of a premonition? I don't blame them for not listening to me. You want to know the worst of it? The truth is, when they forced me aside and made me keep out of it, I was relieved. I felt grateful.''

"You can't blame yourself for being afraid, for being glad it wasn't your responsibility. That's only natural. Anyone would have felt that way in your place.''

"I gave up too easy. I didn't do anything. Even when it became clear they were going to botch it.''

Meghan eased away from him and sat up, her face tight, grim. "Nathan, listen to me," she said. "This memory has festered inside you too long. All that anger—you've twisted it, gotten things screwed around. If you could just listen to yourself, you'd realize how irrational you sound. There were a lot of competent professionals doing their best to save your wife and child. Can you honestly say you could have done better? I'm sorry, but you don't look like Superman to me.''

"No one could have done worse.''

"Hindsight. You couldn't have known that at the time.''

"You don't understand. You don't know how it was. Or me.''

"I'm trying," Meghan said. "I want to understand. Go on, tell me the rest of it.''

He nodded. There was a close, guarded look to his eyes, and he didn't look at her. His voice came out dull and listless, as if a hard shell had fallen over his emotions.

"It was a disaster. The police were still divided. They couldn't stop arguing enough to settle on one concrete plan. So they took the easy way out. They delivered the ransom. A payroll truck drove up to the train and the hijackers came out to get their money and drive the truck to their escape plane.''

Meghan gasped, shocked. "They caved in to the terrorists?''

"Completely. I don't know . . . maybe it was meant as a delaying tactic. Maybe they had plans to grab them at the airport. Who knows what they thought? If they had a plan, they never got to use it. In a matter of seconds, everything fell apart.

"Three of the hijackers moved safely into the truck. They used hostages as shields, all young women. Leah wasn't one of them. I was hiding in the fields, a hundred yards from the train. The police kept the crowds back, but I gave them the slip. I was there, and saw the whole thing.

"It all went smoothly until the fourth hijacker came out. He was shielding himself behind a lovely young girl with long red hair. She'd been beaten. There were bruises on her face and her clothes were torn. She was broken. Even where I was, it was apparent. She was like a wild animal, crazed, out of her head with fear. She couldn't take it anymore.

"The two people they had killed were still lying by the tracks. They had to walk past them to reach the truck. I think one of them must have been a friend or relative of the girl, because when she saw them, something inside her snapped."

"She tried to run?" Meghan breathed.

"No, she folded up," Stand said. "She dropped to her knees and wouldn't budge. The hijacker screamed at her, kicked her, yanked her hair. She wouldn't move. The bastard tried to pick her up and carry her to the truck. She was dead weight; he couldn't do it. He dropped her again and she just lay there, bawling and curling up in a fetal position—I swear she was even sucking her thumb. So he put his gun to the back of her head and blew her face away."

Meghan's breath hissed out sharply. She hugged herself as if freezing, but said nothing, waiting for him to go on.

"The police had marksmen stationed in the fields. One of them decided he couldn't watch that. He dropped the hijacker with a clean shot in the chest. Then hell started. The last two hijackers ducked back inside the train and pulled the door shut. I heard them open fire. The police had to act then. They closed on the train, no sneaking around, just a straight-ahead charge, running and shooting anything that moved. And the hostages were caught in the middle."

It was rushing out of him, the words spilling out as if he couldn't wait to be done with them. "It was a real firefight," he said. "Like an honest-to-God war. Once the police started shooting, they couldn't seem to stop. The hijackers in the truck tried to drive it away. They found out the armor plating was phony; the gunfire ripped it apart. If the hostages inside were alive . . . well, at that point, it didn't matter anymore.

"It was the same or worse for the hostages left on the train. The hijackers didn't even bother to shoot back at the police. They turned their guns on the hostages and sprayed the car. People were screaming. It was so shrill and loud, louder than the guns. The screams—I think I'll never stop hearing them.

"I ran for the train even before the police stopped shooting. It took forever to cover those hundred yards, all the time hearing that noise, that storm of dying. The police killed the hijackers, and still it didn't stop.

"I got to the train first and threw open the door. The police were still hanging back, looking for something else to kill. It was so eerie. The moment I stepped inside, all the noise stopped. Two policemen climbed in with me. They took one look around and vomited on themselves. The place was a slaughterhouse. The floor was covered with chewed-up meat, little that looked vaguely human. Blood was spattered over the walls and there were pools of it on the floor, steaming. A few of the dead had their fingernails ripped off. They'd been scraping at the walls, trying to claw their way out—"

Meghan gasped. "Nathan, please!"

He glared at her as if angered by the interruption. He went on, his voice soft, breathless. "I found Leah at the back. She was on the floor, rolled up against the wall. She was dead. The holes in her chest were already dry. She'd been dead a day or two. I never found out why they shot her. She was a strong woman who wouldn't tolerate being bullied—maybe they found her too much to handle. I like to believe that. I like to think she stood up to them."

Meghan's eyes were dewy, brimming with unspilled tears. "And the child?" she asked hoarsely. "Your daughter, Melissa?"

"I picked up Leah. I couldn't bear to leave her like that. That was when I saw Melissa. She was curled up against the wall, hiding beneath Leah's body. When I pulled Leah off her, she screamed and tried to crawl away.''

"She was alive!''

Stand nodded, his face blank. His voice was flat and lifeless. ''I reached for her and she hissed at me. She fought me as if she didn't know me. I had to drag her out from under the seats. I held her in my arms and said her name over and over and finally I got through to her. She was still alive. It seemed like a miracle. She didn't even look injured. There was so much blood everywhere, but I thought it was her mother's. It wasn't.

''I held her so tight, it must have hurt, but she was past feeling that sort of pain. I was crying, calling her name, yelling it in her face like a madman. She was so quiet, and her eyes, the way she looked at me . . . When she finally spoke . . .

'' 'Where were you?' she said. 'Why did you let them hurt Mommy and me? I called and called, but you didn't come. Where were you, Daddy? Why didn't you come for me? I hate you, Daddy, I hate you.' ''

"Oh, Nathan.''

Stand looked at her and said softly, "Then she died.''

Meghan sobbed quietly. She didn't try to speak. There was nothing to say. She put her arms around Stand and held him, her tears dampening his shoulder. The night was cold and still, broken only by the beat of their hearts pounding, steady, sure, and without mercy.

Sherman sipped an espresso and savored the warmth of the plush, wood-paneled office. The outer wall was entirely glass and he could look down on all of Zurich, spread out like an enormous mural. The offices of Worldview Investments were high in the Kleindeiss Tower. From there, the city looked unreal, like a child's playhouse or a plastic display on a model railroad.

The director was a stolid, bland-faced man with a shock of brilliant silver hair and eyes that were dwarfed by round horn-rimmed spectacles. He looked like everyone's favorite uncle, an easygoing character with a gentle smile and soft voice, the sort who always had candy in his pocket and a bad joke he was eager to share. It was a deceptive appearance that masked a shrewd, calculating mind and a taste for power.

He turned that bland smile on Sherman. "Now, in what way may we assist you?"

"I believe you know that already. Otherwise, I doubt very much that I would be here."

"Quite so. We have checked out the source of your funding and we know what interests you serve. I must say I was surprised that they entrusted Company monies to an agent of MI Six. Perhaps you would explain to me why they did that?"

Sherman hesitated, thinking quickly. How had they got on to him already? They knew he was a British agent, but still they had agreed to see him. Company monies—what was going on here?

"It is matter of mutual concern," Sherman said. "It should hardly be surprising that our nations have decided to cooperate on this venture."

The director nodded thoughtfully. "So, you give away nothing, eh? I understand and appreciate this. I must say, though, I did not expect to do business again with your people so quickly. The earlier transaction was considered successful, I take it?"

"We have no complaints," Sherman said.

The director studied him with a hard gaze. "I find that rather surprising. We were disturbed to hear rumors that the transportation of the product was—shall we say—interrupted."

Sherman smiled easily. "Such rumors do occasionally serve a purpose. It was in our interests that certain parties believed that. It helped to create a desirable confusion."

"I see," the director said, with a trace of admiration. "Then your methods were a considerable success, if confusion was indeed your goal."

"Thank you," Sherman said.

"What is it you wish from us this time?"

"More of the same."

"This is not possible. The product was unique. I thought that was made clear to you before. You already possess all that there is. How can I give you what does not exist?"

"Of course, I understand that. What we had in mind was more in the way of information."

The director's eyes narrowed suspiciously. "What do you mean? Surely there is nothing about the product which you do not know."

"That's true. But we are concerned that we have a premium on that knowledge. We wish to have all records of the product turned over to us. It is imperative that we have exclusive possession of all background materials—the product's provenance, if you will."

The director spread his hands in a weary gesture of futility. "I fail to comprehend why this request is being handled in such an underhanded fashion. If the Company wishes to make use of the MKNAOMI files, why don't they take them through the usual channels? It is their own material, after all. This entire procedure makes no sense."

Sherman blinked, the truth dawning. Suddenly, a great deal was clear to him. "This is a matter of considerable sensitivity, as you can well appreciate," he said. "It requires the greatest secrecy, and methods that may appear unorthodox."

"Of course. But involving MI Six in an effort simply to procure records that can be easily routed through conventional methods seems unreasonably complicated. Ridiculous, actually."

"Confusion," Sherman said. "Confusion again—that is exactly the desired result."

The director frowned and shook his head. "I cannot possibly give you access to MKNAOMI without clearance from the DCI."

Sherman kept his face placid, but his mind was racing. Now he knew his suspicions were correct. "The DCI will say he knows nothing of this," he said. "That is in fact the truth. And it is important that he remain uninformed. It is vital that he retain the option of plausible deniability."

The director nodded sadly. "I had hoped we were finished with such arcane concepts and practices."

"That will never happen as long as we must deal in matters of such political sensitivity."

"Yes, I suppose you're right." The director sighed. "Still, Mr. Sherman, I am uneasy about this. I will have to receive confirmation from some higher source. I cannot turn the records over to you on no more than your own say-so. It is simply expecting too much."

Sherman masked his disappointment. The man was going to stonewall him. He couldn't let that happen, not when he was so close. "Of course, I understand you have to protect yourself," he said.

The director scowled. "It is much more than a simple matter of covering my own backside," he grumbled. "MKNAOMI represents one of our most sensitive and potentially damaging secrets. It has remained secure under our protection for nearly twenty years. I will not risk compromise now. No, Mr. Sherman, it simply isn't on. You can tell them—whatever masters you represent—that if they want MKNAOMI they will have to deal with me more openly and directly. This sort of overcomplicated scheme is exactly how the Company most often embarrasses itself, and I simply won't take part."

A thought struck Sherman, and he smiled smoothly. "Your reluctance is understandable. Of course I don't expect you to simply let me walk away with the documents. I am not here to remove them, simply to verify their existence and pave the way for later dispensation."

"I don't understand, Mr. Sherman. Why should you have to verify their existence? Of course the records exist. The Company knows that."

"Do we, sir?" Sherman asked sharply. "All I have is your word on that. And your reluctance to present them makes me wonder if you're not covering up. Can you put my mind at ease that the records have not been misplaced or forgotten in the twenty years you've hidden them?"

The director puffed up angrily. "You have no right to make such an accusation. The records are secure."

"I have to personally verify that," Sherman said firmly. "I cannot leave until I have seen them for myself."

The director scowled and stabbed a button on his desk intercom. "Wilhelm, come in here, please."

The door opened immediately and a blond-haired young man entered from the outer office. He had a steno pad and a pen, which he held by his side as he assumed a pose of attention. "Yes, sir?"

"Wilhelm, you will accompany Mr. Sherman to the vaults and you will give him the files of the MKNAOMI project. You will lock him inside the vault for fifteen minutes only. Then you will retrieve the files and return them to their proper place. I want an armed guard with you at all times until Mr. Sherman is finished. Do you understand, Wilhelm?"

The young man nodded. "Certainly, sir. Fifteen minutes only."

The director glanced back at Sherman. "I trust that will be time enough to satisfy your curiosity, sir?"

"I suppose it will have to do."

The director smiled thinly. "Yes, it will." He motioned to Wilhelm. The young man led Sherman out.

They rode down to the ground floor, transferred into a different elevator, and continued downward. When the door opened again, Sherman saw they were in a vast underground warehouse. There were crates piled high everywhere, and teams of men worked with forklifts, loading and unloading heavy trucks. Wilhelm had him take a seat on a golf cart and they zipped among the piles of anonymous unmarked crates.

"How big is this place?" Sherman asked, peering around in amazement.

Wilhelm frowned sullenly and did not reply. A few minutes later they turned into a tunnel and traveled a short distance in darkness, then emerged before a compound enclosed by floor-to-ceiling fence wire. Armed guards patrolled the entrance. Wilhelm stopped the cart, got out, and motioned for one of the guards to follow them. He led Sherman through the gate and into a concrete structure with walls a foot thick. Inside were four doors leading to large steel vaults. One of them was open just enough to permit entry.

Wilhelm stopped outside the open vault. He waved at the guard, then pointed at Sherman. "Search him."

"What is the bloody idea?" Sherman protested. The guard ran his hands roughly over every inch of his body. "We're on the same side, you know."

The guard stepped back, nodding that Sherman was clean. Wilhelm said softly, "You will know not to bring anything out. You will be searched again when your time is up. Now kindly step inside the vault. The fifteen minutes will begin once the door is sealed."

Sherman took a deep breath, afraid of being locked in the vault but too proud to show it. He stepped inside and the massive door swung shut behind him. There was a slight hiss of air and the thump of pneumatic bolts being thrown. He shook off his anxiety and looked around the vault. It was not a particularly impressive place, nothing more than a room with large drawers stacked from floor to ceiling on three sides. One of these drawers was open. He went to it and picked up the folder that lay on top. It was a record of the storage of something labeled "Vigo E48R7." Sherman glanced at it briefly, saw that storage had begun in 1969 and continued until October of the current year, when it had been signed out under special order and transferred to Denmark. That was the last entry in the logbook.

It didn't tell Sherman what the bloody thing was. MKNAOMI, the director had called it. That had a faintly familiar ring to it, though he couldn't recall why. He put the log aside and thumbed through the rest of the file drawer, until he came to one labeled "MKNAOMI—VIGO/Test Results & Analysis." He opened the folder and read only a few lines before his eyes widened in horror. Sherman panted and loosened his tie, imagining that the air inside the vault had suddenly become very close.

CHAPTER 17

THE LONDON station of the CIA was a busy place, but Jean had been given an office well out of the way. It was a small colorless room decorated with modern furnishings of glass and chrome. Jean hated it. Every gleaming surface seemed to reflect her face, and she didn't like what she saw. A frown of mounting frustration had settled over her delicate features, hardening as if it might set permanently.

The search for Stand had been under way for weeks, and so far there had been no results. She had scores of operatives looking for the renegade contractor in London and throughout Great Britain. They had checked out a dozen mistaken sightings, but every lead had gone sour. Stand simply wasn't showing himself. He had gone to earth, and where he might be hiding, there wasn't a clue.

She sipped coffee from a paper cup and grimaced. The station was staffed entirely by Americans, but it seemed they had all been in England so long they had forgotten what real coffee was supposed to taste like. Jean pushed the cup away angrily, then instantly scolded herself. It wasn't the coffee. Her nerves were simply frayed. She wondered how much longer she could bear the strain of the search.

She stared at the brimming ashtray, then shrugged and lit another cigarette. She took a deep puff to calm herself and bent over the pages of the daily reports, forcing herself to concentrate, although she knew she would find no sign of

Stand anywhere. It was as if he had stepped off the edge of the earth and vanished.

The eager young man who had been assigned as her aide knocked timidly, rattling the glass-plated door. Jean looked up. "Yes, Roger, what is it?"

"Call for you, Mrs. Frost."

"Take a message. I don't have time right now."

"I think you might want to take this one," the young man said hesitantly. "It sounds important."

"Who is it?"

"I don't know, exactly. It's on the scrambler. Your code only. All I know is that it came through from Switzerland."

"Zurich?" Jean sat up. "Thank you, Roger. Put it through immediately."

"Yes, ma'am. Line three." The young man moved quickly into the outer office. Jean took another quick drag on her cigarette, then picked up the phone and stabbed the blinking button on line three.

The electronic scrambler distorted their voices, making the man on the other end sound a little like a bad Donald Duck impersonator. Jean would have found it humorous under different circumstances. At the moment, she didn't give it a thought.

"Jean Frost," she said.

"This is Wilhelm. We received a visitor today."

Jean felt her pulse race, but she kept her voice cool and measured. "Who was it?"

"An older man, an operative of the British. I have prepared a copy of the credentials he presented. They can be telexed to you on request."

"You're certain he was British?"

"That is definite. His name is Randall Sherman. He came to us quite openly, acting on behalf of a joint effort of your two nations. His credentials were verified. He is a current operative of MI Six."

Jean thought quickly. Stand had many contacts throughout the secret services of Western Europe. It was possible he had been able to persuade one of them to trace the stockpile for him. Stand, it appeared, was not lying low as quietly as she had believed. Jean was chilled by the knowledge that Stand had successfully traced the stockpile's origin to Zurich. The threads of the secret were swiftly coming unraveled.

"Did he inquire about MKNAOMI?" she asked.

"Yes, that is exactly so."

"You stonewalled him, didn't you?"

There was a brief pause when the man hesitated. "I am not sure what you mean. He was permitted to read the file."

Jean swore. "What! You didn't try to prevent that?"

"I was not aware of the man's intentions until after he secured permission from the director to view it," Wilhelm responded.

Jean covered the phone receiver with her hand and called to her assistant. Roger promptly appeared in the doorway.

"I want you to get some records from MI Six," Jean ordered. "Everything they have on a man named Randall Sherman. He's one of their agents."

"Yes, ma'am. You want that by tonight?"

"I want it now," Jean said sharply. "Get going."

She waited until the young man was out of sight, then put the phone back to her ear. "Do you know if this man is still in Zurich?"

"He went directly to the airport and arranged passage on an afternoon flight," Wilhelm replied.

"Back to London?"

"No. He booked a connecting flight to Glasgow. His route was quite circuitous, but the airline records show that to be his eventual destination."

"Damn!" Jean growled. Her fears were now confirmed.

"Mrs. Frost," Wilhelm said, sounding concerned, "I hope I have not done wrong."

Jean took a deep breath. "Thank you, Wilhelm. Your help is much appreciated."

"His flight will not reach Glasgow until very late. It is possible you will still have time to—"

"No, that's all right," Jean said. "I think I know where he's going. We'll find him."

"Very well. Good-bye, Mrs. Frost, and good luck to you."

"Yes, thank you." She sighed. "We'll need it."

Jean put down the phone and sat back, feeling her stomach tighten into knots. She had no doubt Sherman was acting on Stand's behalf. And he was close to the truth, closer than Stand himself could possibly know.

Now it was a race. The secret of MKNAOMI had stood fast for twenty years. Now the walls were beginning to crumble. She had to find Stand before they all came tumbling down.

Stand awoke to find himself alone. The curtains were open and daylight streamed into the room. He climbed from the bed and walked to the window to look out at the street. The sky was clear and blue, so brilliant it hardly looked real. The events of the night seemed far away, and it was easy to believe it had been only a dream. But Meghan's scent still lingered in the room, and he knew it had been much more. His heart felt light, but he was more confused than happy. Unburdening himself to her had been a big step, perhaps a turning point. There was no doubt in his mind that Meghan cared for him and he for her. Where that revelation would lead him was still unclear.

He went into the bathroom and drew a bath in the big clawfooted tub. He sank into the hot water and lay there lazily, remembering how she felt lying next to him, how she held him, and he felt the stirring of something he had almost forgotten. It was hard for him to admit it even to himself. It felt like love.

It was all happening too fast and at the wrong time. There was too much to be done, too many questions yet unanswered. The Company was still looking for him, convinced he was a traitor. Any day they could close in and snare Meghan, too, by implication. It was no good. Somehow he had to get to the bottom of it all. There was no hope of peace until he did.

Reluctantly, he dragged himself from the tub, pulled on his clothes, and went downstairs. The smell of coffee and frying bacon led him to the kitchen. He heard Meghan singing softly to herself, forgetting the words but carrying the tune as if that didn't matter. It was a happy sound, and Stand stopped in the doorway and watched her. She was scrambling eggs over the stove, dressed in jeans and a heavy sweater several sizes too large for her. Her hair was uncombed, but she looked sensuous and attractive, with an air of happiness around her. Stand felt a tug at his heart and was embarrassed. She turned and saw him.

Meghan smiled warmly. "Oh, you're up. I thought I heard you moving around upstairs. Are you ready for some breakfast?" She took the pan from the burner, set it aside, then came over and went up on her toes to kiss him gently. "How are you feeling?"

Stand kissed her awkwardly, feeling uneasy, wondering what she expected from him. "I'm all right," he said. "A little thick-headed from sleeping so late. How are you?"

"Fine, just fine. I saw Melissa off, then called the office and told them I'd be in late today."

"You won't be in any trouble, will you?"

"Oh, I'm sure Jeff will be furious. So what? Let him. Come on, let's eat before it gets cold." He helped her with the plates and pans, and they settled down at the table. Stand ate with a fierce hunger he hadn't been aware of until he sat down. He cleaned his plate, then, at Meghan's insistence, finished the rest of the eggs and bacon from the skillets.

She sipped her coffee and smiled at him across the table. "It's nice to see someone enjoy my cooking. Bill was always hung over and couldn't stomach food in the morning."

"He didn't know what he was missing."

"I think he knew."

"I meant that in more ways than one," Stand said. The words were out of his mouth before he could think.

"Thank you," Meghan said, then laughed. "I think he knew that, too. I kept telling him how lucky he was to have me. I didn't always make things very easy for him, you see."

"He was a fool to leave."

"I used to think so. But in a way, he was the stronger one

for leaving. That took a certain courage, don't you think? And it was the right thing. We were both unhappy, although I couldn't bring myself to face it at the time. It really was best for both of us.''

''You're not very easy on yourself, are you?''

Meghan smiled gently. ''Now, that's an odd question, coming from you. I've had some rough times, but I've never burdened myself with the sort of guilt you've been carrying these last several years.''

''I'm sorry I told you all that last night,'' he said. ''It wasn't fair to dump all my troubles on you.''

Meghan looked down quickly. ''I wish you hadn't said that.''

''Why? What's wrong?''

''Well, I thought your opening up to me was a very special moment. It made me feel good that you could share all that. Now you're sorry it happened. It makes me feel sort of . . . well . . . cheated. I don't regret last night, Nathan. Why do you?''

''Not the closeness,'' he said. ''I don't regret that. Just the timing. I do feel something for you, Meghan. That's the problem. It's more than I'm ready to cope with right now. I'm worried that things are going too fast.''

She took a deep breath, staring at the bottom of her empty cup. ''That was one of the most polite brushoffs I've ever had. Thanks at least for that much, Nathan.''

''Please don't be angry. I'm trying to explain.''

She stood up and grabbed his plate, clanked it down on top of her own, then turned to the sink. ''Of course,'' she muttered. ''What do I have to be angry about? It's my fault, a silly mistake. For some stupid reason, I thought sharing your bed, holding you, letting you pour out your darkest secrets meant something. Forgive me, I won't let it happen again.''

''Meghan, please. I'm just trying to be honest with you.''

The plates rattled together in her shaking hands. ''Give me some credit. You don't have to beat me over the head. It's clear what you're trying to say. We had a few close moments last night in the dark, but now it's lights out. Well, you don't have to worry. I can see pretty clearly in the light.''

Stand jumped up and moved to intercept her. He took her wrists in a firm grip. ''Will you listen for one minute?'' he asked softly. ''I've never shared those memories with anyone before. I wouldn't have done that—I couldn't—if I didn't care for you very much. I do care—for you and Lynnie both.''

''So why did you tell me?'' she asked.

''I don't know. Maybe I shouldn't have. It just seemed right.''

''If it was right, then why the change of heart this morning?''

Stand sighed. ''I came to London to do something very important and I can't allow anything to prevent me from seeing it through. I want you to understand this, so that when I leave, you won't think I'm running away.''

''You have to go?'' Meghan's face was dark, confused. ''I know it's not for medical reasons. That was just a story.''

''Yes,'' Stand said.

''What else did you lie about? Is there any reason I should believe anything you've told me?''

''I didn't want to lie to you.''

Meghan pulled her arms free and dropped the plates on the counter with a crash. ''I thought last night I could trust you,'' she said. ''Now I'm not sure what I think.''

Stand moved toward her, but she glowered. He stopped, his hands loose at his sides, his head bowed. ''Meghan, please try to trust me. I don't want to go, but I have to. It's important.''

''I thought that we . . . what was going on between us . . . was important, too. I guess I was wrong.''

''Please, all I ask is—''

Meghan turned away sharply. ''I'm going to work now. Will you be here this evening, or is today when this mysterious business forces you to leave?''

''I don't know,'' Stand said. ''I think I'll be here for a while longer.''

''Then I suppose I will see you tonight.'' She ran from the

kitchen. He heard her footsteps on the stairs, then the slam of the front door. The silence closed in, oppressive and confining. He stared out the window at the bright blue sky. It seemed brittle and unlikely to last.

Sherman was cold. He cursed Stand for ever getting him involved. On the northwest coast of Scotland, it was miserable, wet and cold, and the wind howled like a wild animal, slashing at him with bared teeth. It was the last place in the world he wanted to be, but he knew the material he had seen inside the MKNAOMI files was too incredible to accept unquestioningly. He had to see for himself.

A policeman in the village of Aultbea helped Sherman charter a fishing boat and accompanied him on the twenty-minute run across the bay. They were quiet as they made their way across the choppy sea. Sherman smoked one cigarette after another. He had given up the habit five years before, but it seemed a good time to start again. He checked the small wire-mesh cage he had brought along, and the two small creatures inside. The rabbits seemed healthy and comfortable enough, though no more happy about the pitching sea than he was. He secured the cage so it wouldn't slide around the cabin, then went topside and stood by the policeman as they neared the island.

It was a bare outcrop of rock, about a mile wide and a mile and a half long. It was black. Every inch of the island had been burned to the ground. The only sign that it had once been inhabited was the charred remains of a crofter's cottage. The island was totally deserted. The reason was well known to both men, and they looked at each other and shivered.

"This is going to be about it, sir," the policeman said, throttling down the boat's engine. "Can't take her in much closer."

"I understand," Sherman said quietly. He picked up binoculars and focused on one of the signs that ringed the beaches at intervals of four hundred yards.

GRUINARD ISLAND.
THIS ISLAND IS
GOVERNMENT PROPERTY
UNDER EXPERIMENT.
THE GROUND IS CONTAMINATED
WITH ANTHRAX AND DANGEROUS.
LANDING IS PROHIBITED.

The sad legacy of Gruinard was no secret. In Britain, it was popularly known as "Anthrax Island," and for good reason. The soil of the island had long been infected with the spores of a deadly disease. It was there, beginning in 1942, that the British began testing biological bombs in the hopes of creating the ultimate weapon to turn the tide of the war against the Nazis.

The potential of anthrax for biological weapons had long been known. Commonly considered a disease of cattle and sheep, it could also be equally deadly to man. Its advantages as a weapon were several—easy to produce, highly infectious, and virtually indestructible. Unlike many other bacterial agents that survived only hours or days, anthrax spores lived for months in carefully prepared suspensions. When contracted, it produced black malignant skin ulcers, and eventually blood poisoning. Inhaled, it resulted in a choking cough, high fever, and respiratory failure. Death was almost inevitable.

In 1942 British scientists exploded the first anthrax bomb on Gruinard. An invisible cloud containing billions of spores drifted over the island and among the flock of test sheep. The animals began to die a day later. They died steadily for a week, chilling proof of the viability and effectiveness of biological warfare weapons. They continued tests through the summer of 1943, concluding only when a dead sheep floated across to the Scottish mainland during a storm, creating an outbreak of anthrax on the coastline. Terrified by the possible ramifications, the scientists put Gruinard to the torch, burning the heather and everything on the island to the ground. The effort was a failure. The island remained sealed off.

The British were not alone in their efforts. American representatives attended the trials on Gruinard and American money funded the continued efforts in biological warfare research and production. In May 1944, an experimental batch of five thousand anthrax weapons was produced at Camp Detrick in Maryland. The main production center for American biological weapons was in Vigo, Indiana, and was capable of creating over half a million anthrax bombs a month. The Vigo center was not ready to go into production until 1945. The end of the war came before the plant was ever used.

The Allies were relieved. The major drawback of the weapons was their awesome lethal potency. Contingency plans drawn up to evaluate their effectiveness against German cities prophesied that over half of those people exposed to the anthrax cloud would die of inhalation, while untold others would suffer the horrible boils, ulcers, and blood poisoning from contamination to the skin. What was most appalling was that anthrax did not readily dissipate. The spores settled into the earth, dormant for years, turning a battlefield into a wasteland unfit for habitation.

What Sherman had learned from his few minutes with the MKNAOMI files was that the American research on biological weapons had not ceased after the end of the war. Anthrax weapons continued to be devised and stockpiled under the auspices of the CIA. It became public knowledge in 1970 when President Nixon ordered all chemical and biological warfare weapons destroyed. When the order was carried out, the CIA withheld an illegal stockpile.

The MKNAOMI file Sherman read was a secret record that the CIA director himself probably was not aware of. A stockpile of a particular strain of anthrax had been created from research at the Vigo center; it was a strain *seven* times more potent than the spores produced during the World War II. It was innocuously labeled Vigo E48R7. Only small quantities had been produced. Half had been kept secret for twenty years in the Zurich underground warehouse. The second half—so the documents had stated—was used in a series of experimental detonations in the one place where the Americans knew anthrax contamination would go unnoticed—on the island of Gruinard.

Sherman was frightened. If even half of what he had read was true, then this grim black island was a killing ground. To set foot on it was to die, but he had to be certain that the documents did not exaggerate. The remaining half of the anthrax stockpile had been smuggled from Zurich in a batch of simple wooden crates. Nathan Stand was the only man in the world who knew where it was—and he was unaware of its lethal contents.

The policeman cut the engine and threw over an anchor. Sherman pulled on a suit of protective clothing. He checked that his oxygen equipment was operating properly while the policeman broke out a rubber raft and tossed it over the side. He and Sherman exchanged a grim look, neither knowing what to say. Sherman took the cage containing the two rabbits and scrambled into the rubber dinghy. He took a deep breath, donned the plastic helmet, fired up the outboard motor, and headed toward the island.

It was unnaturally quiet with the helmet over his head. His breathing rasped in his ears. As he raced toward the beach, he scanned the craggy shore where seabirds liked to nest. There were none to be seen.

He aimed the raft straight at the closest beach, anxious to get the job done quickly. The surf was high, and the raft bounced from swell to swell like an amusement park ride, but he wouldn't slow down. Finally, the beach loomed up. He cut the motor and coasted in the last few yards, then tossed over an anchor when he was nearly on the sand. The raft pulled up short, dragging the anchor, and for a minute he feared he would be cast up on the beach. Then the weight snagged and the raft bobbed in the surf, holding fast.

Sherman wasted no time. He opened the cage and pulled out one rabbit. He hefted it once, then tossed it the short distance to the sand. Quickly, he followed suit with the second rabbit. He sat in the stern, his hand ready on the motor, and watched the two animals scamper out of the water onto the beach. They shook the water from their coats, then darted a short way and paused, lifting their noses to the wind to appraise their new surroundings.

Sherman watched uneasily, not certain what to expect. The rabbits seemed undisturbed. They ran for a few more yards along the sand, then hesitated. Sherman groaned. At this rate, they would soon be out of sight and the whole experiment would be useless.

Suddenly one of the rabbits toppled over. Sherman stared in wide-eyed horror. The creature's belly was covered with black boils, bubbling up before his eyes, protruding as if the skin would burst. The animal panted and jerked in convulsions. The second rabbit skittered a few more steps from its companion, then stopped, coughing a stream of blood. It dropped and lay still. Sherman watched for a few more seconds. Both animals stopped breathing.

Sherman was going to be sick inside his protective headgear. He jerked into action so quickly that he almost tipped over the raft. With one hand he pulled the cord to start the motor, and with the other he drew a knife and slashed the anchor line. He turned the raft hard into the surf. A swell washed over him but he clung grimly to the side and raced the motor until he broke through. He headed out to sea, not caring how the waves bounced him, not caring about anything but getting that black island behind him.

The policeman waved as he drew close to the boat, obviously relieved to see him so quickly. Sherman killed the motor and coasted in,, then caught the rope the policeman threw him and tied off the raft. The policeman leaned over the side and offered a hand.

"No, don't touch me," Sherman said. "Don't touch anything."

The man drew back as if stung, a fearful look in his eyes. He watched silently as Sherman stripped down to his skin and wrapped everything, the protective suit and his own clothes, into the bottom of the raft. He tied it all together as well as he could, his cold hands fumbling over the knots. Then he put one hand and foot on the rope ladder, and with the other hand he stabbed his knife into the rubber tubing.

The air hissed out. Quickly he scrambled aboard the boat as the raft shrank and, dragged down by the weight of the motor, headed for the bottom.

Sherman stood, naked, on the deck of the boat and took one last look at the black island. "Let's get out of here," he said quietly.

"Fine with me, mate," the policeman said. "Let me get you a blanket first. You must be freezing like that."

Sherman shook his head wearily. It didn't matter, he thought. He knew he would never be warm again.

The policeman tied off in Aultbea. Sherman was dressed in fisherman's heavy trousers and a mackintosh, though he still clutched the blanket over his shoulders like a cape.

A short distance away at the end of the pier, a young man slouched against a stone wall, smoking a cigarette and gazing out to sea. Mashed cigarette butts littered the planks below his boots. He had watched them return from the island, certain one of them was the man he waited for.

When Sherman stepped off the boat, the young man removed his watch cap and ran his fingers through his tousled red hair. Far across the harbor, an old man sitting on a bench duplicated the gesture. Then he pulled out a camera with a long telephoto lens and got to work.

The young man replaced his cap and ground out his cigarette. He walked casually to a call box, fished a coin from his pea jacket, and dialed a long series of numbers.

"You were right," he said. "There's been someone here sight-seeing. No, don't worry. I'm on him. He won't get away."

CHAPTER 18

THE TWO workmen wore gray coveralls and snap-brim caps pulled down to protect their faces from the gentle mist. They rolled a green carpet into a cylinder, exposing a freshly dug grave. Hefting the carpet onto their shoulders, they carried it to the canopy that had been erected nearby and set down their load. After looking around in a final inspection, they picked up their tools and moved off toward the small shack at the far end of the graveyard.

Jean watched them go, then swiveled the telescope to inspect the rest of the grounds. She was in a surveillance post in an empty apartment high atop a penthouse that looked down over a quiet back road on the outskirts of Bedford. The graveyard was directly across the road. They had experienced no problem renting the apartment. This outlying sector of the industrial community was predominantly Italian, and they seemed uneager to occupy flats offering a view of neatly spaced headstones. The graveyard was for Protestants.

"See anything?"

Jean straightened up from behind the mounted telescope and shook her head. "No, nothing yet."

"Are you sure he'll show up here?"

"My surveillance team followed Sherman here yesterday. It's clearly a dead drop or a signal site. Stand will have to come to find his friend's message."

"I hope you're right," Gregory said. He looked around

the empty apartment with distaste. "I don't want to stay around here much longer."

Jean frowned at him. "What's your problem? We've only been here a few hours."

"Surveillance is boring."

"We've got it easy. Some agents do this sort of thing for months at a time."

"Not me."

"No," Jean said sourly, "not you." She looked away from him and peered moodily out the window. Gregory was getting on her nerves. He was doing that a lot lately, it seemed, always whining and complaining about every little thing, never offering any real help. He had been involved in the search for Stand from the beginning, but Jean couldn't think of a single instance when he had done anything but get in the way. He didn't seem to be the man she had always thought him to be.

She glanced at him out of the corner of her eye and saw him staring anxiously out the window, his face glum as he absently chewed a fingernail. Her irritation with him began to fade. She noticed that deep worry lines had appeared around his eyes, and the few strands of gray hair at his temples seemed more prominent. The last few weeks had aged them both. The tension was getting tougher to bear, and it wasn't bringing out the best in either of them. It couldn't be easy for him—his head was on the block as much as hers—but she was the one in control. All he could do was stand and watch. It wasn't a comfortable situation for anyone.

"A bunch of cars coming," Gregory muttered.

Jean turned back to the window. There was indeed a long line of cars pulling through the gate of the graveyard, the vehicles moving slowly behind a black hearse.

"Another funeral." Jean sighed. It would be the second ceremony they had witnessed that day. Stand and his friend had certainly chosen a sobering location for their drop site. Jean hoped it wasn't an omen.

The procession of cars stopped near the freshly dug grave. The mourners got out and gathered slowly under the rain canopy. Jean looked away. The idea of spying on people in their moment of grief made her vaguely uneasy. Gregory seemed undisturbed by such notions and pressed closer to the glass, peering down as if glad finally to have something to watch.

"I wonder who the stiff is," he muttered.

"James, really."

"What?"

"Show some respect for—"

Gregory suddenly stood up straighter. "Wait a minute," he said. "Look over there. Someone is standing back by the fence, under the trees."

Jean moved to his side. "Where?"

Gregory pointed with a finger. "See? Back there behind that big tombstone."

Jean squinted to make out the shadowy figure. She let out a little gasp and grabbed the telescope, swung it to focus on the man, while under her breath she offered a silent prayer.

Stand watched from a respectful distance as the casket was lowered into the earth. The widow stood for a moment over the grave. Then the minister took her by the arm and led her away, the family trailing quietly behind. The funeral party slowly dispersed. Stand angled away from them, walking between the long rows of headstones, and approached a small inconspicuous marker. He went down on one knee beside the headstone.

There were fresh flowers atop the grave, two red carnations and one white rose. Stand looked around to make sure no one was watching, then pulled another white rose from out of his coat and dropped it beside the other flowers. He got to his feet and walked away slowly. His heart was pounding in his chest.

In the room overlooking the graveyard, James Gregory straightened from behind the telescope and smiled excitedly. "Bingo! We got him." He grinned.

Jean Frost smiled somberly.

Gregory picked up a two-way radio. "Do we close in?"

"No," Jean said. "I want him followed. Then have a surveillance team watch over him tonight. Tomorrow when he meets Sherman, we can grab the two of them together."

"Are you sure?"

She nodded firmly. "Notify the radio cars, but tell them to be extra careful. I want to know where he's been hiding all this time."

Gregory barked a few terse words into the radio, then threw it down and placed his hands on Jean's shoulders. "This is it, darling. It's almost over."

"Yes," Jean said. "I suppose it is." It was unclear from her tone whether she was pleased or not. She turned from the window, threw off his hands, and left the room without another word. Gregory frowned at the squawking radio, snapped it off with an angry gesture, and hurried after her.

Over supper that night, Stand dropped a casual remark that came out sounding like an announcement. "I'm afraid I won't be staying here much longer," he said.

"Really? So soon?" Meghan asked. She, too, didn't sound as casual as she'd intended. Blushing, she lowered her head and pushed the vegetables around on her plate. "Does this decision have anything to do with us—I mean, with recent events?"

"No," Stand said. "Not at all."

Meghan smiled faintly, trying to make light of it. "What a shame. We were just getting used to having you around, weren't we, Lynnie?"

"I want you to stay, Nathan," the child said flatly. "You're my friend."

Stand shook his head sadly. "I wish I could. It's not my decision, though. There are certain matters that I must see to." He looked up hopefully at Meghan. "My room is paid for until the end of the month. If you can afford not to rent it out right away, I'd like to come back once I've done what I have to do."

"Of course. That would be grand," Meghan said, but she didn't sound convincing.

The rest of the evening went badly. They sat around the living room, Stand pretending to read, while Meghan labored over a manuscript. Lynnie watched one of her favorite comedy shows, but didn't seem to laugh much. She fiddled for a while with a couple of coloring books, then tossed them aside. Turning her back on the adults, she stretched out on the floor and nodded off, her thumb jammed securely in her mouth.

Meghan put down her papers and sighed. "I thought we were past all that thumb-sucking business," she said. "Lynnie hasn't done that in ages. I don't know what's come over her." She put her glasses on the coffee table and bent down over the child. "Come on, sleepyhead, let's get you upstairs."

"No. Nathan," Lynnie protested drowsily.

"Now, honey, he's busy reading."

"I want Nathan to take me."

Stand put his book down and kneeled beside Meghan. "It's all right," he said softly. "I'd like to take her, if you don't mind."

"You're sure? We don't have to obey the little tyrant."

"Please. I want to." Stand smiled awkwardly at Meghan as their bodies brushed together. He bent down and scooped the child up in his arms, then straightened and turned for the stairs. Meghan held his arm lightly, having him pause for a moment while she planted a kiss on Lynnie's head.

"Sleep tight, little one," she murmured. Then she smiled at Stand. "All right, you can see her up now. And thank you."

He moved away quickly. His heart was beating so loudly he feared it would alarm the child. Lynnie shifted in his arms, nestling her head against his shoulder as he started up the stairs. His heart was aching, the old familiar pain, and he held her more tightly than was necessary.

In Lynnie's room Stand held her easily with one arm while he pushed aside a litter of dolls and toys on the bed. He laid her down gently and pulled the covers up to her neck. Tenderly, he brushed the hair from her face. Lynnie's eyes opened, and she grabbed his hand, clung to it fiercely.

"I don't want you to go, Nathan. Please don't leave us."

"I have to, Lynnie," he said. "People sometimes have to do things they don't want to. It can't be helped."

"Please, Nathan. I want you to stay with us. Mummy likes you, she'll let you stay."

Gently, Stand pried open her fingers and tucked her arms under the blankets. "I won't be gone any longer than I absolutely have to be," he said. "I'll come back just as soon as I can. You'll hardly know I ever left."

Her eyes opened wide, warm and trusting. "Really and truly?"

"Shh! That's a promise, Lynnie." He bent low and kissed the top of her head. "Now you go to sleep like a good girl. I'll see you when I come back."

Lynnie rolled over and tucked a favorite doll under her arm. Stand moved quietly to the door. He had taken one step into the hall when the child's voice stopped him. He glanced back and saw her whispering to her doll. "He'll come back," Lynnie said. "I know he'll come back to us. He promised he would."

Stand rushed out. He was halfway down the stairs when the tightness in his chest became agonizing. He slipped and clutched at the rail as if overcome by sudden dizziness. He sat quickly and pressed his face to his knees. The pain shot through him, halting his breath, but there was no stopping the tears. His eyes brimmed and moisture streaked down his face, trailing into his beard.

The sound of footsteps alerted him, but he could not bring himself together in time. Meghan appeared at the foot of the stairs. She glanced up and her face went ashen. She was by his side in a heartbeat. "Nathan, are you all right? What can I do?"

He took a deep breath. "Nothing. It's over now. I'm all right."

"Are you sure? You look terrible."

"Thanks," he said ruefully. "No, it's nothing. I'm sorry you had to see this."

Meghan sat down beside him, their bodies very close on the narrow staircase. "She gets to you, doesn't she?"

"Yes. She does."

"Good," Meghan said. "I'm glad. I hope it gives you second thoughts. I'd use any trick to keep you here with us and I'm not ashamed to admit it."

He stared at her in amazement. "You mean that?"

"You know that I do." She touched his arm tenderly. "Nathan, I think you know what's happening . . . what's starting to happen between us. My life has been so different since you came into it. I don't think it's so wrong to admit it, to come out and say that it feels like love."

"Meghan—" he started, but his voice faltered. His body tensed and he turned away quickly.

"What is it?" she asked. "What's so wrong about me saying it? I know you feel it, too."

"I can't," he said. "It's not right. I have a wife and family. It would be a betrayal to them."

"You think they would want you to be unhappy? I don't believe that."

"No, of course not."

"Why, then, Nathan? What's so wrong? You've grieved for them. You loved them and remember them fondly, but they're gone. Sooner or later, you must start to live for yourself."

"I won't let go of them," he grumbled. "I can't. I can't forget."

"No one's asking you to. They'll always be with you, in your heart. It's right that you remember them and miss them. I understand that. I respect you for it. But no amount of grief will ever bring them back. You've already betrayed them, by denying their death. They're gone, Nathan. You must let them die."

He hung his head sadly. "I don't know if I can do that."

Meghan stood up abruptly. "Then you're not the man I think you are. If you want to remain a coward, hiding in your memories, torturing yourself with guilt, then you're right to leave. I don't want that sort of man here. Look, Nathan, I understand grief. You lost something very precious, the most important part of your life. It hurts; it will always hurt. But that's no excuse for wasting your own life, for giving up. There is no excuse to justify that.''

''Who are you to judge my pain? What do you know about it?''

''I know,'' she said. ''Believe me, I know.''

''You know nothing.''

Her face darkened. ''Is that so? You think you're the only person ever to lose someone you loved?''

''Your husband, you mean?'' Stand grunted. ''You said you were glad that he left.''

''No, not glad. I said it was the right thing. Bill had left me a long time before he actually went out the door. It wasn't so different from what you went through, Nathan—I had to watch him die in front of my eyes. He killed himself with alcohol and self-doubt, killed off the man I loved little by little until one day he was gone. There was a stranger in his place, a stranger full of hate and envy and despair. That's how my husband died, Nathan. It was slower than the way you lost your family, but that didn't make it any less painful.''

''I'm sorry for you, Meghan. Truly sorry. But it's still not the same.'' He groaned and buried his face in his hands. ''This is too much. God, I wish I had a—''

''A drink?''

He gazed at her in confusion. ''You knew?''

Meghan smiled faintly. ''I lived with an alcoholic for five years. Do you think I couldn't recognize the signs? I'm glad, though, that you're willing to admit it to me.''

''I thought I was hiding it well. I've hardly thought of a drink in the time I've been here with you.''

''You do handle it well. You have a strong will, Nathan. I think I sensed that in you—your strength. You can break it, I know you can. You can leave the drinking for good . . . if you want to.''

''It's a frightening idea. I don't know if I'm that strong.''

She said quietly, ''You don't have to fight it alone.''

He looked down and folded his hands together so tightly

that the muscles stood out like cords along his forearms. "Meghan, I can't start a life with you and pretend that the old one never happened. The dreams won't stop. I can't shut off the past that way. If you had been there, seen Melissa's eyes, the pain, the hate . . ."

"She was a child, Nathan. She was frightened, confused. She blamed you for something that wasn't your fault."

"No, she was right."

Meghan sighed in frustration. "I give up. If you'd rather blame yourself for everything, then go ahead. But I don't have to listen." She started down the stairs, but he grabbed her arm and held her back.

"I'm trying to tell you the truth," he said. "I was to blame."

Meghan glared at him and pulled her arm free. "You don't control the world, Nathan. I'm sorry to break it to you this way, but it's time you learned. The world revolves around more than just Nathan-bloody-Stand."

His head snapped up and he almost screamed the words at her. "Dammit! It was me! It was my fault."

"You couldn't stop what happened."

"But they wouldn't have been there, except for me. They wouldn't have been on that train if . . ." He hung his head and his voice became a hoarse whisper. "They were leaving me. It wasn't just a visit. They weren't coming back."

"Because of your drinking?"

"Yes. Because I'm a drunk." He buried his face in his hands, breathing heavily, his chest heaving. His eyes stung, but there were no tears. All his tears were spent.

Meghan wrapped her arms around his shoulders and guided his head to her bosom. Tenderly, she stroked his hair. "Thank you, Nathan," she said softly. "Thank you for finally telling me the truth."

"Now you know," he rasped. "I suppose you'll want no part of me."

"You're right," she said. "I want it all."

Somehow she was in his arms. They kissed, their mouths meeting tenderly. Her lips were soft and cool, compliant.

Then they moved hungrily, with growing passion. The warmth of her body was electric. He tingled everywhere she touched him, as if her skin scorched every nerve it contacted.

When they parted, he expected doubt, but she gazed at him warmly, with a hint of humor gleaming in her eyes. "Are you still sure you have to leave tomorrow?" she murmured.

"Is this what you meant when you said you'd try anything to keep me?"

She smiled. "I meant it. Anything."

He shook his head sadly. "I wish I could. If there were any way—"

She silenced him by touching a finger to his lips. "Then we still have tonight."

"Meghan, no matter what happens, I have to go. I can't make you any promises."

"I don't care," she said. "I don't need promises. We have now. That's enough. It's all I ask for."

They rose slowly and walked arm in arm up the stairs and paused on the landing.

"My place or yours?"

"My room," Stand said. "It's paid for."

She laughed. "I love a man who's sensible about money."

They walked down the hall and hesitated in the doorway, kissed again, slowly and with growing urgency.

Stand held her tightly, and spoke in a trembling voice suffused with passion. "It's been so long since I felt this way. I'm scared, Meghan. God help me, I'm truly scared."

She smiled and prodded him forward with a gentle nudge at his back. "Nathan, it's only love."

They stood beside the bed and undressed each other slowly. Neither wanted to hurry. They lingered over each motion as if to make the night last forever. The silence seemed natural and right.

Stand kissed her and held her tightly. He gently lowered her to the bed and lay by her side. Their hands moved over each other, stroking, exploring to commit every inch of skin to memory.

Then, by silent agreement, Meghan guided him into her. They moved together easily, unhurried. Time hushed, and their hearts pounded in harmony, each surge of blood rippling through them, arousing them to unbearable heights of pleasure.

Meghan began to tremble. She moaned and buried her face at his throat, her breath coming in short gasps. Her legs fastened around his hips, holding him tighter. She threw back her head, her body arching, then stiffened and let out a ragged cry.

At the same moment Stand hissed with a sharp intake of breath. His body convulsed and he clung fiercely to Meghan, shaking wildly until he was spent.

In the warm afterglow, they held each other and talked in low voices. Stand spoke about everything except his work and the reason he had to leave.

"I wish you would confide in me," Meghan said. "It seems like a bad omen, having a secret between us already."

"I want to tell you, Meghan. But I can't. You just have to trust me."

"Will you really come back to us, Nathan? When it's over, when you've done whatever you have to do?"

"I promise."

"All right, then. That's good enough for me." She went to sleep, curled beside him with her head cradled on his chest.

Stand gazed at the ceiling, savoring her warmth and the feel of her body next to him. After a while, he closed his eyes and slept. He dreamed of being alone on a raft, adrift on a calm black sea. The ocean was vast and there was no sight of land, but the night sky was bright with stars, showing the way.

It was cold in the car, but they didn't want to run the engine for risk of someone noticing the exhaust. Jean took the binoculars from Alec Monroe, the captain of the surveillance team, and scanned the line of buildings on the quiet Soho street. "Which place is it?"

"That one between the pub and the Indian restaurant."

She focused the glasses. The house was dark but for a dim glow in a single upstairs window. "You've identified the owner of the property?" she asked.

"It's registered to a Meghan Foster, thirty-seven. She's a widow and lives alone, except for her eight-year-old daughter, Lynn. No record of any kind, and no known prior association with Stand."

"Well, it looks quiet enough," Jean said, handing back the binoculars. "You're certain he's still in there?"

Monroe frowned as if mildly offended by the question. "He's there, all right. He came in about dusk. The woman and the child appeared about forty minutes after that. Since then, no one has entered or left the premises. Our listening equipment has picked up sounds of activity throughout the night. There was a considerable commotion about an hour ago, but it's been reasonably quiet since."

"What kind of commotion?"

"Screaming, banging about. To tell you the truth, it sounded like a fight. Hard to say from our current setup. Someone could have just had the television up too loud for a minute or so." The captain gave Jean a severe look. "We would know more if we could set up properly from a decent distance. I'd like your permission to move in closer."

"Absolutely not," Jean said. "We can't risk being spotted and tipping him off at this point. Under no circumstances will I risk letting him slip away from us again."

"If you're sure this is the man you want, why don't you just move in and grab him?"

"There are two civilians in there," Jean said. "This operation is too sensitive for us to allow any public attention. Dragging people out in the middle of the night is hardly a way to avoid that. It smacks too much of Gestapo tactics. No, we'll wait until tomorrow when he meets his fellow conspirator."

From the backseat came sounds of grumbling. Gregory sat up and tapped Jean on the shoulder. "I would like to get some sleep sometime tonight. It's sure not gonna happen while I'm freezing my butt off in here."

Jean frowned and stared down the street at the dark house. "All right," she said reluctantly. "I guess I've seen enough. We'll check in with you first thing tomorrow, Mr. Monroe. Keep a sharp eye on things."

"That's what I'm paid for," Monroe said. He unscrewed the bulb in the dome light, then signaled that it was all right for them to leave.

"Good night," Jean said, stepping out.

Monroe pulled his coat up tighter as cold air rushed in the open door. "Mind telling me what's so important about this guy? If I'm going to freeze my keester off out here tonight, I'd sorta like to be in the picture."

Jean shook her head. "Sorry. Believe me, you're better off not knowing."

He nodded unhappily. "I knew you were going to say that. That's what they always say." He watched Jean and Gregory disappear around the corner, heading for their warm beds. He sighed and picked up the binoculars.

Meghan and Lynnie were gone when Stand awoke. He suspected that she had gotten out of the way to make his leaving easier and less painful for them all. Stand dressed and packed a few extra clothes in a small bag. He left his larger suitcase in the middle of the bed, where Meghan would be sure to find it. He hoped it would reassure her that he would return. He went downstairs and made himself breakfast, then lingered over it at the kitchen table. He was reluctant to leave this warm house where his life had taken such a startling turn. But it had to be done. He waited as long as he could, then pulled on his coat and slipped outside.

The meeting was in a multilevel parking garage in a busy office district off Regent Street. He stepped off the bus three blocks from his destination and strolled casually past it four times, front and back, before he felt certain it was not being watched. He slipped inside the garage through one of the exists leading to an adjacent office building.

He moved warily among the rows of parked cars, checking each level all the way to the top, then worked his way down to the sixth floor. Most of the cars were parked on lower levels. It was quiet and dark, grim as a mausoleum. Sherman was standing in the shadows behind a massive concrete column. He had his hands jammed in the pockets of his overcoat and looked even more miserable than usual.

Stand walked down the aisle toward his friend, his footsteps echoing hollowly in the cavernous space. He stopped a few yards from Sherman and glanced at him with concern. The MI 6 agent's face was pasty and lined with fatigue. His eyes were red, looked as if they hadn't been closed in a week.

"Well, you kept me waiting bloody long enough," Sherman said, but without his usual bite.

"You look terrible. What have you done to yourself?"

"You'd look like sodding death, too, if you'd seen what I've seen. It's bad, Nathan, worse than you could possibly suspect."

"Tell me."

Sherman coughed, a loud racking noise, and shivered. He hunched his shoulders and collected himself with a visible effort. "It's your own people behind it all, Nathan," he said. "The Zurich clearinghouse is a CIA front. The Erin Dawn doesn't exist. It's a dummy group set up to cover a Company operation."

"Why would the Company use a dummy to smuggle out something from one of their own sites?" Stand asked.

"This job was something they had to keep quiet, even from their fellow insiders. The shipment you intercepted was something they don't want anyone to know they possess. I'm reasonably certain even the DCI doesn't know about the bloody thing."

"What is it, Sherman?"

"Anthrax."

Stand paled. "You can't be serious."

"It's a complete anthrax bomb, with enough nasty little bugs to devastate an entire city. The damned thing's been sitting in storage for almost twenty years. It was made in the late sixties, before you Yanks got touchy about chemical weapons. I saw the records. It was created under the MKNAOMI project; you remember that one?''

"Sure," Stand said. "But it was disbanded over ten years ago. All the CBWs were destroyed."

Sherman shook his head. "Not all. There was one little nasty they kept around, for old times' sake."

"I still can't believe it."

"I wish I didn't. But I saw it for myself, Nathan. I saw the results of a test, a site infected with anthrax. It's not something I ever want to see again."

Stand scowled and ran his fingers through his beard. "I appreciate what you've done for me, Sherman. We have to—" The words stalled in his throat. Stand froze. The garage echoed with a shrill screech. A van and two cars skidded to a stop at the edge of the ramp, blocking the exit. Stand heard a similar noise overhead and knew other cars were moving into position to cut off the ramp leading up. He glanced around anxiously. The elevator behind Sherman had not opened yet, but he could see the lighted floor indicator creeping up to their level. It was no good; he saw it in a flash. All their exits were cut off. He was trapped.

Sherman sighed, a weary sound of resignation and defeat. "I'm sorry, Nathan. It's not my doing."

"I know that."

Stand watched men pile out of the van at the far end of the garage. They went down on their knees and leveled rifles at him with professional coolness. A bell rang softly. Stand turned as the elevator hissed open. A slender figure stepped out. She walked toward them, then stopped a short distance away. The glow of the overhead lamp spilled across her face.

"Why you?" Stand asked.

Jean Frost's expression was neither sad nor triumphant. "I'm responsible. But then, I imagine you had already begun to suspect that."

"I would have come to it," Stand said. "We were getting close."

"Yes, you've done well, Nathan. It's been a long hunt. You might have eluded us forever if you had been content merely to stay out of it.'' She swiveled her gaze to the older man. ''Please step away, Mr. Sherman. This does not concern you.''

Nodding, Sherman turned and took a few steps. He paused as he neared Stand and offered him his hand. ''I'm sorry, Nathan. I guess I'm getting too old for this sort of thing.''

Stand gripped his hand and smiled warmly. ''Thanks, Sherman. Tell them everything, make it easy on yourself. You've done nothing wrong.''

''Good luck, Nathan.'' Sherman dragged himself to the other end of the garage and toward the squadron of armed men. One of them seized him, bent him over the hood of a car, searched him quickly, then took him by the arm and led him away.

Jean walked closer to Stand and watched him as he glanced around, appraising the situation, considering his options.

''Don't try it,'' Jean said. ''You wouldn't get very far.''

''I suppose you have the place well sealed off?''

''There are men at every exit. Phillips, Johnson, Willis— you know all of them.''

''And more to the point, they know me.''

Jean nodded. ''On sight. Of course, you could still try to break out. But think about it for a minute. Those are all Americans, men on our side. You try to run, you'll have to hurt one of them, maybe kill them. You'll have to—because they won't hesitate to hurt you. They're convinced you're a traitor. Some of them are counting on you to try it, praying for it.''

Stand said, ''So what happens now?''

''We walk out of here quietly, together.''

''Just like that? No tricks?''

''You don't have to trust me,'' Jean said. ''But you can read between the lines as well as anyone.''

''If I refuse?''

Her voice was cool and flat, without emotion. ''Then you'll be taken by force and placed in custody. You'll sit in jail until you can be tried for treason.''

"I'll talk. I'll spill everything I know. That means MKNAOMI, the anthrax."

Jean didn't react. "I knew you'd learn about it somehow. Who will believe it, Nathan? Even if you prove it, nothing will change. The Company will hush it up. And you'll never be trusted again. One way or another, it's over."

"That's the best deal you can offer?"

"It's the only way. We're really both after the same thing, you know."

He frowned. "Are we? I still don't know why you were fooling with that stuff. For God's sake, Jean, chemical weapons? What the hell are you up to?"

"I'll be straight with you. Everything will be made clear, I promise."

"Tell me now."

Jean shook her head. "I can't do that, not here. It's too sensitive. We can help each other, Nathan, but only if you come along with me now. Jail or a chance to know the truth—which will it be?"

Stand scowled at her. "Do I really have a choice?"

"Not at all," Jean said. "I've been counting on that."

CHAPTER 19

"WE HAVE him."

"At last. What does the woman plan to do with him now?"

"She's driving him to a safe house in the Lake District. She wanted to take him by herself. I'm going to meet them there later."

"The woman takes no guards with her? Can she be certain he will not try to escape?"

"Stand knows the score now," Gregory said. "He knows he has to cooperate or be tried for treason. There isn't any way out for him. He'll give her the location, sooner or later."

"How many men in the security force at the safe house?"

"None. Jean wants to keep this quiet. No one talks to Stand but her and me."

Falstaff smiled. "Excellent. The woman makes this easy for us. We must move quickly, James. It is time at last for me to meet the troublesome Mr. Stand face-to-face."

Gregory frowned. "How are you going to do that with Jean there?"

"The woman will present no problem," Falstaff said. "You will divert her away from the safe house. Then I and my men will move in."

"Don't you want to wait? Sooner or later, Stand will give Jean the location of the stockpile. That's all you care about. Wouldn't it be smarter for you to stay away from him?"

"I have waited long enough," Falstaff snapped. "It may

take a considerable time for the woman to earn his trust. I have methods which are faster and more certain. Stand will give us what we want to know—that is beyond doubt.''

''How are you going to do that?''

Falstaff smiled. ''You gave me the answer when you told me where Stand has been hiding these many weeks. The time has come for action.''

Falstaff's smile raised a chill down Gregory's back. ''What are you planning?'' he asked. But the other man didn't answer. He turned and walked away. Reluctantly, Gregory tailed along behind. In the back of his mind there was a creeping doubt, a deepening suspicion that he should clear out now, while he still had a chance. But he pushed away the thought. It was easier just to go along and do what he was told, and try not to think at all. Because when he stopped to think, he got scared.

Meghan picked Lynnie up from the elderly neighbor lady who watched the child in the afternoons after school. She took a firm grip on her daughter's hand and walked two blocks at a brisk clip. Lynnie dragged her feet sullenly and pointed down the street to the corner. A group of children played with jump ropes and rusty, secondhand bicycles.

''Please, can I go play for a little while? It's not dark yet.''

''Not tonight,'' Meghan said quickly. She tugged Lynnie up their steps and fumbled in her purse for the keys. ''I want you to stay inside with me.''

''Why can't I play?'' the child whined.

''You can watch the telly while I make supper. Mummy feels lonely tonight, darling. Can't you stay in and keep me company?''

Lynnie stared down the street at the cluster of her friends. The noise of their boisterous screams was a siren lure. She turned away sadly, confused. She knew something odd was going on. Her mother never let her watch television until after the evening meal and homework. She didn't protest anymore. An offer to watch television at this hour was a significant concession. Instinctively, she knew her mother's mind couldn't be changed.

Meghan opened the door and bustled Lynnie inside. The child tossed off her coat and bounded toward the living room and the television. Meghan frowned and bent down to pick up Lynnie's coat. She straightened and turned to close the door. Her heart leaped into her throat when the door swung shut on its own.

A man stepped from his hiding place by the wall. He was a tall menacing figure with his face hidden beneath a black ski mask.

Meghan had no time to think. The next instant she heard a startled cry. "Mummy! Help!" She spun away from the ominous stranger, thinking only of her daughter. She saw Lynnie dart back into the hallway, with two other men in similar masks stumbling after her, grabbing for her.

"Take your hands off her!" Meghan shouted, and tensed to launch herself at them. Too late. The first had stolen up behind her. Strong hands seized her, pinning her arms to her side. A damp cloth was pressed to her face, and she gagged on the choking sweet scent of chloroform. The effect was immediate, dizzying. She wobbled. The room began to spin.

"Dammit! The brat bit me!"

The cry cut through the haze fogging Meghan's mind. She let out a muffled scream as she saw Lynnie struggling in a dark man's arms. The child's face was streaked with tears, and she whimpered. The cloth was forced down over her mouth. In sudden desperation, Meghan drove a sharp-heeled shoe down on the instep of the man holding her. He grunted in pain. She wrenched one arm free, flailed out in blind rage, and struck him across the face, snapping his head back.

"You bitch! I'll make you regret that!"

"She's just a woman. Dammit! Hold on to her."

The third man waved him off. "No," he ordered. "Let her go."

Suddenly freed, Meghan stumbled forward. The room was spinning faster, growing faint, darker. With a cry like an animal growl, she lurched toward her daughter. The men had dropped Lynnie, and she was sprawled out on the floor, pale and still. Meghan took one tottering drunken step toward her, then fell to her knees. She struggled forward, crawling, and reached out to touch her.

"Don't fight it, Mrs. Foster," the leader said quietly. "You will sleep now. No harm will come to your daughter."

Meghan glared up at him. The darkness was all around her, heavy and warm. But for a second longer, she forced it away. Her eyes focused on the leader with a burning hatred. "Don't hurt her," she muttered in a thick-tongued stammer. "You hurt her, I will kill you all. I will—"

Darkness swirled over her head. Meghan finally lost out to it and sagged to the floor.

The leader gazed down at her and slowly peeled off his mask. "She is a fighter, this one," Falstaff said. His eyes gleamed with an odd flickering light. "A remarkable woman. It will be a shame to harm one such as this." He shrugged and waved at the other two men. "Get them outside."

Gregory shifted nervously in the front seat of the van when he heard the door to the house crash open. His mouth gaped when he saw Nazareth with a sleeping child in his arms, and his henchmen carrying a woman. They dumped the two bodies into the back of the van, then climbed in and slammed the doors. He glanced at Gregory and smiled when he saw the incredulous expression on his face.

"Is there a problem, James? You seem disturbed."

"What the hell are you up to?" Gregory asked hoarsely.

"Persuasion, James."

"You intend to use them to make Stand talk?"

"Of course." Falstaff arched an eyebrow. "You don't approve?"

"I . . . I don't know," Gregory stammered. "I don't know what to think."

Falstaff smiled thinly and turned to his driving. Gregory looked away, staring out the window, but seeing nothing. The chill he had felt earlier was back, and there was no way to ignore it, no matter how he tried. And he tried hard.

* * *

Stand was surprised when he saw the safe house Jean had chosen. It could hardly be more different from its American counterparts. It was located in the rugged mountainous region of Cumbria, near Mosedale. Mining had been an important activity in the Lake District for centuries, slate being the primary product. But many of the mines had played out, or become prohibitively expensive to operate, so they were abandoned. It was to just such a place that Jean drove him, to the site of an abandoned mine. Huge spoil heaps of slate were piled everywhere, like crumbling monuments of an ancient people.

There were two buildings, each made of stone. One angled into the sloping hillside, containing the mine itself. The other building was newer, a long, low prefabricated structure resembling an army barracks. Its roof was tin, loosely held together by huge flakes of rust. Though it was apparently of more recent construction, this building, too, had a melancholy look of abandonment.

"Charming," Stand said as he looked around in bewilderment. "What are we doing in a place like this?"

"Don't complain. It's private here, and quiet."

"I believe it."

"And it has a view," Jean said, sweeping a hand to indicate the panorama of black mountains. "I thought you would appreciate that."

Stand said nothing, but actually she had a point. After the crush and clamor of London, the rugged hill country was a pleasant change.

Jean emptied the car of coffee cups, sandwich wrappers, and other assorted trash they had accumulated during the lengthy drive. She pushed it into a paper sack, then carried it a short distance from the buildings and dropped it. The sack disappeared from sight, and it was a few seconds before Stand heard it plop somewhere deep in the earth.

She smiled at his mystified look. "Sinkholes," she said. "The area is absolutely littered with them. The ground opens up in the most unexpected places, cavities that lead down hundreds of feet. There's a virtual ant farm of mine shafts below this whole site. They were all discarded and forgotten generations ago.''

''I get the point,'' Stand said. ''Taking a stroll in the moonlight would not be advisable.''

''Not unless you enjoy nasty surprises.'' She smiled. ''So please don't try to wander off. I'd hate to see you take a fall.''

He frowned. ''In one sense, I think I already have.''

Jean made a face, but didn't reply. She picked her way carefully across the scrabble to the newer building, then stood for a minute by the door, turning a slow circle and studying the ground. Her face suddenly brightened. She leaned down and flipped over a heavy stone. She reached into the space below and came up with a ring of keys.

''You seem to know your way around pretty well,'' Stand said. ''Come here often?''

''Only once before,'' Jean admitted. ''That's why I had trouble remembering where the keys were hidden.'' She shivered in the wind and hurriedly slipped a key into the padlock. The door squealed on rusty hinges as she pushed it open.

Stand followed her inside. It was more inviting than the crumbling exterior had led him to expect. A shell of painted Sheetrock had been erected inside the stone wall, creating a livable space that was plain, but reasonably clean and functional. The furnishings were sparse: a wooden table, several straight-back chairs, and five cots grouped around a large black coal stove. A fire had apparently already been laid, for Jean opened the grate and threw in a match. Cheery flames shot up, sending out a warm glow that immediately made the place more comfortable.

Stand made himself at home, kicking back one of the chairs and planting his feet on the table. He lit up his pipe and smoked while Jean took a can of coffee from a wooden crate in the corner, filled a pot, and placed it on the lid of the stove.

''Okay, now what?'' Stand asked. ''How long do you intend to keep me here in this Mother Earth dream home?''

"That's up to you. Until you tell me where I can recover the stockpile."

Stand frowned. "We could have had this conversation just as easily in London."

"I thought you would appreciate me keeping you out of the Company's hands until this mess could be cleared up more quietly. Or did you forget they want you as guest of honor at a lynching party?"

"No, I seem to remember that. Hardly the sort of thing to slip one's mind."

Jean shrugged and settled into a chair across from him. "All right, then. You know how it plays—you help me, and I help you. It's just as simple as that."

"Not from where I sit," Stand grumbled. "Help you do what? That's what I want to know. What were you planning to do with your anthrax plaything in the first place?"

"I'd rather not tell you that."

"Then we're wasting each other's time."

"I'm not going to wage a biological war on anyone with it," Jean said. "What kind of person do you think I am?"

"Well, excuse me for asking a stupid question, but what else can you do with a germ bomb?"

She shook her head angrily. "Dammit! Nathan, I'm not going to tell you that. How many times do I have to say it?"

Stand dropped his feet to the floor and pushed away from the table. "Don't worry about it. I don't think we need to go through this anymore. You can consider me gone."

"Where do you think you're going to go, Nathan?"

"What's to stop me from going right out that door?"

"And just keep running?" Jean said. "It won't end here, Nathan. You run out now, you'll have to run forever. Do you want to be a fugitive the rest of your life?"

He stood up and glared down at her. "I can live with that. It's better than being a contributor to mass murder."

Jean stiffened, her temper flaring. "Aren't you listening?" she snapped. "I told you we don't intend to use the bomb to hurt anyone. It's monstrous, an abomination. Only a madman would consider using a thing like that."

"What, then? Why do you want it so badly?"

She frowned and bit her lip, turned away from him sullenly. She buried her hands in her pockets and pulled her coat closer around herself, though the stove was heating quickly and the room was not uncomfortably cold.

Stand sighed and said gently, "I'm sorry, Jean, but I can't help you. I won't be a part of this."

Jean's voice rasped, "Sit down, Nathan. You're not going anywhere."

"How do you think you're going to stop me?"

Her right hand came out of her pocket, and it was holding a .32 Baretta. She leveled it at Stand's chest. "I can, and I will. Sit down, Nathan. I don't want to hurt you, but believe me, I will if I have to."

"Jean—"

"Sit down!" she cried, and cocked the pistol. The click of the hammer was sharp in the sudden stillness.

Scowling, Stand moved slowly to the chair and started to sit.

"Back more," Jean said. "Pull the chair away from the table. And keep your hands on your knees where I can see them. Don't try anything, because I'm nervous enough to make this thing go off if I so much as see you blink."

"That's a comforting thought," Stand muttered. He pulled on the chair, scraping the legs across the wooden floor, making a loud screeching noise. He watched Jean's reaction. Her hand was steady, her eyes cool. If she was nervous as she claimed, she wasn't showing it. Cursing below his breath, he sat down and put his hands on his knees, assuming a pose like a schoolboy eager to impress the teacher with his perfect posture.

Jean sighed and uncocked the pistol with her thumb. But she still kept it trained directly at his midsection.

"Do you want me to tie myself up, too?" Stand asked sarcastically. "Or do you intend to watch over me all night?"

"Help is coming," she said. "Any time now. I had hoped we could settle this alone, but I should have known you'd be stubborn and thickheaded as usual."

"Yeah, that's a funny thing about me. I always get up-tight and suspicious when people start pointing guns at me."

"Why don't you shut up for a while, all right?"

A shadow of anger darkened Stand's face. "Tell me something, Jean. Did you intentionally foul things up so Reiger wouldn't make it? Was his death all part of the plan?"

Her face fell. "There is no damned plan. That was an accident. Are you accusing me of working for the other side?"

"Who else, then?"

Jean blinked rapidly, and her gun hand wavered. She raised it again quickly, then opened her eyes wide and stared at him. She trembled and then seemed to deflate, her breath hissing out as if from a punctured balloon. She dropped the gun on the table and buried her face in her hands.

"You're right," she muttered. "This is stupid. What am I doing? God, this is all wrong."

Stand got up and grabbed the pistol. He pulled out the clip and put it in his pocket, levered a shell from the chamber, then put the gun back down. He came around the table and stood over her. "Jean," he said quietly, "the truth now. Tell me what this is all about."

"I want to destroy that thing, Nathan. That's all, nothing sinister, it was all I ever intended. That was the whole idea from the beginning—to smuggle it to a lab where it can be properly disposed of, once and forever."

"I wish I could believe that."

She looked up, and her eyes were dark and troubled. "It's the truth, I swear it. You must believe me."

Stand scowled. "Forgive me for being skeptical, but I've been lied to for so long I don't know if I can trust you anymore at all. If you're telling the truth, then I've been through a lot of trouble for nothing. For God's sake, Jean, why didn't you just tell me?"

"You just said it. I didn't know if you could be trusted. I didn't want you to know the truth. I didn't want anyone to know. That was the whole point. Somehow, I had to get that thing out of the Company's possession and destroy it before anyone learned about it. But it all went sour when you stopped the shipment.''

"I can't understand why you went to so much trouble when you could have made an official request to have the anthrax relocated and properly disposed of.''

"You think I didn't consider that? Give me some credit, Nathan. But how easy do you think it is to requisition something when no one—absolutely no one—even knows it exists?''

"They made the thing, they stored it for twenty years," Stand said. "Someone had to know about it.''

Jean shook her head. "You don't understand how completely a secret like this can be hushed up. The thinking is: What *we* don't know can't hurt us. Administrations come and go. There's always someone new showing up in the White House, in the director's office—it simply isn't safe to trust all those short-timers with this kind of explosive secret. The President doesn't know about it, the DCI doesn't know—no one knows. It's considered safer to pass the buck, to withhold the information. The policy protects the leadership just as much as it protects the secret. Everyone's happy.''

"Ignorance is bliss? That's a policy of national defense?''

"In politics and under certain circumstances, ignorance can be essential.''

Stand growled. "Double-speak, Chinese box rationalizations, lies within lies within more lies. Who is protected by the existence of a nightmare weapon that no one will admit to? You entrusted the anthrax to professional gun smugglers, for chrissakes! What way is that to protect anybody?''

"I know.'' Jean sighed. "I was pretty upset myself when I learned about that scheme.''

"Whose brilliant idea was that?''

"It doesn't matter now.''

"How did you learn about the stockpile?'' Stand asked. "If this thing was such a complete secret, how did you get your hands on it?''

"I met a man named Robert Crimble. He was a microbiologist who was part of the team that built the thing. He came to me and told me the whole story, made me promise to see that it was destroyed. Crimble was haunted by his involvement in MKNAOMI, hated himself for having any part in it. He knew my position gave me the power and opportunity to correct that dreadful mistake.'' Jean paused and raised her head proudly. ''He came to me because he suspected I was someone who cared enough to carry out his wishes, to make certain that this horrible thing was destroyed. And he was right.''

Stand sighed and rubbed at his temples, as if he had gotten an excruciating headache. ''So you proceeded to smuggle out the stockpile and then I came into it. This thing has made my life hell. You allowed me to believe my life was over, that I'd never work again. You didn't bother to tell me the truth, even when I was ready to drink myself literally to death. You didn't even lift a finger when I was branded a traitor and hounded by the same people I served with.''

''What do you want me to say, Nathan? That I'm sorry. Nobody told you to destroy that shipment and to bullheadedly refuse to admit what you'd done to it. You brought it on yourself with your own stubbornness.''

Stand glared at her. ''But it never should have happened. All you had to do was come forward with the truth. You had no business sneaking around, playing at smuggling. That anthrax was transported through populated regions, Jean. What if there'd been an accident? No, dammit! The only sensible thing for you to do was to order the removal officially, so it could be handled by trained experts, with proper safety procedures. All right, so once the Company was alerted, the game would have been up. There might have been leaks, probably a full public disclosure. The country would have been outraged, the Company embarrassed, but the flap would have died down sooner or later. It wouldn't be the end of the world.''

''You're wrong, Nathan. There's much more at stake. It would be devastating. A scandal of this magnitude would tear the Company apart. There's already so much public sentiment against covert activities. If this came out, we'd suffer massive funding cutbacks, additional scrutiny from governmental oversight committees, new legislation to restrict our operations. It would be a disaster.''

''Maybe,'' Stand said. ''But the Company has endured disasters before. It would survive this one. Every government agency is expected to be responsible, to face up to the consequences of its own blundering. There's no reason the Company should be exempt.''

Jean studied him thoughtfully. ''What are you saying, Nathan? That you're in favor of public disclosure? Are you thinking of blowing the whistle?''

''I'm tempted.''

Jean got up and walked over to the stove. She took off the coffeepot and poured some for herself. She didn't return to her seat, but stepped over by the table, leaned back against it, and sipped at the steaming coffee. She had placed herself directly in front of Stand, just a few feet away.

He smiled up at her uneasily and motioned to her cup. ''What's the plan? Throw coffee in my face to blind me, then try to grab back the gun?''

''No, Nathan, nothing like that. I'm through scheming. I'm going to reason with you, simply ask for your help. I have to recover the stockpile. Whatever you did with it, you didn't destroy it. That can only be accomplished in a lab, with careful biochemical procedures. So it's out there somewhere, and it's dangerous. You realize that now as well as I do. You can't leave it. I've screwed things up badly—I admit that—but with your help, we can see that the job is finished. We must, Nathan; it has to be done.''

Stand said nothing. He rocked back on his chair and tugged at his beard in a distracted manner. After a moment, he started slowly refilling his pipe. He lit it and puffed out clouds of smoke, watched them drift around the room.

''Well?'' Jean asked.

''I'm thinking.''

She frowned and raised her coffee cup, then flinched and spilled some on herself as she saw Stand jump to his feet.

''What is it?''

"I heard something," Stand said. "I think someone's coming."

"That'll be James." She put her cup on the table and walked to the door.

"Gregory?" Stand asked, making a face. "I should have known he'd be involved in a balled-up mess like this one."

They heard the crunch of car tires on the rocky soil outside, then waited for a minute, but no one appeared. Jean hesitated a moment longer, then opened the door a crack and peered outside. "It's all right. It's him."

"Swell," Stand said sourly. He frowned, trudged to the stove, and poured himself a cup of coffee. He waited there, glaring as he watched Jean's face.

She threw open the door and a cold gust of wind preceded Gregory as he burst inside. He glanced furtively in Stand's direction, then smiled down at Jean and took her into his arms. He gave her a brief kiss and started to draw away, then hugged her again with a sudden display of emotion. "Oh, Jean—"

"What is it, James? You seem worried."

Gregory nodded sadly. "I have bad news, Jean. You need to call Washington. It's your father . . . he's had . . . I think he may not pull through this time."

Jean shuddered and hugged Gregory tightly, then broke away and grabbed up her coat. "I'll use the phone in the car."

"No good," Gregory said, shaking his head. "It's not working."

"What?" Jean frowned and hurried outside. Gregory glanced quickly at Stand, then turned and went after her.

Jean tugged at the car door, but it was locked and stuck fast. Cursing herself for her stupidity, she pulled out her keys and opened the door, climbed inside. She picked up the cordless car phone and held it to her ear, then shook it angrily, and listened once more.

"Well, darling?" Gregory said as he came up and stood by the door.

Jean threw the phone down in disgust. "You're right. It's

broken.'' She swore and banged her fist on the steering wheel. "Of all the times for this to happen. I feel so helpless. I have to know what's happening to him.''

Gregory leaned inside the car and placed a comforting arm over her shoulders. "Go on, darling. You can be in Mosedale in thirty or forty minutes. You can call the hospital from a pay phone.''

"I can't leave here now.''

"Of course you can. Why not? I'll watch over Stand. He's not going anywhere. The only other car is my van, and I have the keys. He's not going to walk across these mountains at night.''

"You say he's in the hospital?'' Jean asked, weakening.

Gregory nodded. "I'm not sure which one. You might have to try a few to locate him.''

"It must be bad if he's let another doctor near him.''

"Go ahead,'' Gregory said gently. "You have to know. You won't sleep a wink until you're sure he's okay. Don't worry about a thing, darling. We'll be fine here for a little while. Stand knows me; we get along. You go find out about your father; I mean it, go on. I won't take no for an answer.''

Jean leaned over and buried her face at his chest. "Oh, James, what would I do without you? I promise to make it quick.''

He kissed the top of her head, then gently pulled away and closed the door. "Now you take it easy. You won't help your father any by tearing around these back roads and cracking up the car. Promise me you'll take it slow.''

Jean nodded stiffly. "I love you, James. And thank you.''

Gregory backed up and waved. Jean turned the car around quickly and drove off through the hills, scattering gravel in her wake. He watched until the car was out of sight. Then he thumped once on the side of the van and walked back to the building.

Stand was still at his place by the stove, drinking coffee. He grimaced when Gregory reappeared, red-faced and pounding his arms to restore his circulation. "I thought I heard the car,'' Stand said.

"Jean's driving to Mosedale to place a call home. She won't be long."

"You didn't close the door."

"Oh, yeah." Gregory looked back at the open door, but instead of going over to close it, he went straight to the coal stove and held out his hands. "Jeez! It's cold out there tonight," he muttered unhappily.

"It'll be the same in here if you don't close the damned door," Stand grumbled.

"You close it. I gotta warm up. I think I'm comin' down with something."

Stand scowled, but saw that Gregory was determined not to leave the warmth of the stove. Mumbling to himself, he stomped across the room and grabbed the edge of the door. Then suddenly he glanced back at Gregory. "Wait a minute. How did you hear about the old man?"

Gregory looked up and grinned. "I didn't," he said softly.

There was a flash of motion at the edge of Stand's vision, and the next instant a pistol was jammed into the side of his throat. He turned very slightly and saw a huge man with a beefy face smiling at him from the other end of a Walther P-38. The man's smile widened, flashing crooked yellow teeth.

"How'd ya do?" he cackled. "Mind if I come in?"

Stand nodded. "A lot," he said, and swung the door hard, smacking it into the man's brutish face. The man was sent reeling, cracking his head into the doorframe. His eyes rolled back and he slid slowly down to a sitting position, his head hanging loosely to one side. Stand ground his boot into the man's gun hand and kicked the weapon away from him. Then he bent down to pick it up.

That was when the sky fell in. He tumbled over, dropping onto his side, blinking rapidly. The lights had started to flicker. His head was throbbing like organ bellows. He peered up through a deepening haze and focused briefly on a stark white face with the palest eyes he had ever seen. His eyes clouded over and there was nothing at all.

CHAPTER 20

FIGHTING BACK to consciousness was like peeling the scab off an ugly sore. Stand woke slowly, reluctantly. He groaned and held his head as if he feared it might roll off his shoulders. Every heartbeat sent a new pulsing pain darting through his skull. He was still being watched by those pale haunting eyes.

"Who are you?" Stand muttered. "What do you want?"

"That should be obvious, Mr. Stand. I want the stockpile."

"What stockpile?"

"Come now, you're not going to be stubborn, are you? It won't do you any good. You will tell me what I wish to know, eventually. It will be far easier for all concerned if you do not waste my time."

Stand crawled onto one of the hard wooden chairs and sat up cautiously. The world spun dizzily, then slowed, and gradually the room came into focus. He saw a slender, sharp-featured man in a chair behind him, an Uzi machine pistol resting casually in his lap. The large brute he had knocked down was sitting by the table, with the Walther back in his hand. It was trained on Stand. There was a large blue-black bruise forming on the man's temple, swelling and threatening to close one eye. Stand smiled at that.

The pale-faced man kneeled in front of him and examined Stand carefully, flashing a penlight into his eyes to see that his pupils were centered and undilated. He nodded as if pleased. "You do not seem to have suffered a concussion. That is good. I wish your mind to be clear so you will have no trouble answering my questions."

"I'm not answering anything."

"Oh, but you will, Mr. Stand. It would be foolish to believe you can resist me. Tunney will be only too glad to persuade you. I'm afraid you made him very angry with the way you knocked him down."

"It was a cheap shot," the big man interjected. "He caught me off guard."

"Yes, of course," Falstaff said dryly. "I would guess that Mr. Stand is very good at catching people off guard."

"Let me 'ave a go at him. We'll see how bleedin' good he is."

"Patience, Tunney, patience," Falstaff said. He looked back to Stand and shook his head sadly. "You see? He is eagerly hoping that you will prove uncooperative. Despite his appearance, Tunney is quite clever, Mr. Stand, and has a remarkable knowledge of the most frail and painful points of the human anatomy. If you are so foolish as to prove difficult, I will have to permit Tunney to question you in his own rather crude but inventive manner."

Stand looked the big man over and bared his teeth in a grim smile. "Is that the best you could do? You'd better take that gun away from him before he shoots himself in the foot."

Tunney growled and covered the space to Stand in one quick lunge. He swung the pistol, lashing Stand across the face. Stand jerked his head back, turning just in time to deflect the blow, but not completely. A gash opened on his cheek, and he tasted the coppery tang of his own blood as it trickled onto his lips.

"Not bad. You almost hurt me. With a little practice, you might get the hang of it."

The man sneered angrily and raised his hand.

"Enough," the leader barked. "Tunney, sit down. You will not allow him to provoke you."

"I don't let no one talk to me like that," the big man grunted. "I'm going to close his wise-ass mouth."

"You will do nothing of the kind. We will not waste time with your self-indulgences. Can you not see that he wishes to anger you into such actions merely to delay us? Now, sit down and don't move until I tell you to."

Tunney's face was a mask of rage. He glared at Stand, then hissed out a long breath and returned to his seat. Slowly, deliberately, he raised the pistol and sighted at Stand down the barrel. His lips moved soundlessly, mimicking two shots. Boom-boom. He grinned happily.

Stand shrugged, as if he couldn't be bothered with children's games, and turned back to the leader. "He sits on command pretty well. I'm impressed. But I'll bet you don't have him toilet-trained yet."

"You do not fool me, Mr. Stand. You talk too much and your voice is bright and breathless. I can sense your fear."

Stand looked at him squarely and said, "You remind me of a slimy thing I found once under a very flat rock."

A brittle light of anger glittered in Falstaff's eyes, but he kept his voice low and controlled. "Do you still refuse to tell me the location of the stockpile?"

Stand said nothing.

"You are a very foolish man. Foolish men are often stubborn, and I shall not let you try my patience any longer. Fortunately, there are alternative methods that I'm sure will earn your attention. Tell me, Mr. Stand—are you as insensitive to the pain of others as to your own?" Falstaff signaled to the third man. "Oates, show Mr. Stand our other guests."

The man slung the Uzi across one shoulder and walked toward the stove. He paused beside one of the cots and suddenly flung off the blanket. Stand's breath caught in his throat. Stretched out on the bed, trussed and gagged, was Meghan Foster. She glanced about the room and then her gaze came to rest on Stand. Her eyes filled with something dark and unreadable. Stand's heart was pounding. He knew he couldn't blame her if she hated him, loathed him for bringing this terror into her life.

Then Oates tugged the blanket off a second cot, and the pain in Stand's heart became unbearable. Little Lynnie Foster lay sprawled out like a broken doll, eyes closed and very quiet. She was not gagged, but her breathing was uneven and labored.

"You bastard. What did you do to them? They have nothing to do with this."

"I knew you would be difficult. It is regrettable that I must act against children, but such are the fortunes of war."

"What war? What are you raving about?"

Falstaff smiled consolingly. "I knew you would not understand. Only a special few are honored with the gift of enlightenment. Everyone is at war, Mr. Stand, in torment to free themselves of the bonds of the mundane fantasy called life. The people of this world are oppressed, held fast by the chains of their own narrow minds, the shackles of delusion. But soon, very soon, they will know the truth and they will shake off the tyranny of this sordid existence. The world will quake in a holy cleansing of blood and the spiritual release of terror."

"You're mad," Stand whispered.

"No, I am the point at which the physical and the transcendent intersect, the Cross. I have been chosen to show the world that truth lies along a different path. Death is real, not this sentient delusion of the flesh. We die and revert to our natural state. Death is eternal and right. Life is an anomaly. Pain and fear are signs that the soul is struggling to achieve its true state of transcendence."

Stand said quietly, "I would be very happy to help you achieve your final true state."

Falstaff stared at him. "You think you mock me, but you cannot. Your words give me hope. They are an expression of a deeper love that you and the world merely do not yet understand. But I shall bring them the truth. It is my destiny. I was born in death so that I might lead others to that holy and tranquil state. In their fear of me, they shall be united, and in death they shall be delivered."

Stand was breathless, appalled by the depth of the man's

madness. But he struggled to keep his emotions from his face. "I don't understand," he said. "How is it that you were born in death? Who are you?"

Falstaff studied him cannily. "You cannot fool me so easily, Mr. Stand. You are not interested in hearing the truth. You only wish to make me lower my guard, to delay me, perhaps in hopes that the woman will return. Your pitiful efforts will not succeed." He looked at Tunney and made a quick motion with his hand. "Open the trapdoor."

The big man bared his teeth in a wide grin. He went over and pushed one of the cots aside, then bent down and hooked his finger through a small ring Stand had not noticed earlier. He tugged hard. There was a loud groaning of warped wood and rusty metal. Then a trapdoor swung open in his hand.

"One of the abandoned mine shafts," Falstaff explained, confirming Stand's fear. "We discovered it while you were unconscious. I think it should prove helpful to our discussion."

Stand could smell the foul air wafting up from the tunnel, and was suddenly afraid. "What are you going to do?"

Falstaff ignored him and motioned to his henchman. Oates seized a handful of Meghan's hair and pulled her up roughly. "No," Falstaff said. "Take the child."

The man pushed Meghan back down and moved toward Lynnie. Meghan's eyes grew round and she thrashed about wildly, fighting against her bonds. Falstaff watched her futile efforts appreciatively. "This woman has much spirit," he said. "Her passing will be a moment of great cosmic significance."

Stand tensed, preparing to launch himself from the chair. As if reading his thoughts, Falstaff produced a pistol and aimed it at Stand's chest. "Remain as you are. I can easily stop you without killing you. There is only one way you can help them—that is to tell me what I want."

Oates bent over to pick up Lynnie. Tunney stepped in and pushed the man aside. "I want to do it." He gathered the child in his arms and lifted her as if she weighed nothing at all. Lynnie moaned softly in her drugged sleep. The brute glanced over his shoulder to make sure Stand was watching. Then he moved to the edge of the trapdoor.

"Well, Mr. Stand?" Falstaff asked quietly. "The tunnel is over forty meters deep, straight down to a bed of solid rock. It will be a quick end for the child. Even from here, I imagine we will feel her soul passing over."

Tunney held Lynnie over the hole, holding her easily with one hand. She dangled like a puppet as he shook her playfully. The child awoke and let out a cry of terror.

"Ah, that is good," Falstaff said. "She is alert. The moment will be heightened by her fear. Talk now or Tunney will drop her."

Stand could feel Meghan's eyes upon him. She was emitting soft noises, grunts and gurgling, trying to scream around the gag in her mouth. He couldn't face her. Instead, he glared at Falstaff with a steely gaze. "You're dead men, all of you. That's a promise."

"Your threats are meaningless. Say the word quickly or the child is gone."

Meghan rolled off the cot with a thud. Still bound and gagged, she struggled to crawl toward her daughter.

Falstaff sighed. "You had your chance. This is upon your head."

Tunney raised Lynnie high.

"No! Stop!"

Falstaff barked at Tunney and held out his hand. "Wait." He turned to Stand with a broad smile. "You have come to your senses?"

Stand's face might have been chiseled from stone. An expelled breath grated between his tightly drawn lips. "Let her go. You win."

"Of course. It was inevitable."

Tunney frowned, disappointed. He threw the child aside and seized Meghan, dragging her back toward the cot. His hands pawed her breasts roughly. Meghan butted him in the face with the top of her head and Tunney yelped. He touched a finger to a split lip, cursed, and threw her to the floor.

Stand was half out of his chair when Falstaff stopped him

with a sharp command. He waved the pistol, motioning Stand back to his seat.

"No more rough stuff," Stand said. "No one touches them, or you'll never get the stockpile. They both go free or there's no deal."

Falstaff nodded. "They are nothing to me. When I have what I want, they will be released."

Fully awake now, Lynnie whimpered and crawled to her mother's side, huddled up against her. Meghan nuzzled the child, wrapping her body around her protectively. Stand's heart broke at the sight. It was much like an image seared in his memory from a time long ago, when a child named Melissa had spent days cowering beneath the body of her dead mother.

"I'll tell you everything," Stand said hoarsely. "You can have the stockpile. Just don't harm them."

"You must do more than tell me. You will show me where it can be found. You shall personally lead me to the stockpile while the woman and her child remain here. If you try to fool me or to escape, they will die. Make no mistake, their lives will be in my hands until the stockpile is mine."

Stand stared at the two people he loved, curled up on the floor, quivering with fear like two animals cowering in the back of a cave.

"I won't make any mistakes," he said.

Jean drove frantically, bouncing along the rocky trail between the fells. A full moon illuminated the stark landscape, a lonely vista of bare mountains and dark wooded valleys, fast-running streams winding down from the higher slopes. The path had been unused since the mines had closed, and it was rough going, so for several miles she could do nothing but concentrate on her driving. It was not until she left the foothills and pulled onto a paved country road that she was able to turn her mind to the news of her father's illness.

It was well past midnight, and she had the road to herself, so she put her foot down and raced along. Her mind was moving even faster. Her father had been ill for a long time, and she had been dreading this moment, knowing that it would come, but uncertain how to react. It wasn't fair. There was so much they had never learned about each other, so many things they had never said or shared. They had not been close, but recently there had been signs of a developing bond in the mutual intensity they each brought to their work. Jean had never wanted anything more than the assurance of her father's love. Now, it seemed she might never have the chance to earn it.

The end was near for him. She had known that for some time, but clung to a faith in his sheer stubbornness and tenacity, that a man like Daniel McWilliam would not surrender to death easily or soon. But it seemed even McWilliam's formidable will had limits. It was so unfair that his final collapse had occurred when she was far away. Thank God that James had brought her the news while there was still time. She prayed that what she would learn over the phone would be promising, at least that he would be able to hold on until she could reach his side.

Then an odd thought flashed through her mind, and Jean frowned. How had James learned of it? He had been driving nearly all day, as had she, since the early morning capture of Stand. Had he stopped somewhere to contact the Company? If so, why? She wasn't familiar with the van he had arrived in, but she doubted that it was equipped with a phone like the one in her rental car. The phone that had chosen such a damned inconvenient time to break down.

Suddenly it struck her. Jean slammed on the brakes, bringing the car to a skidding halt. James had known her car phone wasn't working. He had told her it was broken before she went out to check it herself. But how could he have known that? The car was locked, and Jean had the only keys.

Feeling queasy in her stomach, Jean got out and walked around the car to inspect the passenger's door. Deep scratches around the lock glowed in the beam of her flashlight. When she inserted her key, the entire lock spun loosely within its housing. She stared at it, her queasiness becoming a sharp tingle of fear. The door had been forced.

Climbing back inside, Jean stretched out on the seat and groped around the floorboards, inspecting the back of the telephone transmitter. It took only a minute to locate the broken wire.

She sat up and closed her door quickly, feeling chilled. It was not the night air that made her shiver. Something was wrong, very wrong. With a sudden certainty, she knew the story about her father was a lie. It had been intended to lure her away from the safe house, to leave James alone with Stand. But why? What possible motive could he have had for such underhanded actions?

Jean's mind raced over the possibilities. She recalled the times she and James had spent together, his relentless curiosity about her work, how many questions he asked. She had always perceived it as a sign of his loving concern, wanting to know about the business that filled so much of her life. Could it have been something more than that, something sinister? She remembered the many secrets she had shared with him, and the spate of embarrassing failures the Company and Office had suffered in recent years, operations thwarted before they had barely begun, agents exposed or captured, communication codes and sensitive information turning up in the hands of the opposition.

James a double agent? It was impossible, unthinkable. Could she have been so blind, entrusting not only her body and soul—but also her nation's secrets—to a man who was a traitor? Her mind reeled at the idea, refusing to accept it.

There was only one way to know the truth. The tires left black tread marks on the road when Jean spun the car in a squealing turn and headed back.

The return drive was even rougher, for Jean warily chose to drive without headlights. Every rock and ditch and sinkhole seemed to turn up directly in her path. She withstood the jolting ride without complaint, so wrapped up with her newly arisen fears that she barely noticed the discomfort.

As the mine site grew near, she slowed the car to a crawl so that the noise would not alert anyone in the safe house. She pulled off the trail half a mile away and hid the car be-

hind a huge granite boulder. She got out, zipping her coat up
tight, and started to climb the nearest fell. It was hard work
clambering up the steep scrabble, but she didn't stop for a
breath until she had reached the summit.

Lying down on the cold stone, Jean pulled out a pair of
binoculars and trained them on the distant safe house. The
van was out front, and all seemed quiet. She watched it for
several minutes, feeling the cold creep into her bones, growing stiff and half numb from remaining so still. She was
about to give up and reconsider another approach when she
spotted a flash of movement by a pile of debris at the corner
of the safe house.

Jean refocused the binoculars and peered intently. A figure
straightened from behind the pile of rubble. It was Gregory.
He stomped his feet and pounded his chest, as if to get his
circulation going again. Then he ducked down once more out
of the wind.

She lowered the glasses, frowning in bewilderment. It
looked as if James were keeping watch. Jean felt certain now
that her fears had been well founded.

A minute later she saw a splash of light when the door to
the safe house opened. She raised the glasses again and
watched as Stand trudged out with his hands tied behind his
back, flanked by one large man and a second, slighter figure.
The second man had an Uzi dangling from a strap around his
neck.

Jean didn't breathe. Gregory appeared from behind his
windbreak and walk out to join the others. A third stranger
came outside and pounded Gregory on the back. They chatted briefly while the big man shoved Stand in the back of the
van and slammed the door. Gregory and the last man climbed
in front and drove away. The other two men didn't wave or
show any interest in the departure, but quickly turned their
backs and hurried to the warmth of the barracks.

Jean lowered the binoculars and watched the headlights
weave though the foothills. With its higher clearance, the van
had an easy time with the rock trail. The van passed by her

hidden car without slowing and rattled on, disappearing from view.

For a minute longer, she lay there stunned and confused. It was clear something terrible was going on. They had taken Stand, and that could mean only one thing. They were after the stockpile. It would be impossible to climb down in time to follow them, and there was no way to guess where they might be taking him.

With a sinking feeling, Jean knew there was only one course of action open, one man she could turn to. She tucked the binoculars inside her coat and started the tricky climb back down to her car. It seemed she would be placing a call to Washington tonight, after all.

The *Doroughty* was a humpback beggar of a boat. Two coats of new paint did nothing to conceal its age or condition. If anything, the paint made it appear more tawdry, like an old hooker trying to plaster over wrinkles with makeup.

Stand scraped his toe along the deck and raised splinters with which he could have speared fish. "Where did you get this bucket?" he asked Falstaff. "At a garage sale?"

"We did not have time to charter the *Q.E. Two*," the terrorist said sourly. "The vessel will remain afloat long enough for us to recover the stockpile, and that is all that matters." Falstaff was not a seaman. They had barely cleared the harbor before he went below to be sick in privacy. Stand was comforted by the thought of his puking up his guts, and he prayed for rough weather.

They sailed from Oban and headed west into the deep Atlantic, to clear the Hebrides before swinging north for the Orkneys, the range of small islands off the northernmost tip of Scotland. It was the long way around, but Falstaff was concerned about secrecy and had ordered the skipper to avoid the congested traffic in the sea lane dividing the Inner and Outer Hebrides.

The *Doroughty* rode smoothly, despite Stand's misgivings about the boat's condition. The first day he spent locked up below with the others. Falstaff lay in his bunk, not moving,

while Gregory, though not as troubled by seasickness, seemed
content to do the same.

The two men Falstaff had taken on, Bradleigh and O'Conner, sat at the table exercising their elbows over bottles of
beer, and their minds over an endless game of gin. They were
divers, rough-hewn men who had learned their trade in the
navy, then went to work servicing offshore rigs in the North
Sea oil industry. Apart from a daily check of their gear, they
seldom left their chairs, playing cards and speaking in a cryp-
tic shorthand, in the way of men who had been together a
long time and knew each other's stories.

Garrison, the boat's skipper, kept to himself in the wheelhouse and showed little interest in his passengers or their
business. He was a tall round man who looked like Santa
Claus gone to seed. His long full beard was gray rather than
white, unkempt and grizzled with tangled split ends curling
and snagging on the buttons of his loud plaid shirt. He chewed
Skoal, packing his cheek every ten minutes or so, but never
spit or even removed it. As far as Stand could tell, the man
ate the stuff.

On the second day out, Garrison called down in a bellow-
ing foghorn voice. "Would ya send the big bearded one topside?" he asked. "The weather's lookin' to take a nasty turn,
and I could do with a good hand to help tighten up the old
girl."

Falstaff groaned and leaned out from his bunk to talk into
the intercom. "In case you've forgotten, Stand is a prisoner.
I'll send Bradleigh up to help you out."

"That one?" Garrison sneered. "I need a sailor, not a
sort who spends his time with the fishes. I'll take Stand.
There's no place for him to go. We're all prisoners until we
make land, don'tcha know?"

"I don't want him looking for a chance to take over the
boat."

"If he does, then all ya have to do is walk in and shoot
him. The wheelhouse is no fortress, and you've the only
shooters aboard, sir."

"All right, all right," Falstaff said irritably, and clutched his nauseated stomach. "Off with you, Stand. But remember, we'll be keeping an eye on you."

Stand wasted no time getting out of the tiny cabin, grateful for the reprieve. He paused on the afterdeck, breathing deeply and taking in the sight of sky and sea. The sea was choppy, and rain slapped at the planking, but the weather looked hardly as threatening as Garrison had suggested.

"There ya be," the skipper said cheerfully when Stand entered the wheelhouse. "Come in, laddie, and close that door. Here, wrap yourself around this lot." He gave Stand a cup of steaming coffee.

"I thought you were concerned about the weather."

"Ach, nonsense, lad. I jest thought ya might like a chance to come topside for a spell. It canna be much fun down there with that lot being sick on themselves. Take a chair, make yourself to home."

"How did you know I'm a seaman?"

"I can always tell. Knew it the moment ya stepped aboard. I could see ya wasn't like the others, even before they told me how's ya was to be shut up and watched over. A sorry lot, they are, but their brass is good, so I'm not complaining."

Stand smiled and drank some coffee. It was black, strong enough to strip paint, and it tasted marvelous.

Garrison reached into a locker and brought up a bottle of cheap Scotch. "Would ya like a touch to sweeten it?"

Stand stared at the bottle for about ten seconds, then shook his head. "No, I guess not."

"Suit yourself, then." Garrison shrugged and splashed a full ounce into his own cup, tasted it, then sat back with a contented sigh. "Ah, this is the life, ain't it, lad? The sea, a good boat, and a cup of something to warm your insides. There's naught better this life can offer."

"I'm tempted to agree," Stand said. "Given a few different circumstances."

"Ah, yes. I'm forgettin' you're a prisoner here, ain't I? Well, that's neither here nor there, as I sees it. I dinna know

why they've snatched ya, and what they're about—and I dinna
care to know. They're payin' me a grand wage, and that's
where me curiosity stops."

"You're making a mistake. You don't know what sort of
men they are. Once they get what they want, they're going
to kill me. And the same is true for you."

"Get on with ya. I can take care of myself. That lot dinna
seem so tough."

Stand sighed and fired up his pipe. "Just a friendly warning; you don't have to listen. But if you're smart, you'll watch
your back."

"It's not drugs, is it?" Garrison asked quietly.

"No, nothing like that."

"Good." The barrel-chested skipper whistled in relief.
"That's one thing I dinna hold for—seen too much of that, I
have, in Africa, the Orient, even here in the Isles, I'm sorry
to say. It's evil what that junk does to a man; rots him inside,
twists his mind all around something queer. I seen men—
good men I shipped with and proud to call mates—go sour
and hungrylike, to where they'd sell their own daughters for
a taste of the needle." He shuddered and took a quick gulp
from his cup. "Naught for me, lad. Whisky and cigarettes,
that's all I deals in."

Stand said, "Alcohol and nicotine—but no drugs, huh?"

"That's right. Jest good clean products that people wants
and needs. And if I can help them get what they wants without the government takin' a bite off the top, then who's the
worse for it? So I says." He saw no contradiction there, and
Stand didn't press it.

They fell into an easy silence then, both of them peering out
at the sea. Rain pounded on the wheelhouse, hammering the
glass in front of them, but the wind and rain only made the cabin seem more cozy. They stared out across the water the way
some people sat entranced before a fire in a hearth, watching
it change form almost like a living creature.

Stand glanced to the west. A course change of a few de-
grees, then straight ahead for a couple thousand miles and he

would be in Innesmore. There was nothing between him and home but open ocean.

"Ya know why I asked ya up here?" Garrison asked suddenly. "I was thinkin' over that name of yours. I heard of a man with that name before—Duncan Stand, it was. He were a salvage man, worked out of Canada and the northeast States."

"My father," Stand said. "How did you hear of him?"

"I think it were in Lloyd's I first saw the name. Accounts of him saving one ship and another. And then I sailed with a man who said he'd worked with him. A right old bastard was what he called him, but he did say there were none better at the game. He worked his crews to death, so this mate said, but they were all happy enough because he knew how to save ships, and there was good money in it. Lord, yes, that's been some time ago. So that's your da, think of that."

"Was," Stand said. "He went down in fifty-four, trying to pull the last three crewmen from a tanker that grounded on a reef called The Serpents."

Garrison clucked sadly, the sound rattling in his mouth like loose dentures. "I'm right sorry to hear that, lad. I never did more than hear or read about your da, but from that I gathered he was a real man."

"He was all of that."

"Fancy me meeting the whelp of Duncan Stand. The world's a funny old place, ain't it?"

"Sure. I'll probably laugh myself to sleep tonight."

A scowl darkened Garrison's grizzled face. His eyes were like the sea, murky and always changing. "I guess I canna blame ya for feelin' that way. It's a right shame we had to meet like this, us caught on different sides-like, but there's naught to be done about it."

"You could always change sides."

"None of that now," Garrison growled. "I'll not sit still for ya tryin' to turn me head. I've taken me charter, and I always see a job through."

"They'll kill you," Stand said flatly. "These men are serious trouble."

Garrison laughed. "And what man isn't trouble to another? I want no more of this talk. Dinna mistake me, lad. It's sorry I am that Duncan Stand's son and I are on the different sides we are, but dinna think that will matter a whit when push comes to shove. I'm gettin' a lot of brass for this trip, and the money's all that matters. It's all that ever does."

"You've sold yourself to the devil, Garrison."

"That so? Well, his brass is good as another's, I expect."

The silence that fell between them this time was more tense, and Stand agreeably changed the subject. "I have to admit I was wrong about this bucket," he said. "The *Doroughty* seems fit and rides smoothly."

Garrison's face split in a wide grin. "Surprised ya, did she? There's a lesson for ya, lad. The old lady's not what she appears, but then ya didn't look too close, did ya?"

"I thought she'd be sluggish and leak like a sieve," Stand admitted.

Garrison was clearly delighted. "Ya only looked topside, lad, and saw exactly what ya was supposed to see. I let her look like an old whore, but the hull is tight and there's Penta engines pushing her along."

"You sneaky bastard," Stand said, with a bemused toss of his head. "You've got a racer disguised as a floating trash heap. What'll she do?"

"Well, maybe not as fast as ya think, but she'll rear up and move right along when I needs her to. Speed's not the end all—there's always a faster boat—but she's quicker than what ya expect her to be, and that's edge enough to see me outta tight spots."

Stand hesitated, then said, "Not the one you're in now. You won't be able to run from this, Garrison. The whole world is endangered by the thing these people are after."

"Of course, the whole world," Garrison said sarcastically. "Dinna I tell ya to leave off with that talk? I think it's time ya went back below, lad."

Stand shrugged and got to his feet. "Thanks for the coffee." He paused at the door and looked back. "Think about what I said. Promise me that much."

The grizzled old smuggler didn't respond. He packed his cheek with a fresh wad of Skoal and busied himself with a compass and a faded chart. Stand turned away with regret, lowered his head, and moved out into the rain.

CHAPTER 21

THE ORKNEYS were a group of small islands separated from the northern coast of Scotland by the Pentland Firth, which at its narrowest point was about six and a half miles. Of the sixty-seven islands, only twenty-nine were inhabited, the total population numbering around seventeen thousand people. Stand led Garrison to one of the westernmost islands where the land rose from the sea in a sheer towering cliff. Bradleigh and O'Conner put down their cards and got to work.

The divers were lowered into the water clinging to a sled, a simple metal platform on the end of a long cable, and Garrison began towing them across the seabed where Stand claimed the *Keegan* had gone under.

It was tedious work, trailing back and forth. Stand stood in the wheelhouse at Garrison's side. Falstaff and Gregory were close behind him, watchful of his every move.

The divers came up twice to change tanks and to warm themselves over cups of steaming tea. The water in this region was warmed by the Gulf Stream, but after hours of immersion, even in their protective wet suits, they were shivering and clacking their teeth as if frozen through.

Finally, in late afternoon, Garrison glanced up and raised an eyebrow at Stand. "Did ya feel it, lad? The old girl gave a slight tug. I think one of them has left the sled."

Sure enough, a few moments later, a bright orange balloon

broke the surface of the sea, and Bradleigh bobbed up beside the marker. They circled and winched in the sled, O'Conner coming aboard alone.

"We got it," he said. "She's thirty meters down, lying on a shelf and sitting up nice as you please. We'll have no problem breaking into the hold."

"Good," Falstaff said. "You may proceed immediately."

"No way. We've been down too long already. It'll wait for the morning."

"That is not good enough. I demand that you begin now."

O'Conner sneered and shook his head wearily. "I don't care what you demand. We're beat. Another few minutes in that water and we'll start suffering hypothermia. No body heat. You lose coordination and your mind gets fuzzy. You stay under when that happens, you slip into a coma and you're good as dead."

Falstaff struck with the quickness of a snake. With his left hand, he shoved O'Conner back, his head slamming hard into the wall. In his right hand a knife appeared magically from nowhere, and he touched the tip to the underside of O'Conner's chin.

"You are as good as dead already," Falstaff hissed, "if you think to challenge my orders. You will do as I command, or die here and now." A trickle of blood trailed down from the point of the sharp-edged knife.

O'Connor glared back defiantly, his voice low and calm. "Then go ahead and do it. Do it now."

Garrison turned from the wheel, his eyes widening in alarm. Stand whispered to him, "Watch closely. This may give you an idea how to plan your future."

Gregory hovered at Falstaff's shoulder. "He's no good to us dead," he said nervously. "We can't bring the thing up by ourselves."

"Shut up, James. Stay out of this."

"You'd better listen to him," O'Conner said. "You'll never recover those crates with one man. Even if Charlie would try it alone. You'll probably have to kill him, too. And then who'll dive on the wreck? You?"

"We have been at sea too long," Falstaff grumbled, wavering. "I want the job finished. There have been too many delays and troublesome interference. I will not have my plans ruined because of your incompetence."

"You'll have what you want," O'Conner said. "In the morning. The job will go fast. By noon, we'll have the wreck emptied. Now, swing around and pick up my partner before he freezes to death out there."

Falstaff pulled back the knife as quickly as he had drawn it. "So be it. But remember, I will tolerate no more delays." He turned his back with disdain, then looked at Gregory and snapped, "Get Stand below. He's not needed up here."

"Won't be long till I'm not needed at all," Stand whispered to Garrison. "Any bets what will happen then?"

"It's your problem, lad. Not mine."

"No," Stand said. "Not yet."

They started as the sun edged over the land, the cliff casting a long shadow that reached across the sea to where they labored. The heavy metal cable was slowly played out, and Bradleigh and O'Conner guided it down to the sunken wreck. Within thirty minutes the signal was given, and the winch started raising the first crate.

They swung it aboard. Falstaff stood on the afterdeck, his eyes gleaming. He made a pretense at remaining calm, but it was clear to the other men how anxious he was. He signaled to them to break the crate open the instant it touched the deck.

Gregory and Stand picked up crowbars and pried off the top, then climbed up on the railing to peer inside the crate.

"Well?" Falstaff asked.

Gregory shook his head. "It's nothing but rocks."

"Empty it."

Grudgingly, Stand climbed into the crate and began tossing rocks over the side. It was hard work, and soon he was sweating underneath his heavy sweater. He didn't mind. Each stone represented another moment he had clung to life. He threw out every last one, until there was nothing below his feet but the bare wood of the crate's bottom.

"Nothing," Gregory called to Falstaff. "This one's not it."

The terrorist scowled. "Throw it overboard to clear room for the next."

Stand and Gregory heaved over the crate, then sat down wearily. Stand watched Falstaff, leaning against the rail, glaring out at the sea and looking pale and miserable. Falstaff's seasickness had been a source of delight to Stand, and he hoped they could prolong it as much as possible. It was a crap shoot—they had only to find one crate out of ten. Stand prayed the stockpile would not appear until the very last one.

But Falstaff's luck was better than that. The second crate was as empty as the first, and the third the same. But the moment they broke into the fourth crate Stand's heart sank.

"There's something different about this one," Gregory said. "It's full of sand."

Stand climbed inside and began scooping it out with an old coffee can. He labored about ten minutes and then the can clanked against something metallic. Gregory motioned excitedly to Falstaff, and the two men gathered around the crate while Stand bailed out the rest of the sand. "Signal Bradleigh and O'Conner to cease work and return to the surface," Falstaff ordered Garrison.

In a little while Stand had cleared out half of the sand remaining, and the object became slowly visible. The divers reappeared, clambering over the side. They joined Falstaff and Gregory in a huddle around the crate.

"Bring it out," Falstaff said softly.

Stand wedged his crowbar under the object and pried it free. He bent down and tugged it with his hands. It was heavy but not unmanageable, and he lifted it clear of the crate, handing it over to Bradleigh and O'Conner. They gently lowered it to the deck.

It was innocent enough in appearance, a small aluminum cask much like a beer keg. There was a pressure gauge on the top, and along one side a black metal box contained what

Stand assumed was some sort of detonating device. He climbed out of the empty crate and edged slowly toward the wheelhouse while the men chattered and congratulated themselves. Falstaff went down on one knee, examining the detonator with a professional eye, and smiled delightedly.

Garrison stood in the wheelhouse door, peering down at the afterdeck with an uneasy expression. "Is that the bloody thing they were after?" he asked quietly.

"I'm afraid so," Stand said.

"What is it, lad?"

"A biochemical bomb." Stand looked up at the grizzled old smuggler. "Do you know what anthrax is?"

"Aye. Me family kept sheep. There were an outbreak of anthrax in the country and three of our lambs caught the nasty stuff. We had to kill and burn the whole flock, we did, even them what wasn't sick. A terrible thing." He frowned thoughtfully.

"Concentrated anthrax," Stand said. "There are enough spores in that thing to kill thousands, maybe millions."

"You're serious, lad?"

"I wish I weren't."

"How did it get here? Where did a thing like that come from?"

"The government. My country and the British developed it during the war."

Garrison scowled. "I shoulda known the bloody English would be behind it." He shook his head grimly. "Well, it's a right dreadful thing, but I canna think I'll lose any sleep over it. It's not on my head what happens to a bunch of cattle and sheep."

"It affects people, too," Stand said.

The burly smuggler's eyes grew alarmed.

Stand nodded. "That thing can wipe out a whole city."

"What do ya suppose he means to do with it, our pale-faced tyrant?"

"I don't know," Stand admitted. "You've seen what sort of man he is. He's insane. What do you suppose?"

"Dear God, what are we involved in, lad?"

"Deep trouble. You know what the stakes are now. Do you still believe they'll let you just walk away?"

Garrison pulled out a round container of Skoal. Slowly and deliberately, he pinched out some of the black tobacco and wedged it in his cheek. His hand returned the container to his pocket. When he brought his hand out again, it was holding a 9 mm Luger. "Move aside, lad," he said gently.

"Garrison, don't—"

"Out of the way," the old smuggler grumbled, his voice firmer. "This is my business now."

Hesitantly, Stand backed toward the rail. He watched Garrison take a deep breath and straighten his back with dignity. "You there!" he called in his deep booming voice. "Stand up and move away from that bloody thing."

The men clustered around the stockpile glanced up. Falstaff's face stiffened in annoyance. "What do you think you're doing?"

"I'm takin' over, is what. Now, do what I says, and easy-like. The first one of ya what moves sudden will find a bullet in his gut."

Gregory trembled and raised his hands in surrender. "Don't shoot. I haven't done anything." Falstaff edged in behind him.

Garrison noticed the movement and growled. "What a right bloody bastard ya are, hidin' behind yer own mates. Move out here so's I can see ya clear."

Gregory glanced around anxiously, saw Falstaff behind him, and quickly stepped aside. Falstaff was revealed in a casual pose, one hand slightly raised. The pistol in his hand coughed three times.

Stand saw Garrison stumble back, all three bullets thudding into his chest. Then Stand threw himself over the rail.

The sea closed over his head, and the cold was like a physical blow, sucking air and strength from his body. He came up again in the last place he hoped they would look for him, directly aft, next to the propeller screws. He took a breath, then pulled himself under the boat. He kicked off the dangerous weight of the water-filled boots, then shrugged off his coat and wrapped it around the propeller shaft. If it started up now, he would be chewed to pieces. He had to slow them down somehow.

He rose cautiously and grabbed another lungful of air, then struck out at the tangent from the boat, parallel to the shore. He swam until his lungs were screaming, and finally angled up, bobbing to the surface.

His head broke through and he gulped sweet air. The boat was north of him, but still seemed perilously near. He heard a sharp cry and bullets ripped into the water around him. He drew in a deep breath and ducked under again. He swam hard, fighting to keep down panic and maintain a smooth steady stroke.

He shot up again quickly, seeing pale blue sky, and gunfire erupted the moment he appeared. He sucked in a breath and submerged again, continuing south. He barely felt the cold now, but he had no strength. It felt as if he had made no progress at all when he had to resurface. He didn't allow himself to look back for the boat, but ducked under and swam on. No gunfire sounded this time. It was a good sign.

The boat would have to raise anchor and winch in the cable before they could follow him. Stand prayed that would give him enough of a lead to make good his escape. At last he felt the current catching him, swinging him toward the shore. He was drifting north, back toward the cliff, but he thought if he swam hard he could make land before being tossed up on those jagged rocks. If he was wrong, then his pursuers wouldn't have to bother with him.

The current seemed to grow stronger the closer to land he came. Stand felt himself tiring, his arms and legs heavy, but he struggled grimly on. The shore loomed up, and he could hear the roar of the surf.

He struck something hard and was knocked aside. Stand raised his head. He was upon the rocks. The current tugged at him, trying to wrench him away, and he was carried side-long onto another boulder. He grabbed at it to catch himself. The sharp-edged stone slashed open his hand and he was dragged away. Like a pinball, he bounced from one rock to another, fighting landward, the frothy white surf closing over his head again and again.

Finally, he caught himself on a pinnacle of stone small enough to wrap his arms around. He hung desperately and lifted his head from the surf, panting deeply, gulping in air. His mind cleared and he glanced around, finding with deep relief that the shore was only yards away. He tentatively straightened his cold numb legs and felt solid ground beneath his feet. Releasing his hold on the stone, he waded through the pounding waves and dragged himself onto the shore.

For a minute, Stand lay there, his chest heaving in exhaustion. Then he rolled onto his back and peered out at the distant boat. He sat up quickly. There was a rubber raft pulling away from the *Doroughty*, moving fast under the power of an outboard motor. Bradleigh was at the controls and O'Conner sat in the bow with a rifle in his hands. They were skimming across the waves, racing directly toward him.

Stand swore and wearily climbed to his feet. He hadn't known Garrison carried a powered raft aboard. His hopes of getting away cleanly vanished. They would be ashore in only minutes.

He turned and scrambled up the slope. He was at the point where the shore began rising to form the cliff, and it took nearly all his remaining strength to scale the thirty-odd feet. When he reached the top, he cursed even more vehemently. The land swept away from the sea in smooth gentle hills. There was an ancient stone fence marking the borders of a farmer's meadow, but otherwise there was nothing, not even a tree for at least half a mile.

He would never be able to beat the two divers in an all-out footrace, not in his weary state. And they only had to get close enough to shoot. There was no choice. He would have to face them there.

Stand glanced back over his shoulder. The raft was drawing close to the shore, Bradleigh angling wide, searching for a safe place to put in. They were so close he saw the anger on their faces. Stand turned and forced himself into a stumbling run, wading through the high heather and gorse to the old stone fence.

It was like hundreds of other such fences to be found all over Great Britain, chest-high and almost two feet across. It was pieced together from loose stones and constructed without mortar, but so meticulously fitted that it had stood for centuries. Stand paused beside the fence and held out the hand that had been cut when he was dashed upon the rocks. His palm was sliced open in a line from his wrist to his fingers. He squeezed the wound viciously, forcing out a stream of blood, letting it drop on the stones. Then he clambered over the wall. He ran another twenty yards, doubled back following his own steps and threw himself down at the base of the fence. He lay there, panting, every sense alert, waiting.

It didn't take long. Stand heard their excited voices as they reached the top of the slope. "Open country. He won't get far."

"Look at the grass. Come on. He went this way."

Stand crouched on the other side of the wall, listening intently. They raced toward him, following his trail of trampled heather. His body was tensed, every muscle primed for quick action. He felt a dead calm as the noise of their labored breathing drew near.

The footsteps pounded up to the wall and stopped. He heard O'Conner almost directly over his head.

"Look, fresh blood. We must have winged him when he was still in the water. I told you I hit him that one time."

"Yeah, sure," Bradleigh grunted. "How do you know it wasn't me that got him?"

Stand listened, gauging the men's positions. The barrel of O'Conner's rifle edged over the wall. Stand's fist closed on a small stone.

"Trail goes off this way," O'Conner said. "Keep your eyes open. He may try to lie low somewhere, but we'll find him. There's no place to hide out here."

Stand rose suddenly, swinging his arm in a wide arc all the way from the ground. He smashed the stone into O'Conner's 'ace before the man could even cry out. O'Conner dropped imply, sprawling over the wall. Stand grabbed the rifle from his fingers and ducked down just as Bradleigh opened fire with a revolver. Bullets sang by in a wild pattern, some glancing off the stone, two thumping into the still form of O'Conner.

Bradleigh let out a gasp, and Stand heard the gun click on an empty chamber. He stood up and leveled the rifle.

"Drop it, Bradleigh."

The man scowled. "You made me kill my mate."

"It's not my doing. You should learn to aim before you shoot. Now toss the gun away. Gently."

Bitterly, the diver complied, throwing the gun into the grass. He took a step toward Stand.

"Stay right there. Don't even think about it."

"How is he?" Bradleigh asked, his voice desperate, anguished. "Did I kill him? I gotta know."

Holding the rifle steady with one hand, Stand reached out and searched for a pulse at O'Conner's neck. He frowned and bent lower. "I think he's still—"

Bradleigh was on him in a flash. The diver leaped atop the wall and launched himself at Stand. A long gutting knife glinted in the sun.

Stand got his arms up, crossing them in front of him just in time to ward off the thrusting blade. He grabbed at Bradleigh's wrist and the two men rolled over and over in the grass, struggling for control of the knife. Bradleigh jolted Stand with a left-hand blow to the side of the head, then rolled atop him, pressing with his superior weight, forcing the knife down toward Stand's throat.

Stand's face contorted with strain. The tip was inches from his neck and Bradleigh pushed it down with both hands, grinning as the knife edged lower. Stand spit. Bradleigh recoiled instinctively, for a moment diverted. Stand acted quickly, forcing the man's hands to the side and smashing his wrist into the stone wall. He hissed in pain and the knife clattered from his grip.

The diver howled in anger and his hands closed over Stand's

throat, his thumbs pressing at the windpipe. Stand struck at Bradleigh's face, but his blow fell short. The diver's longer arms kept him out of reach. Bradleigh laughed and pressed harder. Stand heard the gurgle in his own throat and felt himself starting to black out. In desperation, he arched his back and brought his legs up behind Bradleigh, scissored them around his head, then pushed him away.

Bradleigh snarled in anger. His grasp was broken and the two men pulled apart. Stand rolled over, groping for the knife, but Bradleigh fooled him and went for the fallen rifle. He picked it up and spun, the barrel swinging to bear.

Stand rose on one knee and tossed the knife in a flicking underhanded motion. The blade whistled through the air, flipping one half turn and burying itself in the center of Bradleigh's chest. He fell back, the rifle discharging harmlessly into the air.

Stand walked over and kicked the gun from Bradleigh's hands. The diver scowled up at him, coughed blood, and died.

Stand sat wearily atop the wall for a minute, catching his breath. He glanced out to sea at the *Doroughty*. The boat was slowly pulling away. His effort to jam the propellers had done little good. Now there was nothing to prevent Gregory and his friend from doing whatever it was they had in mind for the stockpile. Or from informing their associates at the Cumbrian safe house that their hostages were no longer needed.

Stand grew cold at the thought and pushed away from the wall. There was no time to be sitting around. He paused long enough to pull the boots from Bradleigh's feet and slip them on. They were a tight fit, but better than going barefoot. He had to move fast.

He walked inland for nearly two miles before he saw a farmhouse. It was a small cottage of whitewashed stone, with a steeply angled roof painted a bright red. He was nearly exhausted as he dragged himself across the fields and pushed through a Judas gate into the yard. There was an old man with a red weathered face pitching straw from the barn onto a wagon hitched to a broken-down tractor.

The farmer stopped when he saw Stand appear. He leaned on his pitchfork and put a stubby pipe between his teeth, then smiled uncertainly. "Now, ain't you a sight?" the farmer said. "Where did ya come from, lad? Looks like ya walked straight up outta the sea."

"There's been some trouble. Do you have a phone?" Stand asked.

"Aye, got one."

"Could I use it? It's important."

"Well, I don't know, exactly," the farmer said, scratching his chin.

"I'll pay for it," Stand said. "I've got money." He reached into his pocket and pulled out twenty pounds. The bills were soggy and stuck together. "It's wet, though."

The farm smiled. "That's all right, lad. Put that away. Seamus McOrbin has never taken money from a stranger in his life, least of all from one in trouble. Now, let's get ya by the fire and something warm inside ya."

Stand smiled gratefully and all but collapsed in the astonished man's arms.

Seamus McOrbin gave Stand a blanket and a cup of tea. He put another log in the hearth, then backed off and smoked his pipe quietly while Stand placed his call. The farmer's eyes opened incredulously when he heard Stand direct the operator to ring a number in Washington, D.C.

The familiar wheezy voice was on the line almost instantly. "Nathan, is that really you? Are you all right?"

"I'm alive, but listen closely, sir. I have a lot to explain."

"Jean has told everything," McWilliam said. "All is forgiven. Tell me where to reach you, Nathan. I'll have someone there within the hour."

Stand sat back, stunned. So Jean had been behind it all. She had gone to her father with the truth, admitting she had duped both of them. The cloud of suspicion was lifted from his head.

"There's only one priority now," McWilliam said. "We have to protect that stockpile."

"It's too late for that," Stand said softly.

McWilliam cursed under his breath. "Go ahead. I'm listening."

"I'll fill you in later. Right now, I have to get back to Cumbria. Send a plane for me."

"That's not necessary. A joint team of SAS and Company men has been watching over the safe house since Jean got word to me."

"You don't get it. They have hostages—people who are important to me."

"Hostages?" McWilliam said, startled. "I know nothing about that."

"It's the woman and child who took me in. Get that plane to me. One way or another, I'm going back. I won't leave them."

The old man spoke softly, picking his words with care. "I sympathize with your feelings, Nathan, but I need you back here immediately. The team watching over the safe house can move in to free the woman and her child."

"No," Stand said. "Not that way. No one goes in but me, do you understand? No one."

McWilliam was silent for a moment, and Stand realized that the phone was shaking wildly in his hand. His heart was beating so hard he feared it would burst through his chest.

"All right, Nathan," McWilliam said at last. "I do understand. I'll pass the word for them to expect you."

"Thank you, sir," Stand said breathlessly.

"Make your way to the beach. A seaplane will pick you up in exactly one hour. It will set you down on Lake Windemere and there'll be a car waiting to drive you to the safe house."

Stand got to his feet, his exhaustion suddenly forgotten. "Make it thirty minutes. I'll be there waiting."

"Be careful, Nathan," the old man said. The phone line clicked dead.

Stand hung up gently. He was aware of the farmer's eyes staring at him. "You heard most of that?"

Seamus McOrbin nodded solemnly. "Not that any of it made sense to me. What the hell are you involved in, lad?"

Stand shook his head slowly. He took out all his money and laid the damp bills on the table beside the phone. "I'm going to leave that here," he said. "Does that old tractor outside run? I have to get to the beach."

"You'll be leaving, I take it?" The old farmer stared down at the money. "And what is this—to buy my silence?"

"No," Stand said. "I won't need it where I'm going."

"And where might that be?"

There was no answer. McOrbin looked at Stand and something cold stirred inside him. He quickly passed a hand across his chest in the sign of a cross.

"What is it?" Stand asked.

"God help me, lad, but for a minute you looked like Death hisself."

Stand nodded. He understood perfectly.

CHAPTER 22

IT WAS nearly dusk when Stand joined up with the team keeping watch over the safe house. A baby-faced SAS lieutenant met him at the car and they covered the last half mile on foot. "Let me show you up to the ridge, sir," he said. "Colonel Parker is most anxious to meet you." He turned smartly on his heels and led him along a winding path between the hills, moving swiftly and surely despite the gathering darkness.

They emerged on a windswept plateau. Stand looked down on the building about two hundred yards away. In the moonlight it seemed quiet and peaceful. There was a glimmer of light showing through one of the boarded-over windows, and smoke billowed from the chimney. They crouched and ran across the ridge. The lieutenant pointed Stand to a field of large boulders. A man knelt behind an infrared telescope. He wore headphones attached to a miniature satellite dish that could pick up the minutest sounds from distances up to a quarter of a mile.

The lieutenant guided him away and they scrambled down the backside of the ridge, out of sight of the safe house. They went a short distance down the slope and came to a campsite. Three small tents were grouped around a fire. One of them was occupied by a man who snored softly.

Colonel Parker was sitting by the fire, smoking a cigarette. He was a small man, barely five feet five, but with an unmistakable strength and authority. His face was twisted in a lopsided grin. When Stand got closer he saw the expression was the result of a knife scar curling up from one corner of his mouth. Parker got to his feet and immediately stuck out a hand.

" 'Evening, sir. We had word to expect you."

Stand accepted the man's firm handshake. "What's the situation here?"

"Quiet. No one in or out. We saw a slender chap stick his head out once or twice, but otherwise they've kept to themselves."

"Good. Then they're still in there."

Parker nodded. "As best we can say. The last radio transmission mentioned something about hostages—a woman and a child?"

"That's right," Stand said. "I'm going to bring them out."

"Yes, so I was told." Parker threw his cigarette into the fire, then looked up at Stand. The solemn expression in his eyes conflicted with the crooked grin at his lips. "I don't really understand why you're here. I have to tell you, sir, it seems a large bit of nonsense for you to tackle those men alone."

"I don't care how it seems to you," Stand said. "That's the way it has to be. No interference, do you get that?"

"I have my orders," Parker said. "You're to be allowed to handle this any way you choose. I will follow my orders, even if they do sound bloody stupid."

"Keep your people back. That's all you have to remember. And the same goes for the Company surveillance. Where are they positioned?"

Parker smiled thinly. "Already cleared out, the lot of them. They left about an hour ago. I think these cold mountainsides aren't exactly the sort of accommodations they're used to."

"All right, good," Stand said. He saw McWilliam's hand in this and was grateful. "I'll need to borrow some of your gear."

"Anything you want. We have a lorry parked some distance back, stocked with provisions and equipment. Give me a list and I'll send a runner for it.''

''Thank you.'' Stand told him the items he needed. Parker roused the man in the sleeping bag and sent him to fetch them. The colonel took a cigarette from a silver case and tapped it several times before lighting it. Stand noticed how Parker automatically shielded the glowing end by cupping it in his hand; it was the habit of a man who had kept secret vigil on many dark nights.

''I think I know what you have in mind,'' Parker said. ''We of course considered the same possibility. The mining company provided some charts, but they're outdated and almost useless. Are you sure you can get in that way?''

''Later.'' Stand sighed. ''I'm too tired to talk about it now. Wake me around midnight. We'll hash it over then, just before I go.'' He stretched out on the ground near the fire, suddenly exhausted, too weary to remain awake a moment longer. He was nervous and his body reacted by demanding rest, recharging itself for the ordeal to come.

Parker nudged him with the toe of a boot. ''Hey, mate, climb in the tent and use a sleeping bag. Don't lie about out here, you'll catch your death.''

The only response was muffled snoring. Stand was already asleep.

''Cheeky bugger,'' Parker said to himself. He pulled the sleeping bag from his tent and draped it over the sleeping Yank.

At midnight, Stand and Parker crept through the hills, approaching the safe house from the rear. They slipped into the second building on the higher slope where the mine shaft angled into the hillside. Stand carried a length of rope coiled over one shoulder, a flashlight, a compass, and Parker's map outlining the layout of the mine shafts.

Parker watched Stand stuff a handful of extra flashlight batteries into his coat pocket. ''What are those for? The ones in your torch are fresh.''

''Flashlight batteries run down,'' Stand said.

Parker caught the tremor in Stand's voice. "Having second thoughts, are you? You sound nervous, mate."

"Don't be silly—I'm terrified."

"I could still come with you, you know."

Stand shook his head. "No good. Just doubles the risk."

"At least let us provide you with a diversion, just a little noise to keep their heads down."

"Absolutely not," Stand said. "I don't want them alerted at all. Besides, I don't know how long it will take me to locate the right mine shaft, or once I do, if it will be accessible to the house the way I think it is. Keep your people quiet; don't do anything that might panic them."

"All right," Parker said grudgingly. "But if we hear shooting, we're not going to sit on our hands and wait for the dust to clear."

Stand nodded. He glanced down the dark shaft and fought back a wave of revulsion. Taking a deep breath, he sighed and held out his hand to Parker. "Well, I guess this is it."

The colonel's eyes narrowed as he took Stand's hand. "Lord, man, you're shaking like a leaf. This woman and child, they must be very important to you."

"Everything," Stand said. Then he turned and walked into the shaft, where he was swallowed by the yawning darkness.

It was his most fearsome nightmare come true. Once he was past the opening, the air seemed to become close and stale. Stand breathed fast, his throat dry. The flashlight emitted a feeble glow, and he could see no farther than a few feet at a time. The deeper he went into the mountainside, the stronger came the urge to flee back to open air and the pale light of the moon.

After about a hundred steps, the floor began to angle downward sharply. The ceiling became lower, barely leaving him room to walk erect. Grimly Stand continued, feeling cold sweat collect in the hollow of his back.

He came to a crossing, where a second tunnel shot off at right angles. He paused, shone the flashlight on his compass, and consulted his map. The readings told him to go right. He took a deep breath and set off, though it took all his strength to make himself turn the corner. Leaving the main shaft seemed an act of finality. He was afraid he would never find his way back to it again. Visions of terror haunted him, and he saw himself trapped in the tunnels forever, wandering hopelessly until the flashlight batteries died and the darkness closed around him for good.

By his calculations he should turn right again, to head in the direction of the house. He walked on for what seemed like miles and passed several connecting tunnels on his left which that cut deeper into the hillside. None led in the other direction. He pressed on, though certain that he had already gone by the point where he needed to turn. The wall on his right continued to be blank, with no opening presenting itself.

Then the tunnel ended abruptly, blocked by a wall of loose stones. A cave-in had sealed off the shaft completely. Dirt streamed down from overhead, as if the remaining structure threatened to collapse as well.

Stand fought down a wave of panic. He spun around, waving the light everywhere, but there was no other way out. He had come to a dead end, and there was nothing to do but retrace his steps. He started back, his mood lightened by the though that he was heading toward the exit. He moved along quickly—too quickly—and had to stop for a minute and collect himself before he broke and ran madly back, thinking of nothing but escape.

Finally he was able to continue, and he made himself go slowly, shining the light carefully on every surface. He came to the last connecting tunnel he had bypassed, and this time gave it a more thorough inspection. He checked the map, but there was nothing to suggest it even existed. He moved ahead cautiously, and the beam of his flashlight revealed a yawning hole. It turned out not to be a tunnel at all, but a vertical connection like an empty elevator shaft. It led only one way. Down.

Sadly, Stand realized it had been foolish to believe he could reach the point he wanted by remaining on only one level. He had to go lower. The prospect filled him with dread.

There was a wooden ladder against one wall of the connecting shaft. Swallowing his fear, Stand started down.

He had taken only two steps when the ladder broke apart in his hands. He fell, a scream rising in his throat, but he dropped only a short distance and landed in soft earth before he had time to utter the cry. He looked around for a minute, dazed, then got up on his hands and knees. He was covered in an indescribable muck, foul-smelling and sticky to the touch. Nausea churned his stomach as he wiped himself off. After a quick check of the compass, he hurriedly set off again.

His watch showed he had been underground for only eighteen minutes, though it felt like an entire lifetime. Stand moved more quickly, trying to make himself concentrate on Meghan and Lynnie, remembering their faces as he had seen them last, bound and gagged, watched over by the leering eyes of the men called Tunney and Oates. Anger burned in his gut, spurring him along, helping him to ignore his own distress.

After fifty yards, the tunnel narrowed sharply. Stand was forced to his hands and knees. His fears deepened. It was everything he dreaded most, the closeness, the darkness surrounding him, the uncertainty of ever seeing daylight again. He heard a strange rustling noise ahead, an odd whispering, but told himself it was his imagination, and in any event it was faint and barely discernible over the loud thumping of his heart.

The tunnel turned sharply right and became so tight that he was almost crawling. Then abruptly it ended, sealed off by an old wooden door. His light flickered over the slats, the hinges coated in rust. Stand paused, panting, and gulped the sour air. The stench there was stronger and the odd noise much louder.

Stand put his ear to the door and listened, but could not tell what caused the strange sounds. He felt the sweat cooling on his face, and realized with a start that air was rushing past him, flowing between the wooden slats of the door. The discovery filled him with sudden hope. If the air was moving that much faster, it must mean he was close to the surface.

With sudden hopefulness, Stand shoved at the wooden door. The hinges squealed, resisting stubbornly. He reared back and put his shoulder to it. The door creaked open a mere fraction, still wedged fast. Angrily, Stand backed up again and drove his shoulder into it harder.

The world dropped out from under him. The door gave way and Stand plunged straight down.

He fell eight or ten feet and landed hard on his back, the air whooshing out of him. He lay stunned, gasping for breath. As his wits returned, he was flooded with new impressions. He flashed the light around, but could see no walls, and he had an undeniable sense of size and space. He was in a large chamber of some sort, the boundaries beyond the reach of his flashlight.

Though his claustrophobia eased, his fear was unrelieved, for the darkness still surrounded him.

He peered up, trying to force his eyes to rid himself of the disturbing impression. A scream clutched his throat. The darkness was coming closer. It was moving!

He cringed in horror, the darkness swarming over him in wave after wave. The rustling noise roared in his ears, and he was breathless with panic. A great wriggling mass, alive and squirming, scratched at his face and snagged his clothes.

Revulsion turned his skin to ice. He struck back at the darkness, swinging the flashlight like a club, lashing out in blind terror. He hit something small and solid, and felt it give way. Then another and another. Somehow, even in the midst of panic, he realized they were bats. Hundreds of them. They darted at him, as frightened as he was. Their soundless cries, the beat of their wings, chilled Stand's blood. They were everywhere, swarming like roaches, threatening to bury him beneath their massed weight.

He growled in fury and swung the light at them, but the more he struggled, the more agitated they became. Stand fought on, driven by fear. He bashed one small creature with the flashlight, connecting solidly. The lens shattered. The light flared for a second, strobelike, then died.

Darkness, total, complete.

Stand rolled over, frantically trying to avoid the lash of tiny claws. He cowered and raised his hands to protect his face, flipping over and over to get away. He stopped when he rolled into something sharp-edged and solid.

Desperately, he fumbled in his pocket, brought out his lighter, and snapped it open. A tiny blue spark flickered to life.

He was in a pile of debris, a trash heap of cans, boxes, and other junk mounded beneath layers of bat guano. The object he'd bumped against was a small wooden crate. He grabbed it and pounded it on the ground, smashing it to bits. Gathering several long splinters, he yanked the map from his pocket and wrapped it tightly around the wooden bundle.

He touched the flame to his makeshift torch and a bright blaze erupted. The white light was reflected in a thousand small blind eyes. Instantly, the bats retreated, showing the fire the respect they had not given the puny electric glow of the flashlight. Stand lurched to his feet, holding the torch aloft. He backed away, slipping and skidding on the slime of droppings that coated the floor.

He could sense the animals just beyond the light and he retreated, swinging the blazing sticks to keep them back. The torch burned with a fierce hear, flaming fragments dropping to the floor.

He backed up until he ran into the wall of the chamber. Groping with his free hand, he moved along it, hoping to find an exit. His torch started to sputter, more of it falling away. Stand kept shuffling to his left, praying that it was the correct way. The glow of his torch was beginning to dim.

Daddy!

Stand heard the soft cry and wheeled around. It was so real it couldn't have been only in his mind. He felt a sharp pang and his eyes fastened on a soft white form, so much like the shroud Melissa wore in his dreams. Then the shape dissipated, thinning to a stream of smoke from his burning torch.

He turned away, but caught himself and glanced back. Something was odd. The smoke hadn't evaporated; it thinned and streamed away, flowing somewhere. Stand edged back, waving his torch, and saw the opening. It was small, barely large enough for him to squeeze through, and low, near the floor, which was why his hand had failed to find it.

Stand held the torch near the opening. The smoke flowed inside and rose swiftly. He poked his head through. It was a vertical shaft only a few feet wide and rising straight up for thirty or forty yards. With a sense of elation, he glimpsed a hinged door overhead. A faint glow shone through the chinks from the other side.

Stand pulled back. Now he noticed the litter of trash was centered in the opening. He knew he had found it. Through a miracle, he had stumbled upon the opening he sought.

Stand felt a cold calm settle over his nerves. The dread of the darkness was forgotten, the bats forgotten. Nothing mattered but the prospect of getting his hands on the men who so gleefully tormented those he loved.

The torch was burning low, its light fading. There was a slithering whisper from the darkness as the bats began to stir. Stand barely noticed. He wedged the torch into the earth outside the opening, and without a moment's hesitation got down on his knees and squeezed into the shaft.

The walls were rough, offering plenty of small ridges and pitted crevices for Stand's hands and feet. The shaft was narrow, just wide enough for him to scale in a chimney climb, his legs braced against opposite walls. Setting his teeth, Stand reached for the first handhold and started up.

Below him, the torch sputtered and went out, leaving him in near total darkness. Stand didn't care. His face was cast in a grim smile as he struggled upward, rising steadily toward the light.

Oates pressed his face to the boarded window, grumbling to himself as he tried to peer out. Tunney sat at the table, his and around an open bottle of whisky, and frowned irritably ⁑t his partner.

"Dammit! Why are you so jumpy? Come away from there ▸efore I rip your friggin' head off."

Oates glanced back at the big man. "I tell you, some-▸ning's gone wrong. They should have been back here long ▸efore this. I got a funny feeling, like we're being watched, ▸hat there's something out there. Don't you feel it?"

"What I feel is a big pain in my ass, and you're it. Sit ▸own and have a drink."

Oates shook his head. "What do you think happened to ▸hem?"

"He's gone," Tunney said. "Wise up, mate. The bugger's ▸one and left us, he has. Got what he wanted and cleared ▸ut, leavin' us to hold the bag. You might as well open your ▸loody eyes. We've been had."

"Quit saying that." Oates glanced at Meghan, lying qui-▸tly on her cot, and the girl sleeping beside her. "They can't ▸esert us. They'll have to come back to finish things."

Tunney laughed bitterly. "No, mate, they's gone. And to-▸norrow we're gonna be gone, too. I'm not stayin' another ▸lay in this soddin' shithole. I'm clearin' out, and if you got ▸ny sense in your head, you'll come with me."

"What about the woman and the brat?"

"What about 'em? You don't think we're gonna drag 'em ▸long with us, do you?"

"No," Oates said softly. "I suppose you're right."

"Damned right I'm right." Tunney rocked back in his chair ▸nd belted down another drink. He swayed unsteadily and set ▸he bottle down with a crash.

"So what are we gonna do with them?"

"Drop 'em down the hole, like I wanted to do days ago."

Oates saw Meghan wince and curl protectively around her ▸laughter. "The bitch is awake. She heard everything you ▸aid."

"Big friggin' deal. What difference you think it makes?"

Oates walked over and peered solemnly at the trapdoor in

the floor. "I still got a funny feeling. I want to clear out o
here now, tonight. If we're gonna do it, let's get it over with."

"Not yet." Tunney took a quick drink and stared acros
the room at Meghan. "Before I do it, I'm gonna get me
piece of that. I'm gonna have something for my trouble, eve
if it's only a piece of lily-white ass."

"You're drunk. You couldn't get it up with a string."

"You fancy her, too, don't you? I seen the way you looke
at her."

"I seen worse," Oates said. He smiled thoughtfully, peer
ing down at Meghan. "Might not be bad at that."

"I'm gonna sit here and have me another drink and enjo
thinking about what I'm gonna do. Then I'll show you. Tha
smart-mouthed bitch is gonna learn what it's like to be wit
a real man for once. It'll be like a gift, ya know, a littl
present to say good-bye."

The smaller man's eyes glittered excitedly. "All right. Lik
you say, we deserve something for our troubles." He pulle
out a coin and jiggled it in his palm. "I'll flip you to see wh
goes first."

"Like bloody hell!" Tunney roared. "You little bugger
I'm the one who—"

Behind Oates, the trapdoor crashed open.

Rising like a vengeful demon from hell, Stand shot u
from the hole. He rolled to one side, reached out, and grabbe
the back of Oates's belt, yanking viciously.

With a startling gasp, Oates fell back, sprawled across th
opening. His legs slipped into the hole and he screamed
hands clutching, scrabbling for a hold.

Stand kicked the man square in the face. Oates droppe
from sight, his scream a jagged cry that ended abruptly.

Across the room, Tunney leaped to his feet and grabbe
for the gun lying on the table. Meghan was up in a flash. Sh
shoved the table in the big man's path, slamming the edg
into his crotch. Tunney doubled over, his breath hissing ou
in a painful gasp.

Stand scrambled to his feet and turned to face the nev

threat. Tunney turned the table over in a sudden rage, knocking it into Meghan, sending her reeling backward.

Stand was on him in two quick steps, diving across the open space and seizing his arm before he could raise the pistol. It went off, loud as an explosion, the bullet raising wood chips from the floorboards. Arm in arm, the two men stumbled across the room like awkward dancers, struggling for control of the weapon.

They crashed through the chairs and cots. One of the chairs caught Stand behind the knees, and for a moment he was off balance. Tunney reached quickly, driving a shoulder into Stand's chest, forcing him back, and pressed him against the glowing coal stove. The touch of hot metal was excruciating. There was a soft hissing noise and the fabric of his coat started to burn.

Tunney grinned cockily and leaned into him more, holding him against the heat. Stand suddenly gave in, letting himself go soft and compliant. The abrupt halt in resistance took Tunney by surprise and he hesitated just the fraction of a second that it took Stand to spin slightly, levering his body inside Tunney's arm span.

Gritting his teeth, Stand put all his weight into forcing their locked hands up and slapping them against the coal stove. The bare back of Tunney's gun hand pressed against the hot iron.

It was bad for both of them, but Stand held on grimly. Tunney's hand sizzled like meat on a griddle, and he howled in pain. The gun slipped from his fingers and dropped to the floor. Stand kicked it into the gaping hole.

The two men broke apart, squaring off like boxers across a ring. Tunney held his wounded hand and glared at Stand through eyes narrowed in pain and wild as a mad dog's. Stand faced his opponent, his hands slightly raised, wearing a smile of contempt. His mind was dead calm. He was in his element, acutely aware of every ticking second, every action drawn out in dreamlike slow motion.

Tunney raised his fists and charged. Stand kicked him on the outside of the knee and the leg buckled. Stand closed in, slipped outside Tunney's guard, and delivered a palm strike to his bulbous nose. He quickly pressed his advantage as the big man stood dazed. He was all flowing motion, one move smoothly leading to the next. His left hand darted out in a smashing back fist to Tunney's face. He followed with an elbow, spun and drove a short jab to the body, burying his fist in Tunney's soft gut.

Tunney doubled over in agony. He straightened abruptly, threw a wild punch that smacked the side of Stand's head, stunning him.

Tunney retreated, grabbed a chair, and came back at Stand swinging it like a massive club. Stand ducked and kicked him in the injured knee again. Tunney cried out and scrambled away in fear. Stand followed, stalking him patiently, his face set in that cold terrible smile.

Tunney turned to flee, then limped quickly across the short gap and made a grab for Lynnie, pulling the child up in front of him like a shield. Meghan was on him even before Stand could react. Even bound and gagged, she fought like a crazed animal, butting and kicking. He had to release the child to free his hands. His fingers snagged the gag at her mouth, pulling it loose. That was all Meghan needed. She leaped on his back and fastened her teeth to his ear, jaws clamped like a bulldog's.

Tunney growled and threw her off with a swing of his arm. His face was a black mask of rage as he spun to finish her with his boots.

The next moment Stand was upon him, his fists a blur, caution forgotten, throwing one punch after another, full roundhouse swings with every ounce of his weight and strength behind them. Tunney stumbled back, feebly trying to cover his face, but Stand stung him again and again, left and right, pounding the man mercilessly.

Tunney crashed against the wall and hung there as Stand hammered him. Stand's breath rasped, but he didn't let up. He heard Meghan call his name and was vaguely aware of the door banging open, of many footsteps, but he was too far gone, driven by a killing rage.

Parker appeared at Stand's side. He watched with a troubled expression, then said softly, "You can stop now, old man. He doesn't feel it, you know."

Stand paused, blinking. He stared at the SAS colonel as if in a daze. Tunney slid soundlessly down the wall and plunked to the floor like a bag of rocks.

"Damned good thing we got here when we did," Parker said. He smiled thinly. "You didn't leave enough for us to clean up after. Where's the other one?"

Stand gazed back blankly.

And then Meghan was in his arms. She held him tight and her tears were hot, spilling on his cheek.

The soldiers untied Lynnie, and she came running. Stand picked her up and held her as if he would never let go. Now the tears were his own. The child wrapped her arms around his neck.

"I knew you'd come back, Nathan," she said. "I knew you would come for us."

"She's right," Meghan said. She smiled gently. "I never doubted it, not for a moment."

Lynnie nuzzled his face and kissed him, smacking her lips loudly against his damp cheek. "Thank you, Nathan. Thank you for saving me."

He held them, breathless, unable to reply, no words for what he felt.

CHAPTER 23

GREGORY AND Falstaff carefully removed a cardboard box from their rented van and placed it on a two-wheeled carrier. Falstaff grabbed the handle and wheeled the box across the parking lot and into the terminal. They merged with the busy crowds in the lobby of Dulles Airport.

Falstaff glanced up at the notices of arrivals and departures. He smiled. Flight 403 would depart on schedule at ten thirty-five A.M. "Everything is going well."

"This is crazy," Gregory moaned. "We have no business doing this. What are you up to?"

"It will all be made clear to you soon, James. Just act and say exactly what I have told you to do, and all will go perfectly, I promise you."

"I don't get it. There are a hundred other more sensible ways to use this thing against the Company. We don't have to try something this dangerous."

"I have spent months of preparation for this moment," Falstaff said. "Every possible difficulty has been foreseen. You have only to follow orders."

Gregory stopped abruptly and blocked Falstaff from pushing the wheeled cart any farther. "No way," Gregory said. "I'm not going through with it. This makes no sense. Have you cleared this with your leaders? There's no way in hell this insane act will aid the Soviet cause."

"You fool. I care nothing for the Soviets. No one tells me what to do."

"What!" Gregory stared at him. "What do you mean?"

Falstaff motioned impatiently. "Out of the way, James. Move along. You have no other choice; you cannot back out now."

"Who are you?"

"I told you, all will be made clear."

"Forget it. I'm out. I don't want any part of this."

"Then I shall kill you, here and now."

"You wouldn't dare. Not here."

"I have nothing to lose. I will tolerate no more of your sniveling cowardice. Proceed, James. Or die. . . . The choice is yours."

Gregory looked into his eyes and shivered. "Dear God, you can't mean it."

Falstaff smiled. "Come along. You know what to do, James. The moment of our destiny is upon us. I can feel it."

They wheeled the crate through the airport and were not bothered until they barged into the exit lane to avoid passing through the metal detectors. A security guard left his post at the detection gate and stepped in front of them.

"Just a minute. Where do you think you're going?"

Gregory flashed his CIA credentials. "Don't make a fuss," he said quietly. "We don't want to start a panic."

"That for real? What's up? I haven't heard about any hijack, or anything."

"There's no hijack. We have reason to believe a bomb has been planted aboard flight four zero three."

The security man gulped. "Damn! No kidding? They'll be boarding four zero three any minute now."

"I want gate five evacuated right away. And have your chief of security meet us there. Well, don't stand there gawking at me, man. Do it."

Gregory and Falstaff pressed on through the throngs of people jamming the wide hallways. No one gave them more than a passing glance. They heard the overhead speakers come to life.

"Arthur Bledsoe to gate five immediately. Code Bravo. Repeat, Code Bravo. Arthur Bledsoe to gate five."

The waiting area by gate five was filled with people lounging uncomfortably in plastic chairs, chatting with friends and loved ones, staring out the large windows at the plane hooked up to the boarding tunnel. A few passengers already formed a line, clutching their bags and holding their tickets at the ready.

At a nod from Falstaff, Gregory stepped up to the attendant at the head of the line and discreetly revealed his card. "Is the crew aboard?"

The young woman paled. "Yes, sir. We were just about to begin boarding."

A stout man in a plaid sport coat rushed up, accompanied by the guard from the metal-detection post. He stepped between Gregory and the attendant, and took him by the arm, steering him away. "I'm Arthur Bledsoe, chief of security. What's going on here? What's this about a hijack?"

"There's no hijack." Gregory sighed.

Bledsoe gave his guard a blistering scowl, then looked back and forth between Gregory and Falstaff. "Then would you kindly inform me what the hell you're doing, telling everyone you're from the CIA?"

Gregory showed him his badge. He was beginning to feel like a detective in a TV cop show. "That's right. Agent Gregory. I want this part of the terminal evacuated now. There's a bomb aboard flight four zero three."

Bledsoe frowned skeptically. "A bomb? Where's the FBI? This is their ball park. Since when does the CIA have anything to do with air traffic security?"

"The FBI is on its way," Gregory said. "You can confirm that with the bureau office in Alexandria if you like. But I want this area cleared first, and I mean everybody—unless you would like to take personal responsibility for the deaths of these people."

The security chief hesitated just a second, then grabbed a phone on the attendant's booth and stabbed three digits. There was a crackle in an overhead speaker. Then his voice rang through the terminal.

"Attention, please—your attention, please. Will all passengers and guests please move quickly and quietly from gate five to the airport lobby. There is no cause for alarm, but we must ask you to leave the area immediately. Please leave gate five at once."

He nodded at Gregory, then pushed the phone at the attendant. "Martha, get all my staff here right away."

There was a loud buzzing of voices as the people in the holding area grabbed their belongings and looked at one another in confusion. Bledsoe moved among them and raised his hands for their attention. He repeated his instructions crisply and started herding them away.

The attendant's nervous voice echoed through the terminal.

"All security personnel to gate five immediately. Repeat, all security personnel to gate five immediately." She hiccuped nervously, the sound amplified explosively throughout the airport, and fumbled the receiver into its cradle.

In a moment, Bledsoe came back, two other men at his heels. "All right, my people are closing off the area now," he grunted, glancing at the flight attendant. "You'd better get out of here, too, Martha."

"Aren't I supposed to stay at my post or something?"

Bledsoe smiled gently. "Martha, how much do they pay you?"

"Not enough."

"Exactly my point."

She took the hint and hurried off without further prompting.

"My partner and I are going aboard now," Gregory said. "We can't wait for the FBI to show."

"What the hell is that thing?" Bledsoe asked, pointing to the cardboard box.

"It's a device to scramble the electronic timer of a bomb."

"Don't look like much to me."

"You do bomb disposal work in your spare time?" Gregory said derisively. "Now just keep the crowds away from here. You do your job and we'll do ours."

Bledsoe grabbed Gregory's arm as he started to turn away. "Hold on. Nobody's going to play around with no bombs until we get the crew off to safety."

"The crew will be necessary to remove the plane to the far side of the airport—unless you want to risk the bomb going off here and taking part of the terminal along with the plane?"

Bledsoe's Adam's apple bobbed as he swallowed dryly. "I sure hope you guys know what you're doing."

Falstaff scowled. "We are wasting time, James." He spun away and began wheeling the crate down the boarding tunnel.

"He's one of those bomb disposal experts?" Bledsoe asked.

"I hope so," Gregory said. "I'll be right beside him."

"Well, better you than me. Good luck. I'm going to get the FBI on the horn and give them a piece of my mind. I can't believe it's taking them so long to show up."

Gregory smiled. "Don't worry. They'll be here soon. I guarantee it." He turned away and thumped down the tunnel behind Falstaff.

Gregory and Falstaff removed the anthrax bomb from the cardboard box. Falstaff had made a few modifications. There were now two cables leading from the black-box detonator. He carried the container onto the plane and entered the cockpit. Three men turned around to look at him in surprise.

"What's going on here?" the captain demanded. "Who are you?"

"Please remain seated, gentlemen," Falstaff said. "No one move. There is a dangerous bomb aboard this plane." He pushed the stockpile into the tight space behind the pilot, then got down on his knees and fastened the two magnetic cups on the ends of the cables to the underside of the captain's chair.

Captain Stewart Hunter, a distinguished-looking man with gray hair and clear blue eyes, craned his head to peer down at Falstaff. "Dammit! What are you doing? What is this about a bomb? I'm not going to endanger my crew! I want some answers, dammit!"

Falstaff muttered from his position on the floor. "Introduce yourself, James."

Gregory stepped forward and pulled a Smith & Wesson revolver from inside his coat. "This should make you understand very clearly. We are taking command of your aircraft, Captain."

Falstaff straightened up and placed a hand on the captain's shoulder as he started to rise from his chair. "Please sit down, Captain."

Hunter grumbled, "I get it. There's no bomb, is there?"

"There is now," Falstaff said. "I have just secured it to your chair. It is triggered by a pressure-sensitive device that will detonate if you try to leave your seat, even for an instant. I hope you are comfortable, Captain. You will remain here for a very long time."

"You're bluffing. It would kill you as well as us."

"I do not bluff, Captain, and I am quite unafraid of death. I have died before. Please keep in mind that if you should think to sacrifice yourselves, it will be in vain. The bomb contains a very unpleasant and potent form of the bacterial agent anthrax. If you move we shall all die within three seconds. Then the wind will carry the spores throughout the eastern part of your United States, killing untold thousands. Unless you want their deaths on your conscience, I suggest that you remain very still."

"You're insane."

Falstaff slipped out a Luger and held the muzzle against the flight engineer's skull. "You will not say such things to me again, Captain. If you do, or if you try in any way to resist, I shall kill this man."

Captain Hunter stared for a moment into Falstaff's pale eyes, then nodded tightly. "I understand."

"Good. Prepare to taxi your plane away from the terminal on my command. But first you will make radio contact with the tower. It is time for me to announce my intentions to the world.''

"Dulles control, this is Global four zero three. We are commencing to taxi to runway two-one."

In the tower, air traffic controller Mark Ford winced and knocked some ash from the cigarette in his mouth as he quickly adjusted the speaker on his headset. "Negative, four-zero-three. You do not have clearance to taxi. Repeat, you do not have clearance."

"Four zero three commencing to taxi."

Mark Ford shot up from his chair and peered out the large windows of the tower. He saw the plane pulling slowly away from gate five. "What the hell are you doing, four-zero-three? You do *not* have clearance. Do you copy?"

"Roger, we copy." Captain Hunter's voice was dry as dust. "Dulles control, you are hereby ordered to shut down all air traffic. Do you copy that, control? All air traffic is to be diverted from Dulles."

"What!!" Ford anxiously waved at his supervisor. "Jim, get over here. Something weird's going on."

Jim Akins rushed across the room and leaned down beside his controller. "What is it?" He glanced at the panel and flinched. "Jesus Christ! What is four zero three doing out there? Pull him back."

"I tried. You tell him." Ford flipped a switch, throwing the radio on a desk speaker. Then he barked again into his headset. "Four zero three, repeat your last transmission."

"You are hereby ordered to shut down all air traffic." Captain Hunter's voice broke from its cool, detached tone. "Do it, guys. This is not a joke. We are taxiing to runway two-one, and there's no stopping us. We have a situation here."

Akins threw a switch and bent over a microphone. "What is your situation?"

Hunter said, "I'll put him on. Just a second. I hope you have a fresh tape in the recorder."

The two air controllers glanced at each other in puzzlement. Then both froze as a new voice crackled over the speaker.

"This is Falstaff. . . ."

"Dear God!" Akins straightened up with a lurch, gazed at the slowly moving plane, then turned and barked to the room at large. "Attention, we have an emergency. Start diverting all traffic to other airports. From this moment on, we are shut down."

Then he picked up the phone. The number for the FBI was taped on top of the receiver.

In the cockpit of the Boeing, Gregory stood as if carved from stone. "Why did you say that?" he mumbled. "Why did you tell them you're Falstaff?"

The terrorist smiled. "Because it is true, James. Are you surprised?"

Gregory stumbled back a step, his mind reeling. His bowels loosed involuntarily, the foul odor sharp in the close cockpit. Falstaff coolly took the revolver from his hand and pushed Gregory away in disgust. "Sit down, James," he said. "You have done your part. Stay out of my way, be quiet, and you may yet live."

Gregory shuddered and said nothing. He saw the captain staring at him, his clear blue eyes filled with loathing and disgust. And Falstaff was still smiling, his own eyes pale and glittering with a cold pleasure, mocking him, laughing.

Gregory stumbled down the aisle and dropped into the first seat, staring blankly at the hands folded in his lap. His mind recoiled, turning deeper and deeper inside itself, fleeing from reality and the bitter truth.

Daniel McWilliam hung up the phone and clutched his chest, breathing in harsh gasps. On the other side of the desk, Jean glanced at him, her knuckles white on the arm of the chair. "What is it? You look terrible."

A final long sigh gurgled moistly in the old man's throat. Then he slowly raised his head. "I want Stand here right away. No excuses. Send a team to drag him here if you have to.''

"He's on his way already," she said softly. Her eyes grew round with concern. "You chartered the plane for him yesterday, don't you remember?"

"Of course. Forgive me. I'm overwrought."

"Something's happened, hasn't it? Does it have to do with the stockpile?"

McWilliam's head nodded heavily. He seemed unable to meet her eyes. "It's the worst imaginable, Jean. Two men have seized a plane at Dulles Airport. They have a bomb on board, and they claim it's capable of wiping out the entire population of the Washington metro area."

"Surely you don't think—"

"The men got aboard by using the Company credentials of an agent named James Gregory. One of them matches his description."

"Oh, dear God."

McWilliam held up one hand. "The other man has identified himself as Falstaff."

Jean raised a hand to her mouth. "Do you believe it's true?" she asked breathlessly. "Do you think it's possible it's Falstaff James has been conspiring with all along?"

"Unfortunately, the man aboard the plane fits the general description we have received from the defector Yanov. We have to assume it's not only possible, but probable."

"It's unthinkable. I can't believe it, I just can't—" Jean's voice broke and she trembled, hugging herself as if feeling a deadly chill.

"Stop it, Jean. Calm down. There's no time for hysterics. We have to prepare to act."

Jean sniffled and raised her head slowly. Her eyes were moist and mascara ran down her cheeks in dark trails. "I'm so sorry," she whispered. "This whole thing is my fault."

"If we want to place blame, we'll have to look back a long way before you were ever involved. Stay strong for me, Jean. I need you help. I need you now more than ever."

"What do you want me to do?" Jean asked, rising to her feet. Her voice was firm again, under control.

"Get on the radio and find out when Stand will arrive. He's the only one who's dealt with these people firsthand. I hate to make more demands on him after all he's been through, but, by God, he's proven he's still the best. And in this case he may be our only real hope."

"I'll get right on it," Jean said, turning away.

"Oh, Jean," he said, as if stricken by an afterthought.

She glanced back. "Yes?"

"Arrange for a car to pick up Stand wherever he comes down, would you? I have a feeling he won't be landing at Dulles."

She was waiting for him when he stepped off the plane. "You?" Stand said.

Jean bit her lip, but held her head up proudly. "Yes, me. Is that so terrible?"

"I guess not. I suppose we were both taken in by him."

Jean scowled at the mention of Gregory. "I trusted the stockpile—I trusted a lot—to the wrong man. It won't help us much to dwell on it now. Besides, we have a lot more important things to discuss."

She rushed him to a long black limousine and filled him in on recent events while the driver raced through the Virginia countryside. The news of the bomb threat was all over the radio, but so far the press hadn't caught on to the anthrax angle.

"How have you managed to keep the lid on?" Stand asked.

"We have been cooperative with the press—to a certain degree. We released an edited version of the recording from the control tower. It makes it clear that he has a bomb and is not afraid of using it, but no mention of anthrax. One reporter has caught on to it, I'm afraid, but Daddy persuaded his publisher to sit on the story. It would only cause a widespread panic, people trying to flee the city, and all for nothing. It wouldn't help anyway. No one anywhere is safe."

"I'm not sure I follow that," Stand said.

Jean opened a panel in the ornate console of the limo's backseat and revealed an entertainment unit that featured a TV, radio, and a cassette tape player. "This is why I opted to use the limo," she said.

"And I thought it was because you wanted to make a good impression on me."

"Sure, that, too," she said, making a face. She held up an audio cassette. "This is a copy of the full, unedited version of Falstaff's demands. Listen and tell me if the voice is familiar to you."

She slid in the tape and punched the Start button. The copy was noisy, but reasonably clear under the circumstances.

"This is Falstaff. I have taken command of flight four zero three. I have installed a bomb, a particularly destructive and horrible bomb that was created by the most unholy alliance of purveyors of destruction on the planet, the United States and Great Britain. This is a biological weapon of awesome lethal potential. It contains a core of the bacterium anthrax, an especially virulent bacterium which was designed by the United States' Central Intelligence Agency under a program known as MKNAOMI. Exposure to the spores is fatal within seconds.

"My first demand is that this statement shall be read on all television networks at seven o'clock this evening. No exceptions to this demand will be tolerated.

"My second demand is the death, before my own eyes, of the Soviet defector known as Sergei Yanov, also called the Italian. He shall be brought before me and publicly executed for all the world to see.

"My third demand is the public admission by the American Central Intelligence Agency of its secret wet squad called the Office. Full disclosure of the Office, its leaders, and a complete history of its covert crimes against the peoples of the world will be included as part of the television broadcasts at seven P.M. Eastern Standard Time.

"My fourth demand is for thirty million dollars in unmarked denominations to be used to finance the continued campaign against those nations and persons who willfully and hatefully enforce unnatural strictures upon the oppressed people of the world. Those who subvert the true and natural order of life and death for their own exploitation and enrichment.

"At seven-thirty P.M. I will offer the television networks, and thus the nation at large, proof of the destructive power I possess. This will be made clear so that all people of the United States will understand and accede to my demands.

"You will have until six A.M. tomorrow to accept and fulfill these terms. If agreement is not reached by that time, this plane will take off and fly inland over the continental United States and will crash on a populated city to be arbitrarily chosen at a time and location of my choosing. If any attempt to hinder or circumvent this takeoff occurs, the anthrax weapon will be detonated, thus exposing thousands of innocent victims to instant death in the immediate region of the Eastern Seaboard.

"In effect, I am holding the lives of all citizens of the United States within my hands. No one can know where or when death will rain from the sky. All citizens, if they value their lives, will now place pressure upon their leaders to see that these demands are met faithfully."

"Well?" Jean asked. "Sound like anyone you know?"

"That's him," Stand said. He smashed his fist down angrily. "I can't believe I was so close to him, but didn't know."

"What do you make of his statement?"

"What do you want me to say? That it's all hot air? He means it, every bit of it. He's insane, Jean."

"Will he go all the way?"

"No doubt about it. Without a second thought."

Jean sighed and hung her head. "I guess Daddy and I were praying that you would have some insights, a sense of his weaknesses."

"He's smart. Look at the way he's rigged the bomb this time. The pilot said it's hooked to his seat?"

"That's right," Jean said. "It's a good way to make sure he had someone around to fly the plane. I can't figure why he didn't wait for the passengers to board the plane. He'd be certain of attention if he had hostages at risk.''

"He doesn't need them," Stand said. "More hostages would be more trouble, more difficult to control. Besides, he figures he's holding the whole nation hostage. That's why he's demanding the television coverage. He knows this is one group of hostages the audience will have real sympathy for—themselves.''

"It's incredible," Jean agreed, shivering. "He really has all of us under his thumb. That plane is capable of reaching any major city on the continent.''

"What's being done about his demand for television coverage?''

"The three major networks and CNN have all provided us with special broadcast trucks, and we've hooked them into the airport cable system. At seven o'clock tonight we'll switch over to local broadcast. We're building four mock television stages, and we have four Company public relations men to read the news.''

"The plane is hooked up to cable?" Stand asked incredulously.

"He allowed the technicians to lay a cable and plug the plane's air conditioning, lights, and the rest of the support system into airport mains. They added a cable television feed. I guess Falstaff couldn't get good enough reception inside the aircraft.''

"And of course he wouldn't want his big moment ruined by a snowy picture," Stand said bitterly. "What about Gregory? He won't be fooled by your stand-in newsmen.''

Jean shrugged. "It's the best we can do. We can't have the networks broadcast the true story. It would create a nationwide panic that would cause more deaths than the explosion of the bomb itself.''

Stand nodded in agreement.

"Do you have any other ideas?" Jean asked.

"Possibly. They're sort of crazy. For one, we're going to need a Hollywood-style special-effects expert.''

"What for?''

"The execution of Yanov. Unless you would rather kill him for real."

Jean looked at him thoughtfully. "That could work, if it's handled properly. What else?"

"That's it for now," Stand said. "I don't know enough about the situation and layout yet. I have to get there and see what's possible. What time is it now?"

Jean glanced at her watch. "Four-twenty. Falstaff has been in control of the plane since ten-thirty this morning. We have less than fourteen hours before he carries out his threat."

"In a couple of hours the news goes on, and Falstaff is supposed to give us a demonstration of the stockpile. I think that's something we'd better see."

Jean nodded grimly. She leaned over and tapped on the glass separating them from the driver. "Speed it up."

CHAPTER 24

THE CONFERENCE room was at the end of the terminal building, and featured floor-to-ceiling windows overlooking the runways. The room was nearly filled by a long mahogany conference table, polished to shine like glass, and marred by coffee spills and cigarette ash from the brimming ashtrays. The room was crowded, jammed with men from a dozen different organizations. Most dominant was the FBI, its agents big burly men with craggy faces who argued quietly among themselves. There were two representatives from the Civil Aeronautics Board, one from the National Security Council, the local police commissioner, and the Washington director of Civil Preparedness.

The most striking members of the party were the two leaders of Delta Force, the military counter-terrorist unit that was specially trained and held in readiness for such events as the one that brought this group together. The Delta men were ominous in black overalls, web belts, and combat boots, hard rugged men with close-cropped hair and stoic faces. If the President made the decision to storm the plane, it would be the Delta men who would carry out the assault. Delta snipers were positioned in various sites all around the airport and along the tarmac, and a special strike unit was resting in the airport lounge, going over their plans, waiting only for the order from the President to leap into combat.

One young man, dressed in a plaid flannel shirt and jeans,

was the most incongruous figure in the room. He was a phone technician, there solely to see that the banks of telephones that had been hurriedly added to the command center functioned properly. It was his responsibility to guarantee that when the President called with his decision, he wouldn't get a busy signal.

Jean was the only woman. The men did not make a point of ignoring her, but she was not invited to take part in the discussion and strategies that were endlessly debated. Neither was Stand. He sat by the wide windows and puffed his pipe quietly, staring out at the plane. Jean sat beside him and chain-smoked cigarettes, compulsively emptying the ashtray after each one.

At seven o'clock the room grew silent. All faces turned toward the bank of television sets that had been installed along one wall. There was a brief flash as the broadcast trucks switched onto the cable, but it was nothing that should attract Falstaff's suspicions. The four TV sets showed the regular news openings that began each network broadcast, then cut to the fill-in news anchors from the CIA.

"Here goes nothing," someone in the room said with a sigh. "Let's pray the bastard buys it."

At the last minute, it had been decided that the anchor for CNN should be a woman. A secretary from the Company Operations division had been hurriedly enlisted for the task. It was a good decision—she was poised and the best reader, by far the most convincing in her role. The three men read adequately, but stiffly, because of nervousness, occasionally losing their place when they glanced from their scripts into the camera.

The first half of the broadcasts was devoted entirely to video packages of how the situation at Dulles had unfolded. It allowed the mock anchors to be on camera a minimum amount of time.

The show was designed entirely to appeal to Falstaff's ego. The scripts stressed how easily he had carried out an ingenious scheme to hold an entire nation at ransom, and the idealistic motivations for his actions. The word "terrorist" was carefully avoided, and the closest they came to describing the real man was in their profile of how dangerous and effective the shadowy figure had proven himself to be. The first half concluded with a compiled history of Falstaff's accomplishments, listing the bomb strikes and numbers of victims killed or maimed in a reign of terror that made the world fear his name.

Stand listened, feeling the anger grow inside him like a smoldering fire, pure focused hatred heating his blood to a fevered boil, making his muscles tighten and quiver with tension.

The video profiles ended and the anchors were back on camera, reading the transcript of Falstaff's demands. They finished the long-winded speech and then pitched to more videotapes showing how government agencies were laboring to comply. There were pictures of a thin, effeminate man being led into the airport flanked by an escort of grim-faced agents. A voiceover explained:

". . . In accordance to Falstaff's demands, a Soviet defector bythe name of Sergei Yanov has been removed from the secret CIA facility where he has been undergoing a long debriefing process by various interrogators. He has been transported to Dulles Airport, awaiting the decision of the President. If Falstaff's request is honored, Sergei Yanov faces public execution at six A.M. tomorrow. . . ."

The next story showed bank officials stuffing banded stacks of money into tall mail sacks. Twelve of the bags were loaded onto an armored Brinks van. They were shown again, unloaded and carted into the airport. The video packages made it clear that the government was scrambling to meet Falstaff's demands.

One by one, the anchors reappeared, reading from identical scripts: ". . . And now, in compliance with Falstaff's third demand, we bring you this public confession, taped earlier this afternoon, by the director of the CIA's secret task force. . . ."

The screens revealed Daniel McWilliam sitting before a plain backdrop. He coughed and took an audible breath, then started to read from the papers in front of him. It was the first time Stand could recall seeing the old man with the blemished backs of his hands fully exposed. There was something disturbingly touching about the sight.

"I am Daniel McWilliam, the acting director of the Office, a secret counter-terrorist organization that functions in co-operation with the American government and the Central Intelligence Agency. In accordance with the wishes of the man who now holds us all captive, I shall now give you a brief history of the Office and its operations, which Falstaff has judged to be crimes. . . ."

Jean and Stand both listened intently. "He said he had to do this personally," Jean explained. "I don't know how he found the strength to go through with it."

They listened as McWilliam began to chronicle an Office operation in early 1984 against the Red Brigade in Italy.

"He's not really going to reveal the history of Office operations, is he?" Stand asked.

Jean smiled. "Relax. It's all fiction. We've had writers cranking out reams of false scenarios all day. There's enough truth to satisfy James, if he's listening, but all the dates and substantive points are made up."

"Your father's a good actor. He almost had me convinced."

"He was going from the taping session to a private audience with the President," Jean said. "He hasn't been out of the house so much in years. I'm worried all this activity will kill him—that is, if we're not all dead tomorrow, anyway."

"What's he going to tell the President?"

"I don't know," Jean replied. "Maybe he has some ideas of his own on how to resolve this problem. I hope so. I haven't heard too many ideas around here that seen promising."

Stand shrugged. "The Delta unit is good. They have a real chance, if they get the green light."

"It's so risky, though. Storming a plane is still little better than a fifty–fifty proposition, no matter how many men or how well prepared they are. They can cut through the hull and disable everyone inside with gas or stun grenades in under twenty seconds . . . but how long does Falstaff need to press one little button?''

"You're a bundle of good cheer,'' Stand grumbled.

They grew silent then, a hush falling over the entire room, as the mock newscast concluded. The anchors stumbled over their closing remarks, perhaps wondering whether to say goodnight or good-bye. It was seven-thirty.

The TV sets flickered and changed to a live shot of the plane. Everyone in the planning room leaned forward as the camera zoomed in closer. There were blurs of motion at a few of the windows, definite signs of activity. Then the rear door swung open.

Falstaff smiled broadly, laughing with childlike delight as he watched the videotaped profiles of himself on the television. "You see, James?'' he chortled. "You see? They honor me with the respect I deserve.''

Gregory stood back, stunned. He knew from the first minute that the newscasts were not genuine. Right off he recognized Lucy Brewster, a secretary from the CIA West Europe desk. She was one of the few women he had actively pursued who had continued to resist his charms—he wasn't likely to forget her. It was clear the Company was up to something and the scope of their efforts astonished Gregory. He knew he should tell Falstaff, but as he watched the terrorist devouring the phony broadcast with such egomaniacal pleasure, he couldn't say anything. It was because of Falstaff that he was in this mess. Falstaff had used him, threatened him, laughed at him. Whatever happened to the two of them now, Gregory didn't care. He knew his life was over. But he would have the last laugh.

Falstaff seemed sad when the half hour was over and the newscast concluded. "They have met the first of our demands, James,'' he said. "You see how they cower?''

"Yeah, sure,'' Gregory muttered, secretly contemptuous, inwardly laughing at this madman's self-absorption. "They're sure running scared, all right.''

A dark look flickered over Falstaff's face at Gregory's tone, but he covered it quickly, smiled, and wrapped an arm about his shoulders. "You are the one who made all this possible, James. It was your fate to deliver unto me the power that has made me invincible. That will never be forgotten. And I am forever grateful."

Gregory lowered his head, unable to speak.

"Come, let us show the world now the power you have delivered unto me."

"What are you going to do?"

"You will see. Bring the two men."

The flight engineer and the co-pilot were both lying on the floor in front of the first seats aft of the cockpit. Their hands were bound, secured to the floor posts of the seat. Gregory bent down and untied them from the posts.

Falstaff smiled at Hunter, who had not moved in hours.

"I trust you will not wander off while we are away, Captain."

"You slimy bastard, don't you dare harm my men."

The terrorist's smile faded. "You are not in any position to issue threats, Captain. I suggest you focus your efforts on remaining very still. Remember, the detonator is extremely sensitive."

Falstaff turned away. Gregory had now freed the two crewmen, and Falstaff came up behind them and touched the barrel of his Luger to the co-pilot's head. "We are going to the rear door now and will open it. The two of you will stand in the doorway as our shields. You will remain still, and you will make no attempt to communicate with those who are outside watching. If either of you so much as raises a finger, I shall kill both of you without hesitation. Do you understand?"

The two men nodded sullenly and moved slowly down the aisle toward the rear door. At Falstaff's order, they slid the door back and stepped up, side by side, to fill the opening.

Falstaff stood directly behind the co-pilot and peered out at the airport. All was quiet, the vast complex as silent as a ghost town. Gregory edged back from the door, reluctant to share the spotlight. Falstaff motioned to him to come closer. "Do not be afraid, James. They cannot harm you. Come, take you rightful place in history."

Then Falstaff turned back and spoke clearly, but without shouting, content that the electronic equipment of his unseen opponents would pick up his voice. "You have wisely complied with the first of my demands. I am pleased. I know there are still those among you who doubt that the awesome power I wield truly exists. Watch now and learn the truth."

With his free hand, he produced a small glass vial and held it high. There was a barely noticeable amount of a dark brown fluid in the bottom. It swirled sluggishly when he shook the container.

Falstaff elbowed between the two crewmen, parting them to give the outside world a better view. "I have strained a small measure of the bacterium from the weapon, no more than a few precious drops. Remember that this was constructed in your own factories of death. Watch closely. You shall see an example of the fate that awaits you if you dare refuse me."

He turned then and smiled gently at Gregory. "The glory shall be yours, James."

"What?"

Without further warning, Falstaff opened the vial. He splashed the contents into Gregory's face, and shoved him out the door.

Jean gasped. In the television image, James hurtled through the air. He cartwheeled wildly and smacked down on the tarmac, landing flat on his back and staring up at the dim twilight sky. The camera zoomed in close on his face.

For a moment nothing happened. Gregory lay deathly still. Then, abruptly, the handsome features began to disappear. In seconds, his face turned dark and bubbles began to appear, great swelling tumors that boiled up and burst open. His skin curled like cooked bacon, the face no longer human, barely recognizable as a face at all.

Jean looked away quickly, sickened. One of the men from

he CAB clamped a hand over his mouth and rushed from
he room.

Stand shook his head and peered out the window, watching
Falstaff retreat inside the plane and the door slam tight.

"He shouldn't have done that. Now he's alone."

"What?" Jean blinked back her tears and looked at him
curiously. "What did you say?"

Stand didn't realize he had spoken aloud. He muttered
gruffly, "I said Falstaff made a mistake. Now he's alone.
There will only be him and me."

It was a long night for everyone. The atmosphere in the
planning room had changed. Tempers flared as nerves grew
edgy. The men argued quietly, in trembling voices that betrayed their uncertainty. They were cowed by the demonstration of the stockpile's potency. None of them had seen
anything like it before, and even the bravest among them
were badly frightened.

Stand claimed a sofa in the corner of the room for himself,
stretched out, and closed his eyes.

"How can you think of sleep now?" Jean asked incredulously.

"There's nothing we can do at the moment. Wake me when
we get the word."

The President had promised a decision by three A.M. The
men in the planning room could debate strategy endlessly,
but the burden of the ultimate decision rested with only one
man. It was not a responsibility any sensible person would
envy.

As the hour drew near, the room became still. All voices
were hushed. All eyes were upon the single red phone in the
center of the conference table.

At two fifty-seven they had surprise visitors. Jean shook
Stand roughly. "Wake up. This has to be it."

The Secretary of Defense stormed inside with all his usual
bluster, his shrewd, foxlike face almost hidden behind a cigar
of Churchill proportions. The man accompanying him moved
more slowly, leaning heavily on a can. A black-suited Delta

lieutenant followed respectfully at his heels, pushing a wheel cart of oxygen.

Jean and Stand exchanged troubled glances. It was her father.

The Secretary of Defense waved his cigar, calling for their attention. His face was grim, his manner solemn. "Gentlemen," he announced, in his sonorous orator's voice, "we have just left a night-long council with the President. After long debate, much soul-searching, and prayer, he has arrived at a decision. The ransom will be paid."

The room erupted in howls of protest, low-throated curses, grumblings, and shouts of derision.

"What the hell—"

"He buckled under!"

"What kind of a yellow-livered coward did we elect?"

Daniel McWilliam limped forward. His shadowy eyes burned with a dark fire, and he peered around, staring down one man and then another, stilling their protests. His will was a force they could not ignore, and his frail body was forgotten in the presence of his authority.

The old man's voice rang out clearly. "If you wish a villain, then you may blame me," he said. "I am the one who persuaded the President to give the man what he wishes. . . ." He paused as the men around him muttered angry curses. He raised his head, proudly facing them all. One by one, their voices died in their throats.

McWilliam went on. "Do not think for one moment, merely because we shall pay the ransom, that we intend for this monster to succeed or to escape. We will give him what he wants only to fool him into a sense of false security. The weapon he holds at our throats is an ominous one; the threat to the people of this nation is grave. Our first and most imperative concern must be to lure Falstaff away. However unpleasant it is for us to appear to bow down to him, the safety of our citizens must come first, before pride, and even before justice.

"Falstaff is but one man. Clearly, he is insane, but he is not inhuman. He has weaknesses, and there is one among us who knows this best of all, one man who has already proven the truth of the monster's vulnerability. David toppled Goliath with but one small stone. In our current dilemma, we find ourselves facing a Goliath capable of destruction such as the world has seldom known. But the monster is proud. That is our edge, our sole advantage. We must strike where he is most vulnerable, in the soft underbelly of his own boundless vanity. The die has already been cast. There is only one among us who can do this. One man, one chance. With your prayers and God's divine guidance, he may prove to be our David.''

The furor that arose this time could not be stilled. The men looked at one another in bewilderment, their voices raised in angry confusion.

"Who is he?" one man shouted, stilling the other voices.

Stand got slowly to his feet. He knew the answer from McWilliam's eyes.

'Me,'' he said.

Stand felt the eyes of the crowd upon him as he moved through the quiet airport halls to the end of the terminal and the service area leading onto the apron. A Delta team was loading the bags of money onto a flatbed luggage carrier. Stand climbed up beside them. "You have it?" he asked.

"Right here, sir," one of the men replied. He handed Stand a shot pistol, sixteen inches long, barely more than a pistol grip with double twelve-bore barrels. An ugly, ungainly weapon, it had been designed for destructive power at close range. At ten yards it could practically tear a man in half, but it had little carry range beyond that distance. It fired a deadly hail of buckshot, hard plastic pellets that could rip through flesh, but would not penetrate the pressurized hull of an aircraft. Stand broke it open and slipped two shells into the chambers.

He swung the gun around for a moment, hefting it one-handed, getting the feel of it.

"I hope you get a chance to use that thing, sir. Tear out a piece of him for us."

Stand nodded absently, absorbed in his task. He took the weapon and a cartridge belt of ten additional shells and jammed them down inside one of the tall sacks of money. He closed the bag and shook it to make the contents settle. When he was content that the weapon was not visible, he took a felt-tipped pen and made a small sign on the "U" of U.S. MAIL on the bag's markings.

He climbed down and walked to a corner of the room where Sergei Yanov sat under a bright light, labored over by a short trim man in a beard and wide rimless spectacles. The special-effects man had been at work on the defector for the better part of three hours, and he was just brushing on the final touches as Stand approached.

"How is it coming?" Stand asked. "It's nearly time."

"Almost there," the effects man replied in a high, chirping voice. "Looks pretty good, even if I do say so myself. I don't normally do the makeup, but heavens, who can't handle a brush and a little rouge? I think it's come out pretty well, don't you think?"

Stand peered closer. There was a faintly visible bulge on Yanov's forehead, a thin layer of flesh-colored plastic. The expert had spread makeup along the edges, blending and shading to make the unnatural bulge almost invisible.

"Looks fine to me," Stand said.

The effects man beamed, then held up a can of aerosol deodorant spray. "Cover your eyes, dearie," he order Yanov. "This is to make certain you don't sweat and ruin all my good work."

Yanov held his hands over his eyes, and the effects man sprayed back and forth across his forehead, the force of spray lifting Yanov's thin hair. "Well, that's it," the expert announced. "He's ready as he'll ever be."

"And you?" Stand asked, looking down at Yanov.

The defector coughed and waved a hand to disperse the clinging cloud of aerosol. "As Jason says. There will never be a time when I am more ready. I am so frightened. I think when I see him again, I shall faint dead away."

"That would be fine," Stand said, smiling. "Fainting

wouldn't be a bad idea. Just so you look dead and stay that way as long as you have to.''

"He will look positively gruesome, I promise you," the effects man said. He squeezed Yanov's hand. "Don't worry. It will all wash off once this horrible ordeal is over.''

"How do I trigger it?" Stand asked.

Jason picked up a small plastic box the size of a pocket aspirin container. There was a single black button in the center of the box. "It's simple enough. You press this at the same time you fire." He handed Stand a gleaming blue Colt Diamondback revolver. "The gun's loaded with blanks. As you know, the discharge can still be deadly at close range, so make certain you aim directly at the skull plate." He spun Yanov around in his chair and tapped the back of his head.

Stand squinted and leaned closer. "Is there something there? I don't see anything."

Jason smiled happily. "That's the whole point. It's hard plastic, flesh-toned, of course, and I matched the wig to his own hair color. The blood bag is right here at the base of his skull, so that's where you should appear to shoot him."

Stand nodded. "No problem. I sure hope this is going to work. You're a brave man, Yanov, for agreeing to go through with it.''

The defector stood up and straightened his bow tie, studying himself in the mirror with rapt attention. "I didn't realize that I truly had a choice," he said. "Do you mean to say I actually could have refused?''

"Only if you don't mind seeing the whole population of Washington die a quick and horrible death.''

Yanov smiled thinly. "Yes, and after I have been here such a short time. What is it you Americans say . . . ? One Soviet moves in, and there goes the neighborhood.''

The commander of the Delta team came over and pointed to his watch. "Are you ready, gentlemen? It's time.''

Stand nodded and turned away as Yanov and Jason embraced.

"Good luck. I'll see you back here soon.''

"I pray that you are right," Yanov said in a dry, husky

voice. He pulled away from the effects man and followed after Stand. They climbed up on the flatbed and sat down atop the sacks of money. The Delta commander pulled on the coveralls of an airport baggage handler, then jumped up behind the wheel of the tractor. He looked back over a shoulder at his passengers.

Stand and Yanov glanced at each other. The defector nodded mutely. "All right," Stand said. "Let's go."

The sky was dark and inpenetrable behind the haze of the blaring airport lights as they moved out onto the apron. A cold wind gusted across the open ground. Stand heard the bleating wail of an ambulance in the distance, the scream cutting through the stillness like a razor edge of sound. He shivered without really knowing why, then felt the uneasiness pass as they slowly rolled out in sight of the lone plane resting quietly on the runway. The familiar anger burned in his gut like a flaring ulcer.

He thought of a young Irish woman, her chest ripped open by a bomb that had torn her twin children into so many pieces they were buried together in a single plastic bag.

He thought of his daughter and the expression of pure hatred on her innocent features when she looked up at him and condemned him with her final breath.

He thought of Meghan and Lynnie bound and gagged, living through days of black horror, never knowing when their captivity would end, or why they had been chosen to suffer. Two caring, innocent people, whose only crime had been to love the silent stranger who had appeared in their lives.

The enemy was a hydra, always the same, though it appeared in many forms. A malignant serpent that slithered in the darkness and drew strength and sustenance from the terror of its victims. The monster had many heads, and when one was severed, two more grew back in its place. He had faced it many times before, in different places and the enemy's diffuse guises, but they were all the same.

There was only one way to slay such a monster. And that was to face it squarely, to resist the impulse of paralyzing dread, to ignore its slavering jaws and move closer, close

nough to see the grim truth of the evil's human core. And
im straight and true for its cruel, black heart.

Stand was ready. He had faced the evil and recognized it
s the same darkness that inhabited every human soul, the
ancer of hatred and envy and despair that was the destroyer
f life. The hydra, despite its many guises, was but one en-
my—and its name was fear.

CHAPTER 25

AT FIVE forty-five A.M., Falstaff leaned over the instru
ment panel in the cockpit and peered out the slanted window
at the activity along the far end of the runway. Following his
instructions, the airport technicians were moving two items
into position. One was a wheeled staircase, which they placed
at the edge of the runway. The second was a flatbed luggage
carrier, laden with twelve heavily stuffed mailbags. There
were two men sitting atop the flatbed. As Falstaff watched,
they climbed down to the tarmac.

Falstaff took a small container from his pocket and shook
out two white pills. He popped them into his mouth and
swallowed. He had been taking amphetamines steadily
throughout the long night, and his eyes had a harsh unnatural
gleam.

Captain Hunter scowled and rubbed at the grime that
coated his own red-rimmed eyes. "Why don't you take a
good dozen or so, just to be sure?" he growled.

"You would like that, wouldn't you, Captain? You would
enjoy watching me suffer in the throes of an overdose, twitch
ing in convulsions as my heart strains and bursts."

"I didn't think you had a heart."

Falstaff smiled coldly and stared out the windows, scan
ning in all directions. "If they come, they will come now
before it is light. But I do not think they will come, Captain

Your people are cowards, and they are smart enough to realize when they have been beaten.''

Turning away, Falstaff bent over the stockpile behind the captain's seat. He touched a tiny hidden spring along the edge of the black box, and a small door sprang open, revealing a single toggle switch inside the hollow compartment.

Hunter twisted his neck to peer back at him. ''What's that?''

''It is an auxiliary detonation control. Surely you cannot believe I would be so foolish as to have but one means of activating the bomb. I have merely to throw this switch—''

He flicked his finger, barely brushing the metal tab, and Hunter winced.

Falstaff straightened, smiling. ''What's the matter, Captain? You appear tense.''

''You bastard. I hope you burn in hell.''

''There is no hell, Captain.'' Falstaff's face twisted in a puzzled expression. ''I thought that you were wise enough to dismiss such childish fables. There is nothing beyond this life but limitless serenity, a state of tranquil oblivion free from the tyranny of the senses.''

''I hope you're wrong,'' Hunter said.

''Really? Why?''

''Because that's too good for the likes of you. I pray there is a hell, and I would gladly enter it myself, if I could drag you along with me.''

Falstaff frowned. ''Foolish captain. You will see. Now make ready for takeoff. It is time.''

Falstaff went down the aisle and bent over the two bound crewmen. He flashed a knife and sliced through the ropes that held them. ''Take your places,'' he ordered.

The co-pilot and the engineer got up stiffly, rubbing at the raw chafed places on their wrists where the ropes had secured them. At Falstaff's prodding, they trudged forward and dropped into their seats.

'' 'Morning, Dave, John,'' Hunter said, smiling. ''You two sleep well back there?''

''No talking,'' Falstaff snapped. He produced his Luger

again and held it out for all of them to see. "You will do no talking that is not necessary for flying the aircraft. Now, prepare the plane."

The men bent over their instruments, going through the ritualistic procedures of a pre-flight check. One by one, the engines fired into life, and the hull shuddered with a pulsing energy. Falstaff watched them all carefully, then peered out at the tiny distant figures at the far end of the runway.

Hunter glanced at his co-pilot and said, "That's it, then. We're set." He reached up for the microphone to call the tower.

"That will not be necessary," Falstaff said. "I am in control. You need speak to no one else."

"Well, then?" Hunter asked.

Falstaff glanced at the chronometer among the bank of instruments and watched it tick to seven o'clock. He smiled.

"Very well, Captain. You may proceed."

Hunter nodded grimly and eased off the brakes. The large lumbering aircraft began to taxi slowly down the long runway.

Falstaff was everywhere, darting about the cabin, checking the surroundings from all angles, peering out windows on both sides. At his orders, Hunter kept their speed at a crawl. The figures at the far end slowly drew closer. One of them moved away from the other and stepped near the center of the runway.

Falstaff frowned and stood by the captain's shoulder, gazing at the distant figure. He leaned forward intently as the man loomed larger and became more distinct.

The man on the runway stood proudly erect, his hands in his coat pockets. He stared at the approaching plane with his head high, like a matador facing down a charging bull.

Suddenly the terrorist stiffened, his breath escaping in an angry hiss. "No, it cannot be!"

Hunter smiled, enjoying Falstaff's apparent discomfort.

"Someone you know?"

* * *

The plane bore down on Stand, but he remained motionless, his rugged bearded face set in a hard smile. His eyes were cool and unreadable as he faced the huge machine. The engines' roar became a deafening scream, and still he didn't move. He wanted Falstaff to see him clearly, to know that he was there by choice and would never back away. The plane came on, and Stand stood steady, unflinching.

At the last moment it veered slightly, passed him by as Hunter eased into a wide turn at the end of the runway. Stand didn't flinch, even as the wash of the plane's engine roared over him, his coat flapping wildly in the rushing airstream.

He watched the plane swing around and head back their way. Then he walked back to the flatbed and stood beside Yanov. "It won't be long now," he said softly. "Are you all right?"

"I am trembling so much I fear my legs will not hold me."

"That's all right. You can lie down pretty soon. When you hear the blast, go down hard. Close your eyes so you won't be watching for the pavement. Just drop and don't move again, no matter what happens after that."

Yanov smiled gamely. "I will do my best. After all, all I must do is die. People do it every day."

"You'll do fine," Stand said. His eyes grew hard as he watched the plane coast up, the pilot swinging the tail around with a fine touch, bringing it to a stop with the rear door within a few feet of the loading stairs.

All was quiet for a minute. Then he sensed motion through the plane's windows. The rear door began to swing open.

"Look frightened," Stand whispered to Yanov.

"Thank you, my friend. An effort is not necessary."

Two men appeared in the doorway, dressed in the uniform jackets of the airlines. Stand recognized the co-pilot and engineer from the televised coverage of earlier events.

Stand called out, "Falstaff, show yourself. Are you such a coward that you must hide behind others?"

The terrorist edged out a few inches from behind the engineer. He peered down at Stand and shook his head. "We meet again, Mr. Stand. At first I doubted my own eyes. It would seem that you are a difficult man to kill."

"Come out and face me like a man."

Falstaff laughed harshly. "You think I can be provoked so easily? How much you underestimate me, Stand. I will not show myself to your marksmen."

"There's no one else," Stand said. "Just you and me."

"Then you are here to carry out my demands?"

Stand pulled the Colt from his right pocket and held it at his side. "I am."

Swiftly, without warning, he raised the gun to the back of Yanov's head. His left hand, concealed in his pocket, pressed the button. There was a sharp crack and the gun kicked high.

Yanov's head snapped forward. A wide hole appeared at the back of his skull and his forehead exploded in a gushing stream of blood and bone. He went over like a tottering statue, his face smacking the pavement. He didn't make a sound, lying still, arms and legs askew.

The effects man had done his job almost too well. It looked more gruesome than some real head wounds Stand had seen. The blood flowed copiously onto the dry tarmac, a startling red torrent that seemed unnaturally bright.

Stand turned from the broken body and glared up at Falstaff. Then he tossed the gun down on the pavement.

"There's the first half of your murderous demands. Why don't you come down and collect the rest?"

"Just a moment," Falstaff called. He motioned with his pistol. "Turn him over, please. I wish to see his face."

"The hell I will, you ghoul."

"Now. I order it—unless you wish to see this man join the Italian in death." Falstaff placed the muzzle of his Luger against the engineer's ear.

Grumbling, Stand went down on one knee and gently turned Yanov over onto his back. As he did so, he deftly took the effects detonator from his pocket and slipped it under Yanov's spine. The defector didn't bat an eye at his touch. With grim surprise, Stand saw real blood at the man's temple. He was breathing very slowly and steadily. Yanov had thrown himself down so hard that he had struck his head on the pavement and knocked himself cold.

The gaping exit wound on his forehead was shockingly lurid. There were flecks of small bleached bone and even bits of soft gray tissue to emulate spattered brain matter. They had brought in Jason from a minor film studio that churned out endless horror films for the drive-in movie market. Apparently, he knew his gory craft well.

At any rate, the display convinced Falstaff. "Very good, Mr. Stand," he said. "You have performed your task well. I sense that he is at peace."

Stand stared back at him calmly. "I suppose it's my turn now," he said.

"No, not yet," Falstaff said. "You have been particularly meddlesome and irritating to me. I have other plans for you. Now, take off your coat and throw it down."

Stand shrugged, slipped off his coat, and let it drop to the ground.

"I do not want you to become overheated," Falstaff said. "You have work to do. Now, bring the money."

Stand nodded and slung one of the bags over his shoulder. He walked slowly to the stairs and started up. Falstaff retreated from view, roughly pulling the two crewmen back with him. Stand reached the top and threw one leg across the short gap between the plane and the stairs. He peered cautiously inside the plane. Falstaff was halfway down the aisle, still behind his two shields. "Throw it inside," he ordered.

Stand tossed the bag down on the floor. He glanced around, quickly appraising the situation. As they had suspected, Falstaff was alone, but he still had the gun to the head of the engineer.

"Now the others," Falstaff commanded. "Make it quick."

Stand trudged back down the stairs and collected another bag. He had never thought money could be so heavy.

Ten more times he tromped up and down the stairs, and he was sweating heavily when he dumped the last bag on the pile against the rear wall of the compartment. He stood in the doorway, his body taut with tension. Now was the moment of truth. From Falstaff's point of view, he wasn't needed anymore.

The terrorist smiled and lowered his gun from the engineer's head. "Take you places," he said to the crewmen. "We will be leaving very soon now." The men glanced at Stand in puzzlement, silently pleading with him, then turned and shuffled to the cockpit, glancing back anxiously over their shoulders.

Falstaff stretched out his arm, training the gun at Stand's chest. "Now, Mr. Stand, it seems we are alone. I thank you for bringing the money. It was most considerate of you to volunteer for this task. Your presence here will save me from the trouble of dealing with you at a later time."

Stand motioned with his head toward the piled bags. "You'd better count it to make sure it's all there. I don't think you would have much luck coming back to demand extra change."

Falstaff laughed. "You think I am so foolish? You wish me to look into the bags?" His face darkened. "Step inside."

Stand grabbed the sides of the door and vaulted inside the plane. Falstaff came slowly down the aisle toward him, the pistol unwavering. "Turn around. Hands on your head."

Stand turned and faced out the door, his hands on the top of his head. Falstaff came warily up to him and touched his pistol to the nape of his neck. He held it there while he patted Stand up and down for hidden weapons. Satisfied, he backed away.

"Open the bags," the terrorist demanded. "All of them."

"What's the matter? They're not rigged."

"We shall see. Open them."

Stand turned slowly and pulled up the first bag. Falstaff was watching him with sharp attention, so he avoided the bag with the small mark. His fingers fumbled with the knotted drawstring. Then he drew the bag open wide and held it out for Falstaff's inspection.

The man's pale eyes became round at the sight of the money.

"Satisfied?"

Falstaff motioned irritably with his pistol. "The others, too. I told you all of them."

"All right, all right," Stand muttered, feigning annoyance. Again Stand opened an unmarked bag.

"Yes, yes," Falstaff barked, barely glancing at the sack's contents. "Faster, I do not have all day." He retreated a step, glancing out the windows on each side.

Stand reached for the sack containing the weapon.

Out at the airport entrance, an ambulance siren howled suddenly, the noise sharp and sudden. Falstaff dropped in a crouch, tensed with alarm. He waved the pistol at Stand.

"Enough. Move away."

Cursing under his breath, Stand stepped back. Falstaff looked over his shoulder and called to the cockpit. "It is time, Captain. Take off and fly north by northwest. You will fly low to evade their radar."

Stand's mind raced, appraising his chances of rushing the man now. Slim to none. And they vanished completely as Falstaff spun back to face him.

"You thought for a moment to charge me, didn't you? You cannot fool me. I can see it in your face."

"As I see insanity in yours."

Falstaff smiled. "You will not provoke me into killing you yet. I know exactly how you are destined to die."

"Let me guess—old age?"

"Make your jokes while you can. Your time in this life is growing short." Then Falstaff turned and, with deadly aim, he shot down the long length of the plane, the bullet shattering the windshield directly between Hunter and his co-pilot, who cried out in fear.

"Now, Captain!" Falstaff screamed. "Or the next shot will splatter the head of your friend upon the glass."

Immediately, the engine roar deepened. The plane vibrated and then began to roll forward, rushing ahead with rapidly increasing speed. The ground outside the open door raced past in a blur.

Stand felt his stomach lurch and stumbled back against the rear wall as the plane lifted smoothly from the ground and angled up into the clouds. He glanced out the door and saw nothing but gray sky. Stand closed the door and locked it tight.

Falstaff tilted back his head and laughed. "We are away. Nothing can stop me now."

"Congratulations." Stand sighed bitterly. The plane was already leveling off, the ground far below, the vista expansive and vaguely unreal.

The terrorist faced him and nodded. "Thank you, Mr. Stand," he said softly. Then he raised the pistol and squinted down the barrel. "For that kindness, you have earned a last request."

"How about your immediate surrender?"

"You do not give up, do you? Something else."

Stand sighed. "All right. A drink."

"Much better." He slowly approached Stand, motioning him back with a wave of the pistol. Stand was forced to retreat. Falstaff slipped the intercom microphone from its cradle on the compartment wall.

"Captain Hunter, maintain a slow cruising speed under two hundred miles an hour. And you will have one of your men bring us a bottle from your galley. Whisky, I should think. Do it quickly."

He turned back to Stand and smiled. "Now," he said softly, "the moment is drawing near. Open the door."

Hunter scowled and glanced at his engineer. "Go ahead, Dave. Do what he wants."

The engineer got to his feet and cast a sullen glance down the passageway. "I've had it up to here with doing what he wants. We have to do something."

He opened his jacket, giving Hunter a glimpse of a fat round cylinder stuck in his belt.

"What's that for?"

"A flare from the emergency kit. I'm going to burn that bastard's eyes out."

"Forget it, Dave."

"No one else is going to help us. We have to do something, or we're all dead. It's up to us."

Hunter nodded reluctantly. "You may have a point."

"We've cooperated for so long, he takes us for granted. He won't be expecting any trouble. Wait until I start back this way. Then black out the cabin lights. That will take him by surprise and I'll jump him."

"Be careful, Dave. He's dangerous."

The engineer smiled tightly. "Careful, hell. I'm going to kill the bastard. He's not as tough as he acts."

Hunter watched his friend go with a grave sense of foreboding.

Stand swung open the door and a stream of air roared through the cabin. The plane slowed quickly and began to buck and jolt, vibrating roughly. He gazed down at a dizzying view of patchwork landscape.

The earth was far away. The pilot was guiding the plane in a slow, steady climb, defying Falstaff's orders and slyly easing into higher air space. Stand gripped the edge of the hatchway tightly. One step and he would tumble into space, falling for thousands of feet to wind up smashed and broken, a small bloody spot on the landscape.

"You are afraid of heights, are you, Mr. Stand?"

"I'm not fond of them."

Falstaff smiled. "Good. Your death will be an especially pleasing moment. You have been particularly meddlesome and annoying to me."

"Nice of you to say so."

"You will not laugh much longer," Falstaff shot back. "In a moment, you will step out that door, screaming in terror as you plummet through the sky, and I will sense your fear for the long seconds it takes you to fall. You are a brave man and because of that the moment of your passing will be especially sharp and vivid. Your fear will be an experience of intense sweetness."

He turned as the engineer came down the passageway. The man scowled at the terrorist with bitter undisguised hatred, as he held out a tall bottle of White Label.

"I had this is my flight bag from the duty-free store. I hope you choke on it."

Falstaff gazed back coolly at the engineer, until the man lowered his eyes. Falstaff smiled and motioned to Stand. "Give it to him."

Grumbling under his breath, the engineer pushed past him and held out the bottle as he approached Stand. "Take it," he grunted. "The same goes for you, you worthless bastard."

"Better than one of those baby-sized bottles," Stand said. "Thanks." He opened the bottle and took a long drink. The whisky glowed warmly down his throat and ignited in his stomach.

"Goddammit! Why don't you do something?" he whispered to Stand.

Stand frowned. "Don't judge what you don't understand."

"I understand plenty," the engineer hissed. "You may be afraid to do anything, but I'm not."

"Don't be a fool."

Falstaff snapped. "Stop this whispering. Come away from him."

The engineer turned back, then gave Stand a final withering look of contempt. "Just stay out of it. We wouldn't want you to get hurt." He stomped angrily down the aisle and Falstaff stepped aside as he started to pass.

Then the terrorist's hand snaked out, grabbed the hair on the back of the engineer's head, and yanked him off balance, jamming the Luger to his throat.

The flare slipped from the man's belt and clattered to the floor. The engineer's eyes opened wide in mute terror. Falstaff picked up the cylinder and shook it in his face.

"What were you planning to do with this?" Falstaff demanded. "Tell me, or I will kill you now."

"Nothing," the engineer stammered. "It was nothing."

"Tell me." The pistol pressed harder, changing the pale skin of his throat to an angry red.

The engineer's eyes were white and wild. His voice trembled and broke in a shrill whine.

"I just . . . I thought I could use it to stop you from killing us all."

"Idiot!" Falstaff released him, shoving him down the aisle, and turned his back scornfully. He tossed the flare to the floor. "You think one man can stop me? Nothing can stop me. I am the Cross, the chosen one. You are nothing more than insects! Step in my way, and I shall squash you. Now get out of my sight. Your face offends me."

The engineer leaned against a seat, panting to catch his breath. His face was ashen and he gazed at the terrorist's back with an expression of doubt and bewilderment that slowly altered to glowering rage. He stood up and straightened his uniform with self-conscious dignity.

Stand watched the man's face and silently prayed that he was wrong about what he saw there. The engineer turned and took two steps up the aisle. Stand breathed a sigh of relief.

Suddenly the lights flickered. The cabin went black.

The engineer spun back, lunged for the terrorist, but at the last second hesitated, torn by fear and doubt. Falstaff twirled to face the challenge. With insolent ease, he swung out his arm and backhanded the man across the face with his pistol. The engineer crumpled, tumbling sideways between the seats.

Falstaff laughed, cackling with insane delight. He peered down at the fallen engineer and slowly trained his pistol. "You fool. You dare to lay hands on *me*. For that, you die."

Stand dove atop the pile of sacks, groping in the darkness for the hidden weapon. His hand dug through the wadded bills and closed on the cool steel of twin barrels.

Falstaff let out a cry of anger and snapped a shot at the sound of Stand's frantic search. The bullet struck Stand like a hammer, spinning him around. He sagged atop the stuffed mailbags, momentarily stunned. Pain and shock left him breathless, paralyzed, and he felt the warm flow of blood down his flank.

Falstaff screamed, tilting his head back and howling like an enraged animal. "You think to defy me! You are dead, all of you! For this absurd effrontery, you have sealed your fate.

I will show the world what happens to those who defy the invincible Cross. And it is on your heads.''

He started up the passageway toward the cockpit. There was a rapid flutter of footsteps and the co-pilot's shadowy form loomed before him. Falstaff raised his hand and fired the pistol straight up at the ceiling. His pale face was ghost-like in the flash.

"Back!" he screamed. "Out of my way. Move back. You cannot resist me.''

Stand regained his senses and sat up stiffly. His shoulder ached like fire, but the pain only crystallized his alertness. He saw the grim spectacle in the forward passage by the dim light from the windows.

The co-pilot blocked Falstaff's way, but slowly retreated. "What are you going to do?'' he asked breathlessly.

"I am going to discharge the bomb. And all the world will know and understand my wrath.''

"I . . . I can't let you do that.''

"You cannot stop me.''

Slowly, they advanced toward the cockpit, the co-pilot steadily giving ground.

"You can't set off the bomb,'' the co-pilot pleaded. "You'll die with the rest of us.''

"Fool. Death will not stop me. I am born of death, and will rise again in the wake of this destruction, stronger than ever. I will be reborn again and again, each time stronger until all the world is a testimony to eternal darkness.''

Stand got up on one knee and raised the shot pistol, but Falstaff was already at the edge of its effective range and the co-pilot was in the line of fire. He had to draw him back. Then his foot brushed the fallen bottle of whisky. He grabbed it and poured alcohol over the mound of mailbags. He groped quickly along the floor and located the forgotten signal flare. He yanked the discharge cord and tossed the flare on the alcohol-soaked money.

The flare burst into a ball of light.

It went up with a loud *whoomph* and a bright bonfire cast a flickering glow throughout the cabin.

Falstaff spun around and screamed in bitter rage.

Stand was a dark figure silhouetted against the brilliant inferno, a silent presence arising from the flames.

Howling insanely, Falstaff raced back at him, firing wildly. Stand felt a tug at his thigh as another bullet tagged him, but he caught his balance and stood firm until the crazed man was in range. He calmly squeezed the trigger and the shotgun coughed white fire.

The buckshot took Falstaff low, halting him in his tracks. The gun kicked up and Stand fired again, the next load striking Falstaff square in the chest, throwing him back like a leaf in a violent wind.

Even as he fell, Falstaff unleashed another shot. The bullet sang past Stand's face, so close he could feel its heat. Instinctively he flinched, stepped back, and dropped as his wounded leg buckled under him. He tumbled onto his back, writhing in pain.

Falstaff moaned softly and rolled over. He looked as if he had been through a grinder. Blood dribbled from a dozen wounds, and his face was laid open to the bone. The co-pilot hissed when he saw the gruesome mask, then shuddered in total horror. The ghastly apparition rose shakily and started to crawl forward, muttering "You cannot stop me, you cannot stop me" in a haunting refrain.

The co-pilot fled from the approaching figure as if it were the devil. Slowly, with unshakable resolve, Falstaff crept closer to the cockpit, fighting with an inhuman determination fueled by rage and the drug still burning in his broken body.

Hunter watched incredulously over his shoulder. As he saw Falstaff grimly bearing down on the cockpit, he suddenly turned and threw full power to the engine, pulling back on the wheel, wrenching the plane up in a steep climb.

Stand gasped in pain as the deck tilted sharply under him and he was thrown back against the last seat. He caught hold of the legs and held on as the plane nosed up ever higher until it seemed they were shooting straight up.

He heard an anguished cry and glanced up the passageway. Falstaff scrambled feebly for a hold on the pitched floor, then slid down the aisle until he crashed into the pile of burning sacks. He lay there, too weak to move. His clothes and hair erupted in flames.

"You cannot beat me!" he screamed. His voice climbed to a shrill screech almost above hearing, a high and breathless wail of agony.

The plane tipped sharply as Hunter banked in a steep turn, and suddenly Falstaff was gone, sliding out the open hatch and tumbling end over end through space, arcing across the sky like a flaming meteor.

Stand closed his eyes. The next thing he knew, the co-pilot was bending over him. "You all right, guy? It's finished. He's dead and gone."

"I've been better," Stand said, wincing at the pain. "Help me to my feet. It's not over yet."

With the co-pilot's aid, Stand limped to the cockpit and settled gratefully in the engineer's chair. The engineer still lay among the seats, unconscious. The co-pilot went back to the cabin to close the Boeing's door.

Hunter turned from his instruments with an uneasy smile and offered his hand. "It's certainly a pleasure, Mr. Stand. I was just speaking to control back at Dulles. They offered their heartiest congratulations."

"Nice of them," Stand muttered, a little drowsily. The co-pilot had given him an injection of morphine from the medical kit, and the drug made his body glow with golden warmth. He felt thick-headed and sleepy, but the pain was merely a curious sensation somewhere far away. "A bit premature, though," he continued. "We still have Falstaff's little gift box to contend with."

Hunter nodded. "Don't I know it. The military is taking over now. They've ordered us to land at Thule—that's an air force base in Greenland. I guess it's the most remote location they could find for us to put down with our nasty cargo."

"What happens when we get there?"

"They're dispatching a team of demolition and biological warfare experts by fighter jets. They should get there before we do. Once we put down, it's in their hands, I guess."

"Fine. They can have it. Anyone who wants it," Stand muttered. He closed his eyes and let his head drop back on the seat.

Hunter ran his fingers through his wavy gray hair. "Can I ask you a question, Stand? Is it true what he said, that this thing was American-made? How did something like this ever happen in the first place?"

But Stand was already asleep.

Hunter nodded thoughtfully as he turned back to his instruments. "Yeah, you're right," he mumbled. "I probably don't really want to know."

The landscape of Greenland was a forbidding desert of snow, ice, and dark barren rock. The landing was routine. Hunter laid the ship down gently. They coasted to a stop at the end of the runway, far from the low silhouettes of the clustered Quonset-style barracks.

"Nice job, skipper," the co-pilot said with a sigh.

Hunter smiled. "Not bad for an old gray-hair."

"You sold me, Captain," Stand said. "From now on, I fly Global."

They peered out the windows at the dark huddled buildings. There was no sign of life. The base appeared to be abandoned. Then they saw a Jeep appear from behind a snowbank and cruise steadily down the runway. It carried a single man in a baggy white protective suit and helmet.

"That's our team of experts?" Hunter muttered. He glanced at his co-pilot. "Well, John, you might as well go welcome out visitor."

The co-pilot nodded and scrambled down the passageway. A viciously cold draft whistled through the cabin as he threw open the door.

He was back a minute later, followed by the disconcerting stranger in his ominous garb. His voice was muffled through his respirator, but the cheerfulness was unmistakable and welcome: "Greetings, gents," he said. "You the guys who called for an exterminator?"

"That's us," Hunter said. "Forgive me if I don't get up."

"Sure thing, Cap. I know the story. Just like you commercial fly boys to sit through a crisis."

"I thought they were sending a whole team to handle this thing."

"That's me. Bombs and bugs, they're all part of the package. No, don't gush at once—I know you're awestruck, but try to save your applause until the final curtain. I'd love to jaw with you some more, Captain, but I think I'd better take a look at this little beauty."

He got down on his knees and bent over the bomb, carefully inspecting every inch. "Boy, this is some job, I gotta tell you. The guy who wired this was a pro."

"Can you defuse it?"

"Well, we'll find out pretty quick-like. Any of you like to step outside while I do a little cutting and snipping?"

"Would it make any difference?" Stand asked.

The face plate glanced up at him. "Not a bit. If this thing goes off, it won't matter if you're here or sucking soup in the officers' mess; the little buggies will get you."

"In that case, I guess we can sit around a few minutes longer."

"Speak for yourself," Hunter said. "I've been sitting so long I've got calluses on my backside. Hurry it up, all right?"

"You got it." The space-suited figure bent over the stockpile. Carefully he laid open a section of wiring. From a pocket on the leg of his suit, he produced a pair of snips. "Well, gents, we got us a fifty–fifty situation. Red wire or blue—anybody got a favorite color?"

The co-pilot paled. "Fifty–fifty—that's the best you can do? I thought you were an expert."

"With bombs, guy, fifty–fifty ain't bad. It beats the odds I was facing before I came here. They pulled me from the poker table of a casino in Atlantic City, and when the M.P.'s showed, I was holding four aces."

"Let's hope you didn't spend all your luck at cards," Stand said. "Cut something."

The helmet nodded and turned back to the bomb. He raised the snips and held them over the red wire. The fingers tight-

ned. Then, at the last instant, he switched to the blue wire
and sliced it neatly in two.

There was a collective gasp from the three men watching
him.

Nothing.

The man straightened up and pulled off his helmet, revealing a freckled youthful face under a tousled mop of red
hair. "You guys play cards, by any chance? I wouldn't mind
a game on the way home."

CHAPTER 26

THE GRAVEYARD was located on the crest of a hill over
looking the Potomac. It was early morning and fog clung to
the Virginia hills, swirling among the dark cedars. The head
lights of the departing cars burned through the mist with a
ghostly glow.

The priest spoke quietly to Jean, then moved away as Stand
stepped up to her side. She glanced up at him, her face pale
but unmarred by tears. Her simple black outfit set off her
beauty in a way that was perversely stunning.

She took his arm and slowly they walked away from the
open grave. "He never knew you succeeded," she said. "He
died when the crisis was still at its peak. It doesn't seem
fair."

"I think he knows," Stand said gently. "I think he knew
what was happening all along. He kept throwing us together
in Lübeck, when the Company was searching for me—he was
trying to help you, but always without tipping his hand."

"You really think so?"

He nodded. "But we'll never be sure. You'll probably have
to face that question again and again—what did he know, and
when? He took a lot more secrets with him than that one."

She looked up at him. "He believed in you. He believed
in you so strongly that he was able to persuade the President
to trust the solution to a single man."

Stand walked along quietly, saying nothing. They reached the ironwork gate, and he peered at the long line of cars vanishing into the shrouding fog. Then he looked down at the woman by his side and squeezed her arm gently.

"The whole thing happened because you were trying to protect him, didn't it?"

Jean nodded and lowered her eyes, sighing. "He was the one responsible for keeping the stockpile in the first place. When the order came in nineteen-seventy to destroy all the CBW weapons, they dumped the stockpile on him and ordered him to quietly hide it for safekeeping. After that, no one would own up to even knowing about it. The whole scandal was left on his shoulders and his own government refused to acknowledge the terrible responsibility it had forced on him."

"Plausible denial?" Stand said. "How much treachery has been performed in the name of saving face?"

"When I discovered the truth, I set out to remove the stockpile and have it destroyed so that black cloud would cease to hang over him. I wanted to spare him the ignominy of history's judgment as the villain who illegally withheld a terrible secret. It would have been uncovered sooner or later. I couldn't bear to see that mar his good name. After all, his life was spent in the service of this country. They would have hated him. The press would have painted him with a black brush, calling him the worst sort of traitor."

"But you went about your plan to destroy the stockpile without telling him what you knew?" Stand asked.

She turned and met his eyes. "That's right," she said firmly. "I didn't want him to know. That way he could have genuinely denied knowledge of it. Plausible denial could have worked for him, instead of against him." She turned and glanced back into the graveyard. "But instead, my meddling created a greater evil, the worst crisis of his life. And he died before it was settled, before you saved us all from the most unimaginable—"

"It's over," Stand said. "Don't let it haunt you forever. You tried to do what you thought was best."

"And I'll continue to do it," she said. "I'll pick up where he left off. The Office is mine now."

"You intend to carry on with the job he started?"

She nodded with conviction. "Absolutely. From now on, it will be my entire life. That's the way he was—that's what it takes." She paused and studied him with a serious expression. "I could use someone like you, Nathan. He said you were the best, and you certainly proved that to me."

Stand shook his head. "Sorry. From here on, I make my own way, and it has nothing to do with this business."

"What do you intend to do?"

"I don't know, maybe teach again. It doesn't matter."

"It will never last, Nathan. A man like you stays at the edge of life, where there are always risks."

"I've had enough of the edge," he said. "I think a warm quiet corner will suit me fine."

She smiled, a glimmer of the magical smile that had so struck him upon their first meeting. "It's the woman, isn't it? The British woman and the child. You intend to go back to them?"

"If they'll have me."

She nodded and stepped away, clinging to his hand one moment longer. "Then I'm happy for you, Nathan. Truly, I am. You found something important, and I hope it works for you. My best wishes to you and your new family."

"And to you, Jean. Good luck."

"If you should ever change your mind—"

He shook his head. She released his hand and walked slowly away with her head high. Edwards opened the door to the long black limousine and she climbed inside.

Stand shrugged, buried his hands in his pockets, and walked down the road to look across the gray winter hills. There was little to see. The fog swirled about him, and there was nothing beyond its blank gray face, like a wall between him and the rest of the world.

He didn't mind. There was nothing for him here. Everything in the world lay thousands of miles away. He turned to face the east. Meghan and Lynnie were waiting for him, and there was nothing to stop him, nothing to hold him back but his own self-doubt, and that had been vanquished. The past was behind him, laid to rest. Tomorrow lay this way. And it wasn't far. Just the other side of the fog.